D1411762

THE BEASTS OF BARAKHAI

DAW Books Presents
the Finest in Fantasy by

MICKEY ZUCKER REICHERT

FLIGHTLESS FALCON

THE LEGEND OF NIGHTFALL

SPIRIT FOX (with Jennifer Wingert)

The Renshai Trilogy:
THE LAST OF THE RENSHAI (Book 1)
THE WESTERN WIZARD (Book 2)
CHILD OF THUNDER (Book 3)

The Renshai Chronicles:
BEYOND RAGNAROK (Book 1)
PRINCE OF DEMONS (Book 2)
THE CHILDREN OF WRATH (Book 3)

The Bifrost Guardians Omnibus Editions

VOLUME ONE:
GODSLAYER
SHADOW CLIMBER
DRAGONRANK MASTER

VOLUME TWO:
SHADOW'S REALM
BY CHAOS CURSED

THE BEASTS OF BARAKHAI

VOLUME ONE OF
THE BOOKS OF BARAKHAI

MICKEY ZUCKER REICHERT

DAW BOOKS, INC.
DONALD A. WOLLHEIM, FOUNDER
375 Hudson Street, New York, NY 10014
ELIZABETH R. WOLLHEIM
SHEILA E. GILBERT
PUBLISHERS
http://www.dawbooks.com

Jacket art by Alan Pollack.

DAW Book Collectors No. 1191.

DAW Books are distributed by Penguin Putnam Inc.

Book designed by Stanley S. Drate/Folio Graphics Co. Inc.

This book is printed on acid-free paper. ♾

First printing, August 2001

1 2 3 4 5 6 7 8 9

To Mikey Gilbert:

You told us you were sick,
and some of us never took
you seriously enough—
but, damn it, did you have to prove it?

Every moment of every day, you are sorely missed.

Acknowledgments

I would like to thank the following people: Mark Moore, Jackie Moore, Koby Moore, Sheila Gilbert, Jonathan Matson, Jo Fletcher, Sandra Zucker, Jennifer Wingert, the PenDragons, my billion or so science professors, and Picasso (who made endless hours of lonely keyboard-time more interesting).

Chapter 1

RACKS of plastic hutches lined the walls of the biology laboratory at Algary campus, each with a test-tube water bottle jutting from its mesh screen lid. Surrounded by wood-topped metal stools, six fused desks/cabinets filled the center of the room, a chaotic jumble of notepads, pens, pipettes, and goggles cluttering their faux wood surfaces. Stomach growling, Benton Collins ladled fresh wood chips into the pan of an empty cage while its usual occupant, a fat white rat, nosed at the corners of the cardboard box that temporarily held it.

The odor of the cleaner churned Collins' hunger into nausea. He flung strands of dark brown hair from his eyes with a gloved hand, smearing wet food mush across his forehead, then immediately berated himself with sarcasm for the habitual gesture. *Smart move. Good thing I wore gloves to protect me from this slop.*

As the sweet aroma of cedar replaced the chemical smells, Collins' gut rumbled again. He had skipped breakfast and lunch, the expectation of a Thanksgiving feast holding hunger at bay. He had promised his girlfriend to do whatever he could to make it to her family's home by 2:00 p.m., to meet her parents for the first time. Collins doubted his skinny, bespectacled self would make much of an impression on an old-money family like the Johnsons, especially reeking of rat and with green-gray smudges of food stick goo across his face. He glanced at his watch. *3:30 p.m.* And he still had an entire row of cages to clean, as well as Professor Demarkietto's notes to review, before he could call it a day. The drive alone would take an hour.

Feeling more like a punching bag than a graduate student, Collins filled the water bottle, placed a few fresh sticks of food in the cage, then hefted the cardboard box. He poured the rat back into its cage. It scuttled about, hurling chips, then hunkered down with a food stick clenched between its front paws. Collins clipped the lid back in place and replaced the cage on its rack. He peeled off the gloves with a snap of latex and tossed them into the trash can. Using a damp paper towel little finer than sandpaper, he scrubbed the grime from his forehead, then washed his hands and drank from his cupped palms. The water sat like lead in his otherwise empty belly. After drying his face and hands, he wadded the paper towels together and launched them, like a basketball, into the can.

Only then, did Collins take a deep breath, close his eyes, and reach for the telephone. Fumbling through the papers for his own organizer, he opened his eyes and leafed to the last page for the home number of Marlys Johnson's parents. He punched it in.

Marlys answered on the first ring. "Hello?" Her tone hardened. "Benton, that better be you."

Seized with a sudden urge to hang up without speaking, Collins forced a laugh. "If I'd been Publishers' Clearinghouse, wouldn't you have felt dumb?"

Dead silence.

Collins cringed. He pictured her: long red hair permed and styled for the holiday, the green eyes that could as easily scald as melt him, the slender legs that seemed to climb to her small-breasted chest. In his mind's eye, he imagined a glare that would send tougher men skittering for cover.

The distant sound of laughter wafted across the receiver, followed by song. The background noise brought Collins back to his childhood, when his parents lived together and his Uncle Harry and Aunt Meg spent every Thanksgiving with them. Harry loved to tell jokes but butchered the punchlines. Meg would try to correct them, laughing so hard that she usually only succeeded in making them hopelessly obtuse. The interaction between the husband and wife always seemed so much funnier than the joke, even correctly told. Collins had spent last Thanksgiving with his mother and her new boyfriend, a paunchy, socially inept engineer with three visiting children he could not control. This year, the two were spending Thanksgiving in Vegas on their honeymoon. Collins' father was touring Europe with his quirky girlfriend, Aviva. Harry and Meg had not invited him.

''You'd better be calling from a cell phone.'' Marlys' frigid voice jarred Collins back to the present.

Collins sighed, hands sliding instinctively to the cell phone, pager, and multitool at his belt. ''I'm still at the lab.''

''Why?'' Her tone implied no explanation short of nuclear catastrophe would suffice.

Collins knew better, but he could not resist another joke. ''The rats invited me for dinner. I couldn't resist . . . food sticks.''

''That's not funny.''

''I'm sorry.''

''Am I a joke to you?''

''Of course not.'' Collins rolled his eyes to the whitewashed ceiling, wishing he had not attempted humor. ''I'd be there if I could, Marlys. You know that. But the power system's been touch and go with all the grain harvests. Lab loses electricity long enough, crash go some of the experiments. Including Dundee's two-million-dollar grant.''

''You're not working for Dundee,'' Marlys reminded. ''Why can't her grad student handle it?''

Collins sat on one of the stools, propping his sneaker-clad feet on another. ''Marly, come on. You know Dave's parents live in Florida.''

''Don't call me Marly—''

''Once they all found out my family wasn't available for the holiday—''

''It's Mar*lys*, Benton, not Marly. And why do you let people take advantage of you?''

Collins gave the expected reply, though he had tired of it. ''Just call me Ben. And it's not a matter of taking advantage. It's—''

''Demarkietto's a slave driver.''

Though true, it was not what Collins had been about to say. ''Well, yes, but—''

''Why don't you just tell him to go fuck himself?''

''Marlys!'' Collins had never heard her use that word before.

''You have a right to a holiday, too.''

Collins hated to remind Marlys of his shortcomings, especially when she had her mother to disparage him. ''A lot of candidates applied for lab positions this year. I was lucky to get one.''

Marlys refused to concede. ''No, Demarkietto's the lucky one. Lucky he could get *any* grad assistant after Carrie Quinton.''

Collins had also heard the rumors, that the beautiful post-doctoral genetics student had disappeared without a trace in an effort to escape Professor Demarkietto's demands. ''I need the money, Marlys. I'm already three payments behind on student loans. And I need the recommendation. Whatever you or Carrie Quinton thinks of ol' D-Mark, he's well-respected in the scientific community.''

Something white caught the edge of Collins' vision.

"Benton, my parents are starting to think you're unreliable."

Distracted, Collins returned to wit. "So is student loan services."

"Benton!"

A white rat scurried from behind the desks, scrambling through the gap in the partially opened door.

"Damn it!"

"Benton! Did you just swear at me?"

"Big problem." Wondering whose ten-year, million-dollar experiment he had just ruined, Collins said, "I'll call you back." Without waiting for a reply, he started to replace the receiver.

Marlys' small voice chased him. "Don't you dare—" Then the earpiece clicked down, cutting off whatever threat Marlys had uttered. Uncertain whether or not he would ever see his girlfriend again, Collins bashed the door open with his shoulder.

The panel shot wide, and the impact bruised his arm even through his emerald-green Algary sweatshirt. Collins caught sight of the rat squeezing beneath the door of one of the unused classrooms provided by grant money. He had once overheard some of the professors discussing the perks of earning such a room, then using it for storage, a badge of honor for bringing in a large endowment. Collins groaned, doubting he could find the escapee amid years of a scientist's accumulated crap.

For a moment, Collins froze, paralyzed by despair. If an experimental animal came up missing on his watch, he would lose his job for certain; and those who graded him might no longer feel so kindly disposed. His thesis might become less valuable than the paper on which he printed it. He would never get a job. His student loans would plunge him into poverty. He had lost his parents to the pursuit of their own happiness, and he had no siblings with whom to commiserate. He had probably just lost his girlfriend; worse, he was not sure he even cared. Suddenly, the idea of becoming a second Carrie Quinton, of disappearing without a trace, seemed the best of all his lousy options.

Collins shook his head, tossing hair the color of bittersweet chocolate; it had gone too long since its last cutting. Driven only by a deeply rooted sense of responsibility, he pulled open the door. Light funneled in from a dusty window that made the room seem full of smoke. Mathematical equations, complicated and incomprehensible, scrawled white across a blackboard. Piled boxes, desks, and chairs crafted strange shadows across the tiled floor. On an open stretch, someone had sketched out a pentagram in purple chalk. A chill spiraled through Collins, and the urge to flee gripped him like ice. He calmed himself with logic. Role-playing gamers abounded on Algary campus, and they often sought out hidden rooms and alcoves for atmosphere. In his college days, he had played some *Dungeons and Dragons* on the roof of Domm Hall.

Collins flicked the light switch. It clicked, but nothing changed. The bulb had, apparently, burned out. He debated leaving the door open to channel in a bit more light, but it seemed prudent to block the only exit. *Rat in a dark storage room. Kind of makes the old needle in a haystack seem like simple hide-and-seek.* He closed the door, pulled his sweatshirt off over his head, and stuffed it under the crack. Satisfied the rat could not squeeze out, he sat on the cold floor, half-naked. *What now? A radioactive, rabid cockroach bites off my three chest hairs?* He glanced around for a cup or empty box to hold the creature until he could transfer it to its cage but found nothing suitable. Accustomed to handling, the rat would likely prove tractable enough to carry in his hands.

Hunger churned through Collins' gut again. Even the rubbery turkey slices Algary's cafeteria served up on holidays seemed like a treat, garnished with ketchup from a can as big as his torso. They would serve it up with some weirdly spiced institutional stuffing, a canned blob of cranberries, and something that vaguely resembled cheese. The denouement: cardboard pie colored some fruity color, as vivid and unrealistic as

Froot Loops. The whole situation suddenly seemed hysterically funny. Shaking his head, he laughed until his ribs ached.

A flash of white ran right past Collins' left sneaker.

"Hey!" Instantly sobered, Collins leaped to his feet and gave chase. The rat skittered between a row of boxes and disappeared beneath a pile of desks. "Hey," he repeated, diving after the retreating tail.

Collins slammed against stacked cartons; they exploded into a wild avalanche. Not bothering to assess the damage, he kept his gaze locked on the rat. His foot came down on something hard, and his ankle twisted. Pain consumed his leg. Afraid to lose the rat, he bulled through it, plunging into the darkness beyond the stack of desks.

The world went suddenly black. Collins blinked several times, seeking a bare trickle of light leaching between boxes or around the irregular shapes that defined the desks. Worried about losing his target, he continued forward blindly, sweeping the space ahead with his hands to protect his head. An occasional squeak or blur of white movement kept him going far longer than seemed possible in such a small room. He got the distinct impression he was chasing his own tail instead of the rat's, caught in a wild spiral of madness constructed from nothing more substantial than stress. Focusing on this current problem kept him from dwelling on the anger his parents aroused, the advantage his preceptor had taken of a miserable situation, his inability to appease the one person he professed to love. His world narrowed to the excitement of the chase.

At length, Benton Collins realized that the passage of time had become more than just a perception. His stomach gnawed at its own lining; dinnertime surely had come and gone. His memory of the telephone call seemed distant, indistinct. His back ached from stooping and his knees from crawling. He reached above his head, his groping fingers meeting nothing of substance. Cautiously, he rose and discovered he could stand without having to stoop. The room remained utterly black.

Collins glanced at his left wrist. The hands of his watch glowed eerily in the darkness: *7:18*. Shocked, he studied the arrangement of hands and hash marks. He could not believe he had been slithering around after a rat for over three hours. The thought seemed lunacy. If true, he should have crashed into a wall or door, should have stumbled over boxes, should have caught glimpses of light through the window. But his world remained dark, and he felt none of the stored items he had seen before while scurrying beneath the desks. *I'm not in the same room. Can't be.*

Vision straining, Collins took careful steps forward, waving his arms in front of him to head off a collision. At length, the fingers of his left hand scraped an irregular wall. He pawed along it for a light switch, feeling damp and craggy stone. *What the hell?* He shook his head, scarcely daring to believe it. *I'm lost in some dark, secret corner of Daubert Labs. But how did I get here?* He sucked in a calming breath, then let it out slowly through his nose. *Must have accidentally crawled through a vent or tunnel or something. No wonder the gamers like it here.*

A sharp squeak startled Collins from his thoughts. He glanced around for the creature, more from habit than true interest anymore. His heart pounded, and a shiver racked him. Rationally, he knew he could not remain lost in a campus building for longer than the four-day holiday, yet disorientation pressed him toward panic. Suddenly, his location seemed the most important piece of information in the world.

Pressing both hands to the wall, Collins chose a direction and followed it to a corner. At some point, he reasoned, he would have to find a door into a hallway. From there, he would surely come upon a part of the laboratory he knew.

A lump formed in Collins' throat. His heart hammered against his ribs, and his thoughts refused to coalesce. His elbow grazed something hard at his belt, and this finally triggered coherent thought. *Pager. Got my cell phone, too. And other stuff.* He fingered the odd assortment of objects in his pockets, identifying keys, calculator, and the lighter he used for bunsen burners and alcohol lamps before ending the silly game. Relief triggered a nervous laugh. *What's wrong with me?* He tugged the phone from its plastic holder, lengthened the antennae, and pressed the lower left button. It came on with a beep, the display revealing the word "on." The indicator showed no signal strength whatsoever. *Weird. Charged it last night.* Collins lowered the phone with a shrug of resignation. *Who would I call anyway?* He considered the situation. *Hello, Dr. Demarkietto? I took a wrong turn, and I'm lost in the lab. Please send Lewis and Clark.* He jabbed the phone back into its holder. His ego preferred no one ever found out about his little adventure.

Collins continued his march along the wall, surprised by its irregularity, as well as his steady footing. He kept expecting to stumble over cartons or furniture, but he continued to walk unimpeded. Then, finally, he discovered a depression in the wall, its surface more like poorly sanded wood than stone. He groped for a doorknob but found none. Confused, he shoved it. To his surprise, it budged. Encouraged, he threw all of his weight against it. The wood panel gave beneath the effort, the hinges twisted free, and it collapsed forward. Momentum dragged Collins along with it.

Collins hit the floor before he realized he was falling, his face slamming into the door. Pain jarred through his nose and chest, and his glasses tumbled. He rolled onto wet mulch that clung to his bare torso and realized he could see now, though blurrily. He lay in a crudely constructed room with a large, paneless window. He fished around for his glasses; his hand came up empty. He saw dust, shattered stone, and moss but no sign of his glasses. Drawn to the window, he abandoned his search to look through it, out onto a plain filled with smeary weeds and wildflowers beneath sky the color of slate. Beyond it lay the shadow of a vast forest. Stunned more by the sight than the fall, Collins spoke aloud. "Where am I?" It looked like nowhere he remembered on Algary campus. Panic returning, he shouted. "Where the living hell am I?"

No answer came. Collins turned and drifted toward the fallen door. His gaze played over an uneven dirt floor, the piled dust displaying his every movement in bold relief: the starburst pattern from the gusts generated by the falling door, every treaded footprint, but no glasses. Collins dropped to all fours, searching diligently around and beneath the fallen door. He found only mud, stone, and moss. Hunger snaked through his gut with a long, loud growl. *Great. What else can go wrong?*

Collins abandoned his glasses for the more driving need for food. He could never remember feeling so unremittingly, miserably starved. He knew he should turn around, should attempt to retrace his steps; but the thought of wandering aimlessly in silent darkness for another three hours or longer, weathering the growing agony in his gut, seemed impossible beyond reckoning. He studied the room. Four stone-and-mortar walls rimed with moss enclosed him, the only exits the doorway into darkness and the window. He cast one last look around for his glasses, but they had disappeared as completely as the familiar rooms and hallways of Daubert Laboratories.

Collins dropped to his buttocks, stunned. Nothing made sense. In a matter of three dark hours, the world had changed in a way no logic could explain. He felt desperately confused, unable to find so much as a thread of logic despite his science background. Either he had plunged into madness or he had clambered into a parallel dimension, much like Dorothy and her Oz. *Only,* Collins reminded himself, *that was fiction.* In the real world, people did not follow white rabbits down holes to Wonderland. Or, in his case, white lab rats.

Only one thing seemed wholly, unutterably certain: he was hungry. Perhaps if he satisfied that single, desperate need, everything else would fall into some sort of proper, or even improper, order.

In a daze, Collins swung his legs over the window ledge

and jumped. He regretted the action immediately. Without his glasses, his depth perception had failed him; and he found himself airborne, surging toward the slope of a massive hill that supported the decaying structure. He hit the ground, right shoulder leading. His teeth snapped shut, pinching his tongue, and he tasted blood. A hot bolt of lightning burst through his head. Pain lurched through his arm and chest. Then, the world swirled around him in alternating patterns of green and silver as he spilled in savage circles down the side of the hill.

Pollen tickled Collins' nostrils. Stems crackled beneath him, stabbing his naked chest, sides, and back. The odor of broken greenery joined the mingled perfumes of the flowers. He wrapped his face in his palms and let gravity take him where it would, sneezing, wincing, and huffling as he went. At last, he glided to a gentle stop. Weeds and wildflowers filled his vision, and his head spun, still several cycles behind his body.

Collins lay on his back. An edge of sun peeked over a horizon he could only assume was the east, throwing broad bands of pink and baby blue through the gray plain of sky. Pale-petaled flowers swayed, intermittently blocking his vision, interspersed with woody stems that he hoped would prove edible and harmless. *Sunrise.* He blinked, the scene senseless. *I couldn't have crawled around that long.*

An interminable, aching groan issued from his stomach.

Collins sat up. *Now what?* He studied the building he had abandoned on the hill, a crumbling ruin of a stone fortress that defied modern construction. If it connected to Algary campus in any fashion, he could not see how. Later, he would explore it for some underground tunnel or well-hidden passage. Food had to come first.

Movement rattled the grasses.

Collins held his breath. He had not gone camping since Boy Scouts, and the image of Jimmy Tarses dumping a copperhead out of his boot remained vivid. No one had teased Jimmy for his high-pitched screams. The rest of them had been equally startled; from that time on, no boy put on any gear without checking it thoroughly first. Now, Collins' skin prickled at the thought. His heart resumed its wild pounding, and he rose cautiously. For all he knew, rattlesnakes might be cavorting all around him.

The rustling recurred, closer.

Collins watched a column of weeds dance, then stop. Hand dropping to the multitool he always kept on his belt, he forced himself to step toward it.

At that moment, the thing sat up on its haunches, peering at him through the grasses. Its nose twitched, its ears rose above the wildflowers, and it examined Collins through enormous black eyes. Collins took one more step, squinting, and finally got a good look at a fat, brown rabbit. It seemed remarkably unafraid, studying him, whiskered nose bobbing.

Never seen a human before? Collins guessed. *Or maybe someone's pet?* He cringed. If he caught the thing, he would have to eat it. If he ever found an owner, he would apologize and replace it; but he had no way of knowing when, or if, his next meal would come. Until he found Algary campus, he would have to make do.

"Here, bunny, bunny." Collins kept his motions fluid and nonthreatening. He held out a hand to it.

The rabbit remained still a moment longer, head cocked. Then, it dropped to all fours and stretched its nose toward Collins' hand.

Collins held totally still, allowing the animal to sniff at his fingers.

The rabbit glided toward him, outstretched front legs followed by a more solid hop of the back ones.

Prepared for it to scratch frantically or bite, Collins reached out and hauled the animal into his arms. Recalling kittens from his childhood, he scooped one arm under its legs, pinning its clawed feet, and used the other to clamp it against him. "Gotcha." The fur felt thick and soft against his chest.

The rabbit made small noises in its throat. Its coat mingled brown-and-gray agouti-striped hair in tufts.

Okay, Alice. You've caught the rabbit. Collins looked at the animal, hating himself for what had to come next. He wished he could keep it as a companion in this bizarre and, thus far, lonely world. *What happens now? The Queen of Hearts shrieks, "Off with his head?"* Though it seemed madness, he spoke to the creature. "You're not one of those magical talking animals, are you?"

The rabbit seemed to take no notice of Collins. It lay in his arms, surprisingly dense, its nose continuously wobbling.

"Because, if you are, you'd better tell me now." Collins carefully shifted the rabbit's weight to free his right hand. Opening the clasp on the belt case of his multitool, he unsnapped it and pulled out the tool. He worked free the knife blade, then looked at the rabbit again. "No? Sorry, bunny. It's over." The words came easier than the deed. Collins hesitated, cringing. He had pithed rats and frogs before, but the idea of slaughtering someone's sweet-tempered pet seemed an evil beyond his tolerance.

Collins closed his eyes. The pain in his gut intensified, an aching exhortation. Opening his eyes to slits, he pressed the blade against the top of its head, just behind the ears. In one swift motion, he drove the point deep into its brain.

The rabbit squealed, a high, haunting call that sent a stab of dread through Collins. Then, it went limp in his arms.

Collins shivered; the lingering horror of the noise weighed heavily on his conscience. He set the rabbit on the ground, his knife beside it. Never having hunted, he did not know the proper way to skin and gut; but he believed his anatomy classes would help. *First, a fire.* Collins pulled up a circle of grass and flowers, picked the driest for kindling, and walked in widening circles in search of twigs. At length, he gathered a handy pile and started the fire with his lighter.

Settling by the glow and crackle of the flames, Collins drew rabbit and knife into his lap and started skinning.

Chapter 2

BENTON Collins had heard rabbit meat described as tough, greaseless, and stringy; but experience clashed pleasantly with the report. He savored its rich, gamy flavor and streaming juices that sizzled in the fire. Succulent as a steak, it satisfied his empty stomach. He had teased out the organs carefully, yet guiltily suspected he had wasted quite a bit of edible meat with the skin. In the future, he hoped he would learn to rescue every scrap; his life, as well as more rabbits', might depend on it. He prepared to sink his teeth into the last leg.

A horse whinnied, sharp and sudden as a whipcrack.

Collins sprang to his feet, whirling toward the sound. Distant figures emerged patternlessly from the forest. He squinted, managing to make out a single, light-colored horse, its rider, and three or four milling people. His spirits soared. "Hey!" he shouted, waving the drumstick. "Over here!"

Their movement stopped. Without his glasses, Collins could not tell if they turned toward him.

"Here!" Collins called louder, waving the remainder of his

food frantically. "Over here." *Human contact, thank God. I'm saved.* He realized his story would sound positively ludicrous, unless others had come to this place through Daubert Laboratories before him. Perhaps some of the gamers did so regularly. Even if no one had, he doubted he would sound insane enough for them to have him institutionalized. *Assuming, of course, this parallel dimension is even at the same tech level as ours.*

Two dogs shot ahead of the people, barking wildly. They bounded into the weeds, leaping like porpoises through the tall grasses toward Collins.

Collins laughed as they approached, the horse cantering after them. A thought struck with chilling abruptness. *What if they're hostile? What if they're members of some primitive warrior tribe that hates everyone?* He discovered eerie parallels in his undergraduate history and sociology classes. People tended to fear differences, to revile what they did not understand. *Oh, come on, Ben. There's no such thing as other worlds. This is twenty-first-century America, for Christ's sake. What's wrong with me?*

Copper highlights glimmered from the horse's sleek golden coat, and its black mane and tail trailed it like streamers. Its rider appeared broad and well-muscled, apparently male, wearing what looked like a thigh-length rust-colored long-sleeved T-shirt with matching bicycle pants and leather riding boots.

The dogs arrived first, sneezing and waggling their tails, snuffling every part of Collins. One resembled a beagle, medium-sized and tricolored. The other towered over its companion, uniform brown except for black on its muzzle. Its ears stuck up in sharp triangles, and its tail curved over its back in a broad, stiff loop. Collins smiled at them, alternately petting each. He offered the last of his dinner to the beagle.

Delicately, the dog sniffed at the meat, whined softly, and retreated. Surprised, Collins held the drumstick out to the other dog. He had never met a large dog that did not gobble down proffered meat in an instant; yet this one also refused, pacing backward and forward nervously. It appeared to Collins as if it wanted the food but dared not take it. Realization seeped slowly into his thoughts. *Probably trained to only accept treats from their trainer.*

The horse skidded to a stop at his makeshift camp, trampling grasses and flowers beneath prancing hooves. Now, Collins could see the crude stitching and deep staining of the man's clothing and the deep saffron of his cuffs and collar. Widely spaced brown eyes studied Collins from coarse, weathered features, and he bore a headful of tangled sandy curls. He reeked of sweat. A sheathed sword dangled from his left hip. The fine-boned mare rolled a blue eye that contrasted strikingly with its buckskin coat and wind-whipped mane and tail. It bore no saddle and only a rope for a bridle, yet it clearly obeyed its rider.

Collins could not help staring back. He could no longer doubt that he had transported through time or discovered a world with no connection to his own. Seeking saliva in a mouth gone painfully dry, Collins broke the silence with a compliment. "Well trained dogs you got there. Wouldn't take fresh meat from a stranger." He brandished the rabbit leg.

The rider leaned forward, gaze sweeping the crafted clearing. Suddenly, he jerked back. He shouted something indecipherable to his slower-moving friends, who quickened their paces.

Collins glanced to his right, trying to figure out what had provoked his new companion. He saw only crushed and broken weeds, his multitool, and the remains of the rabbit. *The multitool*, he guessed. *Probably never seen anything like it.* He continued speaking, trying to radiate trust. "Well trained horse, too. Don't know many people who could ride without—"

Collins broke off as the other four people caught up, panting, with the leader. Though dressed the same, including the swords, they otherwise seemed as different as possible. Two were blonds, both male, one fair and the other dark as cola. One of the brunets was a pale and lanky man with a Roman nose, the other a sinewy, brown-skinned woman with her hair tied in a rough bun. Collins loosed a pent-up breath. At least, they seemed unlikely to comprise a homogeneous group that would hate him simply for his appearance. ''Hello,'' he said.

The people ignored his greeting. The one Collins assumed was the leader dismounted. He and the ample-nosed brunet stood on either side of Collins, examining him intently. The blonds approached the remains of his dinner. A sword rasped from its sheath.

Collins recoiled; but its wielder, the darkest man, kept his back to Collins and the others. He shuffled through the bones, skin, and organs, speaking rapidly in a language Collins could not identify. It sounded like nothing he had ever heard before, even from the international graduate students who shared his campus apartment building.

Abruptly, all of the humans spun toward Collins. Several started speaking at once, their tones frenzied and their gestures savage. The horse's eyes rolled white, and it danced sideways.

The sandy-haired leader stabbed the air with his hand and spoke over the others. Silence followed, but the glare on every face seemed unmistakable.

Collins back-stepped warily, abruptly terrified. His eyes jerked wide, his nostrils flared, and his heart rate doubled in an instant. Drained of thought, he whirled to run and nearly impaled himself on the woman's sword. He stopped short. The metallic rasp of drawing weapons echoed through the clearing. He froze. Then, slowly, he raised his hands in an innocent gesture of surrender. ''I mean you no harm. Friend.'' He hooked a finger toward his naked chest. ''Ben. My name is Ben. Ben.''

Collins felt motion at his flank. He spun. Something heavy crashed against the side of his head. Pain shocked through his skull with an explosion of white light. The impact flung him to the ground. He ducked behind his hands, protecting his aching head. Five swords leveled at his vitals held him in place.

The leader gave a command.

The lighter blond sheathed his sword. He shouldered off his

backpack and rooted inside it. A moment later, he pulled out a braided mass of rope, which he carried to Collins.

Collins bit his lip but otherwise remained perfectly still. His head felt on fire, and he did not know what might antagonize them to finish him off.

The sandy-haired giant motioned at Collins and said something uninterpretable.

Collins shrank further against the ground, head pounding. "I–I don't know what you're saying," he squeaked.

The brunet man exchanged a few words with the leader. Then, he hooked a boot beneath Collins' shoulder and flipped him prone.

Collins did not fight the motion, though it sparked flashes of light through his brain. Behind him, someone seized his hands and roped them together. As the knots tightened, they bit into his wrists. The blonds rifled his pockets, removing everything: loose change, calculator, keys, mechanical pencil, lighter, notes, wallet, the remote keyless entry to Marlys' car. They unfastened his belt, taking it along with his pager and cellular phone. They added his watch and the multitool to their haul. Craning his neck, Collins peered around the nearest of the strangers to watch others scoop the remains of his meal into a sack. Another stomped out his fire. When it seemed every trace of Collins' presence had disappeared into one sack or another, the four men seized him by the arms and knees, hefting him awkwardly onto the horse.

Collins did not fight, recalling the words of his neuroanatomy professor: "In movies, you see heroes bashing guys in the head all the time to knock them out. Truth is, the difference between causing a brain bruise and a deadly hemorrhage is incalculable. Guy goes out longer than a minute or two, it's a murder charge for the hero." If he could help it, Collins would not give these strangers another reason to strike him.

The horse snorted, humping its back. At a warning from the commander, it settled back on its hooves, prancing nervously sideways. The leader spoke soothingly to it, stroking its nose. The mare calmed, docilely allowing them to tie the sacks in place behind Collins. Two people on each side, the sandy-haired man leading the mare, they headed toward the forest.

Every step of the horse jarred through Collins' spine, and he suspected the animal deliberately made the ride as bumpy as possible. It stumbled over invisible stones, losing the delicate grace that had previously characterized its movements. The rope shifted with his slightest motion, grinding into his flesh until he worried it might sever his wrists.

Soon, the forest swallowed the group. Collins found himself in a shade as cozy as an early spring day. Most of the trees closely resembled those he knew: maple, oak, and locust. Others he did not recognize, including one with star-shaped emerald leaves so bright they seemed like polished holographs. His escorts spoke rarely to one another, though he caught them staring at him with evident hostility on occasion. He wondered what about him bothered them so much and, given their wildly different appearances, how they even knew he did not belong among them. The answer came almost immediately. *Duh, genius. Perhaps my complete inability to communicate with them?*

The self-deprecation did little to elevate Collins' spirits. His mind drifted to his telephone call with Marlys. In his current situation, the whole thing seemed foolish. *When I get back, I'll take all the blame. Buy her flowers. Treat her like a queen. She'll forgive me.* The words "if I get back" interspersed themselves into the thought, quite against his will. Apologizing for something not his fault seemed trivial compared to the possibility that these men and woman might be hauling him to eternal imprisonment or death.

Not death, Collins tried to assure himself. *They could have killed me easily enough in the field.* He felt like a suspect whose life now lay in the hands of lawyers and judges. During his first year of college, he had dabbled in radical liberalism. He still recalled trying to convince his father of the "truth" of the prison system. He pictured James Collins in his favorite La-Z-Boy, setting down his newspaper to debate with his son. Gray-flecked, army-short black hair receded from his freckled forehead, and he carried about twenty-five extra pounds, all of it in his gut.

"Prison just hardens criminals, makes them better and crueler criminals."

James had grunted at that. "Not our job to soften 'em, Ben. In prison, at least they're not hurting anyone innocent."

Collins had hardly dared to believe his father could not understand at all. Until his teens, he had always looked up to this man. "But when they get out, Dad, they're worse."

James had given his son a deeply searching look. "Worse than if we let 'em get away with their crimes?" He opened the newspaper again. "I don't think so." He lowered the paper to his knees. "Or are you suggesting executing them all as the alternative?"

The words had shocked Collins. "Dad, the death penalty's barbaric. You know that. And it's not a deterrent."

James had raised the paper again, turning the page with a loud rustle. "It's the ultimate deterrent."

"No." Collins had delved eagerly into the argument. This time, he had clear facts on his side. "No, Dad. It's not. The studies show—"

James' voice became muffled by the newspaper. "I don't need studies to tell me that once a guy's dead he can't hurt anyone any longer. Nothing more deterring than that."

At the time, Collins had given his father up as a lost cause who might never see the light. Now, with his stomach skittishly churning the rabbit meat, his thoughts flying in strange directions, his wrists and back aching, he realized he had discovered that terrifying limbo that precedes a fate wholly determined by strangers. The loss of control alone felt like torture. He could not speak for others, but the terrified wonder would deter him from ever committing a crime. If he ever had the chance.

Again, Collins attempted to steer his thoughts from the depressing possibilities. He concentrated on the scenery. They traveled a dirt path through towering trees whose shade and shed leaves discouraged undergrowth. The branches held vast bounties of leaves in myriad variations of green. Though not as colorful as the bursts of amber, scarlet, and orange that had characterized the autumn foliage in Algary a scant month before, it seemed even more beautiful. The plants seemed to glow with health and, despite mud and dust, looked remarkably clean. The sun streamed through gaps in the highest branches, lending a shimmering glow to the star-shaped leaves and dancing tiny rainbows through clinging droplets of water. In other circumstances, Collins would have enjoyed stretching out beneath the canopy, reveling in birdsong, gaze filled with nature's radiance. Now, distracted by the agonies jolting through his spine and threatening to dismember his hands, and by the uncertainty of whether or not he even had a future, he could only look in mute alarm. He wondered how much more beautiful it might appear with his glasses.

It occurred to Collins suddenly that he should have etched the route they had thus far taken into his memory. If they released him, or he managed to escape, he would have to find his way back to this place. In fact, he would need to keep his wits about him from this point on if he hoped to survive this world intact. *If it's not already too late.* He shook that thought aside. It could only lead to hopeless despair.

The idea proved easier to concoct than to implement. The pathways branched and looped, and Collins lost track of turns that came naturally to his captors. The intensity of his headache muddled his thinking; twice, he found himself drifting into a strange, conscious oblivion. The other pains remained a constant, intermittently overwhelming diversion.

Then, just as Collins began to believe he'd been captured by nomads, the forest opened to pastures and fields. A low wall of corn blocked their way, and the people led the horse around its squared edge. As they rounded the corner, he saw a vast green pasture grazed by several goats, horses, and pigs. Younglings frolicked around them, the different animals intermingling freely in their games. A cow stood by itself, chewing its cud, its round abdomen looking ready to pop out a calf at any moment. Beyond the animals stretched more fields of unidentifiable shoots and, farther, a huddle of buildings that made up a small and primitive town.

Collins took heart at the sight of the animals. A society that accepted people of all appearances as equals seemed likely to prove reasonably broad-minded. For reasons he could only attribute to childhood cartoon watching, the peaceful coexistence of the animals added to the image of tolerance that might prove so important to his fate. The "good guys" always loved a wide variety of animals as well as their fellow men.

The horse trumpeted out a whinny that shook its entire frame. Caught off guard, Collins lost his balance. He toppled from its withers. Instinctively, he went to catch himself with his hands. The rope burned as it shifted across his wrists, and he slammed the ground with his already bruised shoulder. Pain shocked through him. He lay still, eyes closed, teeth gritted. The hands that shoved him back into position disappeared in a dizzying rush of spots that scored his vision. He fell against the horse's slimy neck, panting against pain. *I can't believe this is happening to me.*

The ride continued as a blur of motion and distant voices. Collins remained dimly aware of being carried into a large building and thrust into a cell. The door crashed shut with a metallic ring. He lay on his belly, face pressed against cold stone, and allowed nothingness to overtake him.

Benton Collins awoke in the same position he had lost consciousness. He opened his eyes to a mortared stone wall that smelled damp and as musty as an old book. He struggled to sit, automatically tossing one hand out for balance. He winced against the anticipated pain that movement had caused the last time he performed it, only to find that his arm moved freely. Using his hands, he managed to sit up easily. He examined his wrists. The ropes had scraped them raw, and clear fluid oozed from several places. His head no longer hurt. Dirt splattered his chest and abdomen in smeared patches, glazed with a fine coating of dust. His jeans were damp with horse sweat and grime speckled with short golden hairs.

Collins glanced around his prison, approximately four yards square with bars on three sides. The one across from the only stone wall opened onto a hallway, while the other two separated his cell from the ones on either side. He saw no other captives, which seemed like a good sign. Apparently, they did not confine people on a frequent and arbitrary basis. Once they realized he meant them no harm, they would surely release him.

Two bowls lay on the floor in the front left corner. One held water so clear Collins could see every blemish on the inner surface of the crockery. The other contained what appeared to be salad, dotted with lifesaver-sized and -shaped objects of black and brown. The rabbit sat heavily in his gut, and even the thought of food made him queasy. He wondered how long it would take for anyone to miss him. None of the professors intended to return until Sunday. His parents would assume he had gone to the Johnsons, and Marlys would likely believe he was just being rude. He amended the thought. *Not rude. Passive/aggressive.* A psychology student, she always had a long word, often in unpronounceable Latin, to describe even the most normal aspects of human behavior.

Taking his cue from prisoner movies, Collins examined the bars and lock of his cell. Though pitted in places, they all seemed more than solid enough to withstand any bare-handed assault he could muster. He paced the cell a couple of times, expending nervous energy. Finally, with a sigh of resignation, he sat with his back against the stone wall, his legs stretched in front of him and his throbbing wrists in his lap.

Soon after Collins took his position, two men appeared at his cell. They wore the same rust-and-gold uniforms as the ones who had captured him, but he recognized neither. One looked about six feet tall, with a shock of red hair, pale skin, and wide features. The other stood shorter but outweighed the first by nearly half again as much, most of it muscle. He had hair a shade lighter than Collins' dark brown, and he wore it in a braid. His skin matched his hair almost perfectly. Each carried a sword and what looked like a billy club in a wide belt.

Collins approached, glad for a chance to attempt explanation, though it seemed futile. "Hello," he said in his friendliest voice.

Both men turned.

"My name is Ben." Collins jabbed a finger toward his chest. "Ben."

The men watched him, saying nothing.

"I–I mean no . . . harm." Collins assumed a bright smile, placing his hands casually between the bars on a horizontal support. "I just want to go home." He stabbed a thumb toward the back of the cell. "Home. Understand?"

The men gave no sign that they did. Abruptly, one freed his club, slamming it down on Collins' fingers.

Pain shocked through Collins' hand, and he jerked away instinctively. "Ow, damn it! Why did you—"

The two men were laughing. They glanced at Collins, exchanged a few words, then broke into hearty chuckles again.

Collins withdrew to the back of his cell and slumped against the stone wall. He nursed his left hand in his right. Nothing seemed broken, and the pain dulled swiftly. The agony in his spirit took longer. Tears stung his eyes for the first time in more years than he could remember. *Can't escape. Can't communicate.* He sobbed. *I'm going to die here.*

Apparently having sated their curiosity, and their cruelty, the guards left. A few hours later, others replaced them. These, too, came to study their charge, the first a rangy, middle-aged man, the other a woman of about his age, twenty-three, with silky black hair and a golden tan. They also wore the standard uniform, including the swords and batons.

The thought of repeating the previous encounter repulsed Collins, yet he knew he had to try. He rose, slowly and carefully, edging toward the bars. This time, he stopped beyond reach of their weapons. "Hello," he said miserably.

The man said something to the woman, who nodded. She watched Collins' every movement through intent, blue eyes. She sported high cheekbones, spare lips, and a generous nose. Though not classically beautiful, she had a refinement to her movements and features symmetrical enough to make her reasonably attractive. Though slender, she had a sinewy physique that revealed strength.

It seemed a hopeless question, but Collins asked anyway. "Do you speak any English?"

They did not reply.

"Eng-lish," Collins repeated.

The guards exchanged glances. The male ran a hand through the brown-and-white stubble of his hair and shrugged. He said something in their strange language.

The woman replied, equally incomprehensibly.

"Hurt." Collins hit his left arm with his right hand. He shook his head vigorously. "No hurt." He peeled his right hand away, dropped it to his side, and patted it with his left.

The two watched his every movement.

Collins continued, "Friends." He hugged himself fondly. "Friends?"

"Frinz?" the woman repeated in a questioning tone.

The man put things together more quickly. A frown scored his features, and his crow's-feet sprang to vivid relief around his eyes. "No friends."

Encouraged by their clear attention, Collins explained again. He slapped his left arm again, then looked surprised. "Hurt." He shook his head. "No HURT." He plucked loose his right hand

and patted it again, followed by a self-hug. ''Friends. Yes.'' He bobbed his head eagerly.

The man glared. ''No friends.'' He jabbed a finger at Collins. ''No no no friends.'' He turned his back. ''Yes, *aguryo*.''

Clearly, the guard had understood his pantomime. And rejected it. Heaving a deep sigh, Collins slunk to the back of his cell, dropped to the floor, and buried his head. ''Friends,'' he whispered. ''Friends . . . yes.''

Hopeless terror kept Benton Collins awake far into the night. Despair gave way to rocky acceptance, then to desperate worry. He paced the confines of his cell like a zoo tiger, afraid to try to sleep. When he went still, thoughts crowded him, horrible considerations of what his future held. Suddenly, all the things he had cursed earlier that day seemed insignificant. So his parents had chosen their lovers over their son. He was grown now, and they had a right to lives of their own. It only made sense for the other lab assistants and professors to go home over Thanksgiving, since he had nowhere to go. His student loans—only money. None of it mattered one iota if he never found his way back to Algary.

In the wee morning hours, the female guard reappeared. She stood quietly in front of Collins' cell, studying him. The lantern light kindled glimmers in her pale eyes, but she otherwise blended into the dark obscurity of the prison.

Collins stopped his pacing to look at her. With little hope, he tried one more time, touching a hand to his chest. ''Ben. That's me. Ben Collins.''

''Falima,'' she replied.

''Falima,'' Collins repeated. ''Pretty. Is that your name?''

''Yes. My name is Falima.''

He had not expected a reply; so, when he got one, it stunned him to wide-eyed silence.

''Why?'' Falima added.

Collins found his tongue. ''You–you *do* speak English,'' he said, holding accusation from his voice.

''English,'' she repeated, rolling the word in her mouth as if to taste it. ''Is that what I am speaking?''

''Yes.'' Collins approached the bars but did not touch them. ''And quite well, I might add.''

''You *might* add?''

Knowing idioms, slang, and expressions often confused newcomers to a language, Collins amended. ''Well, I *did* add, I guess. Do all your people speak English?''

''No.'' Falima considered her own answer briefly, apparently recognizing the word from their previous encounter. Her eyes narrowed, and she studied him further. ''No friends.'' She spoke the last two words with a heavy accent that had not tainted her previous conversation.

Collins' heart rate quickened. He had finally found someone with whom he could communicate, and he seemed to be failing miserable. ''Why 'no friends?' '' he asked with genuine concern.

Falima pronounced each word with slow and bitter force. ''You . . . are . . . evil.''

''Me?'' The question was startled from Collins. ''Evil?''

''Yes.''

''Why would you say such a thing?''

''Murderer,'' she hissed. ''Cannibal.''

Collins blinked ponderously, certain Falima had chosen the wrong word. ''Cannibal? What are you talking about?'' A moment later, he wished he had reacted as strongly to the claim of murder. To his knowledge, he did not have a violent bone in his body.

Apparently misunderstanding, Falima defined the word. ''One who eats its own kind. Cannibal. You.''

''I've never eaten a person in my life.'' Seeing the opportunity, he added. ''And I've never killed anyone, either.''

Using her thumb and middle finger, Falima pulled back her locks, black as ink, thick, and shiningly soft. They fell instantly back to the sides of her head. "You killed Joetha, Ben Collins." The blue eyes filled with ice. "Then you ate her. We found the remains in your possession, some in your very hands."

"What?" The suggestion seemed nonsense. "I didn't have—" Realization struck with the force of a speeding truck. "Are you talking about the rabbit?"

"Joetha," Falima corrected.

Stunned, Collins stuttered. "I couldn't—I mean I didn't—know . . ." He trailed off. It seemed impossible that he had discovered a society so tolerant of differences that its citizens considered animals on a par with humans. *Why not? There are people in our world who do.* He recalled incidents of loonies breaking into laboratories, murdering humans to "rescue" laboratory animals that swiftly perished in the wild. "I–I didn't know. You have to believe me."

"I have to?"

"Because it's true. In my world, animals are considered . . ." Collins chose his words with care. ". . . our charges, not . . . our equals."

The blue eyes narrowed, as if Falima found his explanation impossible to fathom. "What is your switch-form?"

The compound word made no sense to Collins. "My what?"

"Your switch-form. Your switch-form?"

The repetition did not help. "I don't understand."

Falima spoke louder and with awkward sluggishness. "YOUR . . . SWITCH . . . -FORM."

Baffled, Collins regarded Falima blankly, then came back with the same volume and tone, "I . . . HAVE . . . NO . . . CLUE . . . WHAT . . . YOU'RE . . . TALKING . . . ABOUT."

Falima tilted her head. Her lips pursed, and she squinted. Clearly, she thought him a moron. "What are you when you are not a man?"

"Not a man?" Collins shook his head. ". . . well, I used to be a boy." He could not help adding, "My girlfriend thinks I still am."

Falima rolled her eyes. "So, you are hiding it. A carnivore of some sort, no doubt. Or a bear, maybe. They are always the ones that fall off their oaths."

Collins threw up his hands in surrender. "I honestly have no idea what you're getting at." He put the scattered details together. "Are you saying that sometimes you're something other than a woman?"

Falima's hands clamped to her hips. "You rode me here."

"I did?" Collins' eyes widened at the realization. "You're . . . you're . . . a horse?" The words sounded twice as ridiculous coming from his own mouth. *One of us is entirely crazy.* He studied Falima more fully, now noticing the minutiae that seemed too clear for coincidence: the large blue eyes, glossy black hair, and golden skin tone. As impossible as it seemed, he believed. Once Collins' mind made that leap, worse had to follow. "Oh, my God!"

"Yes, my switch-form is a horse. What's wrong with that?"

"That rabbit was . . . was—"

"A sweet old woman." Falima's eyes narrowed again. "And you *ate* her."

Collins' stomach churned. Bile climbed up his throat. "Oh, my God. My God!" Though nauseated, he felt certain he could not vomit and desperately wished he could. "Holy shit. My God. My God!" Nothing more coherent seemed possible. "I—" His voice emerged hoarser than he expected. "I . . . didn't know. Where I come from, people are just people. Animals are . . . animals. All the time. Always."

Rage rekindled in Falima's pale eyes, and she regarded Collins like some loathsome insect. "In Barakhai, you are a murderer and a cannibal. And you will be hanged midmorning."

Stunned dumb, Collins could only stare as Falima turned her back on him and strode swiftly beyond sight.

Chapter 3

BENTON Collins sprawled on the floor of his cell, the stone warming to his body. His eyes lay open; he felt incapable of closing them. The irregular, plank ceiling became indelibly etched on his vision: the watermark in the shape of a bottle, the knothole like an ever-staring eye, the spidery crack that emitted a steady patter of water droplets. *You will be hanged midmorning.* The words cycled through his mind, always in Falima's voice, a death knell he had no way to escape. "I didn't know," he said to no one. "How could I possibly know?"

Collins scraped his fingers along the damp stone in mindless circles, his back aching and his wrists throbbing with every heartbeat. *This can't be happening. People changing into animals? It can't be real.* He forced his eyes shut, hoping that, when he opened them, he would awaken from this nightmare. The darkness behind his lids was filled with shadows.

Beyond his control, Collins' eyes glided open to confront the same water spot, the knothole, and the crack. The water plopped steadily against stone.

Collins awakened with no realization of having slept. Only the diffuse glow illuminating the prison revealed that morning had come. Distant voices wafted to him, unintelligible and intermingled with the occasional clink of metal. He sprang to his feet, the movement inciting a sharp pain through his back and right shoulder. The hard floor had stiffened him during the night.

Four men entered Collins' field of vision. They all wore the familiar rust and gold, swords, and batons. They also carried a rope.

Terror seized every part of Collins. He flattened against the back wall of his cell.

The men spoke to one another in their odd language, then gestured Collins forward.

Collins did not move. "There's been . . . a mistake," he wheezed through a throat gone painfully dry. "I didn't know. I . . . didn't . . . know." Enough time had passed that the rabbit no longer filled his belly, a constant reminder of a heinous crime. Yet he found it impossible to eat.

The guards exchanged more words. Then, one stepped forward and unlocked the cage. Two of the men entered, one carrying the rope. The door clanged shut behind them.

Collins measured the two with his gaze. Both stood shorter than his five-foot-eleven frame, and only one outweighed his 155 pounds. However, both moved with a wary dexterity that threatened experience and strength. It seemed as foolish to fight as to go willingly. The first would gain him bruises in addition to his sentence, but the latter would mean he had done nothing to avert his fate. Either way, he had nothing to lose but more pain. He was going to die. *I'm going to die.* Despite the time he had invested in it, the thought seemed beyond comprehension.

The man without the rope, the heavier one, drew a loop in the air with his finger, an obvious gesture to turn.

Collins only blinked, pretending not to understand. It seemed safer than insolence.

The men conversed a moment, then nodded. They lunged for Collins simultaneously. He leaped backward, crashing against the wall with enough force to send pain lurching through his spine and breath huffing from his lungs. A moment later, they had him prone, arms pulled behind him. The ropes tightened around his wrists again, reawakening the previous day's agony. He screamed.

The guards shouted over Collins. The two hauled him to his feet, the door opened, and they all escorted him through the prison hallway. They went through another door, attended by two women in the standard uniform, then emerged into sunshine so bright it seared Collins' eyes. He shut them, allowing the men to guide him blindly, stumblingly forward. Gradually, the sounds of a crowd grew around him, mingled conversations interspersed with an occasional call and sometimes pierced by a bark or whinny. He opened his eyes to slits, seeing a blur of faces, streets, and cottages in a glaze of brilliant sunlight. Then, he caught sight of the gallows towering over the rest, and he forced his eyes fully open despite the pain.

Collins now saw that he walked through a village of mud-and-thatch cottages, shops, and mills. The gathering consisted of a teeming mass of people, as varied in appearance as Americans, except they all wore simple homespun: grizzled elders and slouching adolescents, adults of every age, some clutching children's hands or babies in their arms. The shadow of the gallows loomed over them. Collins pinned his attention on the vast wooden monstrosity. A rope dangled from its uppermost pole, over a high, warped platform with massive, metal hinges. Clearly, the rope went around the victim's throat, then the platform was dropped, suspending him, by his neck, just above the level of the crowd. *Him.* Collins shivered. *Him is me.* He would feel his spine snapping, a moment of excruciating pain followed by absolute and permanent nothingness. *Permanent.* The enormity of death filled his mind with a terror beyond panic, the realization that the world would go on without him in it, that his time on this earth would end, not in years, but in minutes.

Collins reared backward, against his captors, screaming in mindless hysteria. Their grips tightened painfully, nails gouging his arms, then his legs. He felt himself lifted into the air. He squirmed, desperate, howling, aware only of the complete and monstrous need to break free. Though Collins recognized forward motion, the significance of it refused to penetrate the thought-shattering horror that drove his fight.

It all came home moments later.

The noose tickled, then hugged Collins' neck, and he went utterly still. *It's going to happen. It's really going to happen. I'm going to die.* A hopeless rationality filled him, a strange relief from the previous panic. *And I'm not going down in the history books as the hero who faced his end bravely.* His mind slid to a story he had read in junior high, about a man hanged from a bridge who hallucinated a grand escape in the moments before death. He wondered if it really happened that way and realized that no one could possibly know. He would, but he could do nothing with the information. *If only I'd gone to the Johnsons'. If only I hadn't followed that rat. If only I hadn't eaten that rabbit.* Regrets followed, the inability to apologize for small misdeeds, to say good-bye. He thought of all the things he would never get to do: hold a job, marry, coddle his children. *Visit Disney World.*

A man said something Collins could not understand.

Collins laughed hysterically, screwing his eyes shut. Then, the floor fell out under his feet, and he felt himself plunging. He tightened the muscles of his neck and face, bracing for the final impact.

The fall seemed to last forever. Then, a jolt shocked through his groin. Agony cramped his stomach, and he tumbled forward. His nose struck something hard and hairy, driving more pain through him. The crowd roared. Collins forced his lids open. Immediately, wiry hair slashed his eyes, and he shut them again. He felt forward movement, gaining momentum. The noose lay heavy on the back of his neck. He dared a shuddering breath, and air glided silkily, surprisingly easily, into his lungs.

The crowd continued shouting, sounding like they were in an open air sports stadium. Collins sat, splay-legged, on something warm and furry that carried him at a rocking sprint away from the gallows. He remembered the name of the hanging story: "An Occurrence at Owl Creek Bridge," though the significance of knowing it eluded him. Pitching his torso back, without the use of his still-tied arms, he wrenched open his eyes again. His breaths came in pants, due to shock not pressure.

Farm fields flashed past Collins, and forest loomed ahead. Behind, he heard yelling. The noose remained around his neck, trailing a length of rope. He sat astride a horse, its black mane whipping into his face, one golden ear forward, the other flicked backward. A set of saddlebags lay slung across its withers. *Falima?* he wondered, doubting the possibility. She had seemed so hostile toward him the previous night. He eased more steadily onto the horse's back, not caring who or what had caught him, only glad that he had at least a little longer to live.

The horse lunged around the trees, racing between trunks with a speed that quailed Collins. He wished for the use of his hands. Weight shifts and knee pressure seemed woefully inadequate to keep him astride as the animal kept up its breakneck pace on narrow deer trails through dense tangles of forest. Then, as if in answer to his wish, the ropes loosened on his wrists. He fingered them, his exploration rewarded by frayed areas where it had, apparently, broken. He twisted it blindly over fingers, hands, and wrists, hampered by a warm, sticky liquid. Then, the rope fell away, freeing his hands. He pulled the noose from his neck, rubbed his bleeding wrists, and seized handfuls of mane.

The horse loosed a low nicker and slowed, slogging through denser brush and between more tightly packed trunks. Something buzzed past, irritatingly close to Collins' ear. He swatted at it, missed, and turned his attention to the terrain. The horse wallowed through tangles of brush, forcing Collins to flatten against its neck or side to avoid braining himself on leaning deadfalls and shed branches caught in the crotches of other trees. Time and again, he jerked a leg onto the horse's back to rescue it from being crushed.

Collins had done some riding with his high school girlfriend and realized he could steer the animal better than it could randomly pick its way along the trail. Taking up the rope intended to kill him, he fashioned it into a raw bridle, essentially a loop with reins. Gliding up the horse's neck, he flicked the coil around its nose.

The horse made a sound deep in its throat but otherwise seemed to take no notice of the rudely fashioned tack. As panic receded, Collins considered his situation. He rode on a horse that might, at other times, be human, possibly even Falima. The animals he had thus far seen acted exactly like the creatures they resembled in his own world, except for the too-friendly rabbit. *Joetha,* he corrected, cringing. Apparently, while in "switchform," they lost their human memories and fully became animals. He wondered if all humans here had an animal-form, whether he might acquire one if he remained here too long, and how much control they had over the change.

Collins steered the buckskin around a thick, low-hanging branch. It ignored his gentle pull, so he increased the pressure, then drove his opposite heel into its flank.

The ears jerked backward. The horse reared with a sharp squeal, then followed Collins' instruction. The horse's reaction flashed guilt through him. Perhaps the horse did retain at least some of its human understanding. Suddenly he remembered the dogs' unwillingness to share his feast in the field. *They must have some crossover between human and animal time. Otherwise, the dogs would never know they could not eat meat.*

Collins had acted from impulse, accustomed to steering horses with reins and heel strikes. The horses back home had always taken these techniques in stride, a standard and accepted form of communication. Apparently, people here had a different way of making contact with their horses. He had tried talking to the rabbit and had received no response or indication that it understood. In the field, the guards had used a rope on Falima's horse-form, so she had to have some experience with being led. Nevertheless, he resolved not to kick her any more.

Something buzzed past Collins' head again. This time, he caught a glimpse of what appeared to be a large bumblebee or horsefly zipping past him. *Human, too?* he wondered, then dismissed the thought. No world could support even a hundredth as many people as bugs.

Collins turned his attention back to the horse. ''Hello,'' he tried. ''Are you Falima?''

The animal gave no indication it understood, though one ear did rise from its previous position, plastered angrily against its head.

The ride continued for hours, the horse ignoring every attempt by Collins to end it. Pulling back on the rope only made it raise and shake its head. Verbal explanations and, later, exhortations were met with nothing more than a few flicks of its ears. When he tensed to leap from its back, it quickened its pace dangerously, tossing him back into his seat. Eventually, Collins gave up, settling into the most comfortable position his sore thighs could find, flicking off the rope, and allowing the animal to take him where it would.

Finally, deep in some clearly unexplored part of the forest, the horse stopped. It dropped its head to graze at weeds poking around deadfalls and fallen clumps of leaves, then shook its entire body. The sudden movement caught Collins off guard; a grab at the flying mane barely rescued him from a fall. He slid down the horse's side, dislodging the saddlebags and clinging only by his hands. Mane hairs bit into his fingers.

The horse responded with an abrupt toss of its head that tore his grip free, as well as several strands from its mane. Collins dropped to the ground, rolling, hands protecting his head from a chance movement of the animal's hooves. It placidly returned to grazing, paying him no attention at all. The saddlebags lay on the ground.

Carefully, gaze fixed on the animal, Collins eased the saddlebags to him. Made of some natural fiber, the saddlebags yielded easily to his grip, much lighter and flimsier than the leather bags he had used in high school. Its well-crafted shape and metal weights sewn into the central areas kept it in place despite the lack of a pommel. He unlatched one of the two buckles and peered at a bulge of fabric. Hoping for something to replace the sweatshirt he had left to block the door crack in Daubert Labs, he pulled free several pieces. He unfolded a brown dress wrapped around a braided rope halter and lead, followed by a royal blue tunic that looked child-sized. Three knives thumped to the dirt, then a canteen and a stoppered crock. He worked the stopper free and peered inside, discovering a moving mass of what appeared to be enormous bugs. Startled, he dropped the crock. Three black beetles rolled to the ground, bearing a striking resemblance to the round objects he had seen on his salad in the prison cell. One opened its wings, then lifted soundlessly from the ground. The other two followed a moment later, and Collins recorked the crockery.

Collins discovered several more articles of clothing, in varying sizes, including a green tunic and cloak as well as a pair of brown britches that looked as if they might fit him. He pulled the tunic over his head, leaving the lacings undone. It felt odd, the fabric rough against his chest; and it was strangely tight in some places and loose in others. At least it kept him warm. The other pack contained more clothing, another canteen, a parcel of white paste resembling Play Doh, his cell phone and watch, and three pairs of wood-and-rope sandals. He also found a few hard rolls, wrinkled apples, and a wrapped packet of something that looked and smelled like the curds he had tasted on a field trip to the cheese factory in sixth grade.

Collins clipped his cell phone in place and stretched his watch back onto his wrist. It read six o'clock, which was clearly wrong. The sun lay directly overhead. He reset it for noon. Then, needing to relieve himself, he struggled into the weeds. Even as he walked, he realized the ludicrousness of his action. It hardly mattered where he chose to urinate in the depths of a forest. Only the horse would see him, yet he felt odd doing it in front of her, in case she was an intelligent alter ego of Falima. He walked just out of sight to perform his business, then studied the scene around him.

Trees and brush stretched in every direction as far as Collins could see. The intertwined branches emitted sunlight in patches, checkering the forest floor in patterns of gray and gold. In this area, oaks grew predominantly, their distinctive serrated leaves closely resembling the ones in Collins' world. Deep layers of rotting brown leaves lay like foam beneath his feet. He took a long breath of air, savoring the clean dampness. A whiff of smoke entered with it, and he froze. He was an escaped murderer now; he had to assume he'd be pursued.

Whirling, Collins ran back to the horse. A root hooked his foot, sending him sprawling. He skidded through leaf mold and muck, coming to a stop near the saddlebags. Beyond the horse, a campfire burned a cheery, crackling dance. In front of it sat a middle-aged man with skin like milk. From beneath a broad-brimmed hat, white-blond hair fell to his shoulders; and his eyebrows and lashes became invisible in the sunlight. He wore black linens that resembled some of the clothing from the saddlebags. Collins stared, reviving his genetics lessons. Albinism accompanied certain syndromes, including some that dangerously weakened the immune system. But, he recalled, most albinos simply inherited a recessive gene from both parents that left them without melanin.

Shocked by the thought, Collins pushed it from his mind. He

could not understand why he remained so calm when, likely, the other was hunting him. Caught, he would certainly be executed immediately. He whirled to run.

"Come!" the albino said in English. "No run." He repeated, more emphatically. "No *run*."

Curiosity warred with common sense. Collins turned carefully. "You speak English?"

"Little," the man responded. "No hurt." He rose and gestured toward the fire, seeming frustrated with his own limited ability to communicate. "Help you. Bringed here." He shook his head in irritation. "Come."

Still uncertain, Collins took a step toward the other man. A crock rested in the center of the fire, bubbling lazily.

"Me . . . Zylas," the albino said, looking up. Pale blue eyes met Collins' brown ones. "Zylas." He pointed at himself. "Understand?"

Collins nodded vigorously. Then, realizing the action might not mean the same thing here, verbalized his answer. "Understand. I'm Ben. Benton Collins, actually; but you can call me Ben." The horse moved nearer the fire and whinnied.

Zylas reached up and patted it reassuringly.

"Is that . . ." Collins started, wondering if the question might be improper. "Is that Falima's switch-form?"

"Falima." Zylas patted the horse again. "Yes, Falima."

Collins made an intuitive leap. "And you're . . . you're that rat." Hoping he had not offended the man, he softened the question. "Or aren't you?"

"Rat, yes," Zylas returned. "Me rat." His pidgin English clashed with Falima's fluency. Collins found himself wishing for her human form, even if she did seem to intensely dislike him.

"Did you . . . rescue me?"

Zylas nodded, glancing at the cooking food. "Chew rope off neck. Chew rope off hand." He stirred the contents of the crock with a stick. "Falima catched."

"Yes." Collins glided nearer. "Falima caught me. Thanks.

Thank you. Both of you.'' He reached out to pet Falima, but her ears jerked flat to her head, and it seemed safer to remove his hand. ''I don't think she likes me.''

Zylas grinned. ''She'll . . . come around.''

It sounded funny to hear someone who barely knew the language using idioms. Collins guessed Zylas had learned English by example rather than textbooks. ''I–I truly didn't know about the animal . . . transformation thing. Honest. I would never have eaten—''

Zylas waved Collins silent. ''I know. Haven't talked into Falima . . . yet. I been there.'' He made a throwaway gesture. ''She no been.''

Collins filled in the missing words. ''You've been to my world.''

''Yes.'' Zylas wrinkled his nose.

Hope soared, and Collins smiled. ''So you can get me home from here.''

A light flickered in Zylas' soft eyes, and he shrugged. ''Try.''

''All right,'' Collins said carefully. ''Try.'' He reminded Zylas of the obvious, ''Because, if you don't, I'm dead.''

''Yes.'' Zylas went back to stirring.

Expecting something a bit stronger, Collins chewed his lower lip. ''I really appreciate your saving me.''

''Mmmm.''

''And your taking me back to the . . . the way back to my world.''

''All right.''

Collins glanced at the crock, recognizing it as the same one from which he had poured the beetles. ''Um, are those . . . um . . . bugs you're cooking?''

Zylas followed the direction of Collins' gaze. ''*Fraharas*.'' He translated. ''Bugs, yes. Big, hard-shell bugs.'' He added, as if it might matter, ''They clean.''

Collins had not eaten since the rabbit. Terror had kept hunger at bay, but now he realized he would like a bite. *Not bugs.* ''Is that what you eat?''

Zylas bobbed his head. ''Bug. Fruit. Vegetable.'' He said the latter with an extra syllable and an improper emphasis, so it emerged like vejah*tah*bull. ''Fish. Milk. Cheese. Egg—but not with baby in.'' He tossed the parcel of curds. ''These better?''

''Much, thank you.'' Collins popped one into his mouth. It squeaked as he chewed it, but it tasted at least as good as any cheese in his world. He ate three more pieces before speaking again. ''Do all people here become animals.''

''Not *opernes*.'' He considered the translation. ''King . . . and . . . such like . . .''

''Royalty?'' Collins tried.

''Royalty.'' Zylas rolled his eyes as if tasting the word, then bobbed his head. ''Royalty. Others all yes.''

''And all animals?''

''Become person.''

''All?'' Collins put more cheese into his mouth, talking as he chewed.

''All.''

Collins found the contradiction. ''But you said you eat fish.''

Zylas scooped a liquid spoonful of beetles from the crock and slurped it into his mouth. ''Fish not animal.''

Collins' gut churned, and he looked away to keep himself from vomiting. The logic seemed maddeningly circular. All animals became humans, but ''animal'' was, apparently, defined by the ability to transform to human form. ''Anything else living not considered animal?''

The beetles crunched in Zylas' mouth. ''Bug. Plant. Fish.'' He shrugged. ''That all.'' He eased the crock fully from the fire.

Falima wandered off for better grazing, still well within earshot.

''And when you're an animal.'' Collins downed more cheese, keeping his gaze averted. ''Do you remember and understand . . . people stuff?''

"Stuff?"

Collins tried to explain. "Speech, hands, manners."

Zylas scooped and ate more beetles. "Some." He clearly fought for words. "Depend on want. Age. Ex . . . ex . . ." The word would not come.

"Experience," Collins supplied.

"Experience," Zylas repeated. "Experience."

"So the more times you become a rat . . ." Collins trailed off.

"Better . . . overlap."

"Between human and animal forms?" Collins supplied

"Right."

Collins ate more cheese, then asserted. "I think I'd spend half my childhood in switch-form, or even more. Get the hang of it as soon as possible." Feeling Zylas' intent gaze upon him, Collins met the pallid eyes.

"No choice."

"What?"

Zylas used wild hand gestures to punctuate his words, as if this might aid the translation. "Spend half time people, half animal. Change at time, same time, always. No choice."

"Every day?"

"Every day," Zylas confirmed.

Collins tried to understand. "So, half the day you're a rat and half a guy?"

Zylas nodded.

"Do you get to choose which half at least?"

"No choice," Zylas replied again. "No choice at all."

A million more questions occurred to Collins as they rode Falima, for hours, through the woodlands; but he remained silent as Zylas had requested. Sunlight sliced intermittently through breaks in the forest canopy, alternately covered by clouds and branches. Although Collins did not recognize the pathways they took, he had little choice but to trust his new companion. The rat/man had rescued him from execution and did appear to diligently check their route. At irregular intervals, he slid down from his position behind Collins to scout. Some things, Collins could figure out for himself. For example, clearly each person had an individual change time. Otherwise, Falima would have become human at noon, as Zylas had.

Brush rustled. Zylas reached around Collins to lay a pale hand on the left side of Falima's neck. Instantly, she swerved to the right, then went still.

Collins turned to look at his companion. The other man shook his head, gestured at Collins to remain in place, and made a motion near his mouth that Collins took as a plea for quiet. Worried about unseen dangers, he felt his heart rate quicken.

A squirrel appeared on the trail, an acorn clutched between its paws. It gnawed at the nut, flicking its tail in jerky bursts, then continued on its way.

Falima glided back onto the path. Collins smiled at Zylas' paranoia, which seemed oddly stronger than his own. Then he remembered. *That squirrel could be the local police.* As they continued on their way, Collins had to ask, "That squirrel. Was that someone you know?"

"No." Zylas replied into Collins' ear. "*Durithrin.*"

Collins shook his head at the unfamiliar word. "What?"

"*Durithrin,*" Zylas repeated, the word no more comprehensible the second time. "A . . . a . . ." He sighed. "Not . . . city . . . people."

Collins nodded, letting Zylas off the hook, though he still did not really understand. He guessed it was a concept his world did not need, something that applied only to human/beast interfaces.

Collins missed the signal that brought Falima to a stop. Zylas dismounted and disappeared into the brush. Collins remained in place, finger combing the horse's mane and laying the strands in their proper position. Falima stood stock-still, giving no sign she noticed his ministrations. Shortly, Zylas returned. "The ruins." He pointed ahead. "Not far." He flung a hand from Collins to himself, then jabbed it toward the ground.

Taking it as a signal to dismount, Collins slid to the ground. The movement revealed a tightness through the muscles of his thighs and buttocks that would likely become an ache by morning. His wrists had stopped bleeding, but they still dribbled clear fluid and throbbed with every beat of his heart. Both shoulders felt bruised. He looked at his watch. If correct, they had ridden for more than two hours.

Zylas talked softly to Falima and stroked her nose. The horse pawed the ground and snorted. A large insect buzzed past Collins' face.

"Ready?"

Collins looked up, only then realizing Zylas had addressed him. The blue-white eyes lay unsettlingly upon him.

Collins' gaze shifted unconsciously to Falima.

"She not come," Zylas explained, stepping around Collins and heading in the direction he had scouted. "No need."

Collins continued to study the horse, who had lowered her head to graze and seemed to take no notice of the humans' conversation. He hardly knew her; yet, for reasons he could not explain, he would miss her. "Tell her I said 'good-bye.' "

"I will," Zylas assured without looking back.

Collins turned and followed the rat/man through the brush, excitement building with every step. Soon, he would return to the mundane world of troubles that no longer seemed so significant. Staring death in the face, he might not have found courage, but he had found new perspective. Nothing less would ever seem formidable again.

The forest broke gradually to the familiar field of wildflowers and weeds. On the hill, the broken fortress looked positively welcoming. Collins raced toward it.

"Wait." Zylas charged after his impetuous companion. "Wait!" He dove on Collins.

Abruptly driven to the ground, breath dashed from his

lungs, Collins twisted to glare at Zylas. "What the hell did you do that for?"

Zylas' answer was an inclination of his head.

Collins followed his companion's gesture. Just ahead, a ragged line of arrows scored the ground. They had not been there when he had started his run.

"Damn." The expletive left Collins' mouth without intention.

Zylas seized Collins' hand and wriggled back toward the forest.

"Damn," Collins repeated, following. "Guards?"

"Would guess," Zylas returned.

More attuned, Collins heard the second round of bowstrings singing, the rattle and thunk of the arrows landing. He lunged for the forest, Zylas at his side.

There, beyond range of the bowmen, they stopped to study the ruins. Collins saw only the stone building, sunlight flashing from chips of quartz in the crumbling construction. "How did you know?"

"Didn't." Zylas also studied the ruins. "Sense. Smell . . . guess."

Sensed and smelled. It seemed logical to Collins that some of the animal instincts would permeate into the human phase as well. *Thank God.* Now relatively safe, he started to shake, terrified in a way he had not felt when the arrows directly menaced him. *I almost died. Again.* He looked at Zylas, skin white as paper and hair the nearly colorless blond most men loved and many women sought in a bottle. As they retreated back to Falima, he tried to lighten a mood wound as tensely as a spring. "Got any friends who change into rhinoceroses?"

Zylas blinked. "What?"

"Never mind." *A dinosaur or an army tank might do it.*

Falima made a soft, snorting nicker, then pawed the ground.

Zylas spoke to her gently in his own language. He turned his attention back to Collins. "We go." He leaped onto Falima's back, sliding toward her hindquarters to make room for Collins.

Collins' heart felt as if it were sinking into his toes. "Go? But . . ." *But . . . what? What do I expect him to do?* Clearly, approaching directly and in broad daylight could lead only to their deaths. Apparently, at midnight, Zylas would resume his rat form. Then, he could slip past the bowmen. *And do what? Give them all bubonic plague?* He stifled a hysterical chuckle. With a sigh of resignation, he clambered onto a rock and, from there, to Falima. The horse took off, going back the way they had come.

Chapter 4

BENTON Collins mulled the situation over as they rode silently into a deeper part of the forest. Trees glided past in a silken green blur, and Zylas' scouting became a remote background to Collins' thoughts. The fluid motion of the horse also lost significance, though the growing aches in thighs, buttocks, and groin gradually grew too prominent to ignore. His watch read almost 5:55 when they finally stopped in a clearing surrounded by scraggly junipers and scrub pines. Clouds raked across the sky, a gray accompaniment to Collins' dispirited mood. He dismounted beside Zylas. Falima lowered her head and snorted. Zylas stripped off the pack and tossed it to the ground. He unhitched the lead rope/halter from her head and let it fall.

"Now what?" Collins asked, kicking a deadfall at one edge of the camp site. Bark flew amid a spray of rotted wood. A large black beetle with angry-looking pincers scrambled from the carnage.

"Dinner?" Zylas suggested, catching the bug with a swift grab.

"Dinner," Collins repeated. He shook his head and turned to sit on the deadfall. The scream of leg muscles changed his mind in mid-movement, and he struggled back to a stand. Pain made him irritable. "I just lost my appetite." He wrinkled his nose at the beetle kicking madly in Zylas' grip and attempting to twist its pincers to meet the restraining fingers. "Besides, I'm more worried about my neck than my stomach."

Zylas stepped closer, gazing at Collins' throat. "Hurt neck? Sorry. Me tried get rope not with—"

Collins interrupted. "That's not what I meant. I . . . if . . . I have to get out of this . . . this place. My life—"

Zylas frowned and threw his hands in the air. Before he could speak, Collins caught an unexpected movement out of the corner of his eye. He whirled toward it. A naked woman stood where the horse had once grazed. Black hair fell in a satin cascade that formed soft curls around ample breasts. Though not thin, the body looked toned and well-muscled, the curves delicate and in exquisite proportion. Pale eyes made a radiant contrast to the golden/tan skin. She said something Collins did not understand, then snatched the beetle from Zylas, crushed it, and tossed it into her mouth.

Revulsion broke the spell. Flushed from the roots of his hair to his chin, Collins averted his gaze.

The beetle crunched between Falima's teeth, then she said something else to Zylas. He knelt beside the pack, pulled out the linen dress, a pair of something that looked like shorts, and two of the wood-and-cloth sandals. He tossed them to Falima.

Collins heard the rustle of fabric. He focused fanatically on the other man. "Are you always . . . like that . . . when you change?"

"Like what?" Zylas looked from Falima to Collins.

Falima said something simultaneous with Collins', "Like . . . bare. Nude. Naked."

Zylas stuffed clothing back into the pack. "Have to be, you think?"

Collins nodded, swallowing hard. It only made sense. He dared a peek at Falima, who returned a hard glare. She spoke to Zylas again, and he made a throwaway gesture as well as answering with words. Falima stomped a foot, horselike.

"What's wrong?" Collins asked.

Zylas looked at Falima first, urging her to answer. When she did not, Zylas tried. "She have thing . . . mine. Not—"

Apparently even more frustrated with Zylas' broken rendition of English than Collins, Falima interrupted. "The reason I cannot give you your translation stone back is because some *moron* . . ." She glanced pointedly at Collins, then back to Zylas. ". . . kicked me and made me swallow it."

Collins' face reddened again. "I'm sorry. I didn't mean—"

"It all right," Zylas soothed. "Now both can talk and understand Ben."

Falima tossed her head, ruffling her hair so that it fell over her shoulders in inky stripes. "You, barely. Me, I have no interest in speaking to him at all." She turned her back.

Not wishing to engage in another war, Collins ignored the woman for his more cooperative companion. "This stone?"

"Magic," Zylas explained with a word. "Let know all tongue."

Collins accepted the revelation without further questioning. It seemed no more outlandish than humans turning into animals and back, which he had already witnessed. "Remember when I asked about a friend rhino?"

"Rhino*saurus*," Zylas corrected.

"You don't have any in . . . this place? Whatever it's called."

"Barakhai." Zylas sat on the deadfall, examining the hole where he had found the beetle. "Mean 'whole world' our tongue."

"Barra-KIGH." Collins tried to pronounce it correctly, uncertain of the spelling and doubting his companions could illuminate it. It was a lot easier to learn to speak a language than to read it, especially in rat form and on the sly.

"Durithrin Forest be exact."

Durithrin. Collins recognized the word from their previous conversation, applied to a squirrel.

Still ignoring them, Falima pulled food from the pack and stuffed cheese curds in her mouth. Collins glanced at her.

"Very hungry," Zylas apologized for Falima's manners. "Ride most of day. Not time graze."

Falima made a wordless noise around her food.

Collins put aside the issue of how someone who spent half her life as an herbivore and half as an omnivore managed to digest anything but grass. Barakhai clearly followed different natural laws and logic than his biology, chemistry, and physics textbooks. Returning to his original point, Collins cautiously sat beside the albino, this time ignoring his aching muscles. "What about lions? Eagles? Bulls?" He added one he had already seen here. "Big dogs?"

"Know dog," Zylas admitted. "Bull?" His eyes crinkled. "That mean . . . lie?"

Only the shit. Collins dodged the slang to explain as simply as possible, "Man cows. They have horns, and they're big."

"*Pepsa,*" Falima said around another mouthful.

Zylas bobbed his head. "*Pepsa.* Bull. Yes. Why?"

Collins waved away another large, flying insect. The answer seemed so obvious, he could scarcely believe the question. "Don't you people fight?"

"Fight?" Zylas repeated, looking at Falima.

"*Augin telishornil bahk.*" Falima drank from the waterskin. It seemed like a lot of sounds to explain a one-syllable word.

"Fight." Zylas cocked his head to the heavens. "No."

"No?" The answer was nonsensical, especially after the barrage of arrows that had nearly killed them. "They were fighting." He jabbed a hand in the general direction of the crumbling fort.

Zylas followed the gesture with his gaze, eyes shadowed by his hat.

"Different. They *solen ak opernes*."

This time, Falima translated without entreaty. "Royal guards."

Collins considered the foreign phrase. "*Solen ak opernes.*" He remembered now that Zylas had used *opernes* before to refer to royalty. "*Solen ak opernes.*" He quit practicing the foreign phrase. He had no reason to learn their language; he would have to escape as soon as possible . . . and never return. "No one else fights?" he asked dubiously. It seemed beyond possibility. "Ever?"

Falima laid out apples, hard rolls, and cheese, then started peering under rocks and rolling logs.

"Sometime," Zylas admitted, loosening a strand of white hair sweat-plastered to his temple. "Not . . . as group. Not like . . . like . . . king cop."

"*Solen ak opernes*," Collins supplied.

Zylas smiled. "Language go wrong direction."

Collins laughed. He had once watched an exchange between a teacher and an English as a Second Language student via interpreter. At one point, the teacher had used a Spanish phrase that the translator dutifully recited for the Peruvian student—in English. Now, Collins broke bark from his seat with his heel.

Falima rushed in to gather the revealed bugs, placing them in the crock.

Collins wondered how hungry he would have to get to share that meal. "If we could marshal some strong animals, they wouldn't necessarily have to have formal combat training—"

Falima straightened suddenly. "You self-centered bastard!"

The outburst, in perfect English, startled Collins; and he nearly fell off the log.

"Falima," Zylas warned.

But nothing would silence Falima until she spoke her piece. "Is it not enough that we will probably die for saving a cold-blooded cannibal? Do you want more innocents to sacrifice their lives for you?''

Collins found himself unable to reply, though regret filled his stomach like lead, and the bare thought of eating now made him ill.

''Falima,'' Zylas said again, a clear plea to quiet her. He added more in their own language.

''I do not care,'' Falima replied, still in clear English. ''He is a fool and a clod. We should have let him hang.''

Zylas said more, punctuated by broad hand gestures that displayed the anger his tone did not.

Collins tried to defuse the situation. ''I'm sorry. I really am. I am very grateful that you saved my life. I didn't mean to suggest others should die to help me.'' He tried to catch Falima's eyes. ''I don't want anyone to get hurt.''

Falima dodged his gaze. ''What sort of dimwit finds himself in a strange place and immediately kills and eats someone?''

''I'm sorry,'' Collins practically pleaded. He needed Falima and Zylas to help him negotiate Barakhai, but he also desperately wanted a friend. The idea of being alone in a foreign world with rules beyond his understanding overwhelmed him. Nevertheless, he chose to gently defend himself. ''If you came to my world starving, wouldn't you start eating every bug you saw?''

Falima hesitated, clearly seeing the trap. ''You were starving?''

''Yes.'' Collins refused to allow her to sidetrack him. Though no third world orphan, he had gone twenty-seven hours on nothing but water. ''Would you eat the bugs?''

Maybe,'' Falima said, then clenched her jaw. ''Why? Is that murder where you come from?''

The urge to reply affirmatively became a burning compulsion. It would make his point swiftly and efficiently, but Collins never lied well. ''No. But it's disgusting. You wouldn't get hung—''

''Hanged,'' Falima corrected.

Collins blinked, barely daring to believe a person who could only speak his language because of a magical device thought it possible, even necessary, to correct his grammar. "It's hanged? Not hung? Really?"

"Trust me."

Collins returned to his point. "You wouldn't get hanged." It still sounded wrong. "But you might get locked up." He did not bother to differentiate between prison and a mental unit. It would only weaken his point, and at least he had not directly lied.

Another large, flying thing zipped past Collins' head. He smacked it out of the air. "No wonder you can eat the bugs here." It flew in an awkward arc, then crashed into the dirt. "They're as big as—"

Falima's sharp intake of breath cut off Collins' words before he could make a fatal faux pas. Zylas scrambled to check on the fallen creature, Collins presumed to augment dinner.

Zylas scooped it up but did not add it to the crock. Instead, he cradled it in his hand, massaging it with a gentle finger.

Dread crept through Collins' chest in icy prickles. *What have I done this time?* Leaping to his feet, he raced Falima to the thing in Zylas' hands. A tiny hummingbird lay there, its colors vivid against the chalky whiteness of the rat/man's palms. Its body was deep emerald, the wings a lacy lighter green. A patch of pink decorated its throat. The long, thin beak was black. "I'm sorry," Collins gasped out, gagging. "I thought it was a horse-fly. I swear I did. I–I . . . is it . . ." He shuddered at the idea. " . . . dead?"

"Just stunned." Zylas held up his hand, and the bird's wings became a blur. It zipped into the air and disappeared, to Collins' relief.

"He is a menace," Falima grumbled under her breath.

"Honest mistake," Zylas replied.

Collins suspected both of the English comments had been directed at him, though they addressed one another. To his surprise, he appreciated them talking around him rather than in their own language. At least, he felt included. ''I'm sorry,'' he said again. ''I'm really sorry.'' He wondered if he had just destroyed their security or enhanced it. If he alone noticed the hummingbird, and it had been spying, then he might have averted capture. More likely, he had whacked some innocent bystander who would now find him less a curiosity and more a danger to discuss with guards and friends. Collins dropped to the ground and buried his face in his hands. The new lines of thought this bizarre world inspired left him with millions of possibilities and little direction. ''Perhaps . . . perhaps, the guards at the ruins might get tired of waiting for me and give up?''

Falima's amused snort shattered that last hope. Even Zylas loosed a laugh. ''Not likely. Even best time, guard . . . zealous.'' The last word seemed a difficult one for a tyro to choose, and Collins suspected its similarity to the rat/man's name made it easier for him to learn. ''They know you comed from there. Want you.'' He shrugged. ''Not go till get you.''

''They know?'' Collins felt his features grow tightly knit. ''How?'' There seemed only one logical explanation. ''Have others come from my world?''

Zylas glanced at Falima, who shook her head with a grimace. They exchanged more dialogue than Collins thought necessary. Either they had or they had not. If space aliens had visited his town, he could not imagine anyone not knowing.

Finally Zylas addressed Collins again. ''No.''

The answer seemed too simple for the time it had taken to gather it. ''No?''

''Not that either of us knows of,'' Falima clarified. ''The royals might have more information.''

Collins doubted it. If others had come, it seemed likely the so-called royals would have kept him from entering Barakhai in the first place.

Apparently thinking along the same lines, Zylas added. ''If other come, royal not know from where till you.''

Or else I would have found the ruins better guarded. Collins nodded to indicate he understood, then stumbled over an odd thought. "Do your people come to our world often?" He had studied some strange animals, like the platypus, that seemed otherworldly. Perhaps it explained the disappearance of the dinosaurs; somehow they all got zapped to another dimension.

Falima continued gathering bugs. "Zylas is the only one I know of who has gone. And I only just found that out because of you."

Zylas looked at his sandals. "Know one other. Not think more."

"Let us eat." Falima held out the crock, now half-full with crawling insects.

Collins' stomach lurched.

Falima poured water into the crock, replaced the lid, and set it near the food. "Hurry up. Gather kindling."

Immediately, Collins obeyed, glad to find some small way to start repaying his rescuers. He brought back armfuls of dry twigs, choosing wider ones with each pass. The first gray stirrings of dusk settled over the forest, bringing a chilly breeze that stirred the leaves into rattling dances overhead. Oncoming darkness dimmed the trees to skeletal hulks swarmed with fluttering leaves like dark, limp hands. As Collins dropped his third load, he found his two companions squatting in front of a well-arranged tower of kindling with a pile of leaves beneath it. He hunkered down between them. "Be a lot easier if you'd brought my lighter."

"Not need." Zylas reached into his tunic pocket.

Before Collins could marvel over Zylas even knowing what he meant, the albino's hand emerged wrapped around a translucent purple Zippo. Expertly, he flicked the wheel with a callused thumb. A tiny flame appeared, and he used it to ignite the leaves.

Zylas sat back. "Brought own."

Collins dropped to his haunches. "You . . . you have lighters?" It seemed impossible. If Barakhai had that technology, he should see so much more; and it made no sense that they would have an otherworld brand name version even so. Then realization clicked. "You must have got it in my world."

Zylas watched the sprouting flames, brushing aside his cloak and replacing the lighter blindly. "Work hard drag back."

"I'll bet." Collins pictured a rat scooting the Zippo across a dark, dirty floor for hours. He bit back a smile. Zylas probably would not appreciate the humor, and he doubted Falima would either. Reminded of his own devices, Collins expressed gratitude that had gone too long unspoken. He now understood that Zylas must have packed the saddlebags. "By the way, thanks for getting my watch back." He held up his wrist. "And the phone, too." He patted the Motorola StarTAC clipped to his waistband.

"You welcome." Zylas fanned the growing flames with his hat as they danced onto the wood. "Not able get all. Pick good?"

Collins measured his response. No matter how misguided, good deeds deserved praise, not condemnation. "Fine."

Apparently reading the hesitation, Zylas looked up, snowy hair plastered to his head in the shape of his missing hat. "Truth, please."

"Honestly," Collins returned carefully. "I do appreciate your help."

"But . . ." Zylas added, replacing his headgear.

"But," Collins continued dutifully. "Time doesn't make a whole lot of difference." He gestured at his watch, then pulled the cellular phone from its holster. He pressed the button and got no response. "Without a charger, it's not much use." He chuckled. "Even if it worked, who could I call?"

Zylas grinned crookedly. "Do better next time."

"Next time. Right." Collins studied the creases at the corners of Zylas' mouth and realized his companion was kidding. He laughed. "Next time."

Even Falima managed a smile, though she turned away as if

afraid the men might see it. "Why do we not start eating? The main course will come soon enough."

Hungry, Collins nodded. He had eaten only cheese curds since daybreak and not nearly enough of those. They sat and ate most of the apples, hard rolls, and cheese curds in their possession while the bugs bubbled merrily over the coals. They shared the water in the canteens. It tasted dusty and stale, but it slaked Collins' thirst. By the time Falima pulled the hot crockery from the fire, he felt satisfied, not the least bit interested in the boiled mass of recently crawling pests.

Suddenly, Falima stiffened, a handful of dead bugs halfway to her mouth.

"What?" Zylas said.

Falima tipped her head. "Listen."

Collins strained his own hearing. Wind rattled through the leaves, and branches swished softly. Crickets screeched and hummed in a rising and falling chorus. Farther away, a hound bayed.

"Dogs!" Zylas sprang to his feet, kicking dirt over the fire.

Falima stuffed the insects in her mouth, then started shoving loose possessions, willy-nilly, into the pack.

Caught up in his companions' urgency, Collins looked about for stray objects, finding only the lead rope/halter he had used to guide Falima. Snatching it up, he set to using a branch to erase all signs of the camp. "I presume dogs mean—"

"Pursuit," Falima interrupted.

Zylas qualified as he scattered the partially burned kindling. "All horse and all dog is guard."

Falima draped the saddlebags over Collins' shoulders and seized the halter from his hand. "Go! Go! Due north. I will find you. Hide in the . . . the sixth oak."

"But—" Collins started.

"Come." Zylas grabbed his arm and ran. Dragged two steps, Collins stumbled, caught his balance, then charged after the albino.

"What about Falima?"

"She make smell-trail. Catch up." Zylas' pull became insistent. "Come."

Scarcely daring to believe Falima would risk her life for his, nor that Zylas would allow it, Collins did as Zylas bade. "Why the sixth oak?"

"Random," Zylas replied, still running. "Far enough for safe. She find us."

Collins looked back. Falima dragged the crude rope halter through the dirt, then disappeared among the trees in the opposite direction.

"Up! Up!" Zylas shoved Collins into a fat trunk. He crashed against it hard enough to drive the breath from his lungs. White petals showered down over him, silky on his skin, filling hair, mouth, eyes. Amid gasping in air thickened by the cloying perfume of flowers, spitting out petals, and regaining his vision, he managed to seize a low limb. Zylas scrambled over him, quick and agile as a monkey. The albino clambered higher, dislodging more flowers in a gentle rain over Collins, who hauled himself into the sheltering branches. The tree reminded him of a densely blooming tulip poplar or catalpa, but more thickly flowered with fatter, longer petals and indigo centers.

Realization came with shocking abruptness. "This isn't an oak."

Zylas silenced Collins with a hiss.

Collins glanced down. The ground lay barely five feet beneath him. "But Falima won't be able to find—"

Zylas' cloth-covered sandal tapped Collins' cheek in warning. "Hush. Better hiding. Thick and smell."

Collins reached for a higher branch and hauled himself deeper into a suffocating wall of leaves and petals. Zylas' reasoning made sense. The dogs would have a more difficult time catching their scent amid flowers that also concealed them from sight. Yet, he could not help worrying about their other companion. It seemed unlikely Falima could find them either. He tried to think of something he might not have considered; but, even focused on the differences between Barakhai and home, he found nothing. He did not believe horses had an unusually well-developed sense of smell, certainly not keener than hounds.

The barking grew louder, closer, then more insistent. At Zylas' steadying touch, Collins realized he was fidgeting. Adrenaline was driving him to run or pace, foolish urges in their current situation. He looked up. Zylas had climbed even higher. He had had to stretch his toes as far as possible to reach Collins at all. Cautiously, Collins raised a hand to grab an overhead branch. Rapid rustling through the brush stopped him in mid-movement. Below, Falima pressed through a clump of reedy stalks. Something louder slammed the weeds behind her, snuffling.

Falima! Though driven to shout, Collins held his tongue. He swung to a lower branch, then caught the woman's shoulder as she passed.

Falima hissed and spun. Her fist slammed Collins' ear. Fire slashed through his head, and he lost his grip, plummeting to the ground. Pain jarred through his left elbow and hip.

"Oh, sorry," Falima whispered, finally recognizing Collins. She grasped a lower branch and swung herself into the tree.

A hound burst through the foliage.

Collins froze.

The dog skidded to a stop. Young and gangly, it sported long legs, floppy ears, and a tail too long for its body. Patches of brown and white were interspersed randomly over its face and body. Head raised, it opened its mouth.

"No." Collins sprang for the dog, snapping its muzzle closed with one hand and scooping it up under its legs with the other. He could hear its companions baying in the distance, but no others followed it through the brush. Yet.

Clutching the half-grown dog, Collins ran for the tree. It struggled in his grip, making climbing all but impossible. He braced its weight against the lowest branch. Still holding its mouth, he managed to gain a toehold and drag self and dog amid the flowers.

"What are you doing?" Falima asked incredulously.

"Keeping it quiet." Collins loosed the dog's snout. Immediately, it howled. Collins swore and clamped his hand back over its muzzle, stifling the noise. It struggled wildly, clawing at him and trying to duck its head through his grip. Collins clung tighter to the dog, his balance on the tree branch swaying dangerously.

Falima steadied Collins. "You've got to get up higher."

Though true, it seemed impossible. "Here." He thrust the dog's backside at Falima. "Help me."

Muttering something uninterpretable, Falima placed the bulk of the dog's weight on a higher limb. Collins kept one hand wrapped solidly around its muzzle and attempted to climb with the other. Bark scraped a line of skin from his forearm, and the movement unleashed a storm of leaves and petals.

"Easy," Zylas cautioned.

Collins managed to work his way to a reasonably hidden branch. With Falima's help, he steadied the dog in his lap, fingers stiffening on its muzzle. It managed an occasional whine, but he stifled the barks and bays that might bring the hunters. *If they find us, we're dead.* Nevertheless, it never occurred to him to harm the pup.

The barking grew louder and fainter, occasionally mingled with human voices. Collins' breathing turned erratic as he fought not to contemplate the situation. If he did, he might panic, just as he had at the gallows. That image quickened his breathing to pants, and he shoved it aside. He thought instead of grade school autumns, playing tag with friends among the maples and dogwoods.

Over time, the surrounding odor of flowers became more stench than fragrance. The dog's weight seemed to treble; Collins' legs fell asleep beneath it. He passed the hours until full nightfall mentally singing every song he could remember, mostly childhood nursery rhymes, lullabies, and those from his high school musical, *Anything Goes*.

A whistle cut through the night sounds that had risen so gradually, Collins had not realized he was straining his hearing over them. The dog resumed its struggle with a vengeance, pained whines escaping Collins' hold. An explosion of petals and leaves cascaded to the ground. The branch shook violently. Collins fought for his hold, Falima assisting. Finally, the dog ceased its kicking and lay, hopelessly snared, in the tree.

Apparently, the whistle called the dogs home, because the sounds of movement, the barking, and the voices disappeared. For a long time, the three humans and the dog remained silently in the tree. Then, finally, Zylas spoke. "Let's go."

Painstakingly, Collins eased the dog from his lap. It dropped to the ground and immediately loosed a fusillade of barks.

Collins leaped from the branch, jarring a wave of buzzing pain up his legs. The dog whirled, teeth bared, and growled a warning that Collins dared not heed. He dove for it, bearing it to the ground, then grabbed its mouth again. His cramped fingers responded sluggishly, and the dog managed to slash his left hand before he subdued it.

A pair of legs eased into Collins' view. He looked up at a fine-boned stranger dressed in brown and green. He could barely judge height from this angle, but the other seemed small, almost frail. Short, brown hair hung in shaggy disarray, and dark eyes studied Collins with a heated glare.

Collins froze, arms winched around the dog. *Caught*. There was no way he could overpower a dog and a man simultaneously, no matter how slight they were. He cringed, turning the newcomer a pleading look, hoping for some miracle to keep the other from shouting. He found no mercy in the keen brown eyes and lowered his head. "It's over," he whispered. *And I'm going to die.*

Chapter 5

HURL the dog at the man and run! Any action hero would pull it off, but the more rational portion of Collins' mind dismissed the idea immediately. Jackie Chan could outmaneuver a dog; Benton Collins would be lucky to manage two running steps before the animal's teeth sank into his buttocks and the man's shouts brought armed companions to finish what the dog started.

Time seemed to move in slow motion. The stalemate dragged into that strange eternity mortal danger sometimes creates. The aroma of the tree flowers condensed into a cloying cloud, like the worst humidity Collins had ever encountered. His lungs felt thick with pollen.

Displaying none of Collins' caution, Falima and Zylas swung down beside him. A chaos of petals and sticks wound through the woman's thick, black hair. She addressed the newcomer in their musical tongue, and he responded in turn. Zylas placed a hand on the dog, and it resumed its struggles.

Clutching the dog's muzzle tightly, Collins braced himself

against its sharp-nailed paws. Attention fully on the animal, he addressed his companions. "What did he say?"

Zylas helped support the dog's floundering weight. His first word eluded Collins, but the rest came through clearly, ". . . still angry you hit." He paused. "Falima not helping." He glared at her.

As the dog again sank into quiet despair, Collins glanced at the rat/man and tried to fathom his initial utterance. "Yah-linn?" It sounded Chinese to him.

Zylas enunciated, "Ialin. Ee-AH-lin. Other . . . friend."

Falima and the newcomer continued to converse.

"Friend?" Relief flooded Collins, followed by understanding. "He must be . . . the hummingbird?"

Zylas considered, then smiled and nodded. "Ialin. Hummingbird. Yes."

Only then did Collins finally put everything together. He had assumed "Ialin" the Barakhain word for "friend," but it was, apparently, the hummingbird's name. "Ialin," he repeated, then slurred it as Zylas had the first time so it sounded more like, "Yahlin." Collins glanced at Falima, only to find Ialin's gaze pinned on him. *Duh, Ben. You said his name. Twice.* Cheeks heating, he addressed the other man. "Hello and welcome."

Ialin's scowl remained, unchanged.

Falima said something in their tongue, Ialin replied in a sulky growl, then Zylas spoke in turn. The conversation proceeded, growing more heated. At length, even Zylas punctuated his statements with choppy hand gestures and rising volume.

Collins sat, drawing the dog securely into his lap. This time, it barely fought, settling itself in the hollow between his legs. Helplessly studying his companions' exchange, watching it ignite into clear argument, he found himself fondling one of the dog's silky ears. In careful increments, he eased his grip on its muzzle until he no longer pinned it closed. The dog loosed a ferocious howl so suddenly it seemed as if the sound had remained clamped inside, just waiting for him to release it. Collins wrapped his fingers around the slender snout again, choking off another whirlwind round of barking.

All sound disappeared in that moment. Then, leaves rustled in the breeze, and petals floated in a gentle wash. Collins realized what was missing. In addition to birdsong and the dog's cry, his companions' discussion had abruptly ended. He glanced over to find three pairs of eyes directly and unwaveringly upon him.

Collins' face flared red, and he forced a sheepish grin. "Sorry about that." Aware that treating a human the way he had the dog practically defined assault and kidnapping, Collins attempted to mitigate his crimes, at least to his companions. "I'd let it go, but . . ."

Zylas nodded, expression serious. "Cannot." He stroked his chin, clearly pondering. Then, shaking his head, dislodging a storm of petals from the wide brim of his hat, he unraveled a ropy, green vine from a nearby trunk. Carrying it to where Collins sat, he expertly bound the dog's mouth shut. Zylas turned his gaze to Falima. "Know this dog?"

Collins eased away his hand.

The hound's nose crinkled menacingly and it jerked its head, but the vine held.

Falima responded in their language, and Zylas raised a warning hand. "You have stone. Not waste."

Falima glowered.

Zylas' look turned pleading, weary.

"I'd rather Ialin understood than . . . him."

Collins ignored the loathing in Falima's voice and supplied, "Ben."

Falima grumbled something that sounded suspiciously like a snarly teen's "whatever." She switched to English, "We had best move on."

Zylas studied the skeletal shapes of trees against the growing darkness, the crescent moon overhead. "Quickly. I have to sleep soon."

Falima pushed through the trees, Ialin following. The hummingbird/man moved with a flitty grace, individual movements quick and jerky, yet the whole merging into a smooth and agile pattern. Only Zylas remained, frowning at the problem that remained in Collins' lap. Collins elucidated, "He can't bark if we let him go, but he also can't eat or drink if he doesn't find his way home quickly."

"Still think like your world." Zylas grinned. "When he switch . . ."

Collins imagined trying to tie a man's mouth closed and shared Zylas' amusement. ". . . the vine will fall off."

"Right."

Collins rose, dumping the dog from his lap. "Shoo. Go home." Other thoughts dispelled his smile. "But won't he go back and tell everyone who we are and where?"

Zylas' smile also wilted. "Falima say he . . . he . . ." he fumbled for the right word, then supplied one questioningly, "little?"

"Young?" Collins tried, remembering how he, too, had assessed it as a partially grown pup.

Zylas nodded. "Like . . . teenager."

The dog watched them, tail waving uncertainly.

"Probable very dog. Very very dog. Not . . . not retain . . . ?" He looked to Collins to confirm the appropriateness of his word choice.

Collins made an encouraging gesture.

". . . what see in switch-form, not same."

Collins nodded to indicate he understood despite the poorly phrased explanation. Zylas seemed to be struggling more than usual, a sure sign of stress. "Is it possible he might . . . retain . . . some of what happened here after he resumes human form?"

"Not impossible," Zylas admitted.

Collins trusted the decision to his companion, glad the dog made it easier by remaining with them unfettered. Its soft brown gaze rolled from one man to the other, and its tail beat a careful rhythm.

Zylas sighed, air hissing through his lips. His face lapsed into creases that seemed to age him ten years. Beneath the shadow of his hat, his pale eyes radiated troubles, and the white-blond hair hung in limp, tangled strings. "Too tired to make wise choice." He ripped another stout vine from the tree and looped it around the dog's neck. "Keep with us now. Talk. Think." He headed in the direction their companions had taken. The dog balked.

Collins went, too, encouraging the animal by tapping his leg and calling, "Come on, boy. Come on," in a happy tone.

Tail whipping vigorously, the dog followed.

Camp consisted of downing the last of their cold rations, tossing their bodies on layers of moldering leaves, and drifting into sleep. Zylas dropped off almost at once. Falima and Ialin chattered in their incomprehensible language, occasionally glancing furtively in his direction. Though exhausted, Collins found sleep more elusive. He knelt by the tethered dog who no longer required the muzzle tie and had eaten his share of the remaining foodstuffs.

Collins ran a hand along the animal's spine. It quivered at his touch, then lowered its head with a contented sigh. Collins continued to stroke the fur, stopping now and then for a pat or a scratch. The dog sprawled on its side, moaning with contentment. Its tail thudded against the ground, and it wriggled as if to keep every part in contact with Collins' hand. He could scarcely believe it the same beast that had inflicted the gash across his hand.

Thinking of it brought back the pain that desperation and need had made him disregard. Collins examined the wound. Clotted blood filled the creases, making it appear to encompass the entire back of his hand. He spit on a finger, rubbing and scraping until he revealed a superficial, two-inch laceration. He had gotten lucky. He doubted a doctor back home would even bother to stitch it.

The dog whined, sniffing at Collins' hand. It licked the wound.

"Yuck." Collins jerked his hand away, only then thinking of infection. It seemed unlikely this world had a sophisticated medical system, such as antibiotics. *Probably at the level of leeches and bloodletting.* The image sent a shiver through him. He had heard that dog saliva contained natural anti-infection agents, the reason why they licked their own injuries and suffered fewer infections. He wondered whether the benefits of those agents outweighed the germs inherent in any drool of a species that drank from mosquito-infested puddles, groomed itself in unsanitary places, and lapped up horse excrement like candy. *Better,* he decided, *to clean this wound myself.*

Collins glanced at Zylas. The albino slumbered comfortably, the stress lines smoothed from his brow. Collins' watch now read nearly 11:00 p.m. Assuming this place had days the same length as his own, Collins realized Zylas would become a rat again in about an hour. A flash of heat passed through him, followed by a hysterical shiver. Without Zylas' calm reason, he doubted the group would stay together. Apparently, Falima and Ialin hated him, perhaps enough to turn him in to the guards. *They'll hang me.* He wondered if he had now compounded the crime enough for a worse fate, though what fate could be worse than death he didn't even want to imagine. He slumped to the ground, abruptly incapable of anything. Hopelessness overpowered him, a dense blanket that forced his thoughts to a tedious slog. Escape lay only a day's travel away, yet it was beyond his ability to navigate. He still did not know the way. Once there, he would have to battle his way through armed warriors, with only a rat for assistance. *A rat.* A wave of despair buffeted the last of his reason. Twelve hours utterly alone. Twelve hours dodging a hunt he scarcely understood in an unfathomable world. Twelve hours without a friend.

Tears stung Collins' eyes, then rolled down cheeks still flushed with distress. He had so many questions, and he needed those answers to survive Zylas' rat-time. It seemed safest to lay low, to mark time until he had a trustworthy companion to plan with again. He wondered how the people of Barakhai stood the change, interrupting half their lives daily, putting relationships and experiences on hold just as they started to build. Romance seemed impossible without careful coordination of the switching times—if such could even be arranged. He shook his head, the tears flowing faster. He knew so little to be suddenly thrown, friendless, back into an inexplicable world beneath a sentence of death. He had never felt so completely, so desperately, alone.

Leaves rustled. Something warm brushed Collins' cheek. He looked up into the dog's fuzzy face, and it licked tears from his face again. It whined, sharing his discomfort. Collins managed a smile. Even amid all of Barakhai's strangeness, a dog was a dog after all. He placed an arm around the furry body, and it lay down against him with a contented sigh, sharing its warmth.

Falima spoke from startlingly close. "Dogs are good judges of character." She added snidely, "Usually."

Collins tried to surreptitiously wipe away the tears. He did not look at Falima, not wanting her to know about his lapse. "Maybe *you're* the one who misjudged me."

A lengthy pause ensued. "Maybe," she finally admitted, grudgingly.

"About Joetha . . ." Though Collins hated to raise the subject, he knew he would have to resolve the issue before Falima could ever consent to like him. "I truly didn't—"

"I know," Falima interrupted.

"You do?" Collins could not keep surprise from his voice.

"I . . . think I do. It is hard seeing things . . . that way." Falima added insightfully, "Through the eyes of a foreigner."

"Yes." Collins wholeheartedly agreed.

Another long silence followed. Collins thought Falima must

have left as quietly as she had come. So when she spoke, he jumped, turning his tear-streaked face to her. "What were you doing to the dog?" She simulated stroking with her hands, then crouched beside him.

Collins blinked the last of the tears from his eyes. "You mean when I was petting and scratching?"

"Yes."

The answer now seemed wholly obvious, but she seemed to expect one, so Collins reiterated. "Uh, I was, uh, petting. And . . . uh . . . scratching."

"Yes." The word emerged in an emotionless monotone that revealed nothing.

Sorrow gave way to sudden terror. "I always . . . I mean I never thought . . . it's just . . ." Collins gathered his thoughts. "Did I do something terrible? Again?"

"No," Falima reassured. "Not terrible. It is just . . . well, stroking someone. That is kind of . . . personal, do you not think?"

Collins patted the animal snuggled against him, and the dog's tail thumped the ground. He tried to consider the beast as a human, and a strange thought eased into his mind. "Is this a boy dog or a girl dog?"

"Male." The response held a hint of question.

Collins' mind returned to the summer of his freshman year of college, just before his parents' divorce. His best friend from high school, Bill Dusumter, had taken leave from the army at the same time. They had agreed to meet at Bobcat Den Park. When Collins arrived at the picnic grounds, he found several of the old gang sitting around talking. He waved to Diana Hostetler, with whom he had exchanged jokes and a love for the trombone. Dusumter had dated her for a time, their breakup messy; and Collins had avoided pressing for a relationship for fear of losing their friendship. She looked the same as he remembered: dark, shoulder-length hair that shimmered in the sunlight; eyes starkly blue in contrast; high-pitched, freckled cheeks; and a broad, wry mouth. Katie Tonn and Dave Hansen had become a couple, attending Cornell University together. Dusumter claimed to have lost his virginity with Tonn, but none of the three seemed to hold any ill will. Several other friends from high school played a lively game of frisbee. But Collins' gaze fixed on Bill Dusumter, his tomcat best buddy, and the stranger at his side.

Both wore the standard military haircut, matching brown hair buzzed to half-inch prickles. Both were skinny, with lean angular faces; and they both smelled of cigarettes. They wore Levis and T-shirts, Dusumter's red with the name of a local bar and the newcomer's plain black.

Collins' brain worked overtime, trying to divine the relationship between the two. Before he could speak, Dusumter gestured him over, a delighted grin on his face. "Ben. Buddy. How's it hanging?"

Still deep in thought, Collins had to force a smile and missed the opportunity for a snappy comeback. "It's hanging fine. Army treating you okay?"

"Great!" Dusumter gestured toward his companion. "This is Gene." He winked conspiratorially. "You're going to be seeing a lot more of Gene around here."

"Oh." Something seemed wrong, and Collins could not put his uneasiness into words. "Is Gene . . . moving here?"

"Yup."

"Ah." Collins gazed into his friend's eyes and read more there, something exciting and interesting that he would not reveal until asked. Collins felt too dense to find the proper question, whatever it might prove to be.

Dusumter retook his seat. As he did so, he placed a hand squarely on Gene's thigh.

Collins' breath caught in his throat. A million thoughts swirled through his mind in an instant. *Bill's gay?* The thought bothered him deeply, and that troubled him. *I'm for gay rights. I have gay friends. Am I just a hypocrite?* Collins wanted to cry. Few things upset him more than people who preached values to others while cheating on their spouses, fanatics who sabotaged animal experiments then eagerly popped medications born of that research, fiends who labeled women who suffered through an abortion to save their own lives as murderers then encouraged their daughters to destroy the fetus of a man they did not like. *It's easy to cling strongly to morality when it doesn't affect you.* Collins analyzed his discomfort, delving to its source. *I don't have a problem with Bill being gay. It just came completely out of the blue, so opposite from the Bill I knew. I can and will deal with this. It's my problem, not his.*

Collins exchanged pleasantries with his old friend, then headed off to see some of the others. He had taken fewer than half a dozen steps, prepared to step around their scattered purses and backpacks, when Dusumter came up beside him. Grinning, he asked, "So, what do you think of Gene?"

Still shocked, Collins did not know what to say. He barely knew the newcomer, who had not yet spoken a word. "Um," he mumbled. "Seems nice." Unable to meet Dusumter's sparkling brown gaze, he glanced at the backpacks.

"Don't tell anyone else; I wanted you to be the first to know . . ."

Collins braced himself, wishing he had had time to prepare, seeking the most supportive words he could muster in his own panicked moments of shock.

". . . Gene and I are getting married."

Married? Collins whirled to face his friend. Even as he moved, his eyes registered a name on one of the backpacks: "JEAN." *Jean, Gene.* It all came together in that moment. *Just because Bill's fiancée is too skinny to have boobs doesn't mean she's not a woman!* Relief flooded him, not because Dusumter was not gay; that truly did not matter. Collins' solace came from the realization that he did know the man who had been his best friend, that he had not missed signs of misery or need, had not been kept from a significant secret for lack of trust or closeness.

"Congratulations." He caught Dusumter into an embrace, not the least bit self-conscious.

Dusumter's familiar voice hissed into his ear. "Way to keep a secret, buddy."

Now, in an alien world with a dog who was also a man curled against him, Collins smiled at the memory. As weird as the situation had become, it seemed marginally preferable to having made what might have seemed like a sexual advance on some strange woman who, properly and without insult, could be better called a bitch.

Oblivious to Collins' train of thought, Falima continued. "A *young* male, of course."

Great, so now I'm a child molester. Collins cringed. *That makes it much better.*

Attuned to Collins' discomfort, Falima continued, "It is all right, really. He is probably the closest thing to a dog of your world that you will find here. He clearly enjoys the attention, and he probably will not remember much of it in human form."

Collins studied the dog's brown-and-white patches.

"So go ahead and stroke him. If it makes him uncomfortable, he will let you know."

Yeah. Collins glanced at his wound. *Next time, he'll bite my hand clean off.* Tentatively, he petted the dog's back. It sighed and snuggled more closely to him.

Falima smiled. "Actually, I like it when people stroke my nose."

Collins gave Falima a strange look.

"In switch-form, of course." Falima's cheeks turned scarlet, to Collins' surprise. She seemed too strong to let anything embarrass her. "And a scratch behind my ears now and then feels wonderful. Especially when the flies are biting." Her features lapsed back into their tough demeanor. "But I do not like being kicked. In any form."

"I'm sorry," Collins said, meaning it. "It's just that's how we steer in—"

"—your world," Falima finished.

"Yes. In my world. The only world I knew existed until yesterday. I'm very sorry I kicked you. It won't happen again."

A strained silence followed, into which Collins wanted to insert something clever that might finally bridge the gap between them. Instead, a question came to mind. He wanted to know why discussing her petting spots shamed her more than switching to human form buck naked. Wisely, he put aside that train of thought for a safer one. "I guess it's just us till Zylas becomes a man again."

Ialin strolled to them, crunching something between his teeth and carrying handfuls of leaves and stems. He turned Collins a withering, imperious look, then focused on Falima. He remained standing, the only position that allowed the tiny man to tower over his seated companions. He spoke in the language of Barakhai.

Falima's reply took much longer as she, apparently, filled him in on the conversation to date.

With the memory of Bill and Jean Dusumter in his mind, Collins studied Ialin. The hummingbird/man, too, could pass for a slight, curveless woman. For an instant, the thought that he might have made the same mistake twice swept through Collins, banished by the memory of Zylas' use of the pronoun "he" to refer to the hummingbird's human form. *Of course, Zylas' English is rather primitive.*

Falima addressed Collins again. "Zylas will not desert us just because he is in switch-form."

The dog stretched its legs, pressing its back against Collins, groaned, and dropped back off to sleep.

Collins nodded, certain Falima spoke the truth. "I just meant we won't have a way to talk to him until he's . . . until he's human."

"I will." Falima patted her tummy and tossed her black hair, highlights of scarlet, purple, and green shifting through her tresses.

"You will?" Hope rose in a wild rush. "You can . . . you can . . ." Collins barely dared to believe. ". . . talk to each other in animal form?"

Falima held a brief exchange with Ialin that left the man snickering before replying, "Not usually. But Zylas is older. He has good, solid *overlap* between his forms; I know of no one with more. And I still have his translation stone." Her blue gaze hardened. "Thanks to you."

Collins stroked the dog's side, and its tail thumped in gratitude. In addition to a near-flawless grasp of English, Falima had clearly mastered sarcasm. "I'm sorry." He wondered how many times he would have to apologize before Falima would forgive him, hoping she would not prove as difficult to appease as Marlys. *Maybe it's a woman thing.*

Apparently mistaking Collins' attention to the dog for an unspoken question, Falima said, "No, I cannot talk to him. He has little or no *overlap*. He might not even have reached coming-of-age yet."

"Coming-of-age?" Collins repeated. That brought to mind David Fein's bar mitzvah, expanding lip disks, and quests to kill wild boars and leopards.

Ialin made a grunted comment to which Falima responded before switching back to English. "When a child is born, he assumes the same switch-form and at the same times as his mother. He has no *overlap* at all. On his thirteenth birthday, he gets a party. His switch time melds with his personality, *overlap* begins, and, if he is a *Random*, he transmutes."

Collins put up a hand to stay Falima. "Hold it. I was with you up until the thirteenth birthday party. *Randoms*. Transmuting." He shook his head. "What are you talking about?"

Falima eased to a cross-legged sitting position. She spoke painfully slowly, as if to an idiot. "At thirteen, all right?"

Collins did not grace the question with so much as a nod. If he did, he felt certain she would drag a simple explanation into next week.

"A child becomes a man or woman. He gets a switch time . . ." Falima glanced at Collins to see if he still followed her description.

Collins bobbed his head. He knew about switch times from Zylas. "Does some person assign each teen a switching time? Or is it random?"

Falima conversed with Ialin before answering. "Neither. It seems to have more to do with the . . ." She used Collins' word, ". . . teen's personality. It just happens, and it seems to suit the person. *Overlap* between human and animal form begins. *Regulars* tend to learn control faster than *Randoms*, but they also spend more time in animal form."

Collins frowned, shaking his head. "You've lost me again." He considered the problem. "Maybe if you explain what you mean by *Regulars* and *Randoms*." He looked up at the sky. The moon had risen higher, a crescent that scarcely grazed the darkness. Stars spread across the darkness, remarkably similar to the spring pattern of his own world.

"*Regulars* occur when animals of like type mate, whether in human or animal form. A man who becomes a bull, for example, marries a woman whose switch-form is a cow." Falima studied Collins' reaction, and he gave her what he hoped was an encouraging look. This made sense to him. "Since animals can only mate within their type, and they tend not to worry about or understand human conventions when it comes to marriage, *Regulars* outnumber *Randoms* by about three hundred to one."

Collins reasoned, "So a *Random* would come of a union between two humans with different types of switch-forms."

"Right." Apparently impressed by his reasoning, Falima passed it on to Ialin.

Ialin came back with something that sounded gruff, almost warning.

Beaming, Collins struggled to continue. Falima's opinion of him mattered more than he could explain. "Until thirteen, *Randoms* become the animal of their mother. Then, they become . . ." He did not know how to proceed. Logic dictated that boys might follow the father and girls the mother, but the opposite could prove equally true. *What am I doing seeking logic in magic?* Sticking with what the name implied, he tried, ". . . something random?"

"Exactly," Falima crowed. "Though maybe not totally random. It probably has something to do with the physical or emotional makeup of the person. Or maybe the animal-type influences those things. It would be hard to ever know for sure."

"Which are you?"

Falima's open excitement disappeared. Her features lapsed into a mask, and her movements looked calculatedly casual. "What?"

"Which are you?" Collins repeated carefully. "*Regular* or *Random?*"

"All horses are guards," Falima said in a not-quite-indifferent tone. "Senior to dogs. Ours is a respected position, nearly always bred on purpose."

"And you?" Collins pressed.

Falima blinked, now clearly annoyed. "You heard me. You may assume me a *Regular*."

It was not a direct answer, but Collins accepted it. Though he had clearly stepped into dangerous territory, he could not keep himself from asking. "And Zylas?" He glanced toward his companion as he spoke, only to find a set of empty clothing. "He's changed!"

"A few moments ago," Falima confirmed.

Collins studied the britches. He rose with a caution designed not to disturb the dog, drawing nearer to where Zylas had fallen asleep until he found the rat-sized lump stirring regularly beneath linen. "Is he a *Random* or a *Regular?*"

"*Random*," Falima said with a wide yawn. "Do you think we breed rats on purpose?"

Collins thought of the lab. *We do.* "And Ialin?"

This time, Falima dodged the question. "I'm getting tired.

We really should sleep.'' Without awaiting a reply from Collins, she headed away to curl up on a pile of leaves. Ialin went with her.

Put off by Falima's sudden detachment, Collins lay back down beside the dog. Its warmth soothed him, even as he worried for the propriety of his action. At least he could explain it away as a means to keep watch over an animal that might sneak off and report them to the authorities. He wondered about the information Falima had given him and why discussion of the origins of self and friends made her so uncomfortable. He vowed not to press the question the next day. To do so might lose him what little trust of hers he had managed to gain or leave him in the bleak loneliness he had dreaded only an hour ago.

With these thoughts buzzing through his mind, it surprised Collins how swiftly he found sleep.

Chapter 6

BENTON Collins awakened to a sweet but unrecognizable aroma that sent his stomach into a ferocious growl. It reminded him of his mother's freshly baked cinnamon rolls, yet was different in a way he could not quite define. He opened his eyes to a subdued fire surrounding a crock blackened by charcoal. Ialin and Falima spoke in hushed tones, their shadows flickering through the brush at their backs. The sun had not yet penetrated the dense cover of leaves and branches. The two chatted like old friends. Though Collins could not understand a word of it, he noticed that neither wore the tense expression of hostile distrust that had become so familiar to him.

The dog rolled its head to look at Collins. It wagged its tail in greeting, tip stirring the leaves. Ialin and Falima took no notice, so Collins continued to study them in the scarlet-and-amber strobe of the fire. Her golden skin looked beautifully exotic. She had braided her mane of black hair away from her face, though a few strands lay damply against her cheeks. Apparently, she had washed and combed it out earlier that morning. Though lost beneath an overlarge cloak, the curves of her naked body remained vividly in Collins' memory. His mind's eyes conjured the generous breasts, the fine curves, and the well-toned body with an ease that made him flush. He felt himself responding to the image, which abruptly heightened his embarrassment. He tried to quell desire by turning his attention to his other companion.

Ialin rose and walked to the fire, movements odd though never awkward. The words that came to Collins' mind in description: flitty, quick, birdlike fit best, though he found none of them quite adequate. The man reminded him most of Jean, who had become a dependable, almost supernaturally daring, friend over the years. Though small to the point of scrawny, she never hesitated to face off with the largest man. They had once stopped to examine a snake on the road. None of the men in the car would touch it, but Jean had picked it up without a second thought. And, upon discovering that she held a rattlesnake, she had attempted to keep it for a pet. On two occasions, he had watched women leaving a public restroom that Jean had just entered whispering angrily about the man who had dared to walk boldly into their haven.

There was something equally androgynous about the hummingbird/man, and Collins wondered if it had anything to do with the fact that bird gender was difficult to read at a glance. *Or is it?* When he thought about it more carefully, he realized that in many species of birds, like peacocks, blue jays, and chickens, the male and female looked phenomenally different, far more so than, say, horses. Or rats.

Collins shook his head, tired of trying to find rhyme and reason in a world that either had none or, at least, none that he could logically and rationally fathom without the assistance of those who lived it daily. At that moment, he found Ialin returning his gaze with steady yellow-brown eyes. The man said something to Falima, and she looked at Collins as well. For a while, they all simply stared, saying nothing. Finally, Falima's face broke into a cautious, weary half-smile. "Good, you are awake. Come join us."

Collins gave back a genuine grin, glad Falima had actually welcomed him, though it hardly mattered. Soon enough, he would return to his own world and these people would fade into the blurred uncertainty between reality and dream. He had read enough fantasy as a child to know that others, and maybe eventually he, would dismiss whatever adventures he had in this world as the product of distraught imagination. *Assuming I make it out of here alive.* He stood, rearranging his jeans to cover his dwindling excitement. He could taste his morning breath but could think of no way to remedy the problem. He ran a hand through his hair, dislodging wilted petals, twigs, and curled leaves. His appearance and hygiene, he knew, should not bother him; but it did. *At least I probably look better without my glasses.* He squinted, surprised at how easily he found himself getting along without them. He could see better than he remembered, and it sent his mind into another round of unusual thought. *Do I not need them as much as I believe? Am I simply getting used to not having them? Or is it just another part of the magic of Barakhai?*

Using a stick, Ialin eased the crock from the fire.

The dog rolled to its feet, yawned, and stretched. Its tongue uncurled, and the mouth spread wide to reveal rows of surprisingly blunt teeth. Then, finished, it followed Collins to his companions near the fire.

Falima glanced upward, though interwoven branches blocked the sky. "I was about to wake you. I wanted you up before my switch."

"Your switch?" Collins rolled a panic-stricken gaze to Ialin. *Please. Don't leave me alone with . . . him.* He did not voice the concern. He had grown accustomed to Falima's animosity, had even managed to crack it somewhat. The idea of spending time with only Ialin chilled him, colored by his experiences with Jean. He liked Jean, but she also liked him. With Ialin, he could imagine that rattlesnake "accidentally" winding up in his bed. The analogy did not carry well, since any snake here would also be human and, presumably, barred by law and convention from harming others.

"It is coming soon." Falima used an edge of her cloak to ease the crock toward her. Ialin said something to which Falima replied. This time, she deigned to translate. "He wants me to wait until it cools. But I do not get *gahiri* often and do not eat it in switch-form."

"Gahiri?" Collins repeated, surprised to hear a Barakhain word during an English rendition. She had never mixed the two before. Then, he realized the word probably had no equivalent in his language.

Using a stick, Falima ladled a gloppy brown mixture onto a leaf as dark as spinach. It steamed in her hand as she offered it to Collins.

Collins hesitated. Then, worried it might burn her palm if she held it too long, he accepted it. It warmed his grip, its aroma a cross between pecan and currant pie, with a bit of baking potato.

Without seeing if Collins ate it, Falima made similar packets for Ialin and herself. They ate them like tacos, one hand folding the contents together, the other perched below to catch any runoff. He took a delicate bite of just the filling. It burned his tongue, and it took an effort of will not to spit it out. Instead, he swirled it around his mouth, never letting it settle in one place long enough to singe until it grew cool enough to swallow without hurting his throat. Only then, he allowed himself to assess the flavor, sweetly spicy with a subtle crunch he hoped had nothing to do with insects. It tasted sinfully good, like doughnuts for breakfast. He blew on it carefully before daring another bite. This time, he took a chunk of leaf along with the filling; and, to his surprise, it only enhanced the flavor. "Delicious," he said around a heated mouthful.

"The best," Falima agreed. "Most of the ingredients are quite common, but you have to get the *vilegro* seed at the right time.

when you can even find it. It is valuable, too, so we can sell what we do not eat. A worthy find, Ialin had. That is the advantage of a small flying switch-form with a good sense for finding sweet things.''

Falima's description sparked an idea. ''Perhaps,'' Collins started thoughtfully. ''Perhaps Ialin could distract the guards, fly around their . . .''

Before Collins could stop her, Falima translated. Ialin's reply was accompanied by a spark of anger.

Falima laughed. ''Ialin suggests we distract you instead so the guards can catch you easier.''

Collins brows rose, and the look he gave Falima was similar to Ialin's own.

All mirth disappeared. ''He was only kidding,'' she said defensively. She and Ialin feigned sudden, inordinate interest in their *gahiri*.

Collins reached for his own half-eaten breakfast, only to find a large white rat devouring it. Startled, he skittered backward, then realized who had stolen his food. ''Zylas!''

Falima laughed again, and even Ialin could not suppress a snicker. Zylas turned Collins as innocent a look as a rat could muster, then returned to eating.

Falima made three more *gahiri*, handing one to each of her human companions and eating the third. Abandoning his booty, Zylas crawled up Falima's arm to her shoulder, placed both paws on her ear, and squeaked emphatically.

Falima listened for a long time, nodding occasionally with her mouth full of food. She replied in their regular language, stuffed the rest of the *gahiri* into her mouth, then rose. Placing her hand inside her bodice, she plucked a cherry-sized piece of rose quartz from between her breasts and thrust it toward Zylas. The rat took the stone between his teeth, skittered from his perch, and dropped it on the ground near his food. Placing one paw on the rock, he commenced eating.

Collins looked at Falima. ''What was that about?''

In response, Falima only shrugged.

"She can't understand you." Zylas' squeaks now formed high-pitched English words. "She passed the translation stone, and now I have it."

Knowing Falima had swallowed the stone, Collins did not want "pass" defined. "And you understand me?"

"Yes. But the others do not."

Torn between relief that he would not have to make conversation with two people who disliked him and worry that he might have to find other ways to make himself understood, Collins nodded his comprehension. If he could only communicate with one of his companions, he preferred it to be Zylas, even if he was a rat.

Collins glanced at his watch. It read a few minutes till six a.m. "So, what do we do now?"

Falima rose, brushed crumbs from her shift and cloak, and spoke a few words to Ialin, who nodded. She headed into the woods. The dog trotted after her, tail waving like a flag. With a few crisp words and a jab toward the men, she ordered it back. It obeyed, tail low, only the tip still twitching.

"Come here, boy!" Collins used a happy tone, and the dog bounded to him, tail again whipping broadly. He petted it, and it wiggled and circled in excitement. Zylas grabbed up the translation stone in his teeth and scuttled out of the way of the prancing paws. "Falima is switching?" Collins guessed.

Zylas' reply was barely audible. "Yeth." He dodged between the dog's feet to reach Collins and started clawing his way up Collins' jeans. The denim bunched under his claws and weight, dragging them down.

Worried Zylas might pants him, Collins bent, offering a hand to the rat. "Where are you trying to go?"

"'our thoulder, ith 'ou peathe."

Thinking he understood, Collins hoisted Zylas to his left shoulder.

The rat scrabbled off, settling into the hollow between Collins' neck and shoulder. He spat out the stone and clapped it in place with a paw. "Can you hear me better now?"

It suddenly occurred to Collins that Zylas' speech had gone from halting and uncertain to grindingly clear since he had become rat. Though Collins knew it had to do with the magical stone rather than the transformation, the irony made him laugh.

Zylas' claws sank into Collins' flesh. "What's so funny?"

Collins went still, and the nails loosened. Resolved not to laugh or stumble again, to spare himself a gouging, he dismissed the thought. "Nothing important. So," he repeated his earlier, unanswered question. "What do we do now? Try the ruins again? Hope the guards have gone?"

"They're not gone," Zylas replied emphatically. His whiskers tickled Collins' ear.

"You're sure?"

"I'm sure." Not a bit of hesitation entered Zylas' reply.

Collins frowned. "So we have to get past them."

"Can't." The grim certainty remained in Zylas' voice.

"So you're saying it's impossible?"

Zylas did not waver. "Yes."

It went against every self-esteem-building encouragement Collins had received since infancy. "But nothing is really impossible."

"For us," Zylas said, "this is."

Collins opened his mouth, but remembrance of Falima's tirade choked off his words. *Is it not enough that we will probably die for saving a cold-blooded cannibal? Do you want more innocents to sacrifice their lives for you?* He did not want to die, did not want any of his companions to lose their lives, either, especially not for him. "All right." He tried to keep disappointment from his tone, without success.

Zylas clearly read beyond the words. "The guards will not allow us near the ruins. They will patrol now." He shook his head. "You cannot escape through that portal."

That portal. Fresh hope flared. "Could we . . . could we maybe . . . find another portal?" Collins looked up, remembering his companions for the first time since he had asked about Falima's transformation. The buckskin grazed placidly at a patch of weeds, her golden coat glimmering in the patch of sunlight penetrating the forest canopy. Ialin was stuffing Falima's garments into the pack, and the dog lay curled on the ground at his feet.

Zylas paced a circle on Collins' shoulder, clearly vexed. His gaze played over the party as well, lingering longest on the dog. "I don't know of any other portals . . ."

Anticipating a "but," Collins remained silent.

". . . I know someone who might . . ." Zylas went suddenly still. "But . . ." He fell into a long hush.

When Collins' patience ran out, he pressed. "But?"

Zylas skittered down Collins' side, stone in mouth, then leaped to the ground. He darted to Falima's lowered head, dropped the crystal, stepped on it, and commenced squeaking loudly.

The horse pranced backward, trumpeting out a whinny, then another.

Slower now, more thoughtfully, Zylas approached Ialin. Their conversation lasted no longer than the previous one. Finally, he returned to Collins.

Wanting to forgo more scratches, Collins crouched, anticipating Zylas' need. He scooped up the rat and replaced it on his shoulder. "So?"

Zylas spat out the translation stone. "Falima only has a partial overlap, so she's difficult to converse with in this form. Ialin . . . well, Ialin will come around." He made an abrupt motion, as if shaking water from his coat. "Come on."

Having no idea what direction Zylas meant, Collins raised his brows. "Where are we going?"

"We're going," Zylas said thoughtfully, "to visit a good friend of mine."

They rode Falima, Ialin leading from the ground, Collins astride, Zylas sitting in the V formed by his legs. The dog trotted obediently at the horse's heels, apparently used to walking in that particular position. A gentle rain pattered on the leaves overhead, occasional droplets winding through the foliage to land as cold pinpricks against Collins' skin. He did not pressure his companions. Quite literally, they held his life in their hands. *Or rather*, Collins corrected, *in their claws, talons, and hooves.*

Zylas explained as they rode, "Vernon's a good guy. A longtime friend. You and Falima will be safe with him while Ialin and I go . . . elsewhere."

"Elsewhere?"

"To see someone older. Wiser." Zylas shook his pointy-nosed head. "That's all I can tell you."

"Can't I go?"

"No." Even for a rat, Zylas sounded emphatic.

Feeling like a sulky child, Collins grumbled. "Why not?"

"Too dangerous."

Collins looked at the dog who still followed them, tail waving. "For me? Or the elder?"

"Both."

"Oh." Collins considered that answer for several moments in a silence broken only by the swish and crackle of branches, the song of the drizzle on the canopy. "How so?"

"Vernon's a good guy," Zylas repeated, and Collins knew he would get no reply to his previous question. "A longtime friend."

Collins dropped the subject. They rode onward, brushing through wet foliage that left streaks of water across his tunic, jeans, and sneakers. Zylas wandered the length of Falima, pausing to guide her with whispered commands in her ear or to exchange a conversation with Ialin. Collins' watch read ten minutes to nine when Zylas called a halt. He spoke soothingly to Falima; and she slowed, snorting and pawing divots from the ground. Ialin stopped, patting her neck reassuringly. Collins slid from her back. He offered his hands to Zylas, who clambered aboard, little feet warm against Collins' palms. Images of his guinea pig rose to mind, its brown-and-white fur soft as down, its enormous black eyes studying him, and its loud "week, week, week," when it heard his mother making salad. He had named the animal George, which had become Georgie-girl several years later, when he learned how to differentiate gender.

Zylas leaped to Collins' shoulder. Falima dipped her head, nosing for grass amid tiny trees and mulch. Ialin turned his back, perhaps surveying the forest, more likely relieving himself. Three hours bouncing around on horseback had given Collins a similar urge. Working around the rough material of a tunic now as soiled as his jeans, he urinated on a mushy pile of leaves.

"He's getting smaller." Zylas' sudden voice in his ear startled Collins, who jumped. Then, he sounded out the words and grew even more alarmed.

"Wha–what?" Collins stammered, stashing his manhood safely behind his zipper.

"Ialin," Zylas explained. "He's getting smaller. Switching."

Collins whirled to see, finding only an empty pile of clothing which the puppy snuffled eagerly.

Zylas continued, "You'll have to pack his things."

Collins nodded dully, now the only human. With a shock, he realized nearly twenty-four hours had passed since his aborted hanging. Then, too, all his companions had taken animal form, working together to rescue him from death. Approaching the shed clothing, he bent. Zylas scampered down his arm to the ground. Collins gathered the crudely sewn garments, approached Falima, and stuffed them into her saddlebags. He turned to find the pup crouched with its front legs extended, bottom high, and tail wagging cautiously as it urged Zylas to play. Realization glided into his mind. When Ialin appeared as a human, the dog was already in switch-form. Now, Ialin had become a bird again, but the dog remained a dog. "Zylas?"

The rat disengaged from the dog and approached.

"Shouldn't our . . . um . . . unexpected companion have become human by now?"

Zylas twisted his head to look over one shoulder at the puppy. "Not necessarily. *Regulars* spend more time in animal form than *Randoms*." He turned back to Collins. "If he just entered switch-form when he found us, I could even change before he does."

"Really," Collins said thoughtfully.

"We need to get going again." Zylas headed toward Falima. "I only stopped to give Ialin some dignity during his switch."

Collins trotted after his companion.

Zylas stopped by the grazing horse. "A boost, please? I can climb, but it makes her nervous."

Glad to help, Collins hefted Zylas to Falima's back, then mounted himself. Falima's head rose with obvious reluctance. Zylas clambered along her mane and thrust his muzzle into her ear. Falima snorted but resumed her walk through the forest.

Collins recalled that he had set his watch for noon about the time Zylas had become human, and Zylas had switched to rat form around midnight. Falima had turned into a horse at six in the morning and a human at six at night. Ialin changed at nine. That understanding brought a realization: Falima had lied. Aware his companions could and had exchanged information he could not understand, he prodded with utmost caution. "*Regulars*, like the pup, spend more time in animal form?"

Zylas returned to his steadiest position, planted between Collins' thighs. "That's right. And, on average, gain overlap at a younger age."

"Overlap meaning shared understanding and memory between forms."

"Right."

"Hmmm."

"What?"

Collins studied the white rat, suddenly feeling insane. If any of his colleagues had caught him talking to a laboratory animal like this, they would deem him certifiable. *Thirty-six hours in Barakhai, less than a day with animal companions, and it already feels natural to converse with a rat.* "It's just that you seem to have an exceptional amount of overlap."

"I do. Nearly perfect, in fact."

"Why is that?"

Zylas turned a circle, then settled against Collins. "First, I'm older than the others. I apparently have a natural talent for it. And I practice. A lot."

"Practice?" It seemed ludicrous. *Practice what?*

"Rats don't eat much, and any old garbage serves me fine in this form. I pay attention. I have no job. I'm not married. No . . . children." The last word emerged in a pained squeak, and he paused. He turned away for a moment, curling his hairless pink tail around his legs, then regained his composure and continued without missing a beat. "I've concentrated most of my life on enhancing my overlap, with good success." He added, "And it doesn't hurt that I spent my childhood in a similar enough form that I could use most of that training at adolescence rather than starting over. More like a *Regular* without the disadvantages."

Collins recalled that, until coming-of-age, children had the same switch-form as their mothers. "So your original switch-form . . . ?"

Zylas obliged. "A mouse. My father was a blue jay."

Collins laughed, earning a glare from Zylas.

"What's funny?"

Collins did not lie. "It's an odd combination."

The rat's mouth stretched into a grimace that Collins interpreted as a weary grin. "Not in human form." He anticipated a question Collins had not even thought to ask. "And, yes, they were both albino."

Startled into silence, Collins took several moments to craft a coherent question. "Is . . . is . . . it common in . . . in your world?"

"Albinism?"

"Yes."

"No."

"No?"

"I only know of two others." Zylas licked at his fur. "I think that's what brought my parents together. Something in common other than the usual shared switch-form."

"Hmmm." The white mouse came easily to Collins' imagination, the jay with more difficulty, though he had actually seen one at Algary's science museum. He glanced at the passing scenery, mostly leaves and needles, trying to appear casual. The rain had stopped, but droplets still plopped irregularly from higher branches. "What about Falima's parents?"

Zylas continued cleaning himself. "A milk goat and a squirrel, I believe."

A Random. Collins had suspected as much from the start. When he learned *Regulars* kept switch-form longer, it had seemed nearly certain. He wondered why Falima had tried to deceive him. "And Ialin?"

"Owl and shrew."

That combination did not surprise Collins at all. It seemed to fit the hostile, flighty young man. "So, you're all *Randoms?*"

Zylas stopped grooming. "Who told you about *Randoms?*"

"Falima."

Zylas shuddered his fur back into place. "Yes. We're all *Randoms*. Except the pup. Once she came of age as a horse, Falima got fostered to guards."

That seemed odd, though no more so than most of the other things Collins had learned here. "Why?"

"All horses are guards."

"Oh." Collins asked the logical follow-up. "And all rats?"

"We're *vermin*."

It sounded shocking from the mouth of a human rat. "Well, yes, but . . . I meant what job do rats do?"

"*Vermin* were always discouraged from breeding, especially as *Regulars*. The only ones left come out of *Random* unions."

"So your . . . mouse . . . mother . . . ?"

"Also a *Random*, yes. My father, too." Though Zylas did not seem uncomfortable discussing these matters, as Falima had, he did change the subject. "So, tell me about your world. I've seen many things that confuse me. Like why do you keep your white rats in cages while the brown ones run free?"

Chapter 7

BY the time they reached Vernon's ramshackle cabin in the woods, Collins suspected he had raised more questions than he'd satisfied, which seemed only fair. He felt the same way about Barakhai. Falima grazed the clearing. Zylas pulled clothing over his pale human body. The dog romped around all of them, alternately begging pets from Collins and exploring every inch of their new surroundings. Collins did not see Ialin but suspected the hummingbird buzzed nearby, more cautious since being mistaken for an insect and clouted across the forest.

Within moments, the door banged open and a man, apparently Vernon, appeared, britches hastily tied over thick legs, still pulling a coarse linen shirt over his broad, brown shoulders. Though Collins had seen dark-skinned people in this world before, Vernon was the first who closely resembled an African-American in his own world. He sported close-cropped curls, full lips, and shrewd eyes nearly as dark as the pupils. Tall, well-muscled, and bull-necked, he made a startling contrast to the slight albino, who disappeared into his welcoming embrace.

Zylas and Vernon exchanged words briefly. Then, Vernon's gaze shifted across Collins to settle alternately on Falima and the wagging-tailed dog. He shook his head and addressed Zylas with a challenging tone.

Collins recognized "Falima" in a reply otherwise gibberish to him.

Vernon nodded thoughtfully as he laced his shirt. He turned his attention fully on the dog and grunted something.

Zylas merely shrugged.

Collins looked at Falima. By the time he glanced back, Zylas was heading toward him.

"It's settled," Zylas explained, drawing his hat down to shade his forehead. "You and Falima remain here with Vernon. Ialin and I should be back tomorrow."

Collins' gaze rolled to the dog. "What about him?"

Zylas did not bother to follow Collins' gesture. "The dog stays with you. Do what you must to keep us safe."

Collins froze, hoping those words did not mean what he thought they did. He would not murder again, especially a child. He opened his mouth to say so, only to find Zylas watching him with distinct discomfort.

The rat/man held out his hand, fingers clenched to a bloodless fist. Collins watched each finger winch open, finally revealing the rose quartz stone. "You'll need this."

Collins stared at the translation stone. It made sense that he should carry it, as the others could all understand one another, at least in human form. Without reaching for it, he looked at Zylas.

The rat/man's lips pursed to lines as white as his flesh, and he dodged Collins' gaze. His fingers quivered, as if he battled the urge to close them safely around the stone again.

"This is hard for you, isn't it?"

Zylas nodded. "I've rarely let anyone use it, and then only in my presence." He glanced at the stone, and it held his stare. "It's unique and irreplaceable." He finally managed to tear his gaze free, to turn a worried look toward Collins. "It's also illegal."

Collins' brow furrowed. "Illegal?"

"Magic of any kind. The royals hate it."

The words shocked Collins. Shunning such a powerful tool seemed as absurd as locking away the secrets that science revealed. Yet, he realized, his world had done just that for many years now known as the Dark Ages. Despite himself, he found some logic in the realization that technology had brought the atomic bomb as well as computers, pollution along with transportation, thalidomide in addition to penicillin. With the good came the bad, and common sense could dictate none as easily as both. "But, you're all magic—"

"Except the royals," Zylas reminded. "They don't switch forms."

"Right." Collins recalled his companion telling him that, though it seemed ages ago. "Well . . ." Running out of things to say, he reached for the translation stone. ". . . I'll take good care of it. I promise." It seemed ridiculous to vow to protect a rock when he could not keep his own life safe, but he knew Zylas needed the words. "One way or another, no matter what happens, I'll get it back to you."

"Thank you." The lines dropped from Zylas' face, and he managed a slight smile. "I'm sure you will."

Collins took the stone, oddly warmed by Zylas' trust. He wondered if he could ever win it from his other companions.

Zylas made a broad wave toward Vernon, who returned it with a grudging movement of his hand that looked more dismissive than friendly. Ialin zipped out of nowhere to hover at Zylas' left shoulder, then the two headed into the woods. Collins watched them until they disappeared among the trees. When he finally turned back, he saw Vernon leading Falima toward the cottage, the dog trotting at her hooves.

Certain Vernon's cottage would lack indoor plumbing, Collins thought it best to relieve himself before getting to know

Zylas' friend. He dropped the rose quartz into a pocket of his jeans. As he walked to a secluded spot, he allowed his thoughts free rein. His limbs felt heavy, world-weary, and uncertain. He went through the motions of preparing to urinate, thoughts caught up in the realization that he had stumbled into something quite impossible. It amazed him how quickly he accepted companions who spent half or more of their lives as animals, his own transformation from mild-mannered graduate student to hunted fugitive under sentence of death, his need to find some magical doorway back to the world he had once thought alone in the universe. It seemed unbelievable that people spent their lives searching for creatures from other planets when a whole other world existed through a storage room in Daubert Labs.

Collins' urine pattered against dried weeds.

A distant, high-pitched sound touched Collins' hearing suddenly, and he froze. For a moment he heard nothing but the wind rustling through branches and his own urine splattering against dried weeds. A howling bark wafted over those sounds, sharp as a knife cut and followed by another.

Startled, Collins jerked, wetting his left shoe. Staccato words soft as whispers came to him. "This way, this way." "No, over here." "Smell . . . smell target." "Smell." "Smell." "Smell." "Here!" Then a loud, trumpeting voice sounded over the rest, "Hate wood-ground. Go home!"

Uncertainty held Collins in place. Only then, he realized he had wormed a hand into his pocket and clamped it over the worn-smooth rose quartz. *Oh, my God! It's translating barks and whinnies.* A worse understanding penetrated. *They've come for us.* Whirling, he sprinted toward the cabin, securing his fly as he ran.

Vernon met Collins at the door. "Come," he said in rough English. "Hide you."

Collins careened inside. The cottage had no windows. Thatch poked through the mud plastered between the logs. A crooked table surrounded by crudely fashioned chairs took up most of the space. Straw piled on a wooden frame filled one corner and, beside it, stood a chest of drawers. Near that, a trapdoor broke the otherwise solid floor.

Vernon thrust the dog at Collins with a force that sent man and animal staggering. He fell to one knee, arms, chest, and face filled with fur, managing to catch his balance, though awkwardly. Vernon shoved aside the dresser to reveal what seemed to be plain wall until he caught at something Collins had not noticed. Lashed logs that appeared as part of the structure glided open on unseen hinges, and Vernon gestured frantically at the darkness beyond it.

Still holding the dog, Collins dragged himself into the hidden room. Almost immediately, his nose slammed against solid wall, and wood slivered into his right cheek. He barely managed to turn before Vernon smashed the panel closed, and Collins heard the grind of the dresser moving back into position. Worried its claws might make scrabbling noises, Collins continued supporting the dog, one hand wrapped around its muzzle, the other grasping the translation stone.

For several moments that seemed more like hours, Collins stood in the silent darkness. Gradually, his heart rate returned to normal, and worse thoughts descended upon him. *What if they find us? What if they take Vernon away? What if we're walled in here to die?* The tomblike hush of his hiding place seemed to crush in on him, airless and boring, and he stifled an abrupt urge to pound on the door in a mindless frenzy. If the guards caught him, death went from "what if" to stark and graphic certainty.

Shortly, Collins heard footsteps clomping down nearby stairs and realized several people had passed through the trapdoor he had seen, likely into a root cellar. He had heard nothing of whatever exchange occurred in the cottage, but here their voices wafted to him in muffled bursts.

"Why is it that every time we're hunting fugitives, the trail always ends here?" The voice contained clear exasperation.

Vernon's reply sounded gruff. "Why is it that every time you're hunting fugitives, you chase them toward me? I'd thank you to stop. Puts me in danger. Would you like it if I started sending thieves and killers to your—"

The dog shifted, and Collins tightened his hold. If he could hear the men, likely they would hear any noise from him also.

"Cut the crap, Vernon." A loud, irritable voice joined the others. "What did you do with them?"

Vernon's answer dripped sarcasm. "I ate them."

The dog went limp in Collins' arms. The sudden dead weight made it seem twice as heavy, and it took all his strength to lower it soundlessly to the ground. *What the . . . ?*

The first speaker huffed out a laugh. "You're a mouse, Vern. You can barely eat a *hallowin* seed before you fill up."

Worried he might have strangled the dog in an overzealous attempt to keep it quiet, Collins continued to bolster some of its weight. It felt liquid in his arms, all fur and limbs, and he fought for orientation. He no longer had its mouth, which put them at serious risk. He groped for it, swearing silently, overwhelmed by heat. All of the oxygen seemed to drain from the room. His heart rate trebled.

"I'll have you know I can eat three *hallowin* seeds before I fill up."

"Not funny," came the gruff voice again. "This guy we're hunting actually did eat someone. Cannibal. Try and hide him here, he'll probably eat you, too."

"Cannibal?" Vernon sounded shocked. "You're right. That's not funny."

Collins thought his heart might pound out of his throat. The dog became even harder to support, squirming into positions he could not fathom in the darkness. He no longer felt fur beneath his grasp, and that proved the final clue. *God, no. He's switching.* He gripped harder, now seeking a human shape among the movement. *Not now, dog. Please, not now.* He held his breath, awaiting the scream that revealed them.

"I . . . didn't know. I'll do whatever I can to help."

Collins could no longer concentrate on the conversation. He found a human ear beneath a wild mop of hair and lowered his mouth to it. "Please don't make a sound. I'll explain everything."

To Collins' surprise and relief, the boy obeyed. Now he turned his attention back to the speakers, but the voices and footsteps faded away. Vernon's revulsion had sounded sincere, concerned enough to reveal Collins to the guards. His chest clutched and ached. *He doesn't know me, has no loyalty to me.* He cringed, prepared for the worst.

The conversation grew uninterpretable, and Collins realized he had dropped the rose quartz in his struggle to maintain control of the dog. He pressed himself breathlessly to the wall, helpless, waiting for the guards to find him, for the dog/boy to shout, for Vernon to surrender him. Then, the voices faded away. Footsteps slammed up the steps, then disappeared.

More time passed, immeasurable in the sightless, soundless prison. Then, Collins heard the creak of the moving dresser. The door sprang open, and the dull interior of Vernon's cabin blinded him. "Thank you," he gasped out in English. The boy tumbled onto the floor, blinking repeatedly and glancing wildly around the room.

Vernon assisted the boy to his table, talking softly, while Collins fumbled around the hiding space until he found the quartz. He closed his hand firmly around it before shutting the panel. Now that he knew of the false wall's existence, he could see the faint outline of its crack and the indentation that allowed Vernon to pull it open. He shoved the dresser back in place.

Vernon approached Collins, enormous hands outspread. "Hi. Think him . . ." He gestured at the boy, who Collins saw for the first time. Blond hair fell around a heart-shaped, beige face, and brown eyes studied Collins with awed curiosity. Skinny, with long arms and legs, he could pass for a young American teenager if not for his completely unself-conscious nakedness.

". . . think you . . ." Vernon struggled for the word, his English not even as competent as Zylas' pidgin speech.

The boy dropped from his chair to his knees on the floor, head bowed. "Your Majesty."

Collins understood. "*Opernes?*" he supplied. It seemed absurd, and he wondered what about his humble self might give such a noble impression. *My clothes?* The simple homespun his companions had provided clashed with his battered jeans and grimy Nike knockoffs. *My watch?* It seemed more likely until he realized that the boy had made his assumption as a dog. *My scent?* "Why does he think . . . ?"

Vernon's features opened in surprise. "You—you speak . . ." He recovered swiftly, warning in his undertone. "Why does he . . . ? Don't you mean *how?* How does he know you're royal, don't you, Your Majesty?" His lips formed sounds that did not match his words at all, like a badly dubbed movie. Collins had not gained that impression from Falima when she had carried the stone, and he guessed it rendered the speaker immune from that effect.

Clearly, Vernon expected him to play along. Though he did not understand why, Collins would not disappoint a man who had just saved his life. "Yes, of course." He turned to the boy. "How *did* you know?"

Apparently released by Collins' direct questioning, the boy clambered back into his chair. "Only royals don't switch." He studied Collins through liquid eyes, as though the answer should have been obvious.

It should have. Collins tried to cover. "I just didn't know one so young could determine that in switch-form."

"And retain it," Vernon added, almost hastily. "You must have good overlap."

The boy beamed, then blushed. "Not really. Not yet."

For Zylas' sake, Collins did not glance at the translation stone, though he could not help clutching it like a treasure. He could understand Zylas' reluctance to lend it; at the moment, he would not trade it for the Hope Diamond. As he and Vernon took the seats on either side of the boy, he could not help wondering if it proved as useful to Zylas. Nothing required him to visit Collins' world; and, as far as he could tell, all citizens of Barakhai spoke the same language, at least in human form. *But there's more than a little advantage to learning how to communicate with animals, especially here.* He wondered if that explained Zylas' near-perfect overlap.

Unlike Collins, Vernon did not become too lost in thought to remember his manners. ''I'm Vernon.'' He made an arching motion over the boy's head to Collins. ''BentonCollins.'' He slurred it into one word.

''Just Ben's fine,'' Collins said before Vernon could stop him. ''And what's your name?''

''Korfius, Your Majesty.'' The boy stifled a yawn.

''How old are you?'' Collins asked.

''Twelve,'' Korfius replied. His posture improved abruptly as he added, ''Almost a man.''

Barely a kid. Collins kept the thought to himself. ''What do you remember . . .'' He glanced at Vernon for help. ''. . . from . . . switch time?''

Vernon nodded his approval of the query, so Collins turned his attention back to Korfius.

''Not much, Your Majesty,'' Korfius' face reddened again. ''I knew I was with royalty. And a horse-guard.'' His eyes crinkled. ''Though I don't know why or how.'' He looked askance at Collins, who pretended not to see. The less Korfius knew, the safer he remained.

Apparently thinking along the same lines, Vernon rose and gestured at the pallet. ''Why don't you get some sleep, Korfius?''

Collins winced, anticipating an explosion. No near-teen he knew would agree to nap like a child.

But the boy only nodded before glancing hesitantly at Collins. ''Is that all right, Your Majesty?''

Struck dumb, Collins could only imitate Vernon's gesture.

"You sleep, Korfius. I'll be fine. Vernon and I have work to take care of."

Korfius bowed. "Thank you, Your Majesty." Still naked, he headed toward the pallet.

"I've got clothes in the drawers." Vernon walked to the door. "Something in there should fit you."

Collins doubted it. Anything that covered Vernon's enormous form would fit Korfius about as well as a circus tent. "Sleep well." He followed Vernon outside and closed the door. As it clicked in place, he hurriedly tried to explain. "About that cannibal thing—"

Vernon interrupted, leading Collins among a stand of poplar at the outskirts of the woods. "So, what did you eat?"

"Well—"

"Let me guess. A pig?"

"No, but—"

"A cow?"

"No."

"A chicken?"

"No." Turning the details of murder into a game embarrassed Collins. "You don't—"

Vernon whirled suddenly toward Collins. "Give me a hint."

Collins stammered, "I–it was . . . a–a rabbit named Joetha."

Vernon came to an abrupt halt, and terror ground through Collins. "It seems," the hermit started coolly, "that you don't know what 'a hint' means." Apparently to show he meant no malice, he turned Collins a broad grin.

"You don't hate me?"

"Nope."

"But . . . but . . . I ate . . ."

Vernon resumed his walk. "I presume you ate her before you knew about switch-forms?"

The bare thought that Vernon might even consider otherwise twisted Collins' gut. "Yes! I–I wouldn't—"

"Of course, you wouldn't. Who would?"

Outside of a few lunatic serial killers, Collins could think of no one.

Vernon continued, "If you're kind and decent, and I believe most people are, you wouldn't kill someone on purpose. I'm not going to condemn an accident, even if it did result in death."

Collins went speechless with gratitude. He felt tears welling in his eyes.

Vernon politely studied the trees, then chose a deadfall and sat. Shadows dappled his skin, making him appear even darker. "Zylas gave you his stone, didn't he?"

Relieved he would not have to keep a secret from Vernon, Collins nodded.

"He must really like you. And trust you. He's rarely even let me hold it, and we've been friends for thirty years."

"Thirty years." Collins wiped the moisture from his eyes and looked over his companion. The stocky man appeared too young for such a long friendship. "How old are you?"

"Thirty-five."

Collins made a wordless noise that Vernon took for encouragement.

"Our switch time overlaps perfectly. And his mother and I—both mice."

"Yes." Collins intensified his scrutiny, gaze flickering over the broad neck, solid musculature, and whaleboned figure of his newest companion. "So I heard. Hard to believe."

Vernon's eyes narrowed curiously. "Why?"

The answer seemed so obvious to Collins, he found himself simplifying to the level of Tarzan. "Mouse small. You . . . big."

Vernon stretched, sinews rippling. "Sometimes it works out that way. Especially *Randoms*." He smiled. "Would it surprise you to find out my father was a bear?"

"Your mother must have been an amoeba."

Vernon halted in mid-stretch. "What?"

"Never mind." Then, feeling the need to explain at least somewhat, Collins finished, "I'm just thinking a bear would have to combine with something really really tiny to make a mouse.''

''Mama was a skunk.''

Collins' head jerked toward Vernon before he could hide his surprise. ''A skunk?''

Vernon's dark eyes hardened. ''Yeah, I'm half *downcaste*. What about it?''

Surprised by the sudden hostility, Collins raised his hands in a gesture of surrender. ''Nothing about it. I don't even know what *downcaste* means, at least not the way you're using it.''

The softness returned gradually to Vernon's face, then he managed a short laugh. ''Of course, you don't. I'm sorry.''

Collins nodded.

''The *downcaste* are necessary animals relegated to the most distasteful tasks. Creatures the civilized animals wouldn't lower themselves to associate with because they have some undesirable characteristic or habit that makes them . . . repulsive to the *urbanists*.''

''Like skunks?'' Collins asked carefully, not certain he truly understood. He saw nothing essential about skunks. A friend who lived on a small acreage talked about regularly trapping and killing them because more than ninety percent carried rabies in that area.

''Garbage handlers,'' Vernon explained. ''Vultures and hyenas take care of the dead, the only ones allowed by law to eat meat. Goats and pigeons manage the sewage.'' He wrinkled his nose, unable to keep even his prejudice wholly in check. ''They prefer the company of *urbanists* and eat anything.''

''*Urbanists?*'' Collins prompted.

''Creatures who live in cities.'' Vernon drew a leg to his chest. ''Cows, horses, dogs, cats, and such. Some birds.''

Recalling an earlier conversation with Zylas, Collins added, ''*Durithrin*. They also form a social group?''

''The *wildones* include creatures who prefer the woods to others' company.''

Collins realized the stone sometimes translated even those words that worked better in the other language, such as replacing *durithrin* with *wildones*. He supposed *urbanists* and *downcaste* had Barakhain equivalents that would have given him less clue to their meaning. "Deer, squirrels, bears, songbirds . . . ?"

". . . wolves, alligators, wildcats." Vernon shivered. "Once one of those gets a taste for meat, there's no choice but hanging. They *will* kill again."

That explained the severity of Collins' punishment, the lack of a trial, and the intensity of the hunt. *Not like in my world where serial killers are rare and always crazy.* He displayed his new understanding. "*Urbanists, wildones*, and *downcaste*. Your social classes in order of . . ." He searched for words Vernon might not find insulting. ". . . perceived importance."

"Don't forget royals at the top: all human all the time. *Workers* before *wildones*. And, at the very bottom, *vermin*."

With a start, Collins realized that had to include Vernon and Zylas. He swallowed hard, pressing any emotion from his voice. "Define *vermin*."

"Those forbidden to breed with their own kind." Vernon shrugged. "Who wants more mice, rats, snakes, and the like?"

"But you and Zylas—"

"*Randoms*. We weren't made what we are on purpose."

Uncomfortable with the subject, Collins pressed on. "And *workers?*"

Vernon drew up his other leg. "Those who don't quite fit with the *urbanists* but have a high, useful skill to market. Like beavers, who build. Porcupines, the tailors. Moles and weasels, miners, though some would debate whether they go with the *workers* or the *downcaste*.

Collins glanced around the forest, seeing the trees gently bowing in the breeze, the sun glazing every leaf and branch with gold. It seemed impossibly peaceful, hiding the moment when hounds and hunters once again crashed through them, seeking him. He could imagine other specialized creatures: songbird musicians, shrew crop-weeders, bear beekeepers, but he did not question. Closer matters needed discussion, and a realization required voicing. "So you're the other one who's visited my world."

"Several times," Vernon admitted. "With Zylas."

"Why?"

"Why," Vernon repeated, running his fingers through tight curls, straightening them momentarily before they sprang back in place. "Why not?"

Collins suspected that was all the answer he was going to get. "Where's Falima?"

"Hidden." Vernon lowered his legs. "Underground. Too big for your hiding place."

"Agreed." Now, Collins pulled his own feet onto the deadfall, turning to fully face Vernon. "Underground bunkers. Hidden crawl spaces." He spread his fingers. "Why?"

"Because," Vernon said with caution. "Sometimes, good folks need hiding."

It answered nothing. But, for the moment, Collins thought it best not to press.

Chapter 8

BENTON Collins learned more about his newest companion as they headed into the woods surrounding Vernon's cottage. Despite his first thirteen years as a garbage scavenger, Vernon had inherited his father bear's sweet tooth. In addition to visiting another world with Zylas, he had trusted the albino in many situations where common sense suggested he do otherwise. Not the least of these involved treating a horse-guard and a dog-guard to secrets that could get him in as much trouble as Collins and make it impossible for him to help other needy folk in the future.

Known as a reclusive *vermin,* Vernon had few friends or visitors, except when fugitives needed hiding. Luckily, this was not often, so he spent most of his time as he preferred, alone or with Zylas or the handful of *durithrin/wildones* he found worthy of his company. This included Ialin, whom he assured Collins was pleasant and honorable, if flighty, company under most circumstances.

Collins' mind still struggled against the full picture. At times,

Barakhai seemed surreal and distant, at other times too vivid and terrifying. He had discovered a place where dream met savage reality, where nightmare fused inseparably with an existence too obviously genuine to deny. He wanted to get to know his strange companions, at least two of whom already felt like friends. At the same time, he could not find a new portal home too soon. "What are we going to do with Korfius?"

Vernon stopped in what seemed like a random location, studying the trees, shrubbery, and weeds with a wary anxiety. At length, his shoulders fell, his arms uncoiled, and his fingers opened from clenched fists. He turned to face Collins. "I don't know."

Collins studied the site intently, wondering what detail had reassured Vernon. "What are we looking at?"

"Falima." Vernon gestured at scattered leaves piled not-quite-casually in a circle of trees. "Undisturbed. They didn't find her." He headed back toward his cabin.

Collins hated the idea of leaving Falima alone in some underground bunker, but he saw no good alternative. He heard nothing to suggest the location upset her, no thudding hooves against planking, no frantic whinnies. By now, she had probably found a comfortable position to sleep, and disturbing her might prove more foolhardy and dangerous than leaving her in the quiet darkness. He stumbled after the black man. "Korfius?" he repeated.

Vernon shrugged, reminding Collins he had already answered the question.

"What did Zylas say about him?"

Vernon did not look back as the cottage came into view. The thatched roof sagged at the center, and clear gaps had worn through some of the cracks between boards. Wood lay in a neat stack that obliterated the western wall, the one concealing Collins' hiding place. "Zylas called it 'necessary abduction.' Said the boy hadn't changed yet, but ought to soon. Asked if I could help you come up with a story that might convince him not to betray you to the other guards."

Collins considered. "What did you come up with?"

Now, Vernon did turn. "Me? Nothing. I didn't think anything would convince that boy to cooperate. Figured we'd wind up having to do something . . . desperate."

Collins sucked in a quick breath, his mind substituting "murder," though consideration made that doubtful. Little more than strangers to him, these people had already risked their lives and futures for him. Surely, they would not add a capital crime to the lesser ones they had committed for him.

Apparently oblivious to Collins' consternation, Vernon continued, "But the boy made it easy for you, didn't he?"

"How so?" Collins' voice emerged hoarser than he expected.

"Figured you for royalty." Vernon flashed a broad-lipped smile. "That should give you lots of possibilities."

Collins did not share Vernon's confidence. "Except I don't know how to act like royalty."

Vernon laughed, a deep full-throated sound. "Doesn't matter, really. We common folk don't know how royalty acts anyway. We don't intermingle."

It seemed impossible. "Never?"

Vernon dipped his head. "Pretty much. The town leaders take audience now and again, to get their instructions, convey new laws, handle disputes and disasters. Stuff like that." He started walking again. "And we sometimes see a royal guard or messenger, though they're not full-time humans like blood royalty. Only rarely do actual royals choose to walk among us."

"So my strangeness . . ."

". . . could pass for normal royal behavior, as far as a twelve-year-old boy could guess. And he wouldn't know any royal by appearance alone."

"What about my complete inability to speak the language? Don't you think that'll cue him in?"

Vernon stopped at his door to regard Collins again. "Not a problem currently." His gaze dropped to Collins' fist where the translation stone nestled against his fingers. "Probably not later either. All but the most distant of the *downcaste* speaks the language of the *urbanists*. But the *wildones*, the *downcaste*, and the *workers* have languages of their own. And some of the more reclusive species have a tongue based on their animal-speak. Zylas and I sometimes use your language when we want to keep things private. It seems likely the royals would have a private language as well. It wouldn't surprise anyone to find out some royals don't even bother to learn the most common speech of *switchers*." He seized the latch, still looking at Collins. "Ready?"

"Yes," Collins said, though he was not. He doubted he ever would be, however, so now seemed as good as any time.

The door swung open noiselessly to reveal Korfius sitting at the table. His head jerked toward the suddenly open door, he fumbled with something, then chewed vigorously. Crumbs speckled the table, the floor, and the laces at the neck of a shirt that fit him more like a dress.

"Hello, Korfius," Vernon boomed. "Up already?"

Korfius replied with a muffled, "Couldn't sleep."

"What did you say?" Vernon winked conspiratorially at Collins, who grinned. Korfius looked like a toddler caught with a hand in the cookie jar. As glad to have another friend as to discover a wink meant the same thing here as at home, Collins played along.

Korfius swallowed, then cleared his throat. "Couldn't sleep." He looked up to reveal bits of food clinging to his face and a telltale smear of honey on his right cheek.

"Hungry?" Vernon suggested.

Korfius flushed, wiping his mouth with the back of a sleeve. He glanced at the table, realizing he was caught. "Very. I couldn't wait. I'm sorry I took without asking."

Not wishing to embarrass the boy further, Collins added, "I could do with some food, too."

Korfius sprang from his chair. "At once, Your Majesty." He scurried toward the trapdoor and nearly reached it before skidding to a horrified stop. He looked askance at Vernon, who laughed.

"My home is your home," Vernon said, still chuckling, "apparently." He made a broad gesture. "Bring up the best you can find."

Without further encouragement, Korfius lifted the hatch and slid into the parlor. His footfalls echoed on the wooden stairs, growing gradually softer.

Collins oriented as he watched the boy disappear. Clearly, the guards had looked for him and Korfius in the larder, and he had heard their voices as they descended the stairs. He tried to fathom why he had heard them there but not inside the cabin.

As if reading Collins' mind, Vernon explained. "It's not normal to have hiding places, so sound travels oddly. You can hear and be heard by anyone on the parlor stairs but no other place as far as I know. If you have to hide again, though, I'd suggest you stay silent, just in case."

Collins shivered at the thought of cramming himself into that tight, seemingly airless space again. Nevertheless, he found it preferable to hanging. "You can count on it."

"You'd never believe how many times those fools have searched the dresser, leaving me a mess of clothes to pick up." Vernon gestured at the irregularly stained, off-center chest of drawers. Clearly handmade, it occupied most of the eastern wall. "I stash all kinds of clothing in there; people give what they can. Those who can't give wash or patch. You find anything your size, feel free to change. Dirties'll get washed and go to someone else. Or you can get them back next time you drop in."

"I do appreciate your help and your kindness." Collins continued to study the dresser, seeking some indication of the secret area he knew took up most of the space behind it. ''And I hope I don't offend you when I say that I hope I never have to receive it again.''

Vernon turned, brows raised and mouth crinkled with amusement. ''You're welcome. And, yes, I understand.''

Korfius' bare feet clomped up the stairs. He appeared through the opening hugging a variety of flasks and crockery. Straw-colored hair lay in snarled disarray. Streaks of dirt decorated otherwise cherubic cheeks, like war paint, the right still bearing a dab of honey. His gray robe had a tattered hem that dragged on the planking, and its V-neck, even laced, revealed most of his hairless chest. Awkwardly, he dropped his finds on the table. A covered mug rolled across the surface until Korfius caught it and righted it. ''I found lots of stuff, Your Majesty, though not what you're used to of course; but it will have to—''

''All right.'' Vernon interrupted the boy's excited patter. ''Let's see what we have here.'' He lifted and replaced lids, occasionally sniffing the contents. ''Black bread, honey, assorted insects, nut paste, roundfruit, roasted beetles, watered wine, mulled fruit juice.'' He looked up. ''Any of that suit you, Your Majesty?''

A clumsy silence followed before Collins remembered they addressed him. ''Oh. Oh, yes. Honey bread. Maybe some of that nut paste. Fruit and fruit juice, please.''

Vernon started doling out the fare, placing each share directly on the table. ''No beetles, sire? They're the best thing I have, a real delicacy. The big kind with lots of substance and a gratifying crunch.''

Korfius peered eagerly into one of the crocks. ''Real good ones, Your Majesty. Look!''

''That's all right.'' Collins did not care to see. ''I'm not much of a . . . um . . . bug-eater.'' He took his seat at the table while Vernon plopped a golden, viscous fluid, spotted with bits of honeycomb onto a thick slice of dark bread and pushed it in front of his guest. The sweet odor of the honey sent a rumble through Collins' stomach. Instinctively, he thought back to his last satisfying meal and realized, with a guilty start, that it was when he had eaten the rabbit. *Joetha.* The queasy feeling settled back into his gut, though the bread continued to tempt him. Vernon slapped a handful of semisolid brownish glop interspersed with chunks onto the table beside the bread. Oil formed a ring around the edges. Though unappetizing looking, it smelled vaguely similar to peanut butter, which tweaked Collins' hunger again. Two wrinkled balls, stored fruit, rolled across the table toward him, followed by a mug of dull orangish-pink liquid, dense with pulp.

Korfius claimed the chair to Collins' right, clambering onto his knees. "I've had some bread and honey, thank you. I'd just like some of those beetles and a bit of wine, please."

Vernon slopped down a half-dozen insects the size of Collins' first thumb joint. Their black legs curled against their abdomens, and their wings shimmered a pearly aqua, burned to dull black in places. A dribble of saliva escaped Korfius' mouth, but he waited patiently for his host and his fellow guest.

Vernon served himself a bit of everything, then relaxed into his chair. Collins suddenly felt all eyes on him. Apparently, as the presumed royal, he was supposed to take the first bite. Needing cues as to how best to eat the other food, he went for the bread first, taking a healthy bite. It had the consistency of a kitchen sponge, and a hint of mold marred the otherwise pleasant flavor. The honey tasted as fresh and sweet as any he had ever had, though he would have preferred to have strained out all of the comb.

The others started eating, too, Korfius with doglike gusto. "So," the boy said around a mouthful of beetle. "How did I wind up here?" He swallowed. "And when can I go home?"

Vernon's gaze flicked to Collins, and he chewed vigorously.

Collins finished the bite of bread, then set the rest down. He cleared his throat. "Well . . ." If they waited until Korfius became a dog again before releasing him, they probably had half a day before he could report back to the guards. *Unless, as a dog, he can communicate fully with the other dogs.* His ignorance foiled him, yet he could not leave Vernon to handle a problem that he had created. He already depended too much on his companions' charity. "It's difficult. I'm on a top secret royal mission, and I don't know if I can trust you."

"Top secret?" Korfius repeated, features screwed into a knot as he crunched another beetle. Obviously, the term meant little to him, and the translation stone did not leave room for quibbling. Likely, it had portrayed the words "top" and "secret" rather than the compound concept. "Of course you can trust me. Why wouldn't you trust me?"

To emphasize the gravity, Collins thrust all his food aside. "When you're on a mission this secret, you can't trust anyone."

Korfius swallowed, his own food forgotten for the moment, too. "Not anyone?"

"Not . . . anyone."

"Why?"

"Because," Collins leaned toward the boy. "It's so important and so very very secret. If the wrong person found out, if someone told them, thinking he could trust them, or if they merely overheard it, it could destroy the mission."

Korfius swallowed again, harder. "What is the mission?"

"If I told you, I'd have to kill you."

Korfius' features opened, and his jaw fell. Even Vernon turned his head to give Collins a warning stare.

Collins dropped his voice to an urgent whisper. "It's that secret. And that vital."

When the two continued to gape, Collins continued, "The lives of thousands rest in my hands. I can't betray that sacred and dire trust. And I can't let anyone else do it either." He lowered his own gaze to his hands. "I've already said as much as I dare about it."

Korfius bobbed his head, clenching his hands on the edge of the table, knuckles bloodless. "Before I switched, before the hunt. The guards in human form said . . . they said . . ." He looked at Vernon, who waved encouragingly. "A man with your description ate someone."

Collins' thoughts raced. He knew Korfius must have switched to dog form shortly before Collins captured him and that he would understand little of the subsequent details. He should have figured the boy might have known the intention of the hunt. The guards had caught Collins in the process of committing the crime; he could hardly deny it. That would put his credibility, already thin, in hopeless jeopardy.

"Did you . . . did you . . ." Korfius clamped his attention on Collins. ". . . kill . . . and eat . . . that rabbit?"

Collins calmly ladled nut paste into his mouth, stalling. He chewed, maintaining the air of casual innocence, swallowed, took a sip of fruit juice to clear his mouth, then spoke in the most matter-of-fact tone he could muster. "Had to."

Korfius blinked.

"She threatened to tell others about me, about the mission. I hate killing more than anything in the world. But . . ." Collins gave Korfius a look of dangerous sincerity. "In the wrong hands, that information would doom the mission. One life seemed a small price to pay to save thousands."

"I–I," Korfius stammered, voice dropping to a whisper. "I wouldn't tell anyone."

Collins hissed back, "I'm counting on that."

As if he'd suddenly discovered his food, Korfius went back to stuffing beetles into his mouth.

Collins glanced over to Vernon's half-grin.

"Who can't know?" Korfius said between crunches. "Whose hands are the wrong hands?"

"*No one* must know. Where I am, who I'm with, what I'm doing." Collins added conspiratorially, "You're the only one besides my friends who even knows I'm royal."

Vernon wiped his mouth with an edge of his tunic. "Korfius,

here's what I suggest you tell the other guards and your parents.''

Korfius sat up, attentive.

''You fell or got hit or something. You're not sure, but it made you sleep for many hours. When you woke up, you wandered around confused for a long time. Finally, I found you. Fed you. Took you home. Got it?''

Korfius' mouth pinched. ''But that would be a lie.''

''Yes,'' Vernon said simply.

Believing the boy needed more, Collins added, ''A necessary lie. One that will help save the lives of thousands. Do you understand?''

''Sort of,'' Korfius replied, swallowing a mouthful. ''Not really. Not the details.''

''Can't give you those,'' Collins said apologetically, then hardened his tone. ''If you don't agree, you leave me no choice but to . . .'' He trailed off with clear significance.

Korfius hugged himself. When he finally spoke, he used a small voice. ''I want to help save lives.''

Vernon made a noise of approval, deep in his throat. ''So you won't tell anyone about His Majesty or his companions?''

''I won't,'' Korfius promised.

''Good boy.'' Vernon returned to his food, and the others followed suit.

For several moments, they ate in silence, then Collins rose and yawned. ''My turn for a nap?'' he suggested.

Vernon also stood. He walked to the chest of drawers, pulled open the top one, and removed a clay pot. ''Let me show you to the well. You can wash up and change.''

It seemed more logical to wash after the nap, so Collins suspected the older man wanted to talk with him alone. ''Great,'' he said, waving at Korfius. ''See you soon.''

Korfius eyed the beetle jar.

Though Vernon headed for the door, he did not miss the

gesture. "Have as much food as you want," he called over his shoulder to the boy as he exited the cottage, Collins behind him.

The sun slanted toward the western horizon, and Collins' watch read ten minutes until four. Vernon strolled toward the back of the cottage, waiting only until they had clearly passed Korfius' hearing range before asking, "That was brilliant. Where did you come up with all that stuff? About missions and thousands and lives and . . . ?" He showed Collins an expression that bordered on awe.

Collins did not have the heart to tell his companion it came from the meanest B-grade spy movies he had seen in high school. Choosing an air of mystery over idiocy, he reverted to the same understated melodrama that Vernon had laid on him when he asked about the bolt-holes. Cocking his brows, he put on a tight-lipped grin. And left the answer to Vernon's imagination.

Collins awakened to the slam of a closing door and the pound of footsteps on floorboards. For an instant, his mind returned him to the dark enclosure behind Vernon's dresser, desperately clutching a frightened and morphing dog/boy who might give them away in an instant. His lids snapped open to candlelight that held evening grayness at bay in a circle. He lay on the pallet. Korfius sat in the chair Collins had vacated hours earlier, his yellow hair mostly flopped over his right ear, his small hands clasped together on the tabletop. Vernon and Falima stood on the threshold, the man carrying the aroma of cool evening wind and the woman wholly naked. For the second time, Collins caught a glimpse of that wonderful body: the generous, sinewy curves, the pert breasts, and the black triangle between muscular thighs.

Falima glanced at Collins, and her golden skin turned a prickly red. She hid behind Vernon, her discomfort an obvious change from the unself-conscious dignity with which she had carried herself a day ago.

Sensing Falima's uneasiness, Vernon removed his cloak and tossed it over her bare shoulders. She drew it tightly around her while he crossed to the dresser and began sifting through clothing. At length, he pitched out a simple dress of coarse weave, dyed a sallow blue. Falima turned her back to pull it over her head, giving Collins a full view of her round, firm buttocks every bit as pleasurable as what she hid. The fabric fell into place, disguising the exquisite angles beneath a shapeless blob of material. Only then, she returned the cloak to Vernon.

Collins waited until Falima had dressed before sitting up and rubbing grit from the corners of his eyes. His mother had called them "sleepy seeds," but Marlys had broken him of the habit. She felt it best not to refer to bodily fluids, whether liquid or dry, at all. Even earwax made her ill, and a used Q-tip accidentally left on a bathroom ledge sent her into a frenzy. *Marlys.* Collins grimaced. He knew she would not appreciate him staring, or even worse enjoying the sight of, another woman's naked body, no matter how amusing or dire the circumstances.

Vernon and Korfius seemed to take no notice of the process, though the older man prodded the washbasin they had filled earlier that now perched on top of the dresser and waved at the clean pile of clothing beside it. "Your turn," he said in heavily accented English, then winked at Collins.

You bastard. Collins glanced in the indicated direction, then sat. He thrust a hand in his pocket and wrapped his fingers around the translation stone. He withdrew his hand, clutching the quartz to his palm as he removed the travel-stained tunic to reveal his ribby, nearly hairless chest. "Happy?"

Korfius glanced over.

Vernon smiled.

"Not yet," Falima said, mouth widening into a grin.

Now it was Collins' turn to blush. Seeking a distraction, he rose and strode to the basin. He splashed water over his face, abdomen, and armpits, then ran the fingers of his free hand through his hair. Grit rasped against his nails, and twigs pattered to the ground. Without a heavy stream of water and a lot of shampoo, it seemed hopeless. He looked at his companions.

Korfius had lowered his head to his arm, but the other two still watched Collins intently.

All right, I can do this. Collins thought of his two delicious sessions of Falima-watching. *It's only fair.* He reached for his fly, thinking back to his experiences in the locker room. For size, he fell squarely into the average category, and his slender figure only enhanced what he had. He turned around, freed the metal button and unzipped. His pants slid to his ankles. He stepped out of them, then his underwear, baring his backside for his companions.

Collins felt more self-conscious now than the time his six-year-old cousin, Brittany, had pulled the bathroom door wide open during her sister's wedding reception, while he performed inside. He splashed water over his legs and privates, his back to Falima, hoping she had the decency to look elsewhere as he had done for her.

Collins snatched up the fresh, gray britches that Vernon had laid out for him, the fabric rough and scratchy against his hand.

"Turn around," Falima teased.

Collins winced.

"There's nothing to be embarrassed about, Your Majesty." Vernon restored the title and the charade of respect, even as they stripped Collins of all physical dignity. "Those of us who switch see one another naked all the time. There's a lot of . . . normal variation."

Let's get this over with. The longer Collins put it off, he knew, the more Falima would expect when she finally saw him. *And so what? What does it matter what she thinks of . . . that?* Even in his thoughts, he had to use a euphemism, and it intensified the scarlet circles of his cheeks. *It's not like there could ever be anything between us.* Yet, somehow, it did matter. Whether or not they ever came together, he wanted her to like him, to want him, as much as he wanted her. *This is ridiculous. As if a guy like me could ever attract a hotty like her.* Screwing up his courage, he turned, only then realizing that Falima was accustomed to seeing stallions.

Nervously, Collins watched Falima's face as the smile wilted and her pale eyes widened. She back-stepped, gasping.

Collins could not have imagined a more unnerving reaction. "Very funny."

"Wha–what . . . ?" Falima stammered, not sounding the least bit amused. "What happened?"

"It . . . I . . ." Collins floundered with the britches, and it seemed to take inordinately long to find the leg holes. "Sometimes . . . they're all . . ."

Vernon smoothly stepped in to assist. "The cutting," he explained. "The foreskin. We don't do that here."

Collins tied the britches in place, the excess color draining from his face. He dropped the rose quartz into a pocket to speak the word in English that he knew must not translate. "Circumcision." He took up the stone again, so as not to miss anything. "It's a . . . a . . ."

"Royal thing?" Vernon suggested.

"Exactly." Collins appreciated the reminder. In the horror of the situation, they had all apparently forgotten his cover. Otherwise, Vernon would have said "*switchers* don't do that" rather than "we don't do that here." Collins explained, "Keeps it cleaner." *I can't believe I'm discussing the details of my penis in mixed company.* He tried to drop the subject. "So, any place to get a real bath around here?"

"Doesn't it hurt?" Korfius piped in, rising to join the others.

"What?" Vernon inquired.

"That." Korfius jabbed a finger toward Collins' now-covered groin. "Doesn't it hurt to . . . to . . . cut it like that." He added, belatedly, "Your majesty."

Though unnecessary, Collins followed the direction of Korfius' motion naturally. "Oh, that. I don't know. It's done when you're just a couple days old."

"Does it still work, Your Majesty?"

"Work?" All of the blushing returned to Collins' face in an instant. "Of course it works. All the . . . all the . . ." He glanced at Falima, then wished he had not. It only intensified the embarrassment. ". . . functions work. It's just . . . well . . . cleaner, I guess." Again, he tried to redirect the conversation. "Please stop with the 'Your Majesty,' though. No one's supposed to know who I am, remember?" He placed a finger to his lips. "Top secret."

"Top secret." Korfius repeated vigorously. His expression wilted from open and eager to wrinkled disappointment in an instant. "Will I ever get to tell my friends I met a royal?"

Falima placed an arm around the boy. "I've kept the secret a year now. Think you can last half that long?"

Korfius nodded. "Longer even."

"Good boy." Falima tousled the boy's hair.

Collins used the distraction to finish dressing quickly, glad they finally seemed to have moved beyond his genitalia. Now that they had all seen him, he felt like a great weight had lifted from him.

"My turn to nap," Vernon announced suddenly. "Got to get my human sleep time in before the switch."

Collins glanced at his watch. It now read 6:45 p.m., which meant Vernon had a little over five hours before the change; since, according to Vernon, he and Zylas switched at exactly the same time. Collins resisted the urge to ask for an explanation about sleeping. It seemed only right that they would need to do so in both forms.

Collins relished and dreaded the chance to spend some time alone with Falima, to finally explain, one-on-one, his mistake with Joetha. He could get her to understand that she and Ialin had misjudged him, that one error made in good faith, did not make him a monster. For reasons he could not rationalize or elucidate, he needed her to like him. Now, one of his companions slept, but they still had to contend with Korfius. By the time the dog/boy switched, Vernon might already have awakened. *I can't catch a break.*

Korfius and Collins took seats at the table while Vernon stretched out on the pallet. Falima searched the top drawer, then the middle, finally emerging triumphantly with an unwearable rag. She set to work, dusting the surface of the dresser.

Vernon tucked his arms behind his head. "What are you doing?"

"Cleaning." Falima continued without a pause. "For what looks like the first time in years."

"Really," Collins said, trying to save their host's face as well as display the manners his mother had taught him. "I hadn't noticed." Now that Falima had drawn his attention, he saw cobwebs looped and hammocked along the ceiling, walls, and especially the corners. Dust peppered the floors, and food stained the wooden table.

"Of course, you hadn't noticed." Falima redoubled her efforts. "Filth is invisible to males."

The words struck staggeringly close to home. Collins recalled the times his father would pass his room as adequately straightened and let him watch television. His mother would poke in her head, shaking it and rolling her eyes.

"Not invisible." Vernon rolled to his side. "Just tolerable."

Collins rose. "Toss me a rag. I'll help." Sitting had become the most boring pastime in the universe. Though he had never considered himself much of a watcher, he missed television, movies, the internet, video games. It seemed so natural to flick on an electric light rather than search out dust bunnies in the dim flicker of a tiny flame. He suspected even finding a book here would prove nearly impossible. He would rather grade freshmen papers than sit twiddling his thumbs while Falima worked. "What do you people do with your free time?"

"Free time?" Falima repeated as she rummaged through the chest of drawers. "What do you mean by that?"

"Try the bottom," Vernon suggested. "Older stuff there."

Falima slammed the middle drawer shut and opened the bottom one. In a moment, she pulled out the torn remnants of a sleeve. "Here." She tossed it to Collins, who caught it in his right hand.

"Thanks." Collins returned to his question. "You know, free time. Like now. When you have nothing in particular that needs doing."

Falima tossed Collins' dirty clothes on the floor near the door. "I don't know, really. It almost never happens." She scrubbed at the dresser top. "I used to spend all night patrolling or guarding the prison. During the day, I was carrying someone or something. When I wasn't doing either of those, I was sleeping or eating."

"Or searching for food," Vernon said. "Or fixing things that broke."

Korfius added his piece, "Or helping someone find something he lost. Or picking up the slack from someone who's sick or something."

"This situation." Falima made a grand gesture. "This waiting for someone, unable to go outside because someone else is hunting you—"

"Very unnatural," Vernon finished.

"Never happens." Falima dunked her rag into the washbasin and resumed working. "Normally."

Collins thought of all the things his new friends knew nothing about, did not even have the experience to miss: washing machines, dishwashers, music on demand, refrigerators and freezers, vacuum cleaners, cars, ovens, plastic raincoats. The list seemed endless, and he wondered when he had stopped appreciating any of it. No wonder Zylas and Vernon left Barakhai when they could. He suspected they had visited his world more times than they admitted; to have learned even as little as they had managed seemed miraculous. ''Zylas brought a lighter back,'' Collins remembered.

Vernon's deep rumble of laughter surprised Collins. He had not realized he had spoken aloud. ''You should have seen him struggle. Entertained me for an entire day. Still makes me laugh.''

Falima looked up from her work. ''Why didn't he just wait for the switch?''

Vernon propped up his head on one hand, rolling his gaze toward Korfius in a pointed gesture. Though Falima had asked the question, he answered in broken English. ''Only can go as animal. Not switch there.''

Intrigued by the answer, Collins wrapped the cloth around his hand and casually released the translation stone. ''You can't switch? Or choose not to?''

''Can't.''

''Interesting.'' Collins surmised that they had to obey the physical laws of his world once there. *The Law of Conservation of Mass and Energy, perhaps?* He hoped that did not mean he would become a shapeshifter while here, though the thought of soaring like an eagle, swinging through trees like a money, or running as wild and free as a cheetah intrigued him. *With my luck, I'd probably turn into some plodding old tortoise.*

Collins set to flicking at cobwebs with his rag while Korfius watched him from the table. The boy did not seem to miss working at all, enjoying the opportunity to spend the entire day sitting, sleeping, and talking. *And why shouldn't he?* Collins refused to begrudge the seeming laziness. *He probably doesn't get the chance to do absolutely nothing as often as once per year.*

Though he would have preferred listening to Nirvana or Matchbox 20 slamming from a CD in the background, Collins enjoyed the slowed pace as well. For the first time since entering this odd and backward world, he felt almost safe.

Chapter 9

AN hour and a half later, Vernon snored musically on the pallet, Korfius lay, in dog form, with his head on Collins' foot, and the cabin practically sparkled. Falima tossed herself into a chair across from Collins, regarding him in silence.

Feeling the need to speak first, but not wanting to launch into contentious subjects immediately, Collins simply said, "He's a good man, Vernon."

A forelock of black hair fell over Falima's forehead, between the strikingly blue eyes. Her long lashes swept downward, then up again. "Yes."

"Zylas, too."

"Yes."

"And Ialin . . . ?"

"Yes," Falima repeated, as if Collins had spoken the third name in the same tone as the others rather than in question.

Collins smiled. "What do I have to do to get you to use more than one syllable?"

Falima tapped her balled hands on the tabletop. "Try asking

a question where the answer isn't obvious.'' She also smiled, apparently to show she meant no malice.

''All right.'' Collins leaned toward her and addressed his mood. ''Are we really safe here?''

Falima's grin broadened. ''Yes.''

As Falima returned to her ubiquitous monosyllable, Collins groaned. ''All right, then. Let's put this in the form of an essay.'' He cleared his throat. ''Do you believe we're really safe from Barakhain guards here? Why or why not?''

Though Falima could not have understood the reference, she laughed. It was a surprisingly loud sound, full of joie de vivre and mirth, nothing like the dainty bell-like twitters Marlys loosed when she deigned to enjoy one of his jokes. ''As safe as we can be for the moment, I guess. Vernon has a web throughout the *durithrin* community. If the guards remained in or returned to the area, they would tell him.''

That explained why Vernon spoke so freely in the forest as well as in his cabin.

Korfius smacked his jowls a few times, then sighed deeply.

Collins jerked his attention to the dog. ''Do you think *he* understands any of this?''

''No.''

''You're sure?''

''Yes.''

Collins forced his attention from the dog to Falima. ''Positive?''

''Yes.''

Realizing he had cornered Falima into monosyllables yet again, Collins placed the onus on her. ''How can you be so sure?''

Falima slouched. The candle struck red-and-purple highlights in hair otherwise dark as shadow. ''Horses are senior guards, dogs junior. I spent my last twelve years working over dogs. He's too young for much overlap, even if he had put most of his effort into it. But he's clearly . . ." The last word, though apparently enunciated, did not translate.

Collins placed the rose quartz on the table, deliberately removing his hand. "Clearly what?"

"*Lesariat,*" Falima repeated dutifully. She inclined her head toward the translation stone, and Collins placed his palm squarely over it. "Zylas *really* trusts you."

"He honors me more than I deserve."

Falima did not argue that point. "I knew him almost ten years before he let me use it." She turned Collins a telling look. "Now, thanks to you, it'll probably be another ten before he lets me touch it again. If ever."

Collins felt his cheeks warm. "Sorry." He directed the conversation back to its previous point. "What is this *lesar . . . lesar . . . rat?*"

"*Lesariat.*" This time, the stone allowed the foreign word through without attempting translation. "It's a . . . a . . . state of mind . . . of being." Falima sighed, struggling. "The *masuniat* find their animal form an inconvenient interruption. Most don't bother to seek balance or overlap. They live from human time to human time. Some leave themselves notes to allow them to take up exactly where they left off. It's more common in *Randoms*. The *Regular masuniat* often take herbs at coming-of-age to shorten switch time."

Worried about getting hopelessly lost, Collins tried to clarify. "All right. So the *masuniat* try to spend less time as animals and more time as humans."

"Right. The *Regular masuniat,*" Falima reminded. "The more successful the herbs, the more like *Randoms* they become, at least in terms of switch time. Fulfillment would mean they spend exactly half their time human, like *Randoms*."

"And you?" Collins looked pointedly at Falima, who lowered her head.

"You know, don't you?"

"Yeah, and I'm not quite sure why you lied to me." Worried

that he'd never understand Korfius, he reluctantly dropped the matter. "But first, *lesariat*."

"Getting to that," Falima promised. "The herbs have side effects that limit their use. They can cause bellyaches, rashes, vomiting. Even coma or death. They also lessen overlap. So it's a balancing act."

"I'd say so." Collins could think of nothing short of cancer that would make him take anything so toxic.

"The *winariat* accept the change as a natural part of life. They tend to have the best overlap, though that partially depends on philosophy. Some truly believe it more innate to act as animal as possible in switch-form and as human as possible in human form."

Collins saw the direction Falima appeared to be taking. "So the *lesariat* must prefer . . . their animal form?"

"Exactly." Falima beamed at him. "Most have no interest at all in overlap, or they even reverse it. They may bring more habits from their switch-form to their human form. And they take herbs to lengthen their animal time."

Things started to come together. "So Korfius drools. And looks for food all the time."

Falima chuckled. "Exactly. It also helps that I smell the *lesariat* herb on him."

Collins had completely missed that. "What does it smell like?"

"It's . . . distinctive." Falima's lips twisted, then returned to normal. She shook her head. "Ever try to describe a smell?"

Collins bobbed his head and opened his hands in concession. Without a comparison, it could become almost impossible, like taste. For the first time, he realized why so many meats got compared to chicken. It seemed simpler to whiff at their companion sometime after the switch. He studied Falima. The candlelight sparked from her golden skin, revealing smears of grime. Her pale eyes watched him back, striking in their color and depth. Though a bit large, her nose suited her, and the curtain of jet black hair gave her an air of foreign mystery. Though not classically beautiful, she drew his gaze in a way he could not quite explain. He could enjoy staring at that face every morning over the breakfast table, even rumpled, coarsened, and travel weary, for eternity.

Falima broke the spell. "Is it normal where you come from to gawk?"

As usual, Collins groped for humor; but the words that left his mouth surprised even him. "Only when there's something this pretty to gawk at."

"Me?" Falima asked incredulously.

"Of course not," Collins said facetiously. "I meant the gorgeous woman standing behind you."

Falima tensed as if to glance around, then relaxed. "Thank you. But there's no need to lie. I know I'm not . . . attractive."

Stunned, Collins turned defensive. "Of course you're attractive. Where I come from, men would fight over you."

"They would?"

"Yes."

"In human form? Or horse?"

"Human," Collins replied, then added, "In horse form, the girls would fight over you."

Falima blinked several times, obviously confused. "The girls? Why?"

Collins considered briefly. "Because, where I come from, it's almost like a law. Pretty much all girls love horses at some point in their lives. Sometimes forever." He leaned toward Falima. "That's not to say boys and men don't like horses, too. Just not so . . . almost universally."

"Love to . . ." Falima fidgeted, looking at her hands, ". . . eat them?"

"Horses?" Collins shook his head vigorously. "Yuck, never. We don't eat horses where I come from." He had heard people in other countries did, but he saw no reason to get technical.

"But you eat animals."

"Not horses." Collins crinkled his face and shook his head again. He caught sight of Korfius at the corner of his vision. "Or dogs. Or mice, hummingbirds, rats . . ." The latter made him think of the television show *Survivor*, but he did not voice it. There seemed no reason to complicate matters more than already necessary.

"What do you eat?"

Collins spoke slowly, watching Falima's reaction as he spoke each word. "Cows."

Falima winced but continued looking at him encouragingly.

"Pigs, chickens, turkey, and fish."

"Fish aren't animals."

"They are where I come from."

"Oh."

An uncomfortable pause followed.

"What else?" Falima finally said.

"That takes care of about 99.9% of all the meat eaten in the United States." Collins knew he had to mention rabbits for her to believe him. "The rest is what we call game, which you would call *durithrin* or *wildones*. Rabbits, deer, ducks, geese. A few people do bear, squirrel, turtles, possum, snakes, stuff like that. But most people wouldn't consider those animals savory or, in many cases, even edible." He recalled the time one of the international students had brought a tomato-based stew to a potluck that everyone ate with relish, until a rumor circulated that the meat they had sucked down with gusto moments before was actually cat. The ladle never again dipped into that bowl.

"Not horses."

"Not horses." Collins confirmed.

Falima fell silent again, fingers clasping and unclasping on the tabletop.

"This is really creepy for you, isn't it?"

"Not–not really. I mean, I knew—" Falima finally met Collins' gaze. "It's just that sometimes, when you look at me—" A flush crept up her neck. "You look so . . . so . . . hungry."

"Hungry?"

"Right after I change back." Falima rolled her stare to her hands, pinning one with the other. "I don't notice when I'm in switch-form. "It's like you want to . . . to devour me."

Now Collins understood and appreciated that Falima did not meet his eyes. *I do. Just not the way you're thinking.* "That's not hunger, Falima. That's . . ." Words failed him completely.

Now, Falima looked directly at him.

"Well . . ." The word came, but Collins hesitated to use it. ". . . lust."

Falima's expression did not change for several moments, then her brows fell in clear confusion. "What?"

This time, Collins looked away, index finger tracing a stain on the tabletop. "I'm sorry. I do know it's rude to stare at your body, but it's so . . . so beautiful." *And I don't get to see naked women very often.* He had seen Marlys, of course, but only twice. Most men of his time would consider her the prettier of the two: slight, red-haired, high-cheeked, full-lipped and well versed in enhancement with makeup. Yet, for reasons he could not yet elucidate, Falima seemed much more exciting.

Falima's mouth clamped to a severe line. "That's the second time you've called me beautiful."

"You are."

"I'm not."

It was an unwinnable argument, so Collins sidestepped it. "You are to me. Why don't you think so?"

Falima studied Collins, as if trying to read the intention behind an obvious scheme. "I'm a *Random*. I'm muscled like a horse, without a woman's proper softness. My colors match my switch-form better than my human form, which is manifested at night."

Collins felt a grin edging onto his lips and stopped it. "None of those things matter to me."

"They don't?"

"Why would they?"

Falima had no ready answer. "Because . . . because—"

"Because nothing." Collins took Falima's hands and allowed the smile to glide across his face. "You know what I see?"

Falima shook her head.

"I see an athletic woman with eyes like sparkling sapphires." Collins suppressed a wince at his own triteness and wished he had paid more attention in the poetry class he had taken to fulfill his English credits. "A perfect tan. Hair midnight black and as sleek and wild as the sea. Beautiful." He pinned the smile in place. "And a creamy buckskin horse any breeder might envy."

"You do?"

"I do."

"Thank you."

Collins' grin slipped. "No need for thanks. I was simply describing what I see."

"But your words make me feel good."

"I'm glad."

They smiled at one another, and joy suffused Collins. His heart skipped, then quickened. Excitement tingled through his chest in a way he could not recall since his first crush on Betty Lou Finnegan in junior high and, prior to that, not since childhood.

Korfius yipped, breaking the mood. His legs twitched rhythmically, kicking Collins' shin.

Collins slid his feet free, rolling the dog onto his back. Korfius awakened briefly, whacked his tail on the boards, and resumed snoring.

Collins hated to even raise the issue when things were going better than he could ever have imagined, but it needed saying. "About Joetha." An image of his own grandmother came to his mind: her gray-and-white hair falling in curls to just above her shoulders, her small stout form smelling of peppers and cookies, the welcoming smile she had always given him, surrounded by the familiar wrinkles that had come to define unconditional love. She had died two years ago, of natural causes, and he missed her. He forced himself to contemplate some savage serial murderer stabbing her to death, cannibalizing the body. The picture proved too much. Horror dragged through him like a hot knife, and he dropped his head, sobbing, into his hands.

Collins did not hear Falima move, but her warm body enfolded him and her hands stroked his hair like a child's. She rocked him gently as he wept, his tears plastering the rude fabric of her dress against her solid curves. "I'm sorry," he gasped out. "I'm sorry." He wanted to say more, but grief would not allow it. *I killed someone's mother, someone's grandmother. I killed her, and I callously ate her.*

Collins did not know how long he cried into Falima's arms. But, when he finally regained control, his face bore the indentations of every thick fiber. She looked as if she had spilled a glass of water down her bodice, rumpled and pinch-faced.

"It's all right," she finally said.

"It's not." Collins shook his head. "It never will be."

Falima could not deny those words. Collins would have to learn to live with the guilt or go insane.

"A bad thing happened." Falima lowered herself to her haunches. "But the cause was mistake, not malice. Zylas has forgiven you, and so have I. At some point, you have to forgive yourself."

"Joetha's family—"

"—can never forgive you, of course." Falima asked cautiously, "Can you live with that?"

Collins had been about to say "—will suffer," so Falima's question caught him off-guard. He considered. "Yes," he realized to his own surprise. "I can."

Falima rose and returned to her chair. "Then it's settled. We don't need to speak of this again."

Collins liked the way she had phrased it, assuaging his shame but leaving the subject open if he ever felt the emotional need to talk about it. It was a talent he had not known she possessed, and it only made her more desirable.

Collins awakened with a start that left him disoriented to place and time, yet burdened with a decisive thought that usurped all other need for understanding. My friends: Zylas, Falima, Vernon, even Ialin, are good people, better than I could ever be. He tried to imagine himself risking his life and freedom for a murderer on death row, but the image refused to form. He would not do so, even if he knew the man innocent, let alone guilty only from ignorance. He would, of course, come forward to testify; but he would not hazard electrocution by cutting power lines to the electric chair.

Collins opened his eyes. He lay on the pallet in Vernon's cottage, straw poking him through the threadbare blanket, a bundled tunic serving as a makeshift pillow. Falima curled on the floor, snagging the four hours of sleep she required in human form. He would have preferred to give her the more comfortable sleeping place, but maintaining the illusion of his royalty took precedence until they left Korfius in Vernon's care. He saw no sign of Korfius or their host.

As Collins rolled to his right side to face the wall, he found his feet pinned in place. He jerked at the covers, dislodging the dog, who groaned and clambered from the pallet. Freed, Collins finished his intended movement and snuggled back into the straw. He could understand Zylas' assistance. The rat/man might feel responsible for leading Collins into Barakhai and, therefore, the subsequent crime. Vernon clearly made a career out of helping the needy, so perhaps he got some personal satisfaction from hiding Collins. Falima's and Ialin's motivations escaped him completely. *No wonder they're hostile. Zylas must have talked them into it, perhaps against their better judgment.*

Knowing he needed his sleep, Collins forced these thoughts from his mind. He could speculate about their motivations all day and never come near the truth. It was an exercise in futility that he could better solve by simply asking. *Hard enough understanding people of my own world.* Collins pushed his mind to less intrusive thoughts and, eventually, found sleep again.

The next time Benton Collins awakened, he heard low voices. He sat up, the blanket tumbling to his ankles. Zylas leaned across the table, talking softly to Vernon. They made an odd pair, one slight and white as cream, the other powerfully muscled and dark as untouched coffee. Though taught to revile eavesdropping, he strained to overhear. His companions had left him out of conversations about his own welfare so many times that he somehow felt owed the knowledge.

Korfius floundered from beneath the blanket that now covered his head. He flopped to the floor, the cloth fumbling after him in an awkward twist.

The men at the table looked toward them. Zylas said something louder, accompanied by a friendly wave.

Only then, Collins realized his moments of straining could have gained him nothing. Without touching the stone, he could not understand a word of the Barakhain they exchanged. He thrust his hand into the pocket that held the rose quartz, withdrawing it. "You're back," he finally said.

"I am," Zylas admitted. His gaze wandered to the translation stone, and his grin widened. "Thanks for taking such good care of my rock."

Collins returned the grin. "It was nothing," he said honestly. "I really appreciate your leaving it. I couldn't have done anything without it."

Zylas nodded. Collins certainly did not have to explain the merits of the magic to its longtime owner.

"So," Collins pressed for the important news immediately. "Is there another portal?"

Zylas glanced at Vernon, who shrugged, then gave his head

a slight shake. The rat/man's attention returned to Collins. "Not . . . yet. But . . ."

Collins waited for his companion to continue. When he did not, Collins made an impatient gesture. "But . . . ?"

Zylas pursed his lips, then spoke quickly, as if he had to force the words out before he changed his mind. "The elder wishes to meet with you."

Uncertain how to react, Collins asked cautiously, "He does? Why?"

Zylas opened his mouth, then closed it without speaking. He gave Vernon another meaningful look, but the black man turned away, arms folded across his chest. Clearly on his own now, Zylas said lamely, "It's not a simple matter. The elder . . . can explain it better."

"All . . . right." Collins looked from companion to companion, but neither returned his stare. "What do I need to know before I agree to this?"

Silence.

Irritated with his companions' behavior, Collins demanded, "You said my going would be dangerous to the elder and to myself. Don't I have a right to know why before I'm smack dab in the middle of that danger?"

Vernon said gruffly, "It's not you we're worried about."

Zylas placed a hand on Vernon's shoulder, an obvious plea to let him handle it. "It'll become clear, but Vernon's right. So long as you don't do anything foolish or mean . . ."

Like eat some innocent woman? Collins thought bitterly.

". . . you're perfectly safe. The elder . . ." Zylas flicked strands of dirty white-blond hair from his eyes. ". . . has more at stake. We just want to protect—"

Vernon jumped in again. "—the elder."

"Right," Zylas confirmed.

Korfius thrust his nose into Collins' hand. He patted the dog absently, still focused on his oddly behaving friends. "I'm not going to hurt anyone, if that's what you're jazzed up about."

Collins wondered how that translated, but Zylas and Vernon showed no sign of confusion. "I didn't mean to kill Joetha," he said for what seemed like the thousandth time. "It was an awful thing for which I'll feel eternally guilty, but can't we ever—"

Zylas and Vernon made broad motions to silence Collins. "We know that," the albino assured. "We don't have to talk about that anymore."

Vernon stood, nostrils flaring in clear distress. "It's just that you come with . . . certain dangers."

Understanding dawned, dispelling the irritation. "You mean the guards chasing me."

Zylas vigorously nodded confirmation, but Vernon did not let the matter drop. "We don't know you well enough to be sure—"

"Vernon," Zylas warned, but it did not stop his friend.

"—you can keep your mouth shut."

Collins felt the prickle of returning irritation but forced it away. Vernon had a reasonable point. "I owe you all my life at least two times over. I'm not going to give away any secret."

Zylas rolled his gaze to Vernon, who did not seem satisfied. "Can you bind that as a vow?"

Collins blinked, tightening his grip on the translation stone, which didn't seem to be fully functioning. "What?"

Vernon rephrased his question. "Do you have some sanctified words, some gesture, that binds important promises beyond breaking?"

Now Collins understood. *Nothing in my world is so sacred someone can't and won't abandon it.* That answer, he knew, would not satisfy Vernon. He would not break his word because he considered himself an honorable and moral person. Nevertheless, a white lie seemed worth it to appease Vernon. "We have both." He cleared his throat, assuming the most serious expression he could. "I swear to God . . ." It did not sound like enough, so he added, "with sugar on top, that I will . . ." He looked at Vernon questioningly.

Catching the intention of the pause, Vernon supplied the next words, ". . . not divulge the name, location, or even the existence of the elder to anyone ever, no matter what good reason I think I may have for doing so."

"Uh." Collins had no trouble agreeing to the terms, but he could not recall all the words Vernon had used. "I will not . . . uh . . . divulge . . . uh . . . the elder forever no matter what." *Mouthful of mostly long words to express the obvious. He'd have made a good lawyer.* Collins spit on his right hand. "Now we shake on it."

"Shake on . . . it?" Vernon studied Collins' fingers dubiously.

Collins took Vernon's enormous paw of a hand into his own, flicked it vigorously, then released it. He wiped his palm on his britches, and Vernon did the same.

"Done?" the larger man asked.

"Done," Collins agreed.

Vernon muttered something of which the stone translated only, "Weird."

Unable to miss the irony, Collins hid a smile.

Chapter 10

ZYLAS and Collins set off immediately, with the sun still high in the sky. They rode Falima, and Collins caught occasional glimpses of Ialin zipping to Zylas and hovering near his ear. The hummingbird always gave Collins a wide berth, which pleased him as well. The wind carried streamers of Zylas' unnaturally white hair into Collins' face at intervals so irregular he forgot to protect against it. Accustomed to wearing glasses, he rarely reacted in time to rescue his eyes, and the strands whipped across them, stinging, until he wondered if he had permanent red lines across the whites. Adding a buzzing, insect-like bird to the aggravation might have driven him over the edge, from sullen irritation to rage.

Zylas carried the translation stone again, which seemed to make no difference as his other two companions would remain in their animal forms for about five more hours and the rat/man had settled into a nearly unbreakable silence. He led them on a circuitous route that confused Collins utterly. At times, he thought he recognized landmarks they had passed a half hour earlier. They might be traveling in an endless loop for all he knew, and he could not help recalling the Winnie-the-Pooh tale in which the silly old bear and his friend, Piglet, track themselves in a circle, worried that, at each pass, another two creatures have joined the ones they were following. Despite the warmth and humor of this childhood remembrance, Collins found his discomfort growing.

The weather seemed hell-bent on displaying all the happy grandeur Collins' mood lacked. The sun beamed through the trees in golden bands. A breeze danced around the trunks, keeping the temperature hovering at what felt like a comfortable seventy degrees. Crystal-blue sky stretched from horizon to horizon, dotted with a few fluffy clouds that gleamed whitely in the broad expanse of azure.

The ground grew rockier. Falima stumbled. Abruptly jarred sideways, Collins found himself on the ground before he realized he was falling. Pain shot through his left shoulder. Dull aching pounded through his thighs and buttocks, a reminder that he had spent more time riding the last two days than in all the rest of his life combined. He looked up to a hovering hummingbird and a still-mounted Zylas peering down at him, arm extended. "Are you all right?"

"Just fricking fine." Collins had no idea whether the almost-swear word would translate as the real thing or into a somewhat-acceptable substitution like the one he had provided. He clambered painfully to his feet, ignoring Zylas' gesture. "Mind if I just walk for a while?"

"Not at all." Zylas peered into the distance. "In fact, we'll take to the mountains soon. Probably better if we all walk."

Ialin disappeared.

Collins massaged his aching shoulder.

"Only kept us mounted this far to make as small a scent trail as possible. Ialin's seen guards out there, though they don't seem to have located us."

"What about Vernon and Korfius?" Collins asked, worried.

Zylas dismounted, clutching Falima's lead. "No reason to think they're not safe. They've got their stories, and we just have to hope no one convinces Korfius to rat us out."

Collins laughed at the play on words, which seemed to baffle Zylas.

"What's funny?"

Collins saw no harm in explaining, this time. "Rat us out. You're a rat."

Zylas continued to stare.

"Just seemed funny," Collins mumbled, withdrawing back toward his irritability.

"Is that how it translates?"

"Yeah."

Now, Zylas chuckled. "It's not the word I used. We don't have a lot of animal-based slang."

Collins nodded. "Makes sense."

"Ready to continue?"

No, Collins thought but said, "Yes."

They headed into rocky hills that soon became forested mountains. The trail continued to spiral, double back, and loop. For a time, Collins tried to trace the route. When that became impossible, he attempted conversation. "So now will you tell me about this elder?"

Zylas looked up with clear reluctance. "You'll meet soon enough."

Foiled again, Collins bit his lower lip. "How soon is soon enough?"

"Tomorrow evening."

"Tomorrow!" Collins complained, recalling that Zylas and Ialin had made the trip and returned in about twenty-four hours.

Zylas' eyes widened. "Did you want to take longer?"

"Shorter."

"We could arrive a little earlier," Zylas said slowly. "If you won't be uncomfortable with Falima and Ialin in switch-form."

Collins considered. He might perform better with Falima communicative. She seemed to have warmed up to him in Vernon's cabin. Ialin, he thought, might do him better as a speechless bird. "Perhaps somewhere between the two?"

Zylas tossed his tangled hair. "Of course, there's the elder's switch time to consider, too." He rubbed his forehead. "While you sleep, I'll meet with the elder and talk about that."

Surprised to have his opinion considered at all, Collins merely said, "All right." He had not thought about the details such coordination might require, but he should have. He had learned enough under dire enough circumstances. *I should be thinking all the time.* It bothered him to consider that he was, perhaps, not as smart as he believed. He had always done well in school, earning A's and B's with relative ease and not just in rote subjects. Yet he worried that his ability to anticipate and react to life situations might not prove as competent. *What happens when I get out in the real world where life doesn't consist solely of classes and tests?* The thought now seemed ludicrous. *Assuming I survive Barakhai and ever make it back to the "real" world.*

Zylas led Falima up the slope. "Speaking of sleep, we work best when we get half in each form. Thought we could take a break: eat, nap."

Though Collins had slept a solid eight hours, he suffered from hunger, thirst, and physical exhaustion. He supposed he could learn to coordinate his sleep with Zylas', in three- or four-hour blocks rather than all at once. "Sounds good to me."

Despite his suggestion, Zylas continued hauling Falima up the mountainside. "There's a cave not too far. I'd rather hole up on higher ground. Safer."

Collins followed, now aware of his growling tummy, his dry mouth, and the soreness of his legs. He wished Zylas had waited until they'd arrived at the cave to mention food and rest.

Half an hour later, Zylas waved Collins into the rock crevice he had referred to as a cave. A curtain of vines hung over the entrance, swarmed with round pink flowers; and grass softened the floor. Collins touched a wall slimy with algae and moss and immediately jerked back his hand. Warm and moist, the interior seemed stifling after the dry, cool wind that had accompanied them through the day. Falima remained outside, grazing, but Ialin swept onto a ledge and perched. Zylas went outside nearly as soon as he entered, then returned moments later dragging the pack that had rested on Falima's withers. As Collins hurried over to help, Zylas let it flop onto the floor.

"I appreciate that Vernon doesn't want us to starve, but I would have packed a bit lighter."

At the moment, Collins would have carried the pack the rest of the way if it meant a steady supply of Vernon's peanut-buttery nut paste. He helped Zylas unpack enough food to satisfy them both: bread and nut paste, bugs and fruit, roots and berries. They ate well, then settled down to sleep on the grassy carpet.

Collins dreamed of a violent earthquake rocking him in wild, insistent motions. "What? Where?" He leaped to his feet. "Huh?" The world came into abrupt focus, despite his missing glasses. Falima stood beside him, still clutching the arm she had been shaking. Zylas stood near the pack, smiling slightly from beneath his hat brim as he watched the exchange. "Bit jumpy, are you?"

Still slightly disoriented, Collins glanced at his watch. "What time is it?" It read 6:15. Falima would have changed fifteen minutes ago, which would have just given her time to dress and wolf down some food before awakening him. He yawned.

Though Collins had found his own answer, Zylas gave him another. "Early evening. You're a good sleeper."

Collins yawned again. "Most grad students are." He stretched, the pain in his thighs and buttocks even more pronounced. He was glad Falima had taken human form and they would have to walk for a while. "Now, if I could just get some coffee."

Zylas laughed. "Don't have that here. But you're welcome to eat dirt. Tastes about the same to me."

"Let me guess. Not a coffee fan?" Collins sprang forward and hefted the pack before his older and smaller companion could do so. It settled awkwardly across his neck, obviously constructed to balance across a horse's unsaddled withers without sliding. Now, he had to agree with Zylas; fewer supplies would suit his shoulders better. "It's an acquired taste."

"Apparently." Zylas did not fight Collins for the pack. "But why bother to acquire it?"

"For the caffeine." Collins trailed his companions through the viny curtain and into sunlight that, though muted by evening, still burned his unadjusted eyes. "Helps you wake up."

Zylas headed back up the slope. "Why not just take caffeine?"

Why not, indeed? Collins recalled a professor once telling the class that, in the name of avoiding hypocrisy, No-Doz was his morning beverage. It seemed more like an admission of drug addiction than the heroically honest statement the professor had clearly intended. "I actually like the taste of coffee." *Now.* When he first started drinking it, he had diluted it more than halfway with milk. Gradually, the proportion had decreased until he had come to take it with only a splash of nondairy creamer.

"All . . . right," Zylas said slowly. "If you say so."

"It's good." Collins hopped after Falima, who had darted up the hill with a dexterity her horse form could never have matched. "Really. Coffee has a great—" Struck by the ridiculousness of the argument, Collins laughed. *Why am I defending coffee to a man who eats bugs and calls them a delicacy?* "—flavor," he finished. "When it's made right." It seemed rude to leave Falima out of the conversation. Not wanting to lose the ground he had gained with her the previous day, he asked, "So how are things with you, Falima?"

At the sound of her name, Falima turned and shrugged.

"She can't understand you," Zylas reminded.

Oh, yeah. Disappointment flashed through Collins, gradually replaced by guarded relief. As much as he wanted to chat with her, at least, this way, he could not ruin their friendship by saying something stupid.

They continued through softly contoured mountains carpeted with weeds, wildflowers, and evergreen forests. Now, Zylas' diversions became clearer to Collins, as they meandered down and sideways as often as upward, and he often forgot that they traveled through mountains at all. Occasionally, the vegetation gave way to barren rock faces, especially where the walk grew steeper. These proved a minor challenge that would bore a real climber, though Collins found himself guarding every step. A fall seemed unlikely, but it might result in serious injury; and he had taken more than a few missteps in his life on flat, solid ground.

The weather remained clear. That, and a comfortable sleep, vastly improved Collins' mood. He could almost imagine himself on a youth group hike, scurrying up Mount Chockorua with a backpack, a canteen, and a bunch of rowdy boys. The fear of becoming trapped in a world that condemned him as a vicious murderer receded behind a wash of reckless hope.

Collins met Falima's gaze on several occasions, exchanging short nervous smiles whenever they did so. The strange and silent flirtation passed time otherwise measured only by the slow downward creep of the sun. At length, it touched the far horizon, pitching up broad bands of color that blurred and mingled at the edges, cleared to vivid extremes, then dulled into the next. Bold spikes of pink interrupted the pattern at intervals, radiating in majestic lines.

Collins paused on a crest, staring. Evening breezes chilled the sweat spangling his forehead, and he could not tear his gaze from the beauty of the vast panorama stretching out in front of him. He had never seen anything so grand. The few clear sunsets of his camping days he had viewed through forests of skeletal branches that blotted the grandeur with shadows. City lights blunted the epic, almost violent, hues that now paraded before his eyes. In recent years, he had forgotten to look, his evenings gobbled up by essays and lab work, indoor dinners and rented movies.

"What's the matter?"

Zylas' now-familiar voice startled Collins. He jumped, slammed his foot down on a loose stone, twisted his ankle, and toppled. Before the rat/man could move to assist, Collins lay on the ground. His ankle throbbed, but he still managed to say, "What's the matter? The matter is some guy who calls himself a friend scaring me and dumping me on my face."

Zylas drew back, feigning affront. "I never touched you. You dumped yourself on your own face."

"With incredible grace, I might add." Collins rose gingerly and found he could already put most of his weight on his leg. He was not badly hurt. "Don't sell me short, now. I'm excellent at dumping myself on my face."

Zylas agreed, "A real professional." He offered a hand, though Collins had already stood.

"Mind telling Falima it was your fault? She already thinks I'm a clod."

Zylas glanced toward his flank. "I'd do that, but she does have . . . um . . . eyes."

Collins looked around Zylas, only then noticing Falima nearby. She had probably witnessed the entire exchange. He tried to remember which parts of the conversation he had spoken. She could not understand him, but Zylas could come across plainly to both of them. Much like listening to one end of a telephone conversation, she could surely infer much merely from what Zylas had said. *But why the hell do I care what she thinks?* Collins could not explain it; but, somehow, he did. He looked back at the horizon, but the sky's exquisite light show had dulled toward flat black and the first stars had appeared. He rounded on Zylas. "If you must know, I was enjoying that gorgeous sunset. You made me miss the last of it."

Zylas turned his attention westward, with the air of a man so accustomed to seeing radiance, he no longer notices it.

Of course, Collins surmised. *They get sunsets like that every day.* In that moment, he grew less fascinated by the life of a models' photographer. It seemed impossible that staring at beautiful women for a living gradually sapped it of all thrill, yet surely it must. *Does a man ever tire of looking at an attractive wife?* An answer popped swiftly into Collins' mind, though he had never intended to address his own unspoken question. *I don't stare at Marlys the way I used to, and she's only grown more lovely.* In fact, it surprised him to discover that, of all the things he missed most, she barely made the list. *If absence makes the heart grow fonder, then either I don't have a heart or she was never really there.*

Falima followed the direction of Zylas' stare to the now-blunted sunset. She said something, the slight up-tick at the end Collins' only hint that she had asked a question.

Zylas responded in their lilting language, leaving her nodding thoughtfully.

The albino turned his attention back to Collins. "Ready?"

"To go on?" Collins guessed. "Sure."

Zylas adjusted his breeks. "To meet the elder."

Collins blinked. "Tonight? But I thought . . ."

Zylas shrugged. "You requested; I asked." He held out a hand, and the hummingbird alighted, tiny talons gripping his index finger. "Ialin says we've lost the guards. The elder thinks we've muddled the trail enough."

Though he had suspected it, Collins barely dared to believe Zylas had dragged out their journey so much that they could chop off an entire day and not even notice it. "Definitely. I'm ready." Finally, he would find out how to get home. *Home to professors furious that I ruined all their experiments.* He doubted anyone could believe his reason for not taking care of the animals. Each rat had enough water to last several days, and they could go without eating for weeks, if necessary. He wondered if he could get back to Daubert Laboratories before vacation ended; if he cleaned all the cages thoroughly, supplied fresh food sticks and water, no one would know he had gone. The deceit bothered him. It might change the results of some of the analyses, but it seemed preferable to him sacrificing the future he had gone into hock for. A bad relationship, a sundered family, student loans—these all seemed minor inconveniences compared to remaining always a jump ahead of a local constabulary fixated on executing him.

As Zylas headed across a ridge swarming with leafy vines, Collins finally found the argument that might have gotten him to the elder sooner. "You know, Zylas." He tried to keep his voice casual. "I'm the only one taking care of those rats back at the lab for four days."

Zylas continued walking, a stiffening of his back the only clue that he had heard the pronouncement. At length, he spoke. "Are they . . . are they going to . . ." It took a real effort to squeeze out the last word. ". . . die?"

Well, yes. After an experiment, they all die. Collins kept that realization to himself, suddenly wishing he had not raised the topic at all. It seemed cruel to leave Zylas believing he had had a hand in the deaths of a roomful of creatures he considered kin. Initially planning to use the information to help speed things along, Collins suddenly found himself in the position of comforter. "I don't think so. I gave them enough water for at least three days. They might get a bit hungry before the others get back, but they should survive all right." *Great. That accomplished a lot.*

Zylas' movements became jerky, agitated. Falima glided up and gently placed an arm across his shoulders, speaking calmly.

Collins slammed the heel of his palm against his forehead. *Blew that one big time.* He tried to simultaneously rescue his point and Zylas, though the two goals seemed entirely at odds.

"They certainly won't die. Certainly not. But the sooner I get back, the sooner I can attend to them. Clean cages, feed. You know, make them comfortable."

Zylas and Falima made a sudden turn, disappearing behind a crag.

Collins jogged to catch up, then slammed into his companions who had come to a halt just beyond the angle. Driven forward a step, Zylas whirled, while Falima just shook her head and continued studying the cliff wall in front of her. Ialin buzzed into flight.

"Sorry," Collins muttered, then realized the ivy-covered stone in front of him had a central area darker than the surrounding stone. He stared, trying to visually carve clear the outline of the cave mouth that he guessed lay there. "We're here?"

"Yes." Zylas placed a hand on Collins' arm and ushered him forward. "Please, be polite." His tone fairly pleaded, and Collins found it impossible to take offense from the implication. "Respectful. Not . . ." He trailed off, looking more nervous than Collins had ever seen him.

"Not rude?" Collins supplied, with just a hint of indignation.

Zylas finally glanced directly into Collins' face and smiled. "I'm sorry I'm treating you like a child. It's just that . . . well . . . sometimes your people . . . don't handle elders . . . um . . ."

Collins thought he understood. Americans did tend to value youth and vigor more than wisdom. "With appropriate esteem?"

Zylas let out a pent-up breath. "Right."

Falima spoke through gritted teeth, and Zylas translated. "She says that would be a big mistake here."

"I understand." Though tired of reassurances, Collins said and did nothing more. The more impatience he showed, the longer the likely delay. It made sense that the people here showed a deference bordering on awe toward their elders. Given their lifestyle, they likely had few who lasted all that long.

A gravelly voice emerged from the cave scarcely louder than the whisper of windblown vines against stone. "Zylas, Falima, Ialin, please come in. And bring your guest."

No longer able to delay, Zylas executed a bow the elder surely could not see. "At once, Lady Prinivere." He tugged at Collins' arm.

Lady? Collins had to adjust his entire image as he trotted into the cave at Zylas' side. Ialin fluttered ahead, and Falima followed them.

The darkness seemed to swallow them, and Collins blinked several times, seeking some small source of light on which to focus his vision. Afraid to move for fear of knocking into people or furniture, he turned in place to catch the lingering grayness at the opening.

"Forgive me," a sweet but ancient voice said. "I forget that others need this." A ball of light appeared, pulled apart like a chain of glowsticks, then diffused into a pale, sourceless glow. Collins saw a round face as brown as a berry and cast into extensive, deep wrinkles. Dressed only in a loincloth, the old woman left most of her withered flesh exposed. Her breasts hung so low, they covered her slender abdomen. A thick, untidy mop of snowy hair sprouted from her freckled scalp, hanging to just below her ears. Though recessed into hollows, her eyes looked remarkably clear, green as a cat's with the same slitted pupils and full of an ancient wisdom that the wateriness of age could not diminish. Her small nose seemed little more than a pair of slitty nostrils in a sea of pleats. Collins studied her in unbelieving fascination, certain he had never seen anyone quite this old. He barely noticed the furnishings, which consisted entirely of two large chests.

The elder smiled. "I am Prinivere."

Wanting to introduce himself before Zylas could do so, to avoid forever becoming an amalgamation of his full name, Collins found his tongue. "Ben," he said. Despite himself, he added, "Just Ben." He caught himself at once. *Great. Now she's going to call me Justben.* It sounded uncomfortably close to Dustbin, though still better than Bentoncollins or, worse, the Benton Zachary Collins his mother used whenever he got into trouble.

But Prinivere made no such mistake. "A pleasure to meet you, Ben."

"Thank you," Collins said politely, only then blurting a sudden realization. "You speak English."

Unobtrusively, Zylas stepped on Collins' foot.

"I speak all languages," Prinivere explained. She folded her legs, sitting on the floor with surprising grace for one so frail in appearance. "Come join me, Ben."

Without hesitation, Collins dropped to his haunches, then sat in front of the old woman. "Thank you," he said again. Though perhaps not the most suitable response, they were the politest words he knew.

"You're welcome." Prinivere studied Collins in silence then. Her eyes looked tired but very alive, a discomforting contrast to a body that seemed long past its time.

Collins sat very still, feeling like a piece of steak at the meat counter. The long silence that followed made him even more restless. Wondering if it were his job to break it, he looked at Zylas.

The albino shook his head stiffly.

Like a hunter with prey, the movement caught Prinivere's attention. "Who has the stone?"

Zylas crouched beside Collins. "I do, Lady."

The stabbing gaze went fully to the rat/man now, to Collins' relief. "Don't you think it would serve better in his hands?"

Zylas swallowed hard but remained adamant. "I can't afford to lose it. I was hoping . . . can't you . . . ?"

Prinivere leaned forward, and her breasts drooped into her lap. Collins found himself noting this matter-of-factly, the way he might view a fat, shirtless man's stomach overflowing his pants at a sporting event. There was knowledge and venerability but nothing sexual about this primordial creature. "Maybe.

After I've slept, switched.'' She shook her head. ''I think I might be able to.''

Able to what? Collins wondered, but he did not ask. He looked up, only to find the sharp, green eyes back on him.

''So,'' she said. ''What do you think of Barakhai?''

At home, it might have seemed a casual question, a polite query intended to illicit a stock response. Now, Collins sensed a much deeper quality that forced him to think in a way he had not since his companions had freed him from hanging. Driven by desperation, by terror, by need, he had not bothered to contemplate the world and its wonders per se. ''I think,'' he started, and his voice seemed to thunder into an intense and critical silence, ''it's a world with some simple beauty mine hasn't known for some time.'' Though the others nodded, Collins doubted they understood what he meant. ''Clear sunsets, fresh air, water you can drink from its source and not worry about pollution and . . . germs.'' He did not know for certain about the latter. Obviously, the inhabitants drank the water all the time, apparently with no harmful effects; but dogs lapped up muddy, worm-riddled puddles in his world, too. Perhaps the water here teemed with Giardia, amoeba, and other microbes that the animal part of them could tolerate; or they simply survived as long as they could with masses of intestinal parasites writhing inside them. So far, he had drunk the water without getting ill. Only time would tell for certain whether the better part of wisdom would have been to boil it first.

Only quiet consideration filled the hush after Collins' description, so he felt obliged to continue. ''I've met some wonderful people.'' He made a gesture that encompassed Falima and Zylas. Though he did not intentionally leave out Ialin, he made no particular effort to include the hummingbird either. He sucked air through pursed lips, thinking. ''I suppose I might find the rest of the people worth meeting, too, under other circumstances. I can hardly blame the guards for the way they treated me. I had just . . .'' A lump filled his throat suddenly, blocking the words he intended to speak. As he tried to force them out, his eyes brimmed with tears, and he dropped the attempt.

No one came to Collins' rescue, though he thought he caught a subtle nod between Prinivere and Zylas.

Casually, Collins wiped his eyes on the back of his sleeve and changed the subject. "Lady, I don't know exactly what my companions told you, but I came to see you to find out if you knew of any portals to my world other than the one I came through."

"I know," Prinivere said, her voice a dull rasp.

Ialin settled on a shriveled shoulder. Falima lowered herself to one of the chests, listening on the fringes. As usual, she could understand only half the conversation, at most. Collins wondered whether the old woman actually used fluent English or some device translated her words into whatever language necessary for comprehension by every listener. He only knew he used English exclusively and carried nothing to make it sound like anything else.

"You know?" Collins needed clarification, but before he could voice it, Prinivere continued.

"I know the reason you came to me. Your companions told me."

Good. Collins nodded.

"There are no other portals."

Stunned by bad news so unceremoniously and abruptly delivered, Collins froze, speechless. Zylas should have told him that days ago and rescued him from this ridiculous charade. The Barakhains could have kept their beloved elder safe, unmet and unknown, and they would not have wasted time taking some inane, meandering path to her. Gradually, the full implications seeped into a mind already plagued with desperation. They had no choice but to return to the place where Collins had started and find a way past a contingent of archers.

"But—" Prinivere said. That one word seemed to float, alone in a vast vacuum of hope. It felt to Collins like hours passed before she continued, though she never paused. "—I might be able to create a new portal."

Still unmoving, Collins lost his breath. "Create . . . one?" He forced the words out, then gasped in a clumsy breath accompanied by saliva. He choked, coughing so vigorously that Falima leaped to her feet and patted his back helpfully.

Wanting to hear what Prinivere had to say, Collins waved Falima off and tried to control his seizing diaphragm.

But Prinivere did not go on. Turning her attention to Zylas, she engaged the albino in conversation while Collins lost the battle to his cough.

For several moments, Collins struggled, throat raw and full. Finally, the spasms died to a tickle, and he regained control of speech. "Sorry." His voice sounded hoarse and unrecognizable. "Did you say you could create a portal?"

Prinivere spun back to face Collins. "I said I might be able to, yes."

"So . . ." Collins kept his sentence slow to avoid the need to cough again. ". . . you're . . . a sorceress?"

Prinivere's recessed eyes narrowed, so they seemed to disappear into the wrinkles. "Sorceress." She ran the word over her tongue, then shook her head. "Not sure what you mean."

Collins sought synonyms. "A witch." He watched Prinivere's face for clues to her disposition to see if the word had the same negative connotations here as back home. "A magician. A wizard. A person who uses magic."

"No such thing," Zylas grunted. "People, magic." He shook his head. "Don't go together."

Collins suppressed an urge to laugh. *If people turning into animals isn't magic, what is?* He kept the thought to himself. It seemed the populace had little control over the transformation. "*You* have magic," he reminded.

"I carry a magical item," Zylas admitted, though he glanced around as he did so, as if afraid someone outside their group might overhear. "That doesn't make me a user of magic."

In strict terms, of course, it did; but Collins decided it was better not to make an issue of such a thing. "If not by magic, how do you make a portal?" Collins wondered if he might have the means to do it himself.

"Making a portal does require magic." Zylas confused the issue still further. "That's why we need the lady's help."

"But she's not a sorceress."

"No," Prinivere patted her hair into place.

"So you have some sort of portal-making item."

"No such thing." Zylas said.

Clear as mud. Collins sighed and took the chest seat Falima had vacated. "I don't get it."

"You will," Zylas promised with all the believability of a politician a week before an election. "You will."

An undertone in the albino's voice made Collins wonder if he wanted to.

Chapter 11

PRINIVERE wandered to the farthest corner of the cave to sleep while Collins discussed matters fervently with the one companion who did understand him and insisted on translating for the one who did not. Twilight faded from the opening and the cave so gradually that, even in a darkness that might have seemed solid under other circumstances, Collins found himself able to differentiate between the gray silhouettes of his companions.

"Let's talk about those rats back at the lab." Though redirected several times, Zylas always returned to the matter Collins now fervently wished he had never raised.

Collins sighed, certain he would have to change his major. After this day, he might never find the courage to euthanize another experimental animal. *That, or fill my home with pet rats, mice, guinea pigs, and monkeys.* He imagined the look of horror twisting his landlady's meaty features; she screamed at the sight of a large spider. "They'll be fine," Collins insisted with a finality he hoped would satisfy his companion—this time. "They've got plenty of water till my preceptor gets back.'' *Is that today?* ''At most they'll go a day without food, and their cages will stink a bit.''

Zylas' expression remained taut.

Collins laid an arm across the albino's shoulders. ''Look, man. There's nothing we can do about it, is there? The whole school's getting back tomorrow. Believe me when I say every biology professor at Algary will head straight for the lab.'' *Where they'll see the crappy job I did and flunk me on the spot.* More concerned for his future than the temporary comfort of a bunch of laboratory rats, Collins again sought a topic switch. ''So what's the big secret about Prinivere anyway? I mean, besides the fact that she's a woman when you had me believing she was a man.''

Zylas shrugged off Collins' arm. ''*Lady* Prinivere,'' he corrected in a bristly voice. ''And I don't recall ever calling the lady a man.''

''Not directly.'' Collins admitted. ''But you did refer to her only as 'the elder.' Never even used a pronoun as far as I remember. Didn't correct me when I called her 'him'.''

''That's you assuming, not deception.'' Zylas paced to Falima and joined her on the chest.

Depends on what the definition of ''is'' is. Collins shook off the presidential comparison. ''You can claim you didn't lie. But not correcting an assumption you knew was false *is* deception.'' He straddled the opposite chest, facing Zylas directly. ''Are you going to tell me it's different in your world?''

Zylas conceded with a sigh. ''I'm sorry. Vernon thought that, if we never made it to the lady, any information you had that the guards might get would be . . . misleading. He's a smart man, and it seemed safest at the time.''

Falima poked Zylas' back, and he turned to translate.

A sensation of being watched spiraled through Collins suddenly, and he shivered, glancing toward the cave mouth. ''You've managed to deflect my question again, I notice. What exactly—" The hair on the nape of his neck prickled. A realization of intense and imminent danger grasped his gut like an icy hand. His heart raced into wild pounding, and words caught like a sticky lump in his throat. Panic sent him lurching to his feet, and he skittered to the cave mouth before logic trickled between otherwise ravaged thoughts. *What the hell?*

Pressed against the stone wall, Collins glanced back into the cave. Zylas and Falima had also risen, their backs to him. Though they had not run, they did seem agitated. A dinosaur-like creature took up most of the back of the cave: long-necked and -legged, covered in greenish-black scales that seemed to glow. Plates jutted from the neck, back, and tail, which ended in a ragged scar. "Dr–dragon?" Collins stammered out the only English word that might suit this massive animal. Though he knew it must be Prinivere's switch-form, he could not force himself to reenter the cave.

Ideas rushed back into Collins' mind. Memory came first, of a girl he had dated in college. A fan of aliens, angels, and conspiracy theories, she had once brought him a book that "conclusively proved" the existence of dragons. For the purposes of domestic harmony, he had read it, a pseudoscientific account filled with blurry photographs, anecdotal sightings, and misconceptions a freshmen science student should see through. He had tried to argue the biological impossibility of a heavy, four-legged creature with wings. If dragons did exist, he had asserted, they would look like pteranodons. Wings had served as the forelimbs of every flying animal throughout history.

Now, Collins stared upon a creature that defied every biological tenet. Big as a school bus, it had to weigh tons. Strong hind legs ended in massive, four-clawed feet. The forelimbs had three toes, each with talons that closely resembled curved knives. Leathery appendages near the shoulders clearly represented folded wings. It bore little resemblance to the serpents of the Chinese New Year's parades, its body blocky and its snout more like that of a Doberman. It bore none of the decorative finery, no streamers, beards, or spinners. The ears stuck up, shaped and proportioned like a horse's, jet black in color. Eyes like emeralds lay recessed deeply into its sockets.

A voice entered Collins' head, seeming to bypass his hearing. **I won't hurt you. Come.**

Collins pawed at his ears, willing them to work properly; his life might depend on it. The reassurance, apparently the dragon's, did not soothe. He found himself incapable of taking a step closer to a creature that could shred him, crush him, or bite him in half without breaking a sweat.

Zylas took several nervous steps, bowed to the dragon, then hurried to Collins. "You're insulting Lady Prinivere," he hissed.

In response, Collins pressed his back more tightly to the wall. Vines tickled his arms, and stone jabbed his spine. He tried to explain, "She's a . . . she's a . . . a dragon."

"Yes."

"We . . . we . . . don't have . . . dragons . . . in my world."

"Neither do we."

The ludicrousness of that statement finally broke the spell. Collins turned his head slowly toward Zylas to grant him a judgmental stare. "I beg to differ."

Zylas took one of Collins' hands in both of his. "Except Lady Prinivere, of course. She's the last."

Collins looked at the hand clamped between Zylas' and hoped the albino did not plan to try to drag him back into the cave. He wiped his other sweating palm on his britches and tried to screw up his courage.

"The others were killed off centuries ago."

"By knights, no doubt." Collins resorted to his usual haven, humor, to orient his failing rationality.

Zylas tugged gently at Collins. "Huh?"

"Never mind." It seemed worse than senseless to try to explain legends at a time when reality had gone beyond them.

"It's all right. Really. Come meet her."

Collins looked at the dragon, still hesitating. Falima faced the dragon, clearly engaged in conversation, arms waving at intervals. If Prinivere responded, she did so without opening her mouth. "She could eat us all in the same bite."

"Eat us?" Zylas rolled his eyes. "She's constrained by the same laws as the rest of us. Can't eat any meat, remember?"

"Who could stop her?" Collins muttered, but he did take a step forward. Prinivere posed no more threat to him than the guardsmen, and she might hold the only key to his escape. He managed another step.

Zylas released Collins' hand. Falima turned, impassively watching her friends approach. As he drew closer, Collins noticed details he had missed on first inspection. The glow that outlined the dragon seemed as feeble and tattered as a dying star. Most of the claws looked jagged, broken beyond repair. Scars marred her scaly hide in several locations, the worst a mottled, irregular patch in the right chest area. She moved with a slowness that suggested long-standing fatigue. Her dragon form had clearly aged along with her human one.

Actually, it's my human form that aged along with the dragon form. The words whispered into Collins' brain, unspoken.

Collins jumped, heart racing again.

Yes, I read minds. That's how I know every language.

Collins had not yet recovered enough to ask the question she had already answered. Remembering that he needed her, he forced calm. *If she predicts my future thoughts, too, why bother to communicate at all?* "Wouldn't it be easier if you just told me how this whole conversation's going to come out?"

Prinivere exhaled a loud snort that Collins interpreted as a laugh. **I don't usually anticipate. It's just, after a few centuries, you figure out what any human would ask. Never met one yet who didn't wonder how I get into his or her head.**

Collins glanced at his regular companions. Zylas and Falima sat on one of the chests, whispering back and forth. He wondered how much of the conversation they could hear.

All of it, Prinivere said before Collins could formulate the thought into words. **But Falima doesn't understand your side of it, and Zylas has to guess the thoughts I'm responding to.**

Zylas looked up and waved to Collins, apparently to confirm Prinivere's explanation.

Though he knew the question impolite, Collins had to know. ''So how old are you anyway?''

''—my lady,'' Zylas added, teeth clenched in warning.

It's fine, Zylas Prinivere swung her long neck toward the rat/man. **In his world, they rarely use titles. He means no disrespect.** She swiveled her head back to Collins. **I'm one thousand seven hundred thirty-six years old.**

Collins blinked, for the first time glad his mind went blank. ''One *thousand?*''

Seven hundred thirty-six.

''Ah,'' Collins said, pinching his arm. The mild pain did not reassure him. It seemed equally possible that he had just dreamed it, too.

Zylas cut in, voice soft, words uninterpretable to Collins. If Prinivere responded, he heard none of it.

Finally, the dragon addressed Collins directly. **Come here. I'm going to attempt some magic.**

Hoping she meant the portal, Collins obeyed. He tried to look composed, but his steps turned more mincing the nearer he came to the dragon and he found himself trembling. Falima cleared her throat, and Collins dropped to a startled crouch, glancing wildly toward her. Ialin stood in human form between his other two companions.

Falima made an impatient gesture toward Prinivere.

Collins followed the movement to its natural conclusion. He did not know how long it had taken him to move as far as he had. It had seemed only seconds, but Ialin had had time to switch and fully dress. Collins closed his eyes, hoping that would allow him to walk blindly into a dragon, yet its massive presence still pressed vividly against his memory. Opening his lids, he forced himself to step up to Prinivere.

She gave off a not-unpleasant odor that Collins had never smelled before. It might come from something she ate, some nearby plant or fungus, even from something trapped between her claws. But, for Collins, the musky allspice aroma would forever define dragon smell.

One foot stretched toward Collins, slowly, nonthreateningly, and settled firmly on his head. At first, he felt nothing but the presence of that huge appendage, a claw dangling across his left cheek and ear and another tangling in his hair. Then, gradually, he recognized something indefinable flowing into him, like electric current without the jolt. The foot grew heavier over time, and he found himself expending increasing amounts of energy to remain standing. Finally, the strange feeling ended, replaced entirely by the full weight of a massive foot crushing him toward the ground.

Zylas, Falima, and Ialin dashed forward, hefting the dragon's claw and shoving Collins from beneath it. The foot flopped to the cave floor, and the dragon sank to the ground. Pain ached through Collins' neck and shoulders. As he massaged them, rolling his head, he noticed the dragon was lying still, unmoving. "Is she all right?"

Zylas rushed to Prinivere's side.

Falima responded. "She's very old. Even a simple spell like that one leaves her drained."

Collins nodded, still studying the dragon. Then, realization struck, and he jerked his attention to Falima. "Hey, I understood you. I know what you said, and—"

Ialin rolled his eyes.

Not wanting to look the fool again, Collins considered. "That must be what the magic she did was all about."

"Lucky guess," Ialin grumbled.

"She's sleeping," Zylas announced. "We'll have to stay and keep her safe until she's strong again."

It seemed only fair. Prinivere had exhausted herself for him, and he owed her at least that much. Nevertheless, Collins could not stay the icy seep of disappointment overtaking him. "The portal," he said to no one in particular, now far enough beyond shock and confusion to realize that Prinivere would only have assumed he needed to communicate with the people of Barakhai if she knew she could not get him home soon.

Collins anticipated a verbal onslaught from Ialin about how he should feel grateful for what the dragon sacrificed for him, but it did not come. The hummingbird/man stood in silence, letting Zylas answer.

The albino patted one of the chests, then sat. Collins came over, taking the place beside the one person he trusted completely in this world.

Zylas stared at the ceiling for several moments, collecting his thoughts before beginning. "I'm as *masuniat* as they come . . ." He paused.

Collins remembered *masuniat* as the word for people more entrenched in their human than animal forms. He nodded his understanding.

". . . I don't know a thing about magic except what the lady has told me. But—" Zylas glanced around at his companions' expectant faces. "As I understand it, the spell she just threw is a particularly simple one. She's old, even for a dragon; that and simple healings are the extent of her magic nowadays." He turned the tender look of a grandson upon the sleeping creature. "I wouldn't dare ask her to do even the spell she just cast again. Next time, it might kill her."

"She made your translation stone," Collins suggested.

Zylas shook his head. "She has made translation stones, but not mine and not in the last few decades. Making spells portable, casting onto rocks and crystals, takes a lot more energy than just throwing a bit of magic at someone." He displayed the piece of quartz. "And I told you mine's unique. Centuries old and very special. A family heirloom."

Ialin balanced, cross-legged, on the other chest, listening. Falima sat beside Collins, opposite Zylas. Attempting to anticipate

Zylas' point, Collins considered whether or not creating a portal would require an item. He clung to the memory of Prinivere stating that she might have the power to make one.

"We already know Lady Prinivere does not have the strength to magic another stone."

Collins could not hold back the significant query any longer. "A portal?"

Zylas bit his lip and met Collins' gaze, clearly measuring his reaction. "Or make a portal."

Collins felt horse-kicked. "But she said—"

Zylas raised a forestalling hand. "There is a crystal, already made, that can enhance her magic."

Though reborn, Collins' hope remained guarded. It seemed that every time something started going his way, something worse intervened. "Don't tell me. It's in the possession of an eight-headed hydra."

"No."

"A werewolf?"

"What?"

"A giant; the minotaur; Medusa; titans; the bogeyman; a fire-breathing, man-eating demon vampire unicorn." Having exhausted his repertoire of monsters, Collins fell silent, hands folded across his lap. Anything they mentioned now had to sound puny in comparison.

All three regarded him with open-mouthed curiosity.

"So." Collins broke the silence. "From who or what do we have to get this crystal thingy?"

"Um," Zylas said, licking his lips. "We think the king has it."

"And there's no 'we' to it," Ialin added sulkily.

Surprised he had actually gotten things close to right, Collins brought up the matter he had expected to come to light first. "Couldn't we just ask someone with younger magic for help?"

Zylas smiled weakly. "Lady Prinivere has the youngest magic we know of."

Shocked, Collins leaned backward. ''You mean you know someone *older?*''

Ialin slapped his own forehead. ''You numbskull! She's the only one with magic any of us knows. She's the last dragon. Ipso facto, the last user of magic.''

Surprised to hear Latin from his alien friends, Collins let the insult pass. He wondered what Ialin might possibly have said in Barakhain that the magic would translate into ''ipso facto'' rather than ''therefore.'' Collins went for funny. ''So, in your quaint lovable way, you're trying to tell me that only dragons have magic.''

''Exactly.'' Ialin ignored the sarcasm.

''And Lady Prinivere is the last dragon. And as far as practically anyone knows, she doesn't even exist.''

''Right,'' Zylas confirmed.

That left an enormous gap in Collins' understanding. ''Then why would magic be illegal?'' He patted Zylas' pocket to indicate the translation stone. ''Wouldn't people just assume it doesn't exist?''

This time, Falima answered. ''Because of item magic, rare stuff left behind from the days when dragons were commonplace.''

''Centuries ago,'' Collins remembered. ''Does the king know about Lady Prinivere?''

''No,'' they all chorused with a suddenness and expressions that revealed such a thing would prove catastrophic. Zylas added, ''What a horrible thought.''

Certain they meant that the king would have Prinivere executed, Collins continued his questioning. ''Does he know this crystal thingy is magical?''

Still wide-eyed and pursed-lipped, the others fell into an uncomfortable hush before Zylas answered. ''We don't know.''

Collins tried to put everything together. ''So, if I fetch this crystal and bring it back, Prinivere can make a portal for me?''

Nods circumnavigated the room.

Finally, something Ialin had said sank in. "What did you mean, 'there's no "we" to it?' That I have to get this thing all by myself?"

Ialin flicked his head in a birdlike fashion. "You're not as stupid as I thought."

Collins smiled. "Thanks. That's the nicest thing you've said to or about me so far." He looked accusingly at Zylas. "Let's face it. A magic amplifier doesn't just help me. Long after I'm gone, you can use it to make and do all kinds of things. Why wouldn't you guys help me get it?"

Falima developed an inordinate interest in her feet. Ialin yawned, leaving only Zylas to answer. "We don't really know what this crystal can do. It's possible it only works one time." He glanced at the others for help, but Falima headed across the cave to check on Prinivere and Ialin got caught up in a luxurious stretch. "But mainly, it's because the royal chambers can only be accessed by stable people."

Still in half-stretch, Ialin clarified. "Meaning people without a switch-form." His tone suggested that he did not believe Collins fit the other definition of "stable."

"We *switchers* would get caught for sure," Falima added from across the room. "And killed. But you . . ."

. . . *are already condemned to die?* Collins believed he had uncovered the real reason, one his companions would never say aloud.

". . . won't set off the security. If you did get caught, you could pass yourself off as minor nobility come to learn, to valet, or to assist," Falima finished.

"Sure. Except I know nothing about any of those things." Collins could not stop himself from arguing, though it would do him no good. If he wanted to go home, he had to get this crystal. He might die in the attempt, but remaining in Barakhai without the support of his friends also would result in his swift demise. He might just as well charge the archers guarding the other portal and get it over with swiftly.

Ialin addressed the spoken thought. "You don't have to know much about nobility. Just the fact that you don't switch should keep you safe there. Who would suspect you're not of this world?"

Collins refused to put too much faith in that explanation. "Perhaps the royal archers guarding the portal?"

Ialin interjected, almost too quickly. "From what I heard while spying, they just know there's something magical there that bears watching. They're not going to let anyone near it."

Collins tried to logically consider what the authorities in his world would do with something similar. "Until someone explores it thoroughly?"

"More likely, wall it up so no one can use it or get hurt by it. Seek a way to destroy it."

Collins looked to Zylas, who shrugged and nodded. Though he knew American politicians and scientists would feel compelled to explore any anomaly until they gleaned every possible detail, he could understand where a civilization still in its more primitive stages might prefer avoidance to investigation. *Especially a place where magic and dragons are, or at least were, real.* So far, the only ones who believed he had come from another world were people who had traveled there and their closest companions. Apparently, the authorities had not figured out the purpose of the portal, though likely their study and discovery of it came as a direct result of the crime he had committed nearby.

The idea of breaking into a heavily guarded castle seemed impossible, yet Collins saw no better alternative. The archers at the first portal had shown their clear intent to kill anyone who approached it. Also, traveling back toward the town that had condemned him as a murderer and a cannibal seemed like sure suicide. Depending on the communication between areas, the royals might know nothing of his crime. If the crystal had properties beyond helping Prinivere make him a portal, so much the better. He owed his companions at least that much for risking themselves to save the life of a stranger. *A stranger*, Collins reminded himself, *who has yet to show a suitable amount of gratitude.* "Of course, I'll fetch that crystal," Collins promised aloud. "And I hope it works a lot more than one time. I appreciate your helping me. You guys deserve it and more." Collins smiled at another thought. "In fact, after I'm home, I'll see what I can find for you. Things like Zylas' lighter that make life a bit easier."

No real breeze blew through Prinivere's cave, but a tangible rush of relief followed Collins' pronouncement.

Returning from her visit to the sleeping dragon, Falima turned to practical considerations. "Of course, we'll get you to the castle. And describe as much of the layout as we know."

"Of course." Now that he had so valiantly volunteered, Collins refused to consider details. So long as the break-in remained abstract, he could bask in his friends' adulation and convince himself he would soon get home.

Zylas became a rat at midnight, his white fur easy to spot even in the dense gloom of a cave at night. He crawled off to sleep with the dragon, while Falima and Ialin discussed keeping watches. Since they made no effort to include him in their conversation, Collins stretched out on the floor near the entrance and tried to sleep.

The hard floor bit into his back and shoulders, no matter how frequently he shifted his position. The possible challenges that awaited him, alone and in strange surroundings, kept intruding on thoughts he desperately tried to keep dull and commonplace. The sheep he counted mutated to dragons. The map of his childhood home became an Escheresque maze-castle filled with weapons and monsters. Conjugating high school Spanish verbs became so simple, it could not hold his attention. He considered the reason; he had always struggled with them in the past and should only have gotten rustier over time. *It's the dragon's spell.* Understanding dawned with a suddenness that brought him fully awake again. *If this thing's long-lasting and crosses worlds, I've got a brilliant career as a translator.*

Oddly, that thought soothed him where others had not. Now he had work to fall back on should his professors blackball him from science forever. Even if he managed to talk his way out of their wrath, having wasted millions of dollars in grants, translation could earn him the spare cash he needed to handle his student loans. *If it lasts,* he reminded himself before excitement ran away with him. *I should be so lucky.* It occurred to Collins that he had to survive Barakhai first, which brought him back to the circle of worry that had, thus far, held sleep at bay. With a sigh, Collins began the battle again.

Chapter 12

A SHAKE awakened Benton Collins from a dream, heart pounding, wildly aware. He sprang to his feet to face Falima, who retreated in a scramble.

The cave mouth remained dark. Ialin sat on a chest with his chin in his hands, a grin of amusement on his homely, androgynous features. The dragon shimmered slightly in the darkness, still sleeping. He saw no sign of Zylas.

"What's wrong?" Collins asked.

"Nothing's wrong," Falima replied in a sheepish tone. "I just thought you'd want to get up before I change."

"Oh." Collins glanced at his watch. It read 5:30 a.m. The fatigue that should have greeted him upon first awakening seeped in on him now, accompanied by a multitude of pains spread across every part of his body. *Why?* he wondered, stretching out his throbbing arms. He glanced at the wound the dog had inflicted, but it had scabbed completely, leaving no redness and only slight bruising. It bothered him less than the twinges coming from what seemed like every other part of him, especially his back.

Gradually, Collins' mind caught up to his instantly alert body. *Of course I hurt. I slept with nothing but clothes between me and an irregular stone floor, I fell off a horse, and I rode for hours.* He rubbed an aching hip and continued a conversation that had stagnated while he considered. "Good idea. You've only got a half hour of human time left." He could not help glancing at Ialin, with whom he would share three more hours as a man. They would have to converse, he felt certain, since he could talk to no one else. *Or can I?* "Zylas' stone lets him understand animal speech as well."

Falima had anticipated the question. "His stone is unique. Most, and the spell, only work for human languages; though the lady said you might get some basic idea of an animal's mood." She studied him, brows rising in increments. "If that's necessary." It seemed more question than statement.

Collins shrugged, disappointed. "It can't hurt." Not wanting to look stupid, he added. "Though, when a horse draws its ears back and raises a hind foot, or a bird screeches and lashes out with its beak, or a dog growls, I can get a pretty good notion of their bent toward me."

Ialin chimed in, "Those are pretty obvious signs." He added with heat, "Of course, when a man slaps me halfway to Carterton, I get a pretty good idea of his bent toward me, too."

"That's not fair," Collins protested. "I thought you were a bug."

"Joetha, too, apparently."

Assaulted by irritation, Collins dismissed the comment with a sharp wave. "Can't we ever get past that?"

"Past it?" Ialin's voice went crisp with angry incredulity. "You killed and ate someone. How do you get past that?"

Collins did not know, but he had managed. Zylas, Falima, Vernon, Prinivere, and even Korfius had managed as well. He emphasized every word, and they emerged in clear snarls, "It . . . was . . . an . . . accident."

"Ialin," Falima said, in the same warning tone Zylas used to use when she verbally assaulted Collins.

At that moment, the rat skidded into their midst, squeaking savagely. He dropped the translation stone to the floor and planted a paw on it. "Cool it, guys. She's awake."

While Collins still marveled at how flawlessly the two translation devices merged even into slang, the others hurried or scrambled to the dragon's side.

Prinivere stretched her long, scaly neck, peering at the three in front of her with ancient eyes. **I'm fine,** she broadcast, with no more sincerity than the claim usually held in America. Even without physical words, her weakness came to him clearly. **A few more hours, and I should have the strength to fly. I appreciate your watching over me.**

"We appreciate the magic, my lady," Zylas squeaked, right front paw on the crystal.

The dragon reached out an enormous claw and seemed to enclose Zylas in it.

Fear clutched at Collins, though he knew she meant him no harm.

When Prinivere removed her claw, she left Zylas as he had been, except for a tousle of fur between his pink velvet ears. "Near-perfect overlap. I'm impressed, Zylas."

"Couldn't have done it without you and this magic," Zylas threw back the compliment, jiggling the translation stone with his paw.

"And constant practice," Falima added. "Don't go getting too humble, even in the lady's presence."

Zylas twitched his pointed nose at Falima, who excused herself and headed for the cave mouth.

Knowing she had gone to switch, Collins walked toward the group to give Falima more privacy. As they passed one another, Falima whispered, "Ialin will come around."

Collins bit his lip to keep from laughing. They were precisely the words Zylas had used about her and Ialin at various times. It hardly mattered, then or now. He only had to get along with the hummingbird long enough to steal the magic-enhancing crystal and get himself through the new portal.

Prinivere recovered more slowly than even she seemed to expect, though her loyal attendants, a horse and a rat, showed no signs of impatience. Ialin set to describing the layout of the palace to Collins in a straight, matter-of-fact manner that precluded gibes or personal affronts. Apparently, the keep had two irregular lines of curtain walls: the outer with six mural towers and two gatehouses, the inner with gatehouses directly in line with those of the outer wall, but smaller. Both walls had full-length, crenellated parapets. Between the walls lay a grassy outer courtyard, grazed by herbivore servants and horse-guards while in their switch-forms. In addition to the keep, the inner courtyard contained a stables/guard barracks, gardens, kennel barracks, and a pond.

Head overflowing with sketched diagrams and verbal descriptions, Collins sat back on his haunches. "How do you know all this?"

Ialin gave him that well-rehearsed stare that proclaimed Collins the dumbest man alive. "We're a hummingbird and a rat. How do you think we know?"

The three hours until Zylas' return to man form passed more swiftly than Collins expected as he tried to cram the information Ialin gave him into every nook and cranny in his brain. Comparing the situation to the night before finals helped, but the unfamiliar castle terms required defining, making the whole even more complicated. Collins could not help remembering why he had chosen a formulaic, theoretical, and logical field rather than one based mainly on memorization. He gained new respect for historians and geographers.

Falima grazed outside throughout the lesson. At nine, Ialin returned to bird form, and Collins heaved a grateful sigh. Anticipating three hours of blessed relief and silence, he drew the travel pack to him in search of breakfast. Crouched in front of one of the chests, he placed each item on its lid: first a hunk of brown bread, the jar of nut paste, and a wrinkled applelike fruit. He rummaged for a stick to spread the paste, wishing he had his multitool. It had served him well in many unexpected situations, from using the pliers to straighten a damaged cage clasp to cutting open the otherwise impenetrable plastic packaging that entombed so many small electronics.

Collins discarded the thought of using his companions' utility knives on food. *No telling what's on those blades.* Instead, he went to the cave mouth to find a suitable stick.

At Collins' sudden appearance, Falima raised her head and nickered. Remembering an earlier conversation, he strode over and scratched her between the ears. She closed her eyes and lowered her head, half-chewed stems jutting from her mouth. The sun beamed down from a cloudless sky, igniting red highlights in her tangled black forelock. Collins finger-combed it back in place with one hand, while the other continued to scratch.

Collins' stomach rumbled, and he abandoned his ministrations with a final pat. "Pretty girl," he cooed, feeling like an idiot and wondering how much of the encounter Falima would remember in human form. Locating a thick twig near his feet, he picked it up and returned to the cave.

Prinivere lumbered outside. Collins froze, fear twitching through him despite his knowledge and his efforts to keep the emotion at bay. He stepped aside, shoving his shaking hands into his pockets to hide them. The stick jabbed his thigh through the fabric, and he loosed a grunt of pain.

I'm going to find food, Prinivere announced, though whether at him or everyone, Collins could not tell. **Be back by the time Zylas changes.**

Collins nodded his reply, though the dragon had already swept past him. He had no idea what something so large might eat in the vegetable family to sustain herself. Though some of the largest dinosaurs had been herbivores, the paleontologists surmised that they had had to eat constantly to keep themselves alive. So far, he had not seen the dragon consume anything.

Carrying his spreading stick, Collins returned to his food, only to find Zylas nibbling at the bread. He stopped short. ''You know, in my world, finding a rat eating your food might just be the grossest thing imaginable.''

''Great,'' Zylas squeaked, his paw on the translation stone and his mouth leaking crumbs. ''More for me.''

''Ah,'' Collins reached for the nut paste. ''But I'm a biology student. I could eat a block of Swiss in a pathology laboratory over the smell of formaldehyde while mice used the holes for a maze.'' The medical student from whom he had stolen the quote had added a nearby dissected cadaver and that, if hungry enough, he would devour the animals with the cheese. Under the circumstances, Collins felt it best to leave those parts out.

Despite his bold words, Collins got himself a fresh piece of bread on which to spread the paste. He doubted Zylas could carry any of the rat-borne illnesses of his world without infecting himself in human form, but he saw no need to take chances. ''So what, exactly, does a dragon eat?''

Zylas finished a mouthful of bread. ''A whole lot.''

''No doubt.'' Collins dipped the stick into the jar and slapped a glob onto his bread. ''A whole lot of what?''

''People,'' Zylas said without hesitation.

Collins jerked his attention to the rat, hand still on the bread. ''What?''

''I'm kidding,'' Zylas said. ''Of course, she eats the same things everyone else eats. Plants, fish, bugs.''

''Oh.'' Collins swallowed hard. ''That's not funny.''

''Sorry.''

''In fact, it was downright insensitive.''

"I'm sorry," Zylas repeated. "I have *near* perfect overlap. Apparently, my rat sense of humor isn't as careful as my man sense of humor."

The guilt of his crime revived, Collins discovered a lump in his throat that made eating a chore. He pulled a bladder from the pack and sucked a mouthful of a sweet-and-sour fruit juice that contained a hint of alcohol. Expecting water, he nearly choked on the contents. "What the hell is this?"

Zylas jumped from the chest to Collins' lap, then skittered up his arm. He stuck his entire, furry head through the opening, then retreated with golden droplets clinging to his whiskers. He returned to his place, and the translating stone, before speaking. "It's a mix, one of Vernon's special recipes. Don't you like it?"

Collins had not given a thought to his opinion of the unexpected taste. Now, he considered, savoring the aftertaste on his tongue. If he had to guess the ingredients, he would have said grape juice, apple juice, some lemon, a dash of something exotic, like guava or mango, and a touch of dry wine. "Actually, I do. I just wasn't expecting it." He turned his thoughts back to Prinivere. "She'd have to eat an ocean of fish, I'd guess."

Zylas bobbed his head, splashing the golden droplets. "She usually does most of her eating in her human form, but I'd guess she had to 'refuel' from the spell."

Refuel. Collins liked the translation, though it could not have been the actual word Zylas had used. His respect for magic grew tenfold in an instant.

"Are you ready to learn the interior of the keep?"

Collins groaned. "Can't we wait till you're . . . human?" He had looked forward to three hours of eating and quiet or, at most, gentle conversation with Zylas alone.

"Once the lady fully regains her strength, we need to move on." Zylas eyed the pack. "Could you get me one of those beetles, please?"

Collins shoved a piece of bread in his mouth. He opened the pack, rummaging for the bug jar.

"It's best you have the general layout down by then. We can review and discuss strategy en route.

Collins found the covered crock and pulled it out. He opened the lid, watching the horde of grape-sized insects crawl over one another, then placed it on the chest beside Zylas. He chewed and swallowed. "Are you sure this is really the easiest way?"

Zylas placed his nose into the crock, then withdrew suddenly, sneezing. "You mean sneaking into an unsuspecting castle and removing a small object?"

"Yes."

"As opposed to taking on a phalanx of archers ordered to kill?"

When Zylas put it that way, it seemed clear. "Well . . ."

"Near a town that found you guilty of murder and sentenced you to a hanging they damn well know they didn't manage to complete."

"All right. I get it."

Zylas again stuck his face into the beetle crock. His squeaks echoed through the confines. "Of course, if you'd rather stay here with us forever . . ."

It was not an option. Even if his days were not numbered by how long it took the guards to catch up to him, Collins doubted he could live without the conveniences to which he had become accustomed: electric lights, refrigerators, modern medicine, pizza. He sighed at the thought. How much simpler his life could become if he did stay, but it would become so much better with a portal that allowed him to bring back the occasional Tylenol or Twinkie. Finally, he stated what he knew was true all along. "I can't possibly stay."

Zylas withdrew. "Would you mind getting one of those out for me, please. Every time I try, I get the whole bunch of them glomming onto my face."

Collins reached into the crock and pinched out a single beetle. Gingerly, Zylas took it from Collins' grip with his teeth, whiskers tickling.

Collins replaced the lid. "You going to want more?"

Beetle clamped between his teeth, Zylas silently shook his head.

Collins returned the jar to the pack, smiling at how normal it now seemed to feed bugs to a talking rat. Only a couple of days ago, he would have considered it absolutely understandable to find himself locked in some loony bin for even imagining such behavior.

While Zylas ripped into the beetle, Collins studied the bland interior of the cave. The dark, irregular walls surrounded a comfortable area, with nothing but the two chests to break the monotony. "What's in the boxes?" he asked, surprised he had not wondered sooner.

Zylas abandoned the partially eaten beetle to answer. "Personal things, I'd venture. Clothes maybe, though the lady rarely wears any. Food, certainly. Baubles."

"Baubles?"

"Things friends and intimates have given her through the ages."

"Her hoard?" Collins suggested.

Now, it was Zylas' turn to question. "Hoard?"

"Money," Collins explained. "Silver and gold trinkets. Gems. Jewelry." He came by the information through his brief stint of role-playing. "It's generally believed in my world that dragons like shiny things and objects of value."

Zylas abandoned his repast, red eyes positively glowing with excitement. "So you once had dragons in your world, too?"

The rat/man looked so happy, Collins hated to disappoint him, but he would not lie. "Only in myth and fairy tale, I'm afraid."

The light died in Zylas' eyes, and he returned to eating.

"Sixty million years before people, we did have dinosaurs. Those were giant lizards, some of which bore a resemblance to dragons."

"Really." Zylas spoke around a mouthful of bug. "Did they use magic?"

"Most had brains about the size of your lunch." Collins addressed the question more directly, "It seems highly unlikely."

Zylas made a wordless noise.

Collins returned to his point, "Anyway, in the stories, dragons keep hoards of shiny treasure which they guard fiercely."

"It has to be shiny?"

"Apparently." The details of legend seemed unimportant to Collins.

Zylas shook out his fur. "Well, that's not like dragons here. At least, it's not like the one I know. She doesn't have much interest in . . . material things, except as they pertain to causes."

"That's good to know." Collins could not see a long-term use for the knowledge. "If I ever write a story or start role-playing again, I'll keep that in mind."

Zylas finished the beetle, licked his paws, then cleaned his face with them.

Collins returned the leftover rations to the pack. Zylas waited only until he shoved it aside to ask, "Ready?"

"For what?" Collins asked cautiously.

"To learn the inside of the castle."

"No," Collins said, settling down on his buttocks. He doubted his answer mattered, however.

True to Collins' hunch, Zylas began. "The lowest floor contains the storerooms and dungeons . . ."

The lesson droned on for hours while Falima continued to graze outside and Ialin made occasional buzzing appearances. Benton Collins got his first break when Prinivere appeared at the entrance. The green-gray scales looked ruffled, the leathern wings droopy, the ancient eyes dull. She dragged wearily back into the cave, finding her sleeping corner, and flopped to the ground.

Zylas abandoned his lesson in the middle of a sentence and rushed to the dragon's side. Ialin fluttered in after her, hovering at her eye level.

Savoring a few moments alone, Collins sighed and remained in place, unable to hear their exchange. His head whirled with information: kitchens and workshops on the ground floor, above underground storage rooms, food cellars, and the dungeons. The second story held the library and great dining hall, the third the servants' quarters. Every floor had what Collins understood to be a primitive bathroom, translated as "garderobe." Apparently, both dragon spell and translation stone considered it an English word, though he had never heard it before. He imagined it had not entered common American parlance; though, with their known penchant for fart, belch, and bathroom humor, it would have worked well there. Zylas described it rather like a park potty: a thigh-high platform with a hole in it. The rat/man seemed to think it might prove a suitable portal for entry, escape, or for secreting the magical crystal. Though not averse to tossing the stone down the hole, Collins would rather eat bugs than retrieve it afterward. And using it as an exit was not even a remote possibility.

Zylas knew nothing about the two uppermost floors because of their warding against *switchers*, but he surmised they held the private quarters of the royals. The roof was crenellated, with crossbowmen and ballistae protecting it, and the winding stairwell proceeded a story higher, to a trapdoor that opened onto the top of a guard tower. Heavy ironbound oak doors opened onto each floor and the roof in both directions, though the four to the two upper stories did not admit *switchers*. Apparently, if a commoner so much as touched it, the door would sound an alarm and latch up tight.

Unable to put any logical explanation to such a system, Collins had to assume magic. *Unless other portals exist, and folks from civilizations more advanced than ours have come.* He shoved the thought aside. *Zylas would know that. Hard enough accepting magic. Do I have to put some* Planet of the Apes *twist on this?* Collins had once read that "advanced science is virtually indistinguishable from magic." The average man on the street could not explain how a toaster or a microwave worked, and a significant portion of the population considered the simple running of electricity through wires a miracle too technical for understanding. He himself found the concept of fax transmission fascinating and incomprehensible. *The source doesn't matter. I just need to know how it works on the macro level.*

Shortly, Zylas returned, translation stone clutched in his jaws. He scurried up Collins' arm to his shoulder and spit out the quartz to speak directly into the man's ear. "She says she just needs a short nap. Then she should be strong enough to return home."

"Home?"

"A different cave," Zylas explained. "She has several residences. Safer." He pawed the rose quartz into a more secure position. "Better you know as few as possible, too."

Collins nodded agreement, then glanced at his watch. It read a couple of minutes until noon. "You'd better get off me. A full-grown man would definitely put a strain on my rotator cuff."

"Don't worry. I'm going." The last syllable was muffled by the translation stone, and Zylas scrambled to the floor. He settled himself by the pack to wait.

Knowing his companion would emerge from his switchform naked, Collins politely turned his back. Experience told him it was unnecessary. Accustomed to the change from birth, the Barakhains apparently did not view nudity as a vulnerable state the way full-time humans did. But the gesture made Collins feel more comfortable and respectful, and his discussion with Falima made it clear that embarrassment could be reawakened by the wrong stare.

Stealing the few moments during which the change distracted his companion, Collins left the cave. Clouds pulled like lace across the sun, dimming it to caramel. Falima whinnied a soft greeting. Flies settled in a line along her spine, and the skin of her legs wriggled to dislodge others. Scraggly mountain grasses drooped from her lips, growing shorter as she chewed.

Collins clambered up an enormous rock near the cave mouth and looked out over the crags. Tree-loaded mountains stretched as far as he could see, sunlight glazing their needles and leaves. Peaks and boulders thrust between wide patches of greenery. Absently, he stroked Falima's back, dislodging the flies into angrily buzzing chaos. She swished her tail, black hairs like wires stinging across his bare arm. He shifted to a crouch to avoid another lashing and massaged the fur behind her ears. Her head sank, eyes closed, as she enjoyed his caress.

Collins shut his own eyes, imagining himself running his hand through the soft, black curtain of Falima's human hair. The strands glided through his fingers like silk while he massaged the tension from her upper back. He could see himself sliding his hands to her breasts, her turning her head to meet his kiss.

''Ben!'' Zylas' voice shattered the guilty pleasure of Collins' reverie.

Startled, Collins jerked, lost his footing on a smear of slime, and plummeted from the back of the rock. The landing jarred through his ankles, and he slapped his hands on the rock to protect his face.

With a surprised whinny, Falima sidled away, eyeing Collins with wary caution.

Collins waited for the pain to fade before peering over the granite at Zylas in man form. ''What did you do that for?''

Zylas studied Collins blandly from the shadow of his hat. ''I presume my transgression was . . . um . . . speaking your name?''

Collins stepped around the rock, brushing dirt from his tunic. ''The transgression part was sneaking up on us.'' He glanced at Falima who shifted from hoof to hoof, still watching him with suspicion. ''On me.''

"You were facing me," Zylas defended. "I thought you saw me."

"I had my eyes closed."

"Ah, my fault." Zylas smiled, clearly meaning none of it. "Falima was right. You are jumpy."

That being self-evident, Collins did not deny it. "Wouldn't you be, too, if you had to do what I'm going to have to do?"

"Maybe." Zylas continued to pin Collins with his gaze. "But you'll do better calm."

Easy to say. Collins grunted.

"Trust me."

Believing Zylas' description of the inside of the castle was firsthand, Collins did not argue. At least Zylas had had rat form to hide behind. Sneaking became much easier for someone the size of Collins' fist. "What did you want?"

Zylas made a gesture Collins could not fathom. "We need to finish your lesson."

Collins groaned. "Can't we take a little break?"

Zylas tensed, glancing around at the sun glimmering from chips of quartz in the rocks, the brilliant blue of the sky, and the sparse, delicate clouds. "I suppose so. I just want . . ." He stared off into the distance, stiff and still. ". . . you . . . to succeed."

"Why?" Collins spoke softly, afraid to frighten Zylas away from the truth. It seemed too important to the albino to solely hinge on Collins' survival.

The left corner of Zylas' mouth twitched. "Because I . . . like you. I want you to make it home safely."

"That's it?"

"That's it."

Collins did not believe the answer, though he knew of no reason for Zylas to lie. Experience suggested the rat/man wanted the stone for whatever magic remained in it after Prinivere created the portal. His own cynicism conjured a frown. *He rescued me from hanging. He's risked his neck for me several times since. Shouldn't he get something for his effort?*

The thought was less comforting than Collins expected. Nameless dread edged through the soothing world he had built with friendships, trust, and the understanding that a way existed for him to go home. He was missing something that his companions found too obvious to tell him, something he did not even know enough about to ask, something that might determine whether or not he survived the world of Barakhai. A breeze dragged a strand of mouse-brown hair into Collins' eye and sent a wild shiver through him. He only hoped the omission would not prove a fatal one.

Chapter 13

WITH Zylas pacing like a maniac, Benton Collins found it impossible to enjoy his break, despite the beauty of the day and Falima's soft nose and fur. Jorge Martinez, his lab partner during freshman year, had been fond of the expression "fake it till you make it." For half an hour, Collins tried to follow that advice, ignoring his agitated companion to focus on the calm animal that was his other one. But, over time, Zylas' frenzy became contagious. Falima pranced dangerously, forcing Collins to give her some space. With a sigh, he headed back into the cave, Zylas following. "Respite finished?"

"Sadly, yes." Collins searched for his memories of the castle's description. He glanced toward the chests; but, deciding he would rather have a backrest than height, chose a seat on the floor near the exit instead. He wriggled backward until his spine touched stone. "What do you want to talk about?"

Zylas removed his hat and pulled white hair away from his face, holding it behind his head. "First, I want to hear your version of the castle, make sure you've got the details. Then we can start discussing strategy.''

Collins nodded, simultaneously lauding and cursing Zylas' thoroughness. The constant need to concentrate made him dizzy, but he knew his life might well depend on careful attention to details. He drew a verbal picture of the castle walls and grounds, the moat, the tents and outbuildings in the courtyards, the location of every door and portcullis. As he did so, he tried to put a visual image to his narration, a more difficult process than he expected. Most people learned better from pictures than words, but he had always found his memory worked the opposite way. It made him better at standardized tests, where every concept was reduced to text; but it meant he had to work harder than his peers in the hands-on world of the laboratory.

Collins shifted his focus to wards and guards, then switched to the interior. There, he faltered, requiring Zylas' assistance to recall which room lay where, who or what he might encounter there, and the best routes to the upper levels which most likely housed the magical crystal. Frustrated, Collins tried to sidetrack Zylas for a few moments. ''How do you know so damn much about this place?''

''Been there,'' Zylas said, barely an explanation.

Collins guessed, ''Did you work there? A servant, maybe?''

''Vermin? Invited into the castle?'' Zylas laughed with a mirth so genuine, Collins could not help joining him.

Ialin zipped into the cave, buzzing frantic circles around Zylas. The laughter broke off abruptly. Zylas sprang to his feet, expression tense, edgy, with a touch of fear.

''What?'' Collins also rose, but Zylas waved him back and silent. The albino crept toward the cave mouth, head cocked.

Suddenly, a hound bayed, the sound close.

Collins jumped, heart hammering.

Zylas charged from the cave toward Falima. ''Get the lady out!''

Out? Out where? Uncertain whether Zylas intended the command for him or for Ialin, Collins ran toward the dragon. Before he reached her, a brown-and-white dog bounded into the cave, barking madly. Toenails scrabbled against stone as it attempted to stop. Instead, it skidded, long legs buckling, ears flopping. It bashed into a chest, which sent the dog caroming practically into the dragon's lap. Prinivere jerked awake, wings unfolding, a hiss escaping her massive mouth between rows of pointed teeth. Whatever she actually ate, nature clearly intended her to be a carnivore.

The dog let out a squeak of surprise, followed by a string of desperate whimpers. It scuttled backward, bashing into Collins' legs, then rolled its eyes to him in terror and hope. Thrown to a crouch, Collins met the dog's gaze and recognized him instantly. "Korfius!" He dropped to his knees.

Still loosing panting whines, the dog crawled onto Collins' legs.

"Zylas, it's Korfius." Collins petted the dog all over, as it tried to fit its entire body onto him.

Zylas hauled Falima into the cave. "I don't see or hear any more dogs. He's either way ahead of a pack or alone." He glanced wildly around the cave. "When's his change time?"

Collins glanced at his watch, which read nearly 1:00. He recalled how Korfius had switched forms in his arms while hiding in Vernon's false wall. "I'd say just about now."

"Now?" Zylas leaped to Collins' side with an abruptness that sent Falima into a half-rear. "We've got to get him out before—" He grabbed the dog by the nape of the neck, and Korfius let out a startled yelp.

Zylas pulled, dragging the dog from Collins' lap. Korfius' dark eyes implored Collins. He planted his feet against stone, and Zylas struggled to move him. "Help me here, would you?"

Collins stood, uncertain exactly what to do. Korfius threw his head back and forth, trying to break free of Zylas' grip, which tightened as he surely worried about getting bitten. Korfius' form blurred.

Zylas cursed.

Falima whinnied tensely, then bolted from the cave.

Zylas let out a string of curses, which translated strangely as everything from bodily functions, to disasters, mythical creatures, and filth. He let go.

Korfius writhed as his forelegs became arms, features grew or disappeared, fur receded. Soon, a naked boy on all fours replaced the dog form, stammering a single word, "Dr–dr–dr–dr–dragon. It's a dragon." He looked directly at Collins. "I saw a dragon." He whipped his head to Zylas. "A real dragon." Finally, he turned his attention to Prinivere. "Dragon." He rose with slow, careful movements and drifted toward her as if in a daze. "Excuse me, but are you really a dragon?"

I am, young man, Prinivere returned. **My name is Prinivere.**

Zylas paced, wringing his hands.

Unself-consciously naked, Korfius bowed. "Deeply honored to meet you, Lady Prinivere. I'm Korfius."

So I gathered. The dragon settled back down. Only then, Collins noticed the black hole behind her, apparently the escape Zylas had wanted him to use. He wondered why he had not seen it before and decided the dragon had fully stolen his attention. Most of the time, her enormous, sleeping form had blocked it.

Falima trumpeted out a neigh.

"Now what?" Zylas muttered, rushing to the entrance just as a savagely panting Vernon threw himself inside.

"I'm . . . sorry," the black man gasped out. "I . . . tried to . . . stop . . . him, but . . ." He paused for several beats to concentrate on breathing. ". . . he's quick."

"Got one hell of a nose, too." Zylas held out a hand to assist his friend, but Vernon chose to remain on the ground for the moment.

Korfius drew himself up proudly. "Best sniffer in my brigade."

Collins remembered how Korfius had found them in the

flowering tree when the other hounds had not. He nodded. "No doubt."

"A dragon." Korfius seemed incapable of getting past that word. He turned stiffly to Collins. "Your Majesty, you keep interesting company." He bowed. "And I am at your service."

Collins glanced at Zylas, who nodded with wary encouragement. "Korfius, I've already told you the best way to serve me."

"I know, Sire—"

"Just Ben," Collins reminded.

"I know . . ." Korfius clearly struggled mightily, but managed to blurt out, "Ben. But I want to help, to be a part of this." His wide-eyed gaze fell on the dragon again, though he did not say the word this time. "A guard superior, a royal, and a . . . a dragon." The reverent tone gained strength with each naming. "I'm staying with you. Seeing this through. You might need me!"

Once more, Collins glanced at Zylas for support. He wished the other man would say something. After all, Zylas was more likely to have the necessary knowledge to handle this situation; but Collins also knew that maintaining the illusion of his royalty required him to speak. "What I don't need is a couple of worried parents sending an entire guard force after me." It seemed almost moot, as they already tracked him on a murder charge. "Nor do I need to add a kidnapping rap."

"Parents?" Korfius laughed. "Don't worry about my parents. They're extremely *lesariat*. I'm from a litter of seven . . ."

Collins took his cue from Zylas, whose eyes went round as coins and whose lips glided open in clear surprise.

". . . and as far as they're concerned, they raised me. I'm on my own."

Though it seemed easier with his parents out of the equation, Collins could not imagine any mother not worrying about her missing child. *Put it in animal terms,* he reminded himself. *Once the puppies hit somewhere between six and ten weeks, the parents often don't even recognize them.* Cynically, he wondered if whoever was in charge of the city would prove more diligent about his ''best sniffer'' then the parents were over their missing septuplet. Zylas' reaction made it clear that multiple births were not the norm, despite the time spent as animals. From the way Korfius stated it, Collins guessed that the ones more anchored in animal form had a higher likelihood of more than one offspring at a time. ''Well, then,'' Collins said, surprised by his own words. ''Perhaps I *could* use your help.''

Zylas' jaw, already dangling from the litter comment, now positively fell. ''Um . . . Ben. Could I speak to you for a moment?''

Though tempted to say ''no,'' which would leave Zylas completely defenseless, Collins excused himself from Korfius, telling the boy to put some clothes on, and then followed his pale companion to the cave mouth.

Zylas barely waited until they got beyond hearing range. ''What the hell are you doing?''

Collins wondered if the concept of hell as he knew it actually existed in this world, then shrugged off the thought. None of his companions seemed overly religious, and he saw no need to create a possible rift. ''What do you mean?''

Zylas kept his voice at a bare hiss, though he clearly would have preferred to yell. ''I mean, you just invited a kid along.''

''What did you want me to do?'' Collins finally realized what his subconscious had much earlier. ''Send him back to whatever that town was that's hunting us knowing all about your precious lady?''

Zylas swallowed hard.

''Well?''

''That,'' Zylas said thoughtfully, ''can't happen.'' A look of sharp terror took over his features, so intense that Collins felt fear prickling up his spine as well.

Collins fell silent, uncertain whether he wished to encourage Zylas any longer.

''What are we going to do?''

You're asking me? Collins raised his brows, throwing the question right back to his uncomfortable companion.

"They'll hunt her down and kill her."

Collins continued to study Zylas. The other option, killing a child to keep her secret, seemed even more heinous. "Zylas," he started carefully, not at all certain where he planned to go from there.

"You're right," Zylas interrupted. "We have to keep him with us. And quiet." He stomped a foot. "Damn! Why did he have to . . ." He trailed off with a noise of frustration.

"I'm sure Vernon did everything he could."

"Yeah. I trust—" Zylas' nostrils flared. "We've got to get out of here." He looked past Collins. "If one dog could follow our scent, others could."

Collins was not convinced of that.

"Or, they might just follow *his* scent."

That seemed much more likely. "Can Prinivere travel?"

"She should be able to make it to another of her . . ." Zylas ended lamely, ". . . places now." Apparently seized by another thought, he added, "In fact, she should go now, before she switches."

About eighteen hours had passed since Collins had seen Prinivere in human form. Somehow, he doubted she had to take any drugs to keep her dragon-time longer. Given that she could use all her higher functions as a dragon, plus magic and a vastly extended life-span, he suspected she considered it her more advanced form.

Zylas headed back toward Prinivere. "My lady," he said as he moved. "Forgive the abruptness of our departure, but I think it best if we all go as soon as possible." He put a subtle emphasis on the word "all" which Collins took to mean he wanted her to know that she should take off also.

He's just a boy, Prinivere sent, Collins presumed to him and Zylas, at least, and certainly not to Korfius who still stared at her with undisguised awe. **Don't do anything rash.**

"I won't," Zylas promised. "Unless it becomes absolutely necessary. But we can't risk . . ." He glanced at Korfius, as if to read how much of the one-sided conversation he might fathom, ". . . you. And I don't know many . . ." he hedged, as if seeking a code word, then brightened. Casually, he removed the rose quartz stone from his pocket and set it on an irregularity in the rocky wall. He switched to broken English, surely aware only Collins and Prinivere could understand him. ". . . child can't hold secret. Will . . ." He struggled, then touched the stone. ". . . caution." He removed his fingers and returned to English. "But if it comes to a decision—your life or his—I have no choice, my lady."

I'm old, she reminded.

"But got at least as many years left as he." Zylas inclined his head toward Korfius. "And need—" He struggled again; but, this time, did not resort to the translation stone. "—other life depend—" He glanced at Collins and fell silent, then scooped up his stone and returned it to his pocket. "Let's go," he growled in clear frustration.

Collins remained silent throughout the exchange, quietly putting the details together. Clearly, Korfius' finding them threw Zylas into a terrible dilemma. He had to keep Korfius quiet about Prinivere, not just for the duration of Collins' time here, but forever. Collins did not envy him that position; he could not kill a regular dog, let alone one who became a boy at intervals. Yet, Zylas had a loyalty to Prinivere that transcended Collins' understanding.

Collins and Zylas packed their gear in a tense hush punctuated only by occasional sighs from the rat/man. Collins did not press, certain his companion would speak in his own time. He did not have the words to comfort, so the best he could do was to listen.

Korfius seemed to share none of Zylas' consternation, chattering at the dragon with an exuberance Collins could not ever remember having. Apparently, the dragon answered him privately and with infinite patience, because Korfius kept bouncing and talking, often not waiting long enough for Prinivere to possibly have addressed the question before zipping off another. Shortly, they had everything, and Zylas signaled for everyone to go.

Korfius obediently bounded from the cave, Zylas and Collins behind him and Ialin hovering anxiously. Falima made no complaint as Zylas lashed the pack to her back then assisted Korfius astride, still talking.

"I can't believe I'm helping a royal and a dragon. A real dragon. I can't believe there really even is a *real dragon* to help. A real, live dragon."

Zylas looked as tense as a depressed spring.

Collins placed a hand on Korfius' calf. "Listen, little buddy."

Korfius turned him a happy look.

"Remember how I told you this was secret?"

"Yes, I . . ." Korfius turned thoughtful, features screwed up in apparent pain. "Oh. Does that mean . . . ?"

"Yes," Collins said firmly, though the boy had never completed the question. "You can't tell anyone about Lady Prinivere."

"Ever?" The word seemed driven from his lips.

"Ever." Collins confirmed in a voice he hoped brooked no further questioning.

"Not even—"

To emphasize the point, Collins did not let Korfius finish. "Not even."

"But I didn't get to—"

"Doesn't matter. Not anyone. Ever." Collins dusted his hands to show the matter had ended, with no further discussion necessary or desirable. "It's as simple as that."

"Oh," Korfius said barely audibly. He hunched, disappointment clear from his stance as well as his features. "Well. At least, I'll get to help?" His tone suggested defeat, and he clearly expected Collins to burst his one last bubble.

"Of course, you can help," Collins said cheerfully, though he had no idea how. Knowing he would likely have to give Korfius a "busy" job, he added, "There are no small roles in the service of good and justice." He rather liked the sound of his own words and wondered whether he had just created them, as he believed, or if his subconscious had revived it from some long-ago comic book.

"I can't believe I met a . . ." This time, Korfius caught himself before he said, "dragon."

Collins made a "zip your lip" motion.

Though he could not understand the reference, Korfius apparently got the implication. He mimicked the gesture and fell silent.

As they headed off in a new direction, Collins glanced around. "Where's Vernon?"

Zylas continued to look worriedly between Collins and Korfius. "He'll get the lady off safely, then head back home." He held Collins' gaze. "We need him there."

Uncertain whether Zylas meant in general or for some reason related to their current mission, Collins did not press. Zylas clearly wanted to speak as little as possible about such matters in the boy's presence.

For the first few hours, they traveled in relative quiet. Then, Korfius drifted off to sleep, body sprawled across the pack, arms dangling on either side of Falima's neck. Collins paused to redistribute the boy's weight, to tuck limp hands beneath the weighted center, and to smooth hair from his eyes. Korfius mumbled something unintelligible but did not fully awaken. Collins now found himself able to continue without worrying constantly over the child's safety.

Finally, Collins went to Falima's head, where Zylas used the lead rope to haul her generally westward. "You know, between his only spending seven hours a day as a boy and the need to get sleep in both forms, he might just as well be a full-time dog.

"*Lesariat*," Zylas reminded in a grunt. "That's the whole idea."

Suddenly, Collins found the answer to a question he had asked himself earlier. *Of course their civilization has stagnated for longer than a century. When you spend half or more of your life in animal form, it has to take all your time just to do the things necessary for survival. Who has time for innovation?*

Zylas glanced at the boy, apparently to ascertain that he slept. "Let's get back to planning."

Collins nodded, surprised to find himself eager. The more he understood, the better his chances for success. The several hours of walking had proved just the break he needed. "Let's start with the moat."

Another day of travel brought them down from the mountains to a road that hugged the base and a broad expanse of forest. Collins realized they could have avoided the crags and steppes simply by following the path, which most people surely did. He did not begrudge the course they had taken. Though longer, even without the looping detours Zylas had taken to foil pursuit, it only made sense for Prinivere to live where few humans dared or bothered to go. *On my world, she'd probably hide out on Everest.* He amended, *Or, perhaps, the tenth, eleventh, or twelfth highest mountain might not have quite as many determined climbers.*

They entered the forest just in time. Clouds that had stalked and threatened through the night broke open to release a splattering downpour. Rain roared against the canopy, occasionally rolling through to soak them with icy pinpoints or sudden streams of runoff. It continued into the evening, adding jagged bursts of lightning and rolling booms of thunder to the symphony of nature's pique. They ate from a pack growing welcomely lighter, and Collins appreciated that his companions found the insects the most desirable of their fare. By now, none of those remained, and they feasted on the foods he liked best: dried fruit, nut paste, and bread.

With Korfius in dog form, Collins' companions discussed the upcoming castle break in freely. Caught up in the plans, Collins listened and joined in eagerly. Though the approach changed several times, the idea that he might not succeed never entered the conversations. Heartened by his companions' confidence, Collins found himself just as certain that he would prevail. The crystal would make it back to Prinivere, she would open the portal, and he would return home to face the consequences of his absence—gladly. He only wished he could take his new friends with him. The image this conjured made him laugh. *Wouldn't that be interesting?* He curled up to sleep, dreaming of castle spires and a talking plesiosaur entrenched in a moat of blood.

Early the following morning, Ialin raced back to Collins and his friends: a rat, a horse, and a dog. "It's just ahead."

"The castle?"

"Yes, the castle." Impatience touched Ialin's tone, his small, thin body in constant motion. "Up ahead. Come look."

As Collins went to do so, the other man added, "Carefully, now."

Collins obediently moved slowly in the indicated direction, trying to avoid crackling leaves and snapping twigs.

Ialin pranced an anxious circle around him. "Come on."

Collins stopped, studying the little man. "I can be quick or careful, not both. Choose."

Ialin sighed. "Careful." He flitted ahead, still clearly fretful, though he no longer rushed the only other companion in human form. He paused to peer through a gap in the foliage.

Collins counted Ialin shifting from foot to foot seven times in the few seconds it took him to come up beside the hummingbird/man. He wondered if the speeding metabolism required by a quick and tiny bird extended to his human form and made the world seem to move that much slower. He glanced through the gap, vision obscured in serrated chaos by overhanging leaves. Not far ahead, the forest opened to a vast plain of grass grazed by sheep, cows, and goats in a myriad array of colors. Chickens and ducks waddled through the herd, scooping up the bugs dislodged by shambling hooves.

Beyond the animals, a ring of brackish water surrounded a high stone wall with teethlike turrets and circular platforms. An even taller wall peeked over the first, visible only as jagged shadows. Above it all rose the castle, looking very much like the pictures Collins remembered from the postcards of friends who had chosen world travel over higher education. Each corner held a square-shaped tower that loomed over the turreted, rectangular roof. Every part was constructed of mortared stone blocks. It looked exactly as Ialin had described it, yet it defied all of Collins' expectations. The grandeur held him spellbound, struck by the work that must have gone into its construction, the eerie aura of power that accompanied a living fossil. The pictures his friends had sent were of crumbling ruins that barely compared with the reality of a functioning, real-time castle. "Wow," he said.

Ialin loosed a sound, half-snort and half-giggle. "Zylas said you were a people of few words, but I never realized just how few."

Collins tried to explain, gaze locked on the castle of Barakhai. "It's amazing. I've never seen anything like it."

Ialin withdrew, and Collins followed. "Where does *your* king live?"

As Collins returned to his animal companions, he tried to explain, "We don't have a king. We have a president who's elected—"

Ialin made a gesture to indicate he did not understand.

"We pick him."

"Who's *we*?" Ialin asked suspiciously, sliding the pack from Falima's withers. He eased it to the ground.

"We." Collins made a broad gesture to indicate everyone. "The people. All of us." It was not true in the strictest sense, as the 2000 presidential election could attest, but Collins had no intention of explaining the electoral college to a man struggling with the meaning of "vote."

Ialin dragged the pack deeper into the forest. "Regular people picked your leader?"

In rat form, Zylas galloped after Ialin. Korfius thrust his damp, icy nose into Collins' palm.

"Pick," Collins corrected the tense and scratched behind Korfius' ears. His family had always had a dog and at least one cat. His current lifestyle did not lend itself to pets, but he hoped to get one of each as soon as he graduated. "Every four years, we decide on a new one."

"And everyone agrees?"

At the same time, Zylas squeaked, "How do you keep one from taking over. From declaring himself leader for life?"

More worried about getting safely into and out of the castle, Collins found himself unwilling to get into a long discussion about American democracy. "There are whole enormous textbooks written on those very topics. It's not my field of study, but the system's worked reasonably well for at least the last two hundred years." He rushed to add, "Now, if we can get back to the matter at hand."

Zylas scurried up Collins' arm to his shoulder. "Ah, so now you're the one who only wants to talk about the castle."

"Yeah," Collins admitted, still stroking the dog. "Guess I'm a natural crammer." At the confused look on Ialin's face, he explained. "I tend to avoid things I don't want to do until a deadline looms. Then, I dive into it to the exclusion of everything else."

Ialin shrugged and began setting up the camp. "How odd."

"Not where I come from. Not for students, anyway."

Zylas spoke directly into Collins' ear. "I find I tend to remember things longer and better if I learn them slowly over time. And repetitively."

Collins flushed. "Well, yeah. I didn't say cramming was a smart thing." Realizing they had veered off the topic again, he redirected the conversation. "Any recent ideas on how I'm going to get into this castle?"

At first, Collins thought Ialin turned to look at him. Then, he realized the smaller man's gaze did not directly meet his own. He was, instead, consulting the rat on Collins' shoulder. "As a matter of fact," the man in human form started, "we have one."

Interested in what they might have discussed on the sly, Collins tipped his head toward Zylas to indicate his interest.

"Well," Ialin started, sitting on the only blanket he had, thus far, laid out. "Town guards sometimes come for brief training with the king's warriors. From what I understand, it keeps the king informed about the goings-on in his holdings and gets some elite training for the guards."

"Yeah?" Collins encouraged, not yet sure how this could apply to him.

"They usually come in pairs," Ialin continued. "So if we send you in riding Falima, no one should question it. Usually, a guard wouldn't let anyone but a royal or another guard sit on them."

Collins considered. "Falima let *me* ride her."

With a wave of his paw, Zylas dismissed that argument. "After she went 'renegade' by saving you, all bets were off."

That seeming self-evident, Collins shook his head. "No, I mean before the rescue. She carried me to the . . . the dungeon." He swallowed, fighting a forming image. A swirl of the desperate parade of emotions that had struck him there returned to haunt him.

"Because the other guards told her to do it, I presume," Ialin growled. "And I'll also wager it wasn't a comfortable ride."

Remembering, Collins winced. "You'd win that bet."

"Anyway," Ialin said, returning to the subject, "if you rode in on Falima, no one would think to question that you're both guards."

Collins still saw a gap in the logic. "Unless word of Falima turning . . ." He used Zylas' word, or at least the one the translation spell and stone turned it into, ". . . 'renegade' has reached this far."

Ialin wiped his mouth with the back of his sleeve. "Oh, we have to assume that."

"We'll disguise her," Zylas explained, whiskers tickling Collins' ear.

Collins' mind conjured images of a horse wearing a huge plastic nose, mustache, and glasses combination. The usual methods of disguise: clothes, haircut, contact lenses, perhaps a fake scar or two would not work here. They could not even sneak into the relative safety of careful cross-dressing. "As a horse? Or a woman?"

Ialin gave Collins another one of his judgmental stares. "We'll do the horse part. She'll have to handle the woman herself. We'll send the pack, so you can put anything she'll need in there."

Collins looked doubtfully from the grazing horse to the pack near Ialin's feet. "Won't I have to know something about the town I'm supposed to represent?"

"Not as much as you think," Zylas said.

Apparently missing Zylas' words, spoken low and directly into Collins' ear, Ialin said, "Just a bit."

Sensing Collins' tension, Korfius whined, butting the now-stilled hand.

Absently, Collins continued his ministrations while his two older companions outlined their plan.

Chapter 14

COLLINS' watch read 5:00 p.m. when he rode Falima across the well-cropped grassy field that separated the outer curtain wall from the forest. He tucked the watch into his pocket, wishing he could have left it behind with Zylas. Pulling out impossible technology at the wrong time might give him away, but he relied upon it to determine a proper and consistent pretend switch time, to keep track of Falima, and to have a clear idea of how long the whole process was taking him. The black fur beneath him was disorienting after several days of riding a golden buckskin. Having never heard of bleach, his companions found it impossible to lighten Falima's coloring, so had chosen to make her body the same coarse ebony as her mane, tail, and points. Apparently, jet black was one of the most common horse colors in Barakhai and should not attract undue attention.

At switch time, Falima would make herself scarce. The dye might carry over into her human form, though probably not with much consistency. Apparently, some items in the pack would allow her to touch up blotches or to change her appearance in other believable fashions. Collins hoped he would recognize her, though it did not matter. His escape plan and hers did not hinge upon one another.

Sheep looked up as they passed, baaing noisy greetings. The goats proved more curious, approaching them to sniff, bleat at, and chew the cloth shoes his companions had provided in place of his Nike look-alikes. The horse's ears went flat backward, and she emitted occasional warning squeals that sent the goats scattering, though they always returned. The cows paid them no attention at all.

As they crossed the plain, Collins got a clear view of the outer wall, and he steered Falima toward the attached roofed structure that clearly represented the gatehouse. A massive construct of plank and rope pressed against the stone wall, apparently the drawbridge. Collins pulled up in front of the gatehouse, at the edge of the moat. Insects skittered over the surface of the water, leaving star-shaped wakes. Far beneath them, fish glided through the transparent pond, apparently accustomed to having no place to hide.

The gatehouse consisted of two of the round towers that interrupted the wall at regular intervals, with a straight stretch of stone no wider than the drawbridge between them. On the roof of each tower stood two guards dressed in white-chested aqua tunics, the top portion decorated with designs that looked like thinly stretched clover to Collins. Black belts held their uniforms in place and supported long, thin swords in wooden sheaths. All four watched Collins' approach with obvious interest, though they raised no weapons. One called down in a strong, female voice, "Who's there?"

Collins had initially assumed they were all men, so the speaker caught him off guard.

When he did not answer immediately, the woman's partner boomed out, "You were asked a question, good sir. Are you deaf or rude?"

Collins dismounted and bowed, hoping they would attribute

any violated protocol to his foreignness. "Just tired, sir. I am Benton." It seemed ironic that he would use the full name he had so many times asked others to shorten. He had often wished his parents had named him Benjamin, like every other "Ben" he had ever met. His current friends had assured him that Benton fit this world much better than Ben; and, by using his real name, he would not forget it, as he might a pseudonym, in the heat of a chaotic moment. If he accidentally did call himself "Ben," it would follow naturally as a proper shortening or interrupted utterance. "And this . . ." He made a flourishing motion toward Falima, "is Marlys." It was another alias he would remember, though he knew it made things harder for his companion. He dared not use anything approaching her real name, as it might trigger suspicion. "We've traveled a long way under less than ideal circumstances."

"From where?" the woman asked, and the others leaned forward for the answer. Now, Collins was able to get a good look at all of them. Mail peeked from beneath their collars and sleeves, and helmets pinned down their hair. Their faces ranged from the male partner's dark brown to the woman's café au lait to the paler khaki of the guards in the other tower. Wisps of sable hair escaped onto one man's forehead, but the others kept their locks bunched beneath arming caps and metal helmets.

Collins used the town name Ialin had given him, "Epronville. We've come to do our shift for the king."

"Where are your colors?" one of the pale men asked.

Anticipating the question, Collins had a ready answer. "Bandits. That was part of our less than ideal circumstances."

The woman's partner snorted. "Bandits robbing guardsmen. You're right. You do need a shift here. Some competent training."

Collins feigned affront. "Do you think we don't feel foolish enough? You have to rub our noses in it?" He wondered how the slang would translate. "Perhaps you'd like to bring the whole guard force out here to point fingers and laugh at us?"

He simulated the guards, jabbing a digit toward Falima. "Ha ha ha, simple rube guards can't even keep *themselves* safe from bandits." He dropped his hand. "And, by the way, don't bother to mention we faced off six of them."

The dark man made a gesture of surrender. "Take it easy. I meant no disrespect." The tight-lipped smirk he tried to hide told otherwise. He turned and disappeared from the tower.

Keeping his own expression neutral, Collins congratulated himself on his acting. He had managed to divert the guards from the issue of the missing colors. The fact that it made him look weak did not bother him at all.

The fourth guard reappeared at his position. Then, a ratcheting, clanking noise ground through Collins' hearing. The drawbridge edged downward, adding a squeal of massive, rusty hinges to the din.

"You'd best move back," the woman instructed. "Or you might get crushed."

Collins led Falima away from the moat, hoping his failure to exercise the proper caution would pass for small town ignorance rather than a complete lack of knowledge about castles. He knew Barakhai had only one such fortress, that the dwellings of the outlying superiors consisted only of mansions with the barest of defenses. When he considered their system, it seemed miraculous that they managed even that much. At most, the people had only eight hours a day to accomplish any work along with such necessities as eating and general personal care.

Suspended by two sturdy chains, the drawbridge dropped across the moat with a thud that shook the ground. Falima loosed a low nicker, prancing several more paces backward.

"Easy girl." Collins rubbed her neck soothingly, feeling the warm sweat that slicked her fur. He glanced surreptitiously at his palm, worried the moisture might disturb the dye. Though caked with dirt and foamy horse sweat, his hand remained free of black smudges. He breathed a sigh of relief.

Gripping the lead rope more tightly, Collins drew Falima to

the drawbridge. She eyed the board warily. Collins stepped up first, hoping that would ease her concerns. One front hoof rose, then settled on the wood. The other followed. She took a step forward, hoof clomping on the board. Another carried her directly over the moat, and a hollow sound rang through the drawbridge. With a snort and whinny that left Collins' ears ringing, she stumbled back to solid ground.

Afraid the horse's lurching might toss him into the water, Collins skittered after her. "Falima, honey, it's all right," he whispered. "It's all right. You need to come."

Falima trumpeted out another whinny.

"Not much overlap," one of the guards guessed.

"Some." Collins remembered what Zylas had told him. "But she's still pretty young."

One of the guardsmen took pity on the weary travelers. "First time across is always difficult. Just keep trying. If necessary, I'll get someone in switch-form to show her across."

"Thank you." Collins did not try to lead Falima again but just stood at her head murmuring reassurances and stroking behind her ears. He knew horses would go almost anywhere if they saw another horse safely make the journey ahead of them. A friend had once told him she trained colts to cross streams and puddles by having them shadow a staid old trail horse. "Ready, Marlys?" he finally said out loud, suddenly wishing he had chosen another name. It seemed to stick in his mouth, desperately out of place. It reminded him of how he and his elementary school friends had become so used to Michelangelo referring to a mutant ninja turtle, they giggled wildly when it came up on an art museum field trip.

One hand grasping the rope at the base of Falima's chin, the other clutching the cheekpiece, he urged her forward with him. He did not know how people encouraged horses in Barakhai; but, back home, the position gave him unprecedented control over an animal large enough to crush him. He remembered a favorite saying of an old girlfriend, "He who has the horse's head has the horse.'' It applied to leading horses, grooming and immunizing, as well as reining, but he could not help getting a *The Godfather*-like image of the amputated head resting in someone's bed.

With Collins close and urgent, Falima raised a foreleg high, then placed it on the drawbridge.

''Good girl,'' Collins encouraged. ''Good good girl.''

Falima took another step, the thunk of its touch sending a quiver through her. This time, she did not attempt to withdraw, but took another hesitant step onto the surface.

''Come on, honey. You can do it.'' Collins reverted to a pet name, which allowed him avoid the whole ''Marlys'' issue. He hoped Zylas and Ialin had called it right when they claimed Falima understood enough in horse form to get the gist of the plan. He kept imagining her becoming human surrounded by king's guards with no memory of how she got there and, in a wild blithering panic, giving them all away. Surely, they had talked to her before the change, while he slept. *Surely nothing.* So many of his friends' motives appeared bizarre or inscrutable, it seemed senseless to even speculate.

Collins continued to cluck encouragingly as Falima took more steps onto the drawbridge. Head bowed nearly to her knees, she studied the surface and her own hooves as she moved, her steps never growing confident. At least, she continued forward. In fact, her pace quickened as she clearly attempted to get past the portion of ground that felt and sounded unstable to a horse's ears.

When they came to the part of the drawbridge on the far side of the moat, Falima's demeanor returned to normal. She clopped through the opened double doors and into the gatehouse with little more than a glance.

The woman guard and one of the men from the other tower met them in the span. Doors shaped like cathedral windows opened onto the towers, while a heavy set of ironbound oak doors blocked further entry in the direction of the castle.

The man raised his right hand in greeting. ''I'm Mabix. Welcome to Opernes Castle, home of King Terrin and Queen Althea, high rulers of Barakhai.''

Zylas had prepared Collins with the names, though the albino had warned him to stay alert for changes. The royals did not discuss coups and ascensions with the regular folk as a rule, though the information eventually reached even the lowliest *outcaste.*

King Terrin and Queen Althea. King Terrin and Queen Althea. Collins worked to fix the titles in his mind, only then realizing he had completely forgotten the name of the man in front of him. For a moment, he teetered on the decision of whether to let it pass and fake it or ask for a repeat. Then, deciding it best to look the fool now rather than later, he pressed. ''Thank you, kind sir, but I'm afraid I didn't quite catch your name.''

''Mabix,'' he repeated without offense. ''This is Lyra.''

The female guard dipped ever so slightly to acknowledge the introduction. Though a motion of respect, it fell short of an actual curtsy which, Collins presumed, she reserved for royalty. ''Lyra,'' Collins repeated. ''Mabix.''

''Now,'' Mabix said, getting down to business. ''If we could just see your writ.''

Collins fought a grin. Other than a utility knife, the saddest bit of rations, and a ragged change of clothes, the presumably forged paper was the only thing his friends had given him.

''Or,'' Lyra added with just the barest hint of suspicion, ''did the bandits get that, too?''

''Over my dead body,'' Collins said, hoping it sounded as emphatic in Barakhain as English. He thrust a hand into his tunic and emerged with the crumpled paper covered with flowery scribbles. The spell that allowed him to speak fluently apparently did not extend to the written word. *With my luck, it's probably really gibberish.* A sudden thought rose. *Or worse, calls the king a pickle-nosed bastard.*

Mabix examined the paper, Lyra looking over his shoulder.

They both nodded. Now, Collins got a good look at their uniforms, the patterned white ending just below their breastbones. Joined by impressively straight stitching for a world without machines, the aqua material fell just past the knee. Mail showed at the collar and arms, while high boots of stiffened cloth covered their legs. They wore bowl-shaped metal helmets.

Once they had the writ, the two relaxed visibly, which left Collins wondering where Zylas had gotten it. Because his friends had initially rescued him in animal form and they switched naked, he had seen all their personal belongings in the saddlebags he found tied to Falima that first day. Vernon had packed them much fuller; but, if the mouse/man had stuck in such a thing, it meant they had known how he would infiltrate the castle ever since they left the cabin. He wondered why they had not discussed it with him sooner. *They also didn't let me know the gender of an elder who turned out to be a dragon until I saw her with my own eyes. Why does this surprise me?*

Lyra and Mabix pulled closed the massive doors through which their guests had entered. As they banged shut, a ratcheting sound echoed through the small enclosed room, the drawbridge lifting. Other than a bit of diffused sunlight filtering through cracks in the wooden construction, the room went dark. Falima danced, whinnying her discomfort. Collins patted her, whispering nonsense in a steady patter while Lyra and Mabix slid the bolt on the door behind them and pushed the panels open. Light rushed in, accompanied by the sweet odor of young plants and the mingled sounds of answering neighs, whines, barks, and human voices.

Falima squealed out another whinny, the shrill sound reverberating painfully in the still mostly enclosed area. She charged for the outside, and Collins let her go. Peering beyond her, he saw an emerald stretch of well-grazed grasses crisscrossed by pathways. Several horses, a few mules, and a goat placidly ate, though the nearest ones looked up as Falima joined them. She snorted, nostrils widened as if to suck in all the unfamiliar smells, then lowered her head to graze.

Collins glanced around as the guards ushered him into the outer courtyard. Now, he could see the towers that looked round from the outside had flat backs that turned them into semicircles. Behind the wall-wide crenels and merlons lay battlement walkways paced by guards in the same uniforms as his new companions. Small buildings lay pressed against the wall, their construction wooden except for the stone backings they borrowed from the wall itself. Shingles or thatch topped them. Directly ahead, Collins saw another double-towered gatehouse, larger than the one they had just exited. Another crenellated wall ringed the still distant castle.

Lyra rushed ahead to the second gatehouse. Mabix looked at Falima. "She can stay here if she wants."

Collins considered. He liked the idea of her only needing to escape one wall should he fail at his mission. "That's up to her," he said casually. "She's due to change shortly and should be quite capable of making the decision by herself." He removed the rope halter and placed it in the pack, debating whether or not to remove the whole thing and carry it himself. Not wishing to burden himself when Falima remained clearly untroubled by it, he left it in place.

"So what's the news from Epronville?"

"From—?" Collins stopped himself from saying "where?" "—Epronville?" He laughed to cover his mistake. "Never much happening there." He could have kicked himself. He felt trapped by the easiest, most casual and obvious question in the universe, one he had even anticipated. Larger concerns and the need for haste had made him forget the problem he had initially raised. Now, his ignorance undid him, leaving him unable to even fabricate a credible answer. He had little idea of the size of Barakhai, let alone its various towns and cities, could not guess how intimately they intertwined, and what might serve as news. In some cultures, information about who had married whom or which babies had survived the winter was welcome knowledge as far as a man could travel. "At least compared with here."

Uncertain whether his last comment had helped or only dug him deeper, he switched to a different tactic. "No matter what I say, Marlys will contradict me." Those were the first words since he arrived at the castle that rang surprisingly true. "I'm always wrong."

Mabix chuckled. "Sounds like you two are married."

"Marlys and me?" Collins was as struck by the next words that escaped his mouth as Mabix was amused by them. "What a horrible thought."

Now Mabix laughed openly. "Often that which a man protests the most will or should come to pass." He winked, and Collins was again struck by the similarity of that gesture to his own culture. "At least according to women."

Lyra returned, the gatehouse doors now open ahead. "What was that?"

Mabix shook his head. "Nothing you need to hear."

Lyra sighed, speaking in a tone that implied confidentiality, though Mabix could surely hear her. "Something between men, no doubt. I'm tired of that."

For the first time, it occurred to Collins that he ought to see as many female guards as male since, presumably, the horses gave birth to as many fillies as colts. He made a mental note to ask Falima about it later, though he managed to devise a possible answer from his own experience. Likely, the women spent more of their human time house- and child-keeping. Or, perhaps, the women did more of the routine guard chores that did not involve the possibility of direct combat. The less industrial and enlightened a society, in general, the less it could afford to emancipate its women without endangering its survival.

Lyra led them through the second gatehouse and into the courtyard that surrounded the castle. Here, he saw less grass, though a few horses did graze around the scattered buildings. Gardens took up most of the space, paths winding between them. A vast variety of vegetables flourished in crooked rows, and Collins saw none of the tended panoramas of flowers he expected from his visits to the arboretum. Each and every patch grew edibles of some type, from herbs to roots, fruit trees to vines. He did find some attractive blue flowers, but these grew in a planned line, obviously the source of some delectable seed. *Perhaps vilegro.* Collins remembered the name of the plant Falima had turned into a sweet treat called *gahiri*. Here, too, buildings cropped out from the wall, kennels, guardhouses, and stables in remarkable abundance.

All of that flashed across Collins' sight in the instants before his attention became riveted upon the castle. Like some massive university, it stood grandly, towering over its walls and gardens. Sun rays skipped across its surface, igniting glimmering lines of quartz and mica. The four square towers at the corners stood like sentinels, their tops crenellated with antlike figures of guards pacing atop them. A stone-cut stairway led into the open door.

Falima clomped through the gatehouse to pull up beside Collins. While he studied the structure, she grazed with an aloofness indicative of indifference.

Mabix spoke, "Magnificent, isn't it?"

Only then, sound returned to Collins' world, and he heard the background noises of giggling children, conversation, and animal sounds of a myriad types. In response, he only nodded.

Lyra drew up. "So, what's the news from Epronville?"

"Fine," Collins murmured, still staring.

Mabix laughed. "You'll get more from her when she switches, I'd warrant. This one seems due for some sleep." He jerked a thumb toward Collins, which finally seized his attention.

"Sleep's fine." Collins yawned broadly, remembering Zylas' advice. "But I'd rather some food. I switch soon, too, and I'd like to grab a bite of something substantial before I'm committed to grass."

Mabix and Lyra nodded vigorously. "I'm with you on that one," the woman muttered. He had clearly struck a chord.

"That's where the dogs have the advantage." Lyra headed toward one of the barracks. "Though I don't know many who'd admit it so freely."

Collins supported the confession for the purposes of creating camaraderie with those who believed themselves his peers. "Right now, I'm so hungry I could eat a . . ." He doubted the spell would translate as "horse," but he dared not take that chance. ". . . tree."

Mabix completed what was, apparently, a common saying, ". . . two shrubs, three beehives, and a garden."

"That, too," Collins added, to his companions' amusement. He found himself liking them and hoped his theft would not reflect badly on them or cost them their jobs.

The man inclined his head toward one of the buildings. Reminded of their purpose, he and Lyra started walking. Collins and Falima followed.

They stopped in front of one of the guardhouses, animals noting their passage with curious looks. Collins felt like he had entered a dim, creepy house where the eyes of pictures seemed to fix on anyone who passed. "Bring your pack," Mabix said. "I'll show you to your quarters." Without waiting for Collins to obey, he shoved open the door and entered. "Hope you two don't mind sharing."

Collins tried to sound matter-of-fact. "Not at all." He supposed it made sense to part-time animals that they house men and women in the same barracks, even the same rooms. He wondered how many accidental marriages and out-of-wedlock births this created in buildings at least half full of stallions. He undid all the clasps, clips, and ties with Lyra's assistance, shouldered the pack, and trotted after Mabix.

The door opened onto a common room strewn with clothes, bits of food, and half-finished games of chess and dice. Crude, mismatched furniture, mostly constructed from crates and barrels, interrupted the vast chaos. If not for the lanterns instead of overhead lights and the lack of a television, it could have passed for the recreation room of most men's dormitories. Smaller doors led off in several directions. Crossing the room, Mabix knocked on one of the doors before opening it.

Through the portal, Collins saw a square, windowless room the size of a large bathroom. Three rolled up pallets leaned in one corner, a pile of chamber pots in the other. A chair crafted from a quarter-cut barrel stood pushed against a wall. A cushion affixed to a circular piece of wood lay on the floor beside it, apparently the seat.

Mabix squeezed past Lyra and Collins in the doorway, picked up the cushion, and pointed into the seat. "You can store your gear here."

Where? Collins followed Mabix and examined the chair. He saw a hole where his backside would usually go, creating a good-sized hollow that ended with a thick wooden bottom. Clearly, it served as a neat storage area as well as a piece of furniture once the cushion was balanced on top of the opening. About to say something about the cleverness of its inventor, Collins held his tongue instead. For all he knew, everyone had these in their homes.

Mabix noticed Collins studying the arrangement. "Convenient, huh?"

"Very." Collins let a bit of his respect seep into his tone.

Lyra added, "Craftsman who came up with that design won himself a permanent place on the king's staff.

Mabix bobbed his head. "A *Random*, too. On the king's staff. Can you believe it?"

"Wow," Collins replied, holding back a storm of questions he could never ask his *Random* companions. He swung the pack to the floor, feeling trapped. He had to leave it so Falima would have clothes and access to the makeup, but he hated to risk losing it. Suddenly, he realized he had no reason to hide that piece of information. "You know, I think I'd better put it back on . . ." He caught himself about to say "Falima." ". . . on Marlys. She gets cold easily and likes to dress as soon as possible." He had originally planned to say she felt uncomfortable naked among strangers but liked what came out of his mouth better. *How do you like that? I can think on my feet.* A less wholesome thought followed, *Or am I just becoming a better liar?* Winning over Korfius and Vernon had certainly given him plenty of practice.

Collins looked at the pack, as if noticing it for the first time. "She's due to switch pretty soon." He wondered if he had just made a crucial blunder. As partners, they ought to know one another's habits well enough that he would never have removed the pack in the first place.

But, if Lyra or Mabix thought the same way, neither revealed it. They headed back outside without another word or anything Collins would consider knowing glances. Falima grazed placidly among a small group of horses and one mule. As he reattached the pack, Collins found himself wondering about the long-earred animal. In his world, they came from breeding a donkey with a horse and were always sterile. He wondered how that applied here and how it affected the creature's human form.

Stop it! Collins blamed nervousness for his thoughts taking off in a trained but unhelpful direction. *Focus!* Casually, he poked a hand into his pocket, seized his watch, and glanced surreptitiously at it around folds of fabric. It now read 5:50 p.m., only ten minutes before Falima's switch. He needed to draw the guards away from her so she could have the privacy necessary to affect her disguise. "Now, about that tree I plan to eat . . ."

Mabix laughed, taking the hint. "I'll walk you to the dining hall. It's getting on toward dinner anyway, so you'll have a chance to meet a good bunch of the guards and staff."

Lyra made a throwaway gesture, and Mabix nodded. "She needs to return to her post." He took Collins' elbow, steering him toward the castle as Lyra headed back toward the gatehouses. "I'll have to get back myself, as soon as I've got you settled in. Can you do all right on your own?"

Still stuck on the realization that he would share the dining hall with a crowd, Collins forced a nod. "I'll do fine." He hoped he spoke truth. He was hungry, but he would have to feign starvation. So long as he had his mouth full, he would not have to answer questions. He only hoped dinner would not consist of a plateful of bugs as large as puppies. His mind conjured images of enormous beetles, crisply browned, legs stretched upward with turkey caps on all six drumsticks.

Mabix stopped suddenly, halfway down the courtyard path to the castle. "Didn't you say your partner would switch soon?"

The query put Collins on his guard, though it seemed foolish to lie. "Yes. Yes, I did."

"Won't she want to join us for dinner?"

Collins thought it best to leave Falima alone, at least for the change. "No," he said, fighting down an edge of terror. "No, she . . . she doesn't like to eat right after. The combination of rich food piled on a bellyful of grass." He wrinkled his features. "Bothers her."

"Interesting," Mabix said with the air of one who has found himself in the same situation many times but never had a similar experience. "But maybe it's different for us daytime humans. That's never bothered me."

"Me either," Collins agreed. "But it bothers her."

Mabix accepted that explanation, and Collins hoped he would not have to make up many more. The more implausibilities he forced them to consider, the more suspicious they would likely become. Though he enjoyed having a reasonably kindred soul, he was just as happy that Mabix would have to leave. Spreading his stories farther apart might make them harder to penetrate.

Mabix led Collins up the castle stairs, muddy with shoe and boot tracks, to the open door. Voices wafted through, a disharmonious hum of myriad conversations. Suspended by chains, a wooden cross-hatching hung overhead like the sword of Damocles. Collins' new knowledge of languages allowed him to give it a name, a raised portcullis. He had seen them before, in every swashbuckling movie that required a castle. Always, the heroes, from the Three Musketeers to Robin Hood dived beneath the closing grate at the last possible second, while guards' swords rattled futilely on the portcullis behind them. The very object meant to trap them saved them instead.

The door opened onto a spiral staircase that wound clockwise upward and also went downward. Cold funneled from the lower areas where Collins knew the dungeons and storerooms lay. Mabix took him up, past one landing with a set of doors opening on either side. Collins knew the right one led to the kitchens, the left to workshops. The noises grew louder as they continued their ascent, and Mabix stopped at the next set of doors. He opened the right one, revealing a vast dining hall, its grandeur surpassing Zylas' description. At the far end of the room, a smaller table stood on a dais. At it sat ten people in splendid silks and satins, their robes trimmed with gold lacework or embroidery. The women wore nappy dresses and capes, the men fine tunics and sashes, doublets, and robes.

Three massive tables stretched between the door and the occupants of the dais, filled with people whose dress, demeanor, and appearance spanned a gamut that would once have seemed to Collins beyond possibility. Dogs of varying shapes and sizes wound freely around the diners or hovered beneath the tables. Tapestries and banners hung from every wall, their colors a rainbow mix of pattern and picture. Above them, cathedral-cut open windows revealed a balcony blocked by waist-high handrails. Men and women in matching aqua-and-white plaid looked down over the diners, clutching oddly shaped instruments and conferring with one another.

"Impressive, isn't it?"

Mabix's description jarred Collins from his daze. He made no apology for staring. He was supposed to be an awestruck bumpkin. "Wow." It finally occurred to him to evaluate the food he had trapped himself into eating with gusto. He could not see what occupied the gold and silver platters of the head table, but the regular folk scooped a gloppy substance, with hands and spoons, from what appeared to be stale slices of bread that served as plates. Servants wove between the tables, refilling goblets, and plopping down fresh bowls of stew for the guests to ladle onto their bread plates.

"That's King Terrin at the head table," Mabix said, gesturing toward the central figure, a burly man with wheaten ringlets and a full beard." In order, that's the constable, the pantler, an adviser, the butler, the queen's steward, the prince, the queen, the king again, a princess, another princess, the king's steward, another adviser, the children's steward, the ewerer, and one more adviser."

The list came too fast for Collins to follow, but that did not matter. He did not intend to remain here long enough to care who he had seen and met.

"Find a seat on one of the benches at any trestle table. Whoever's next to you can help you with the proper procedures."

Collins nodded. "Thanks." He suspected he could teach them a thing or two about manners. Unlike those at the head table, the commoners lacked forks. They all used spoons and fingers, even in the communal bowls holding the only course. They shared goblets as well. Though he had no intention of eating a bite of what he imagined was a worm stew drenched in spider guts, he did take a seat for the sake of appearances. He chose the place between a demure woman in a stained white apron and a thin man animatedly engaged in conversation with the guard on his other side.

Mabix stepped around to a cluster of uniformed guards sitting at the center table. He chatted with them briefly, then they turned toward Collins. Pinned by their stares, he froze, abruptly afraid; but Mabix's cheerful wave dispelled his tension almost as soon as it arose. *Of course, he would have to tell someone about Falima's and my arrival.*

A boy rushed in to place a slice of bread in front of Collins. Dark and stiff with blue-green mold along one edge of crust, it did nothing to stimulate his appetite. The same boy laid out a spoon beside it.

"Thank you," Collins said.

Blushing, the boy bowed, then hurried to assist another diner.

Mabix trotted from the room, back onto the staircase, then disappeared.

The musicians launched into an upbeat song, and the conversations died to a hum. Harp, lute, and fiddle braided into a sweet harmony filled with riffs and runs. Collins looked at the bread plate, then at the woman beside him. "Excuse me," he whispered. "Where would I find a rest room?"

Silently, the woman lifted a hand to point beyond the royal diners. Only then, Collins noticed a door in the far wall that surely led to one of the garderobes Zylas had described. She hissed back, "If you don't want to walk past the royals, there's another one in the library. Just go out the main door, across the landing, and through the cross door. The only other exit from the library is the garderobe."

"Thank you." Collins rose and headed back the way he had come. Once in the staircase, he crossed to the library door. He had his hand on the ring before he remembered his interest in the rest room was only diversionary. *What better time for exploring than when most of the staff and royals are gathered in the dining room?*

Quickly, Collins scurried up the stairs. He reached the next landing, heart pounding, and paused to regroup. A tall window overlooked the castle grounds, a ledge jutting from it. He perched on it, glancing down at the courtyards. Horses sprawled, bathing in the sunshine while others quietly grazed. A gardener pulled weeds, feeding them to a spotted goat as he worked. A pair of dogs frolicked with a young colt, barking at its heels. It charged them, as if to crush them beneath its hooves, then turned aside at the last moment, leaving the dogs to whirl and charge after it again. Collins tore his gaze from the scene to turn his attention inward. The doors on either side should open onto the servants' sleeping chambers, which meant he had one more floor till he came to the first warded area. He resumed his climb.

The next landing also held a window overlooking a slightly different view of the courtyards. A calico cat curled on the ledge, the resemblance to Collins' first pet uncanny. Like Fluffy, this cat had one black ear and one white, its body covered with blotches on a chalky background, tail and paws darkly tipped. The memory brought a smile to his lips. "Here kitty, kitty," he said softly. "Here girl." The scientist in him came out to wonder whether the same rules of genetics applied here. He knew cats carried color genes on their X-chromosomes and, at most, two different hues on each X. Since males only had one X and females two, and calicoes had three colors by definition, all calicoes were either female or the uncommon XXY, a usually sterile male mutation.

The cat lifted its head.

Collins approached gently, fingers extended. The cat sniffed curiously. He lowered his hand to its back, making a broad stroke. The cat arched, a purr rumbling from it. It jammed its head into his cupped hand.

Smiling, Collins stroked the entire length of the cat, enjoying the soft rush of fur beneath his palm. He missed having a cat terribly. Studies showed that petting an animal naturally lowered blood pressure and relieved stress. He could scarcely recall a time when he needed a natural tranquilizer more. He scratched around the animal's ears, ruffling its fur into a mane. Its purr deepened to a roar.

Only then did Collins realize what he was doing. *Oh, my God, I'm stroking a human woman!* He cursed his lack of caution. Caught up in his memory of Fluffy, he had completely forgotten that no creature here was what it seemed. He withdrew his hands, and the purr died immediately. The cat bounded down from its perch with a thud that made him cringe, then twined itself against and through his legs.

Collins back-stepped. "That's it for now, kitty. I've got work to do." Reaching for the door ring, he pushed it open. Every cat he had ever owned had to run through any newly opened door no matter where it led, but this one did not attempt to enter the royal bedchambers. Warded against *switchers*, it would not allow her entry. Seeing no movement inside, Collins headed in, pulling the door shut behind him. His heart rate quickened again, and any stress-easing that petting the cat might have achieved disappeared. His pulse pounded in his temples, and sweat slicked his back. He had just reached the point of no return. No logical explanation could cover him now.

Much smaller than the great dining hall, the room contained a curtained bed with a shelved frame, a chest, a stool, and a chandelier with a dozen white candles. A massive tapestry depicting a hunt covered most of one wall. Collins dredged up the description of the crystal: a smooth oblong rock the size of a peach with five, smooth edges of different sizes, milky blue in color. The room held few enough furnishings that it would not take long to search.

Collins walked first to the bed, suddenly struck by something that had gotten only his passing notice when he had glanced at it. *A hunting scene?* It seemed an impossible thing for a society that considered the killing of animals murder. He jerked his attention back to the tapestry. It was clearly old, a museum piece faded nearly beyond recognition. Washed to shades of gray, its figures blurred into the background. Yet Collins had managed to take away a solid impression, and he struggled now to find the details that had previously caught his eye. Men on horseback raised spears, while a pack of dogs harried some huge, indiscernible animal.

You don't have time for this, Collins reminded himself. Tearing his gaze from the tapestry, he opened one of the drawers. Stacks of neatly folded tunics in a variety of colors met his gaze. He felt under and between them for a hard lump, glad for its size. Anything smaller might require him to rifle the room, which would definitely cast suspicion. If possible, he wanted to get the stone without anyone noticing it, or him, missing.

Drawer by drawer, Collins checked through the king's clothing, intensely aware of every passing second. He had no more than an hour to search before he either had to furtively withdraw or find a hiding place and hope he had a chance to look again, perhaps at another meal. A better thought came to him. *While they're sleeping.* He shoved the last drawer shut and cast his gaze around the room again. It seemed worth losing a few minutes of trying to find the magical stone in order to locate a haven. The drawer-base meant no room beneath the bed, and its position flat against one corner gave him no space to squeeze beyond the curtains. Even if the chest did not surely contain something, it would prove a tight squeeze even for his skinny frame. Two other doors led out of the king's chamber.

Footsteps thundered on the staircase, growing louder. *They're coming.* Terror scattered Collins' wits, and he bolted for the far doors in a desperate scramble. Seizing one at random, he shoved it opened and hurled himself through. He skidded across a polished clay floor. His shoulder slammed into a low shelf. He sprang to his feet, braining himself on an overhanging lip. He bit off a scream, teeth sinking into his tongue. Dizziness washed over him in a blaze of black-and-gray spots. He caught a blurry glimpse of what he had hit, a wooden board atop a bench with a hole cut into the wood. *Bathroom.* He whirled to face four men with drawn swords.

Collins' skin seemed to turn to ice. His head throbbed, and he tasted blood. He retreated, raising his hands to indicate surrender. Wood pressed into the backs of his calves, and he stopped, forced into a sitting position on the bench. "I won't fight. Don't hurt me." His vision cleared enough to reveal faces familiar from the dining hall, including the goldenrod hair and beard of Barakhai's king.

Chapter 15

COLLINS froze, pressed against the garderobe, with three swords hovering in front of him. His mind raced. He braced himself for the rush of panic that had assailed him just before his near-hanging, but his thoughts remained strikingly clear. The world seemed to move in slow motion, while he mulled the situation. *If I go with them, they'll execute me. If I fight, they'll kill me.* There appeared no choice at all, but memory assisted him. Falima had claimed only the king's guards could use weapons, which meant, in most situations, they only had to raise them in a threatening manner. Since they had come through the door, these three had to be royalty, even less likely to possess true combat knowledge.

Based on this train of thought, Collins took a chance. Hands up, features displaying honest terror, he begged. "Please, don't hurt me."

The men edged closer. As they did, Collins dove beneath the raised swords. His shoulder crashed against the king's legs, staggering the Barakhain and sending pain screaming through Collins' arm.

"Are you all right?" The men instinctively went to the aid of their king.

Collins rolled to his feet, then made a crouched sprint back into the king's bedchamber.

Terrin bellowed. "Get him!"

Collins cleared the room in three running strides, then wrenched the stairwell door open and hurled himself through it. Only then he realized he had just tossed himself into a mass of armed palace guards. "Shit!"

"Get him!"

Collins flailed wildly, arms connecting with flesh in several directions. His vision filled with a chaotic forest of arms, legs, and swords. A fist slammed his cheek, and cold steel sliced his hip. Pain clipped through the site, and he howled, balance lost. He felt himself falling, control utterly beyond his grasp. He tumbled, stone steps slamming bruises across his back, his face, his limbs. He grabbed for support, fingers opening and closing like fish mouths, capturing nothing.

"The portcullis!" someone yelled, the sound a dull echo amid the shouts of the guards.

A clanking reverberation joined the other crisscrossing sounds in the tubular stairwell. Collins caught his fingers in cloth. He jerked to a stop, clinging desperately to this anchor, chest and belly splayed across several stairs. Then, the stabilizing object whipped suddenly upward, breaking his grip. Before Collins' dizzy mind could register that he had been clasped to someone's leg, it swung back. A heel struck him in the eye, stealing vision and sending bolts of white light flashing through his brain. He tumbled, fully out of control again.

Collins had so many wounds, it all numbed to a single overwhelming agony that encompassed his entire frame and made coherent thought impossible. He registered only the savage plunge and the rumble of voices dulled by a steady ringing. He forced both eyes opened. Ahead, he saw the falling portcullis, with barely a body length remaining between it and the floor. *I'm a Musketeer.* On all fours, he launched himself for the opening.

It disappeared as he arrived. His face found delicious freedom an instant before the heavy wooden portal slammed into his skull. Vision shattered, hearing crushed by buzzing, limbs too heavy to lift, he lay in place fighting a losing battle with unconsciousness. His neuroanatomy professor's words cycled through his mind: *The difference between causing a brain bruise and a deadly hemorrhage is incalculable. Guy goes out longer than a minute or two, it's a murder charge for hero. A murder charge for hero . . . a murder charge for hero . . .*

Hands seized Collins' britches and tunic, hauling him back to the landing. *Got to stay conscious.* The movement proved too much. He closed his eyes, and darkness descended upon him.

Collins awakened to a limbo that dissolved in a fierce rush of pain. His breath emerged in agonized grunts, and he dared not move for fear of worsening any of them. Tears dribbled from his eyes. His mind seemed to work, though hopelessly overwhelmed by a throbbing headache and distracted by his myriad other wounds. "Oh, God," he managed to huff out. "Oh, God."

Collins opened his eyes, but they refused to focus. He blinked several times, catching a blurry impression of metal bars, a stone floor, someone standing nearby. The presence of another human might mean imminent danger, but Collins found himself unable to care. At the moment, they could slowly dismember him and he would consider it a favor. The cold of the stone floor seeped through his clothes, offering some relief from the bruises on his chest, arms, legs, and abdomen. His lids became heavy, and he let them drift closed. Once he did, sleep overtook him again.

Collins did not know how long he drifted in and out of consciousness, but he knew he had awakened on several brief occasions. His dreams had seemed more surreal than usual, taking him from home to school to Barakhai in moments that defied logic or consistency. He thought he remembered someone sewing the gash in his hip, the pain flowing into the mass that had come to define his current existence. Now, when he opened his eyes, the world came into instant focus. Prone on the damp, stone floor, he felt stiff as well as physically anguished. Enclosed by three stone block walls and one barred gate, he saw no other cells. Shackles and collars hung from chains, apparently the usual method of separating, controlling, or punishing prisoners. Collins shivered, certain he could not tolerate that kind of treatment in his current condition. *As opposed to what? Hanging?*

Having visually explored his quarters, Collins glanced beyond them. Two guards sat in the space between his cell and the door to the stairwell, watching him. Both men, they wore matching uniforms that differed from the ones of the tower guards. They had mail but no helmets, and the white portion of their tunics carried no design. A slight blond with swarthy skin and dark brown eyes, the one on the left followed Collins' every motion. The other, a dark brunet kept his sword drawn and in his lap. Though he had no reason to know, Collins guessed them to be dog-guards. A station below, they likely would wear simpler uniforms.

"Hello," Collins tried.

The guards studied him blankly, without replying.

Collins attempted to move. He hurt in every part, but he bulled through the pain to gather his limbs beneath him. They all seemed to function, at least, and he did not believe he had broken anything. *A small miracle.* He ran his fingers over his hip, through the tear in his britches, and touched a line of knots that confirmed his waking realization. Someone had tended the sword cut, stitching it in whatever clumsy, dirty fashion they did those things here. If it did not fester, it would scar badly.

The irony raised a grimace. *So my executed corpse has a boo-boo.* He shook his head at his own stupidity. *Like it really matters.*

Only then did it occur to Collins to worry about Falima. He drew some solace from his solitude. Zylas' floor plan did not include two dungeons, so they should have brought her here if they'd captured her. *Unless they executed her.* He shoved that thought aside. *They'd have far more reason to execute me, and I'm still here.* He wished he could leave things at that, believing Falima safe and well; but reality intruded. He could imagine that treason might carry a stronger and swifter sentence even than murder. Or, as a trained warrior, she might have fought in a more directed and lethal manner than he had managed.

"Hello," Collins said again, not certain where to direct the conversation. He desperately wanted to know Falima's fate, but he did not want to place her into danger by mentioning her if the king and his guards had not yet made the connection between them.

The guards continued to study Collins in silence.

Collins eased himself into a sitting position, grimacing and grunting with every movement. Using the wall for back support, he regarded the guards with the same intensity as they did him.

The quiet stalemate continued for several minutes before a knock at the wooden door sent both guards leaping to attention. Wishing he could still move that fast, Collins remained in place.

The door winched open cautiously, and a helmeted head poked through it. "Jiviss?"

"Here, sir," the blond said with a salute from around the door.

The newcomer glanced at Collins. "Has he changed?"

"No, sir," Jiviss said.

Collins disagreed. He had awakened and even managed to sit.

"The king wants to see him. In the upper quarters."

Jiviss shrugged, hiding the motion behind the door.

"Shackles?" the brunet said, his voice unexpectedly hoarse.

Jiviss returned to his scrutiny of Collins. "I hardly think they're necessary. In fact, someone's going to have to carry him, I'd warrant."

The newcomer frowned. "He fights, I'll deliver his bloody pieces to the king myself."

Tired of being discussed in the third person, Collins promised, "I won't fight." Realizing he would say the exact same thing if he did plan to fight, he added. "I can't fight. Just breathing hurts." He sucked in a deep lungful of air, sending agony shooting through his ribs, and reassessed the possibility that he might have broken something.

"He's not going anywhere." Jiviss seemed convinced that Collins' anguish was no act. He added emphatically, "And he is, apparently, royalty."

That caught Collins by surprise, though he swiftly realized it should not have. They had captured him in an area magically prohibited to *switchers,* and he guessed they had kept him in the dungeon long enough to ascertain that he had no switch-form. Even though the king did not know him, what else could they assume?

The helmeted man's demeanor softened. "You're right, of course." He addressed Collins directly. "Sir, you need to come with me. The king wishes to speak with you. No one will harm you if you come freely." He stepped fully into the area, revealing the aqua-and-stretched-clover pattern against white that Collins had first come to associate with royal guards.

Using one of the hanging chains for support, Collins clambered to legs that felt like rubber. *I'm sure he does want to speak with me. I've got to be a real puzzle.* "I'll come freely." He realized he had not done anything terrible yet. The king might forgive a relative's unauthorized presence in his room, especially when he found nothing missing. Collins felt certain his encounter in the stairwell had hurt no one so much as himself. As long as nobody made the connection between him and the man who had cannibalized a rabbit/woman, he might bluff his way out of serious punishment. He only wished he had the knowledge to convincingly fake it and wondered how much of his ignorance he could blame on the head injury. *It's not over yet. I still have a chance.*

The horse-guard took a ring of iron keys and shoved one into the lock. It clicked, and he stepped back. "Come."

Collins limped toward the entrance. Every muscle felt strained or bruised, and he tried to find a gait that caused the least amount of pain. Finally, he reached the exit. The horse-guard moved aside, drawing the door with him, and Collins exited into the guards' area. He waited there for them to cue him.

The horse-guard opened the wooden door. The brunet went into the stairwell first, then the helmeted man gestured for Collins to follow. He did so, and the two men settled into place behind him.

Clinging to the wall and scattered torch brackets in lieu of absent handrails, Collins made slow progress up the seemingly endless flights of stairs. He appreciated that the clockwise spiral kept the bracing wall always at his stronger right hand, though he knew the masons had never had him in mind for their construction. Likely, it had more to do with defense. Invaders running up the steps would have their sword arms hampered while defenders coming down would gain the advantage.

At last, the procession stopped, and the brunet knocked on the door opposite the king's bedchamber. It opened immediately to reveal a woman close to Collins' age. He recognized her from the dais table in the dining hall, introduced as one of the king's advisers. She wore a blue velvet dress with colorful embroidery and lace trim that complemented a slender but curvaceous figure. A hammered gold chain around her neck dipped into her bodice. Dark blonde curls fell to just past her shoulders, and strikingly pale eyes made her high cheeks and full lips seem rosier. She was the most beautiful woman he had seen since his arrival in Barakhai, perhaps in his life.

"Bring him in," she said, her voice a lilting alto. "Then wait outside, please."

"I'll see myself in." Collins hobbled into the room, while the guards settled in behind him and closed the door. Two cathedral windows lit the room, tapered from the inside to the out so that by the time they opened, they had narrowed to slits. The lowest part of the windows began at twice his own height from the floor. A cloth-covered table in one corner held a candle in a silver holder, a pitcher, and two goblets. Three padded chairs took up most of the center of the room.

The woman gestured at the chairs, and Collins took one gratefully. "Would you like a drink?"

"Yes," Collins said without bothering to ask about the contents of the pitcher. He had consumed nothing for at least fifteen hours. Thus far, pain had kept his mind from his belly, but he hoped his internal organs would resume functioning soon.

The woman crossed the room to the pitcher and filled both goblets.

It occurred to Collins that they might have poisoned the drink, but only briefly. They had had plenty of time to kill him if they had chosen to do so. In a spy movie, it would contain truth serum, but he seriously doubted anyone in this world had the wherewithal to create sodium pentothal. "Thank you."

She carried over both goblets, handed one to Collins, and sat in the middle chair.

"Thank you," Collins repeated, sniffing the pinkish liquid. It smelled faintly of alcohol and more strongly of fruit. "What is it?"

"Watered wine. Or more aptly, wined water. You'll find it's a bit safer to drink than straight city water."

Collins stared. This woman did not talk like any Barakhain he had met before.

She set her goblet on the floor beside her chair, rummaged through a pocket in her dress, and pulled something out. "You look like you could use some of these, too.'' She opened her fist to reveal a flat metal pillbox with *Advil* emblazoned on the side.

Collins' eyes widened, and understanding struck like lightning. ''You're . . . you're . . . Carrie Quinton.''

''Yes.''

''Demarkietto's previous assistant.''

The woman smiled. ''How is ol' D-Mark anyway?''

The use of the professor's nickname dispelled all doubt. ''Oh, my God.'' Collins chugged down his drink, too thirsty to set it aside. ''Oh, my God. How . . . how . . .'' He meant to ask about her arrival and subsequent life, but he only managed to finish with, ''. . . are you?''

Quinton laughed. ''Well enough for a woman trapped in a godless, primitive, louse-infested world . . .''

''. . . that considers bugs a delicacy,'' Collins could not help adding.

''Actually, those aren't bad, once you get used to them. Aside from fish, milk, and eggs, they're the only source of protein.''

Collins grimaced. ''I think I'd stick with the fish, milk, and eggs, thank you very much.''

Quinton rattled the pill case. ''Go on. Take them. You look like you owe money to two guys named Guido.''

Collins imagined he had to look a fright, bruised from head to toe, coated in travel grime, scrawny even before he skipped a few meals. He accepted the case and flicked it open to reveal four enteric-coated tablets of the proper size and shape. They even had *Advil* clearly written across each one, which fully allayed his suspicions. He dumped three into his palm, put one back, then popped the two remaining into his mouth. Quinton refilled his goblet, and he drank them down with the full contents. His belly felt stretched, but the meager calories in the two drinks only aroused his hunger. ''Thanks.'' He thought back to something Quinton had said, ''Once I find what I came for, you're no longer trapped. We can go home.''

Quinton met the news with none of the excitement Collins had anticipated. "Is that what Zylas told you?"

Shocked by her knowledge, Collins stammered. "Wh–what?"

"Zylas. The white rat." Quinton studied his expression. "Or did he give you another alias?"

Quinton fumbled at the chain around her neck. "This is what he sent you after, isn't it?" She dangled an irregular peach-sized hunk of bluish-hued quartz from the necklace."

Collins could not find his tongue. "How could you . . . ? How did . . . ?" He licked his lips. "What . . . ?"

Quinton answered one of the unspoken questions. "I was working alone in the lab, and I followed a white rat here. Sound familiar?"

"Very," Collins admitted.

Quinton dropped the stone back down between her breasts, giving Collins a casual glance at well-shaped cleavage. "What did Zylas tell *you* it was for?"

"It?" Collins probed, averting his eyes too late.

"The stone."

"Oh." Collins turned cautious, bewildered by the situation. "He said it would get me home."

"It won't."

The abrupt cold pronouncement sank Collins' hopes and raised too many quandaries. "How . . . how do you know?"

Quinton smiled. "I'm still here, aren't I?"

"Yes, but," Collins started, then caught himself. He had suspected that his companions had withheld information, but he had trusted them enough to believe it nothing significant. Now, he knew they had lied outright. Zylas had claimed no one from Collins' world had come to Barakhai before him, yet he sat talking to evidence of that deceit. *Unless she's the one who's lying.* Lives might be at stake depending on what he revealed. He shoved aside rising irritation. It made no sense to get angry until he knew for certain who had betrayed him. "You're still here, indeed," Collins finished lamely.

Quinton crossed her legs. "Zylas told me he needed that stone to rescue innocent people from the king's brutal regime."

"He did?" Collins clamped his hands over his spinning head, the abrupt movement awakening a whole new round of pain. He tried to sift logic from a sea of bewilderment, to find the truth hidden amidst so many lies. He studied Quinton. "Can you prove you're who you claim to be?"

Carrie smiled. "He's good, isn't he, that rat." She reached into the folds of her dress and extracted a battered wallet. She tossed a handful of cards into Collins' lap.

Setting aside the goblet, Collins sifted through the pile. Among Visa, Hallmark Gold Crown, and PetCo P.A.L.S. cards, all in the name of Carrie A. Quinton, he found two with picture identification. A Missouri driver's license showed her with shorter hair and a crinkled, quizzical expression. The student photo ID held a more flattering picture of a smiling Carrie Quinton with permed hair and the familiar pale eyes. No doubt, this was the same woman. Collins gathered the cards and returned them.

"Convinced?"

Collins nodded.

"Bill Clinton was president when I left." Quinton stuffed the cards back into the wallet. "You'd have a new one now."

"George Bush," Collins said.

"Again?"

Collins opened his mouth to explain, but Quinton waved him off.

"Kidding. I know it's gotta be George W. And no surprise, there. They knew that years before the election, before I left. Not sure why we even bother to vote."

Collins wondered what Quinton would think if she knew about the legal and political wrangling that had resulted in that squeak-by victory, but decided not to broach the subject. They had more important things to discuss, matters of faith and survival.

Quinton continued to vocalize proofs. "Before Clinton was Bush, Reagan before him, and Jimmy Carter the smiling peanut guy was president when I was born. And you and I are the only ones in Barakhai who know the difference between a dominant and a recessive gene."

"All right." Collins made a gesture of surrender. "You're the real deal. Now tell me how you wound up here."

Quinton gathered her cards, replaced them, then shoved her wallet back into its pocket in the folds of her dress. "I told you. I followed a white rat. He gave me this." She withdrew a hunk of white quartz from another pocket and deposited it on the arm of her chair. "I assume you have one, too?"

Collins did not reply.

Quinton continued, "He convinced me to try to steal this." She inclined her head downward to indicate the crystal. "I got caught, found out the truth, joined the right side." She shrugged. "Been here since."

Collins gripped the sides of his chair, the implications sinking deeply into him. He ran a finger along the stone. "It's a translation stone?"

"The guards searched you but didn't find yours." Though not a question, it begged answering.

Collins thought fast. Just because Quinton came from his world and time did not mean he could trust her with information that might harm people who, though more alien, he had come to consider friends. She would never buy that he had learned the language so quickly, and she apparently did not know about Prinivere. Recalling Falima's early dilemma, he tried, "I . . . swallowed it."

Quinton reclaimed the stone. "You did?"

Seeing no reason to swear to a lie, Collins shrugged. "The guards didn't find it. Did they?"

Quinton studied the rock. "I just didn't know it could work that way."

"Try it," Collins suggested.

The woman's features remained pinched with doubt. "Doesn't it . . . well . . . eventually come out."

Worried they might start collecting and examining his excrement, Collins shrugged. "Mine hasn't. Maybe it got stuck, but it hasn't come out. At least, not yet." Needing to change the subject, he questioned. "So you're saying Zylas—?"

"Maybe I will try it." Gaze still fixed on the stone, Quinton did not seem to realize she had interrupted. "As soon as I'm with someone who can't understand every word I say without it." She smiled. "You don't know how long I've waited to talk to someone in English. I mean real English. And to hear the answer in good old English, too."

"Real English?" Collins laughed. His aunt and uncle had once visited Great Britain, returning with quaint stories of loos and lifts, windscreens and tellies. "I'm not sure anyone outside the United States would call what we speak '*real* English.' Not enough u's, for one thing. Slangy and sloppy for another."

Quinton smiled. "It's real enough for me." She slapped the stone down on the arm of her chair, deliberately not touching it. She stretched luxuriously, showing off a long, lithe, and very feminine figure. It seemed almost impossible that she and Falima came from the same gender and species, though, in a way, they did not. "So," she purred. "How is Zylas doing?"

Collins shrugged, too vigorously this time. The movement ached through his body. "He seemed fine, but I have nothing to compare it with."

"Too bad."

Collins' brows rose. "You don't like him, I take it."

"No," Quinton admitted, then clarified. "Oh, he's charming all right. Friendly, easy to get along with, seems like a real straight shooter, right?"

Collins recalled times when he thought the rat/man might

be hiding things from him; but, for the most part, he found the description accurate. "Yeah. Are you saying it's an act?"

"You betcha. And a damn good one."

"Why do you say that?"

Quinton met Collins' gaze with directness and sincerity. "Because he's a famous troublemaker, a rebel leader with plans to destroy the natural order and the kingdom."

"What?" Laughter jarred from Collins before he could think to stop it.

"It's not funny." Quinton's horrified expression gave Collins instant control.

"I'm sorry."

"He lured me here. He lured you here." Though it seemed impossible, Quinton's gaze became even more intense. "And I was not the first."

Now, Collins could not have laughed even had he wished to. "What?"

"Don't you remember?"

Collins shook his head carefully, though it still increased the ache. "Remember what?"

"The janitor. The one who disappeared about five years before I did."

Collins tried to recall. "The papers said he ran off with a young coed. Left a shrewish wife and three in-and-out-of-trouble teenagers to make a new, secret life."

Quinton's expression remained stony. "Want me to show you his body? And the coed's, too? Her name, by the way, was Amanda."

"Not . . ." Collins gulped. ". . . necessary."

"Before that was the kid who played that weird game, what's it called?"

Collins knew who Quinton meant. "*Dungeons and Dragons.*"

"Yeah, that's it. Got too wrapped up in the game and lost track of reality."

"Wound up in a mental institution, as I recall."

Quinton finished, "Rambling about ancient ruins, magic, and *people who transform into animals*."

"Oh . . . my God."

Quinton fell silent and pressed her hands between her knees, letting the whole scenario sink in.

"Oh, my God," Collins repeated. "Damn." His mind moved sluggishly. "So you're saying that my following Zylas was no accident?"

"Nor me." Quinton leaned forward. "He led us here on purpose."

Collins had to admit it seemed right. He remembered chasing the rat into the proper room, losing it several times, only to find it again by what seemed like impossible luck. "Why?"

"To get this." Quinton dangled and returned the blue crystal again.

"Why?" Collins repeated.

"I don't know." Quinton sighed. "No one here does, but it has to have something to do with the rebels' plan to overthrow the kingdom."

Collins slumped in his chair, his world crumbling around him. Nothing made sense. The people he had dared to trust, to whom he owed his very life, were frauds. *True, Zylas saved my life; but it was his fault I needed it saved in the first place.* Other past uncertainties clicked into place. *No wonder he shushed the others when they grumbled about my underwhelming gratitude. And why he didn't dare hold Joetha against me.*

Apparently noting his distress, Quinton softened her tone. "I'm sorry. They had me fooled, too."

"They?" Collins repeated, not wanting to believe Falima had had a hand in the deceit, although she surely must have.

"Zylas and his accomplices. Different ones than you would have met. We caught the snake and the chipmunk."

"And?"

"And what?"

Collins had to know, could not help substituting Falima,

Ialin, and Vernon for the snake and the chipmunk. ''What happened to them?''

Quinton hesitated. ''You can't expect traitors in a primitive society to be treated with any more leniency than in our own.''

Collins filled in the detail Quinton had implied but not voiced. ''They were killed.''

''Painlessly. And with decorum.''

Collins blinked. When he had faced execution, he had turned a dignified ceremony into a panic-stricken tussle. Decorum seemed insignificant when the end result was one's own death.

Quinton's voice seemed to come from a distance. ''Are you hungry?''

Barely noticing the abrupt change of topic, Collins nodded.

Quinton rose and crossed the room. She placed a hand on the door latch, then smiled without tripping it. Instead, she turned, walked back to her seat, and scooped up the translation stone. ''Oops.''

Collins lowered his head into his palms, thoughts a desperately unsortable swirl. He listened to Quinton's footsteps as she crossed the room again, heard the door winch open and a soft conversation ensue.

The panel clicked shut, and she returned. She wandered behind Collins, her delicate hands settling onto his shoulders. ''Where were we?'' she asked.

Collins spoke into his hands. ''Discussing execution.''

''Ah.'' Quinton kneaded the knotted, aching muscles of Collins' neck, and he winced. ''We'll come back to that. Am I hurting you?''

She was, but her massage also comforted, a grueling mixture of pleasure and pain. ''No,'' Collins lied, uncertain why. ''It feels good.'' In his most testosterone-driven, adolescent moments, he had imagined a woman this beautiful touching him, concerned for his pleasure. The reality of it seemed well worth the torment. ''You want to leave, right?''

''I did.''

For the moment, Collins pushed aside the change of heart that answer suggested. "Why didn't you?"

Quinton's hands smoothed the tension from Collins' coiled muscles. "Tried. Couldn't find my way back, even with the kingdom's help."

Collins twisted his head toward Quinton, wishing he had some bulk to the muscles she was working over. Most women claimed they did not like the bodybuilder look, but he had yet to meet one who preferred his bony carriage. Despite the distraction, he found a discrepancy that made her claim seem ludicrous. "The king knows exactly where that portal is. He's got a contingent of archers parked right in front of it."

"What?" Carrie's hands stilled. "That's ridiculous."

Collins swiveled halfway around in his chair. "Is it? I saw them. They shot at me. Tried to kill me."

"The king's archers?"

"Yes!"

"Dressed in white and blue-green uniforms?"

Collins considered, forcing his mind back to the scene. Everything had happened so quickly, and he had worried more for his life than anyone's clothing. "They . . . didn't have a set uniform. They just wore any—"

"Who told you those were the king's archers?"

Realization dawned. "Zylas."

"Who had reason to keep you in Barakhai?"

Collins slumped back into his seat. "He wouldn't—"

Quinton restarted her massage. "Don't you think that if the king knew the location of the portal, he would *want* you to leave, not stop you? Don't you think he would work to close it, to stem the flow of outsiders sent by the renegades?"

Things Collins had not closely considered before became suddenly vitally important: Zylas' and Falima's discussion before claiming they knew of no others from Collins' world, the surreptitious exchanges between his companions when he received Prinivere's spell, the many little things that did not quite add up and often left him wondering if he were "missing something." He remembered Falima's deceit, trying to make him believe her a *Regular* rather than a *Random*. "Does this have something to do with the *Regular/Random* thing?"

"Not exactly," Quinton said. As Collins became accustomed to her ministrations, he noticed the pain less and the enjoyment more. "Most of the renegades are *Randoms*, though I think it's only because they tend toward instability. More undesirables are *Randoms*, since no one tries to make them on purpose. Of course they tend to be more likely to have a criminal bent, to not like authority or government."

It seemed logical that the least satisfied would seek the most radical changes, but that did not justify the events of the last several days. Zylas had seduced Collins here, knowing that others he brought had died for a cause in which they held no interest, understanding, or stake. Thanks to the renegades, Collins had to live with the guilt of having not only murdered but eaten an innocent woman, with the hysterical memory of having nearly died on the gallows, and with the knowledge of having become a thief as well. Rage finally stirred. "What does he want that stone of yours for anyway?"

"We don't know." Carrie admitted. She ran a hand through Collins' hair, fussing the overlong, grimy strands into proper position. "We're waiting for the dragons to mature."

"Dragons." Collins perked up at the word. "But they told me dragons were extinct." Carrie's fingers in his hair sent a shiver of desire through him that reawakened the aches the *Advil* had relieved. *At least one part of me still works.* "Was that another lie?" Though he now intended to reveal some information about the renegades, his vow to Vernon still bound his conscience. He would not give up Prinivere without a compelling reason.

"Dragons are extinct," Quinton confirmed. "But the king confiscated two *Randoms* who transformed into dragons at coming-of-age. The law compels him to kill them, but he just couldn't bring himself to do it. He's hoping that, raised and handled properly, they won't harm anyone."

"Wow."

The pace of Quinton's speech quickened, revealing excitement. "They're young now, babies by dragon standards. I figure they're maturing about one human year for every twenty. It seems the people here grow according to their slowest maturing form, and dragons—" Apparently realizing she had taken over the conversation, Quinton laughed. "Sorry if I'm boring you. I find them absolutely fascinating."

"I'm a bio grad student, too," Collins reminded her, interest piqued. "Are they male or female?" Simple statistics suggested a fifty-fifty chance they would come up opposite genders.

"Both," Quinton blurted, then laughed and corrected. "One of each, that is, not hermaphrodites. I get to train and, eventually, breed them."

Collins stared. "The king wants *more* dragons?"

Quinton's hands dropped back to Collins' shoulders. "Not yet. But I'm working on him." She squealed. "Can you imagine? I'm thinking they're egg layers, but they're definitely warm-blooded; and I think I'm seeing rudimentary nipples. Probably the closest thing to dinosaurs we'll ever see, don't you think? Imagine what we could learn from them."

Quinton's excitement was contagious. Though intrigued, Collins found himself distracted by troubling thoughts. The people to whom he had believed he owed his very life had actually placed it into danger. Those he had trusted as friends had lied to and betrayed him, played him for a fool. He pictured Falima; her silky black mane and startlingly pale eyes no longer seemed so beautiful when he knew they housed a soul that had used him, that found him unworthy of truth or trust, that pretended to like him while manipulating him like a brainless puppet. Zylas apparently made a career out of deception. *A rat, indeed. I should have seen through it.* His blood warmed, grew hot, and seemed to boil in his veins. "I'm with you," he said evenly. "Breeding dragons, finding the portal, going home."

"Revealing the traitors?" Quinton added.

Collins squirmed. *I owe the bastard nothing.* "What do you want to know?"

Chapter 16

MOMENTS later, Benton Collins sat in a pillowed chair nearly as comfortable as his father's old La-Z-Boy in front of a table laden with food. King Terrin occupied a similar seat across from Collins, and Carrie Quinton held a place to his left and the king's right. A large slice of white bread slathered in honey took up most of Collins' plate, surrounded by an array of berries in colors that ranged from deep ebony to brilliant green with stripes of indigo. He had chosen his meal from the myriad of dishes at the table, and many of the ones he bypassed still called to him. The warm aroma of sweet spices mixed with mashed, orange roots reminded him of pumpkin pie, and he instinctively reserved that for dessert. Though he had never cared for spinach, the buttery aroma of the assorted greens beckoned, and a platter of cubed fish smothered in a spice that resembled curry lured him to try it next. The complete absence of anything insectlike thrilled him, clearly a dispensation extended by the king.

Hunger got the better of Collins' caution, and he found himself incapable of concentrating on protocol. He dove into the meal with gusto, glad his choice of bread made sorting out the crude utensils unnecessary. As he gradually went from famished to merely interested in the feast, he deferred to Quinton's manners and worried more over what the king might think of him. The man held the power of an entire world. He could promote with a word, execute with a gesture. Collins wished he had taken the time to grill Quinton on how to handle the situation. He knew next to nothing about royalty in general and less about Barakhain royalty in particular. A poorly chosen turn of phrase, an improper glance—anything might constitute a capital crime, Collins realized. Days ago, the simple act of filling his belly had condemned him to the gallows; and, then, he had not had the arrogant and arbitrary whims of a king to consider.

King Terrin seemed nearly as uncomfortable as Collins. He shifted in his chair and examined the food choices of his companions with hawklike intensity. Collins could not help noticing the lack of servants, guards, and food tasters, which he might have attributed to a genuine show of trust if not for the fact that they now sat in the room above the one he had shared with Quinton. *Switchers* could never make it through the door.

As Collins mopped up the last crumbs and filled his plate with all the delicacies he had missed, the king cleared his throat. "I understand your name is Ben."

Collins froze with the warm bowl of mashed, cinnamony roots clutched between his hands. "Yes, sir." *Sire,* he reminded himself, but it felt too weird to say aloud. He remembered the time he had gone for jury duty, equally stymied by the requisite, "Your Honor." He had grown up calling his parents' friends, and several of his teachers, by their first names. Titles implied a hierarchy that Americans prided themselves on never having to consider. All men and women, he had heard since birth, are created equal.

The king did not seem to notice the lapse of protocol. He looked at Quinton with darting brown eyes, as if begging her to assist him with the same propriety with which Collins struggled. He cleared his throat again and stroked the stiff amber curls of his beard with thoughtful motions. "And you come from the same place as Carrie?"

"Yes, sir," Collins said again, still incapable of forming his lips around "sire." That started to bother him. Since titles held little meaning in America, he thought he should be able to speak them as easily as any name. He wondered if it had to do with the same damnable honesty that kept him from saying "I love you" without long consideration and absolute certainty or singing the "dear" in Happy Birthday to a stranger. *Didn't keep me from lying to Korfius at all.* That reminded him of the boy, another innocent caught in Zylas' and Falima's game. He should make certain Korfius did not get punished for a forced and contrived association. He shoveled the mashed roots onto his plate, then replaced the dish, only then realizing the king had asked another question.

"I'm sorry." To demonstrate the sincerity of his apology, Collins forced out the proper title. "I'm really very sorry, Sire. I missed what you just asked."

Without a hint of offense, the king repeated, "Do you know how you got here?"

Now that he had heard the question, Collins needed it interpreted. "I'm not sure what you mean, Sire." The title came out easier the second time. "I walked here under my own power. I was following—" He glanced at Quinton, wondering just how much the king already knew. The guards had escorted him directly here, and he had waited less than ten minutes for Quinton and the king to arrive. If she had briefed him on their conversation, it had not taken long.

Quinton nodded encouragingly.

King Terrin finished the thought. "You were following a white rat."

"Yes," Collins admitted, his food forgotten for the moment. "I'm not the first, I understand."

The king bobbed his head as Quinton had done, blond curls pitching and raising. The movement released a wave of musk. "There were three before you, including Carrie. The first two came together and got killed breaking into the castle."

Terrin did not elaborate, and Collins found himself less curious about the details than he expected. He did note that the first visitor, the *D & D* player, apparently never even made it to the castle.

"Then Carrie came, and talking with her brought sense to the matter." The king leaned forward, as if to share something private. "That rat, that agitator . . ." His gaze became distant, and he shook his head with a suddenness that revealed intense emotion: anger or frustration. ". . . He's been a thorn in our side for years. Circumvents every law, fights order at every step, despoils every logical decree."

Collins bit his lip, struggling to see Zylas in this new light. Though enraged that the rat/man had tricked him, he could not help liking him. "Why?"

"Why?" the king repeated, straightening. "Why, indeed." This time, he consulted Quinton with his gaze.

Quinton responded with a flourishing wave. "Because it's the job of the royals to civilize a society of animals."

Literally, Collins realized and cringed. Though he had flirted briefly with idealistic anarchy, that phase had not lasted long. His politics had grown more centrist the older he got. And, while he still considered himself a democrat, no one would mistake him for an over-the-top liberal. He now accepted the necessity of leaders to maintain order and civility.

"And, sometimes, we have to make laws that place priority on safety over freedom."

It was the very definition of governing, creating laws that restricted the rights of individuals for the good of the community. "We have those, too," Collins said, not even trying to tack on the "sire." "I understand so far."

Quinton chewed and swallowed, her bites small and delicate. "For obvious reasons, enforced vegetarianism is essential."

Collins shuddered, once again reminded of his lapse in this regard. He covered with humor, spearing a piece of fish. "Sort of a lacto-ovo-ichthy vegetarianism."

Quinton smiled around her food. "Right."

Joy accompanied the realization that he had finally found someone to whom he did not have to explain a biology-based joke. He suspected the translation magic turned his description into "milk-egg-fish vegetable-eating" for the benefit of the king.

The king glanced between his guests. "Certain types of animals cannot control their appetites for meat."

"Carnivores," Collins said to Quinton.

"Some carnivores," Quinton corrected. "Cats and dogs, for example, have civilized to an omnivorous state. Like natural omnivores: foxes, bears . . ."

". . . people," Collins inserted.

Quinton nodded. ". . . they can be taught young to avoid meat. Scavengers, like vultures and hyenas, serve as a sort of cleanup crew and can get away with eating carrion, though most people find it as disgusting as we do. Herons, egrets, and 'gators eat fish. Lots of things can live off bugs. But certain animals . . ." She trailed off with a shrug.

Collins ate the piece of fish. Soft-textured, fresh, and lightly spiced, it tasted better than anything he remembered eating in a long time. "Like, say, lions? Wolves?"

"Exactly." Quinton shook back blonde tresses that shimmered like gold in the candlelight. "They got executed into oblivion long before His Majesty came to power." Speaking of the king apparently reminded her of his presence. She jerked her attention to him, and her cheeks turned rosy. "I'm sorry, Sire. I didn't mean to take over your explanation."

The king grinned gently, swallowing a mouthful. "Continue." He made a regal gesture. "You're doing marvelously."

"Anyway," Quinton continued awkwardly. "The only way

carnivores come up is through *Random* breedings. Quite rare, but their danger is significant. On average, they kill six times before they're caught, so the law calls for destroying them as soon as the switch-form manifests."

"At thirteen," Collins recalled.

"At thirteen," Quinton confirmed.

Collins considered the implications, features crinkling. "So they execute innocent kids to avoid future crimes?" He turned his attention to the king as he asked the question.

Terrin studied his hands in his lap, without meeting Collins' gaze.

Quinton rescued the king. "It's an unfortunate circumstance, a fully avoidable one. People understand the risk they take when they breed *Randomly*, and it's always a conscious choice made in human form. Animals cannot interbreed outside their species."

"I saw a mule in the courtyard."

Quinton smiled. "Always the scientist, aren't you?" She laughed, the sound light and bellish, very different from Marlys' rare twitters or Falima's uninhibited, horsy guffaws. "Me, too. Mules are considered *Regulars* since their switch-form is completely predictable when a donkey and a horse mate. They're also sterile, so there are no future offspring to consider."

Collins set aside his fork. "Wouldn't it be better to at least try to train these carnivores to eat bugs and fish?"

"Tried." Quinton rubbed the base of her fork. "Never succeeded."

Collins felt as if time had receded and he had returned to his argument with his father over the death penalty. "But what if one can do it? Shouldn't you at least wait until they commit a crime before irreversibly punishing them?"

"Let them kill someone else's child?" The king sounded anguished. "Six of them on average?"

"No," Collins said, still unable to reconcile the idea of confining someone, let alone inflicting the death penalty, simply because statistics said they would probably commit a crime. If the United States worked by the same rules, the jails would be overflowing with inner city black males, the ones destined to overcome poverty, prejudice, and cultural fetters lost along with those consumed by these conditions. The great ones, like Colin Powell, like Martin Luther King, would never have the chance to change the world for the better. "But . . . but . . . what about . . . ?"

Quinton tried to anticipate his question. "Ever see a tiger in a small zoo cage?"

Collins dropped the larger point to picture the striped beasts wandering in mindless circles. "Yes. They pace. But, if they could talk, I doubt they would say they prefer death."

"The ones of this world would disagree, according to the history books. A previous king tried imprisonment, and suicides resulted. Others begged for death rather than life in a cage."

Collins' doubt must have shown on his face, because Quinton turned defensive.

"Step out of the we-know-what's-best-for-everyone American persona for a moment. Dorothy, you're not in Kansas anymore."

Surprised by Quinton's sudden switch from empathetic listener to cut-the-crap critic, Collins forced himself to think in a different way. She had a definite point, one Falima had made much earlier. He had to stop judging Barakhai by twentieth century democratic standards.

Quinton's tone softened slightly. "You have to remember, we're talking about boring, nothing-to-do dungeons here. No phones, no gyms, no TV, and no conjugal visits."

"Why not?" Collins asked. At Quinton's "no one's that dumb" look, he clarified. "I mean why no conjugal visits?"

"No birth control, either," Quinton reminded. "Does Barakhai need more vicious carnivores to further crowd its dungeons?"

Collins had to insert. "But *Randoms* are random—"

''Not completely. There's a definite genetic component to what they become.'' Quinton spoke to her area of expertise. ''Not strictly Mendelian, I don't think, but—'' Apparently realizing Collins had exploited her own interests to throw her off track, Quinton returned abruptly to her point. ''How many ladybugs do you think it would take to fill up a full-grown lion, anyway? Hard enough supplying adequate protein for the innocent people. According to my studies, iron deficiency anemia is rampant here. I'm surprised they don't see more kwashiorkor, too.''

Collins went quiet, picturing large-eyed, African orphans with skeletal limbs and enormous bellies caused by the severe protein malnutrition she had mentioned. In fact, Quinton had several valid points.

''Our rich society gives us a lot of leeway these people just don't have. You notice a lot of small people here? Nutritional adequacy's a constant battle in an undeveloped society, and the kids can't just pop a Flintstone's with Iron.'' Quinton's blue eyes seemed to drag Collins' gaze deep inside of them. ''You can't coddle murderers when you can't properly feed the loyal and innocent. Kapish?''

''Kapish,'' Collins said in a small voice, turning his attention back to his meal. As he ate, he wondered how much of their exchange the king had understood and whether or not he found any of it offensive. Abruptly remembering what had brought them to this point in the conversation, Collins attempted to turn it back to his original question. ''What does all this have to do with Zylas anyway?''

Quinton and King Terrin traded glances, and the king took up the explanation again. ''He had a daughter.''

The rest seemed obvious. ''A carnivore?'' Collins guessed, chest tightening and food once more forgotten. His mind formed an image of the albino standing in stunned silence while guards hauled his little girl away to die, his face a white mask that defined abject, depthless sorrow. He remembered the earlier tears when Zylas mentioned not having a family.

''Yes,'' King Terrin said.

Collins could not help saying, ''Poor Zylas.''

The king pursed his lips, head falling. Quinton's jaw tensed, and she wrested the discourse from him again. ''I thought the same thing. At first. Then I discovered how many daughters and sons, mothers and fathers died because of his . . . his junta. His rabid schemes to destroy the Barakhain hierarchy, to ravage the kingdom and the royal family have resulted in so many deaths: guards, his own followers', innocent bystanders'.'' She tried to catch Collins' gaze; but, this time, he dodged her. ''Bystanders like Bill the janitor and Amanda the coed. Like me, almost. And you.''

Collins swallowed hard, head ringing. The information he had gained revealed so much he had never suspected, explained so many of his former companions' nudges and lapses. *Zylas, Falima, how could you do this to me?* He felt like a lost child.

The king's voice was soothing, fatherly. ''What happened to the horse, Ben?''

The horse? Collins was momentarily puzzled by the question, and then understanding hit. His nostrils flared, and his eyes widened. *He means Falima. They know! They know who I am. What I did.* ''The horse?'' he repeated, trying to hide his nervousness. Perhaps he had misunderstood.

''The one who saved you from the gallows,'' King Terrin said, without malice. ''The buckskin who goes by the name of Falima.''

''The gallows,'' Collins repeated, a tingle passing through his neck where the rope had once lain, and a shiver traversing his body. ''You. . .'' it emerged in a desperate squeak, ''. . . know?'' He added quickly, ''Sire?'' This did not seem like a moment to skimp on propriety.

''Of course we know,'' Quinton said. ''And unlike the renegades, we're not going to lie to you. Didn't you think Olton would let the king know about a murderer on the loose?''

''Olton?'' Collins did not know whether Quinton named the place or an informant. Though it did not matter, he focused on the detail to delay the moment when he discovered his fate. Whether they sent him back to that town or performed the execution here, he would end up just as dead. He wondered why they had not just left him to rot in his cell rather than bring him here to talk to Quinton and the king. Within a moment, he had the answer. *Because they plan to get as much information as possible from me first.* His manner grew guarded.

''Olton's the town that sentenced you,'' the king explained. ''We'd still like to know about the horse.''

Collins could not get past the matter of his future, or lack of one. ''Are you going to hang me?''

The king and Carrie Quinton jerked. Simultaneously, they said, ''What?''

Collins rose, scarcely daring to believe how calm they remained, how surprised they seemed that he might worry about his neck. ''Are you sending me back or performing my execution here?''

''Neither.'' The king's leonine head swung up to follow Collins' movement. ''As soon as Carrie and I figured out what you had to be, I pardoned you.''

Quinton added, ''Didn't you notice no one was chasing you anymore?''

''I . . .'' Collins started, sinking back into his chair. ''I thought we just eluded them.''

Quinton's wispy brows rose nearly to her hairline. ''Eluded human-smart hounds? Please.''

Collins could scarcely believe it. ''So I'm not going to be hung?''

''Hanged,'' Quinton corrected. ''The past tense of 'hang' when you're killing someone is hanged. Laundry is hung.''

How do you like that? Falima was right. ''Thanks. My grammar really is more important here than whether or not I'm flung off a platform so a heavy rope around my neck *chokes me to death!*''

Quinton's lips twitched at the corners. ''Sorry. Just one of those pet peeve things.'' She added, ''If you were actually going to get hanged, I wouldn't have said that.''

Collins grunted, still sarcastic. ''Of course not. That might have seemed . . . well . . . tacky.''

The smile became genuine. ''Just so you know, if they had to drag you there, you'd be *dragged*, not drug.''

With his life spared, Collins enjoyed the banter. ''But a load of laundry would be drug?''

''Dragged, too,'' Quinton said. ''It's always dragged. Drug is a noun or a verb, but the past tense of drug is drugged.''

''Not drag?''

''The doctor drag her prior to surgery.'' Quinton laughed. ''Nope, doesn't work.''

Though not a part of it, the king smiled broadly at their friendly exchange.

Growing remarkably comfortable, Collins had to wonder whether or not *he* had been drugged. ''Not that I'm complaining, Sire, but why did you pardon me? You didn't know me.''

''Ah, but I did.'' King Terrin turned his gaze to Quinton. ''Once we figured you for an *Otherworlder*, Carrie could innocently explain all your actions.''

Collins poked at his food, considering. ''I spoke a completely different language.'' He popped some mashed roots into his mouth, delighted by the flavor. He tasted cinnamon and allspice in a mixture halfway between sugared pumpkin and sweet potato.

''That was a big clue.'' Quinton pushed her plate aside. ''Also, that you made no attempt to hide your crime from the guards showed you had no idea you did anything wrong.''

King Terrin reached for the serving bowl of mashed roots.

"You killed and ate in human form. Murder rarely happens like that and cannibalism never."

Though he craved more of the root dish, Collins put his fork down. He schooled his features. "I want you to know I'm very very sorry about what I did. I've suffered a lot of recriminations, tears, and soul-searching to deal with it, and I still have moments of heart-wrenching regret. If I had known—"

The king raised his hand. "You would not have done it. I understand."

"Thank you, Sire," Collins said, this time without difficulty. If his original companions had forgiven him this easily, they could have spared him and themselves a lot of bickering and discomfort. "I don't have the words to express how much I appreciate your understanding."

The king ladled root-mash onto his plate. "You need say nothing more."

As it sounded as much a command as a suggestion, Collins obeyed.

The king sat straighter in his chair, steam from the root-mash twining into his beard. "You have a choice, Ben. You may stay here and become another adviser."

"A generous offer, Sire," Quinton inserted, and Collins wished he had had the chance to say that first.

"Or you may show us the way to the portal so that you and Carrie, if she wishes, may return to your home."

I'm going back. Excitement trembled through Collins. *I'm going home.* "Thank you, Sire," he said, not voicing his choice because his quick decision to leave might offend the king.

Quinton clutched the front of her dress. "So you know the way to the portal?"

"I—" Collins started, then stopped with nowhere to go from that point. "I . . . don't you . . . I mean . . ."

No one jumped in to help him.

"The way to the portal?"

Quinton's hands sank to her lap.

Collins shook his head to clear it. "Shouldn't be that hard to figure out. It's in a set of ruins on a hill not far from Olton. The guards caught me in a field close by. They should know."

The king and Quinton exchanged glances.

Quinton shook her head. "We sent guards to where you got caught. I remembered coming in through ruins, too; but the only ones they found that looked right took us nowhere."

Collins crinkled his eyes as the impossibility of the statement overtook him. "How can that be? How many ruins are there?"

"A lot." The king answered before Quinton could. "Centuries ago, the kingdom sat in that very area, sprawling for miles, with cities and towns at myriad locations. You can't go there without running into the ruins of something."

Collins' eyes slitted further. "Maybe if Carrie and I went with your guards, Sire. Taken place to place, surely we'd recognize—"

"Tried that," Quinton interrupted. "Amazing how similar a crumbling pile of stone and mortar can look to another crumbling pile of stone and mortar. Over hundreds of years, things get picked through until nothing of value remains for a landmark."

Collins shook his head, maintaining his confused expression. "But Zylas uses the portal again and again, so there must be some way to recognize it." He considered his next utterance, not wishing to offend. "Men do have . . . some advantage in the spatial relations realm."

Quinton adopted a deep, broken caveman speech. "Girls talk, men logic. Ugh." She pretended to scratch herself, apelike. "I got a 780 on my math SAT, I'll have you know. That's about an eyelash from a perfect 800."

Glad he had not resorted to the word "superior," Collins tried to make amends. "I'm not saying women are dumb, just that their brains are wired different from men's. Not worse," he added swiftly, "just different."

"Different*ly*," Quinton said.

"Differently." Collins accepted the correction without comment, especially since it served to make his point. "Look, women have that extra X chromosome that protects them from hemophilia, color blindness, and a whole host of other deadly diseases. They live longer. They've got an advantage when it comes to verbal and nonverbal communication. Men had to get something."

"Testosterone?" Quinton suggested.

Collins knew his only hope now lay in self-deprecatory humor. "I mean *besides* the drive to kill each another."

Quinton laughed, opening the way for Collins to finish.

"And it just happens to be a better handle on how one object relates to another."

"Which is why guys never ask directions."

"Exactly." Collins grinned. "To do so would be abdicating our maleness, our one claim to . . . to equality."

The king, who had quietly feasted on the roots while his guests argued the merits of gender, finally spoke. "I'm afraid I can't let you leave the castle, Ben. At least, not yet."

Collins' smile wilted. "I'm a prisoner?"

The king laid aside his fork. "Not at all. You're free to go anywhere within the fortifications. The guards will politely stop you from going farther."

Although Collins had no plans to go anywhere, the idea of a restriction bothered him. "If I'm not a prisoner, then why?"

King Terrin did not bother to consult Quinton this time. "We've been honest with you. Dangerously so. We can't risk you rejoining the renegades."

Collins weighed the king's words. The man had a point. He thought of Zylas, picturing the fair skin and soft waves of tangled, snowy hair beneath the ever present broad-brimmed hat. The pale blue eyes had always seemed so wise, so desperately earnest, a strange contrast to the inscrutable red beads he looked through in rat form. They had formed such a swift, strong friendship based on the mortal danger they had shared. Danger,

Collins now knew, contrived by the very man he had seen as a savior. He thought of Falima, unable to suppress a smile. That evening in Vernon's cabin when they had finally reached an understanding, that camaraderie could not have been feigned. *And Vernon*. Collins still had difficulty reconciling the enormous man to the tiny mouse he became. Vernon had mentioned that he remained in mouse form, and Zylas a rat, whenever he visited Collins' world, even if he passed his switch time. Collins wondered if that had something to do with a difference in the physical laws in effect in each world. *Thank goodness gravity, at least, works the same.*

Realizing his thoughts had rushed off on a tangent, Collins redirected them. He knew the king wanted him to give up as many of the renegades as he could. They already knew about Zylas and Falima, so he did not need to worry about betraying them. He doubted he had any information about those two that the king did not already know. Collins saw no reason not to surrender Ialin, too. The tiny man had treated him with persistent hostility despite the trials he and his friends had deliberately caused for Collins. The realization irritated him. *At least Zylas and Falima had the decency to acknowledge their debt to me.* Which brought him to Vernon. There, Collins found a real dilemma. The mouse/man clearly dedicated his life to assisting people of many types, often without explanation or reason. Daily, he put himself in danger to help others, and he apparently did it from innate kindness rather than any expectation of reward.

I thought Zylas was a good guy, too. Collins grimaced at the realization. For reasons he could not fully explain, he believed Vernon truly had no ulterior motives. And then there was Prinivere. He realized how important knowing about her would be to the king, yet he also liked her. His vow to Vernon, though a sham, ached inside him. He had promised to keep her existence a secret, and his word meant more to him than he realized. Though the ceremony of spitting and shaking had no real significance, the fact that Vernon believed it did brought it to a whole new level. And Korfius was completely innocent. These thoughts rushed through Collins' mind faster than he expected. "I need time to sort all of this out before I make an irreversible decision."

"Understood." The king seemed unperturbed by this response. "And until then, you must see why we need to keep you here."

Collins did understand. "Yes, Sire." Politeness seemed the best policy. "And I appreciate your hospitality." Though no one had threatened or even suggested it, Collins realized they held a trump card. If he refused to cooperate, they could reinstate his death sentence. He appreciated that they made it look like his choice, though, in the end, he truly had none. On the other hand, he saw advantages to leaguing with Barakhai's royalty. Quinton's presence, alive, well, and happy showed the king rewarded loyalty. He and the geneticist had spent time alone together. Even if the king had some way of listening in on their conversation, Quinton had shown that she could switch to English simply by setting aside the stone. Surely she would have warned him of any hidden agendas or cruelties of King Terrin or his staff.

Aside from holding him at sword point and in a cell, both understandable under the circumstances, they had, thus far, shown Collins nothing but kindness. They also seemed almost brutally honest in their dealings with him. In exchange for some information about people who had lured him into mortal danger and then accepted credit and trust for rescuing him from it, he would get a pardon, a way home, a beautiful companion to corroborate his story and maybe even, through a shared experience no one else could understand, a life partner. That he could pick and choose who he exposed and no one could know that he had done so proved the icing on the cake.

Collins needed time alone to think, and the king of Barakhai happily granted that request.

Chapter 17

BENTON Collins awakened to the scattered glaze of sunlight through the slit of his window. He sat up and stretched, regretting it immediately as a wave of suffering washed through him. His bruises and strains had stiffened during the night, but time and sleep had erased the sharp edges of pain. He lay in a bed of simple construction, just a wood frame and blanket-wrapped straw, but it far exceeded the one in Vernon's cottage. The cloth had warmed to his body through the night, and the idea of leaving the snuggly cocoon formed by his coverings seemed onerous. He glanced around the room. A chest of drawers filled most of one wall, full of clean clothing he looked forward to pulling over a body too long enmeshed in the same grimy tunic and britches. They had allowed him a bath before bed, a luxury more welcome even than painkillers or sleep. A table sat in the middle of the room, a basin of fresh water on its surface and a chair at its side.

A single pounded knock echoed suddenly through the chamber.

"Who is it?" Collins called.

He received no answer; but, shortly, another knock hammered against the door.

Guessing the wood was too thick to admit voices, Collins hopped from the bed, dressed only in a long, linen sleep shirt. He pulled the wooden panel open to reveal a guard who took one look at his garb and averted her eyes. "Sir, there's a woman who wishes to see you." She gestured lower on the spiral staircase.

Collins poked his head through the opening. A short, chunky woman stood there, glancing at and around him nervously. He did not recognize her and wondered what she wanted. "All right." She stood too far away to address directly, though she surely heard him. "Tell her I'm coming as soon as I dress."

The guard continued to avoid looking at him. "Very well, sir." She withdrew.

Collins closed the door and examined his sleep shirt. It fully covered him, and he guessed it made the guard uncomfortable only because of its purpose. It reminded him of the discomfort of barging in on a woman in her bra and panties, though the same woman in a bikini on the beach seemed perfectly decent. *All of which is ridiculously moot in a place where people see one another naked all the time.* He amended the thought, *Except the royals, of course, and I'm now considered one.* He rummaged through the drawers, pulling a crisp tunic, a thin long-sleeved shirt, and britches from piles of similar ones dyed different colors.

Collins threw off the sleep shirt and tossed it on the bed, smoothing the blankets into reasonable order. Since the bedroom was on the top floor, no maids could enter to clean it. He wondered if the king also made his own bed or whether lower level royalty or children served as menial labor in these "safe" areas of the castle. He pulled on the clean clothing, fitting the shirt under the tunic and tucking his watch neatly beneath the sleeve. Now that the king knew what he was, he saw no need to hide the device; but he had no intention of trying to explain it to every curious guard and servant who noticed it. He pulled on the boots the king had given him, made of soft cloth stiffened with wooden battens.

By the time Collins exited, the guard had left; and only the strange woman remained. He excused himself to use one of the garderobes. Returning, he joined her on the spiral staircase. She fidgeted as he approached, and her hands moved into various positions before finding a haven in the pockets of her dress. She wore her chestnut hair short, and sunlight struck highlights of blonde, black, and red through the strands. She had brown eyes so pale they looked almost yellow, and they dodged Collins' with uncomfortable caution. "My name is Lattie. Could we talk outside?"

Collins nodded, glad to move from the stuffy confines of the castle to fresh air and sunshine.

"I'm sorry I woke you." Lattie led the way down the stairs, past a pair of guards who stopped chattering and watched them go. "It is late morning, and I thought—."

Collins tried to make her feel at ease. "I was up. Just hadn't bothered to dress yet." It was essentially true. He had awakened before the knock. He did not press her for her business, though curiosity pounded at him. He had only just become a welcome member of the royal entourage that night, and it seemed impossible that people in the king's employ would already seek out his advice. *Of course, now is the best time. Once they have a taste of my uncanny wisdom, they'll all know to steer clear of it.*

After passing several more guards and servants, Lattie and Collins departed the castle, through the open portcullis. The sun beamed down, too warm for the long shirt he had chosen to hide his watch. The sweet odors of grass and pollen wafted to Collins' nose, a pleasant change from the stale smells of old food, mustiness, and mildew. Horses in a variety of conformations and colors grazed the grassland, while dogs wound among them. A group of children squealed and giggled as they threw balls as much at as to one another. Gardeners weeded, joined by goats and geese who carefully plucked around the healthy plants.

Lattie stopped walking, glancing around to assure no one stood close enough to overhear. "Before we go any further, I want to apologize."

Collins' shoulders lifted in a questioning shrug. "Apologize? For what?"

Lattie looked down. Collins followed her gaze to the wood and cloth sandals on her feet. "I–I'm the one who got you . . . hurt."

Collins let his gaze stray up her thick legs, over the bulges of belly and breasts, to her round baby face. "What do you mean?"

"I reported to King Terrin when you went in his room." Lattie shuffled her feet in the dirt. "I didn't know you. I worried . . . I mean . . . the king's own room."

"It's all right." Collins reassured, needing to know. "How did you see me?"

"You . . . you . . ." Lattie's gaze fell back to her footwear. "You . . . stroked me. It felt . . . it felt very nice."

Stroked her? Collins pursed his lips as his mistake became utterly clear. *The cat on the window ledge.* "It's all right," he repeated. "You had no loyalty to me, and I'm sure the king believes you did right."

Lattie sucked in a deep breath and let it out in a slow, relieved sigh. "Thank you for your forgiveness." Her attention remained on the ground, and she continued to shuffle. "I'm going to switch-form soon, and I wondered if you would . . . if you would . . ." She seemed incapable of finishing.

Collins smiled, believing he knew the rest. "You want me to pet you some more?"

"You must think me very forward."

"Not at all." Collins wondered what the cats in his world would say if they could talk. "Where I come from, once you choose to own a cat, your lap belongs to them."

Lattie finally met his gaze, her eyes moist with horror. "Own?" she repeated.

Oops. Collins laid blame the only place he dared. "Sorry, I'm new to your language. I meant, if you live with a cat, it gets your lap whenever you make one. Cat hair becomes an accessory and a condiment. When you're not petting them, they're rubbing against you, even if that means lying on your book, marching across the table, or standing in your plate."

Lattie's eyes fairly sparkled, and she asked not quite casually, "Where are you from?"

Collins laughed. "Too far for you to go, I'm afraid. I'm not even sure I'll ever get back there." Not wanting to explain, he returned to the original topic. "Actually, I find petting animals calming, so I'd enjoy it as much as you do."

"Really?" Innocent excitement tinged the word.

"Really," Collins replied, meaning it. He still had a lot of thinking to do, and experience told him he could do so in a calmer state and more clearly with a contented cat purring in his lap.

Lattie circled Collins with a sinuous grace, her earlier nervousness lost. "I know a place. A private place, in case some of the others don't understand. It's got catnip, too."

"Catnip. Hmmm." Collins did not know what to say, as he had no particular affinity for the stuff. In fact, he would not even recognize the growing plant; despite his science background, he had only a passing interest in botany.

Caution tainted Lattie's otherwise excited demeanor. Clearly, Falima had a point about the dubious propriety of petting Barakhain animals.

Collins raised his arm, allowing his sleeve to slide back just far enough to peek at his watch, which read 10:50 a.m. So far, everyone who switched did so on an exact hour, which seemed like an uncanny coincidence until he remembered he had reset his watch by Zylas' switch time. Presumably, Lattie would transform at 11:00, and he refused to take her into his lap until that happened. So far, he had remained faithful to Marlys, though he already planned to break up with her if he ever managed to see her again. Carrie Quinton's behavior suggested he might have a chance with her, and he had no intention of ruining that opportunity to appease a cat.

Lattie led Collins toward the inner gatehouse. Guards stood in the towers, looking over the outer courtyard. The doors were open, allowing free passage between the courtyards. A man led an oxcart through the passageway, the vigorous, young beast effortlessly hauling a load of hay. A sow slept in the pile, two piglets of varying sizes nosing around her. Lattie stepped aside to let them by, then gestured Collins through the gatehouse.

Collins paused, watching the cart creak and rattle toward the castle, not wanting anyone to think he was trying to escape. At Lattie's urging, he continued, looking up as they headed into the outer courtyard. The guards remained at their posts, giving him only a passing glance. He eased out a pent-up breath, realizing that the king must consider both courtyards available to the castle staff. More horses and dogs occupied the inner areas, along with guardhouses, stables, and kennels to house them; but they moved freely between the two areas.

Lattie continued walking, leading Collins along a path through the grasslands, past mixed herds of sheep, cows, and goats, to a shaded garden filled with a mixture of flowering plants and covered by a fringed cloth canopy built against one stone wall. Tall thistles stretched into makeshift walls on either side, blocking the garden from general view and making it appear as if it had no safe entrance. Bees buzzed by on their way to and from the flowers, and butterflies flitted in colorful circles through the air.

Lattie brushed through an area that looked impenetrable. Beginning to wonder if he had made a dangerous decision, Collins followed. Thorns glided from his sleeves, rattling against his heavier britches and tunic, then parted to reveal a simple garden. Unlike the tended patches of the inner courtyard, this one grew relatively wild. Flowers of countless hues intermingled patternlessly, and vines twisted through them to overflow from the low stone frames. In the center sat a clay bowl on a stand, looking very much like a birdbath, though the canopy did not admit rainwater. Beetles and bees hovered around it, and Collins caught a sweet, unfamiliar scent beneath the already clashing perfumes of the various flowers.

Collins turned to question his companion, only to find her gone. Soft fur tickled his ankles. He rolled his gaze downward to the plump calico he had discovered in the castle stairway window. The issue of the bowl's contents would have to wait until he met with Carrie Quinton again, since his current companion would remain an uncommunicative animal for at least the next twelve hours.

Collins wandered farther into the garden until he found a carved granite bench. He sat, leaning against the smooth back. Cold seeped through his britches but could not penetrate the double layer of his shirt and tunic. The cat leaped up beside him. Before he could even find the most comfortable position, she clambered delicately into his lap, curled into every contour, and purred.

Laughing, Collins stroked the multicolored fur, immediately drawn to memories of his childhood. In those days, his parents had made a handsome, seemingly happy couple. Fluffy had had her choice of laps, preferring Mom's but accepting his when she was not available. Though third choice, Dad enjoyed his time with the cat, often devoting his full attention to stroking the silky fur, examining the ears for ticks or lice, the body for scratches.

Collins forced his thoughts to his current situation. Essentially alone in a sweet-smelling garden, caressed by spring breezes, his wounds dulled to a tolerable ache, a refreshing sleep just behind him, he felt contented and clearheaded. During the night, his thoughts had shifted and resettled. He liked the king and the beautiful woman who shared so much in common with him: a student trapped in a world where magic usurped laws that had once seemed utterly obvious and infallible. People changed into animals, stones and spells allowed otherwise impossible communication, massive dragons not only existed but cast magic and flew. Pardoned from the gallows, he no longer felt the anxious rush to return home to Demarkietto's demands, his imminent breakup with Marlys, his parents' self-indulgence. He wondered if anyone even missed him yet, aside from the inconvenience of dirty rat cages and experiments lost to unintentional neglect.

Carrie Quinton filled his mind's eye. Beautiful, graceful, intelligent, she seemed the perfect woman . . . and way out of his league. Yet he dared to hope that their shared interests and experience might bring them together. Like the veterans of Vietnam, they had become part of a world that strangers would never understand, that would likely taint their lives for eternity. That alone would have to bring them together, if not as a couple, at least as lifelong friends. Her decision to touch him, her gentle kindness, gave him hope where once he would not even have dared to consider a relationship possible.

Necessarily, Collins' thoughts went to Zylas and his crew. The king's and Quinton's explanations brought so much that had once seemed fuzzy to brilliant clarity. A million tiny details that had eluded him or that he had tossed away as unimportant now worked their way to the fore. Clearly, Zylas had deliberately brought him to Barakhai. He remembered how the white rat had kept appearing just when he had lost hope of ever finding it. Zylas had led him directly to this world; and, he now knew, others before him. All the things Collins had gratefully accepted: Zylas and Falima saving his life, returning his watch and cell phone, feeding and clothing him, protecting him from taunts and disdain, had become a sham. Zylas owed him all of that and more. One simple discovery, that Zylas had deliberately lured him here, turned the whole relationship, the whole matter, on its ear.

Lattie rubbed against Collins' hand, purr insistent. He increased his attention, running both hands the full length of her silky body, dislodging fur to spin wildly through bars of sunlight. So many glances, so many stifled comments and other-language exchanges gained meaning. It now seemed clear that he would give up Zylas, Falima, and Ialin to the king; but other things still needed consideration. He believed Terrin would understand Korfius' decision to join them, given that it mostly hinged on loyalty to the royal line, to which he believed Collins belonged. Though Vernon likely had some understanding of the scheme, Collins liked him and hated the thought of getting him into trouble. As to Prinivere, he needed to understand more about why dragons had become extinct. Given the greatness of her age and the withering of her magic, she seemed harmless without the enhancing stone. Perhaps he could negotiate for her life as well.

The thistles to Collins' left rattled. He glanced toward them, hands stilling on the cat.

Lattie butted his hand.

The plants quivered again, the movement too broad for wind. A yip wafted to him.

The cat froze, attention now on the sound as well.

Suddenly, a dog burst through the foliage. Ears swung down beside an ebony head, followed by a long-legged black body. It launched itself at Collins.

Lattie's body swelled to twice its normal size, and she yowled a warning. Her claws sank into Collins' leg.

"Ow!" Collins sprang to his feet, dumping the cat. She scrabbled wildly, raking gouges into his already bruised thighs. The dog hurled itself into Collins' emptied lap, all legs and tongue. The cat raced into the gardens. The dog flew after her, tearing up plants and flinging dirt with every bound.

Collins charged after the animals, trying to stop them. "Hey!" he yelled. "Down, dog! Get down!" He watched helplessly as Lattie scrambled up a canopy post, the dog yapping at her heels.

"No! Bad dog!" Collins lunged for the dog's neck, but it bounced out of reach, still barking at the cat.

Lattie made it to the top, but the give of the canopy turned her motions into an awkward stagger and roll. The dog pranced around the stake for several moments, keeping just beyond Collins' reach. Then the cat lost her footing, tumbling to the center of the canopy where she thrashed desperately. The dog continued leaping and barking at the overhead lump in the fabric of the canopy. Lattie yowled in terror. Abruptly, the dog raced from the garden.

For a moment, Collins breathed a sigh of relief. Then, realizing he could not rescue Lattie from beneath the canopy and that the dog might know another way to get to her, he sprinted after the dog. Thistles jabbed his legs, ripping his right sleeve, and vines snagged his ankles. He fell on his face, rolling from the brush to the freedom of the grassy courtyard. He saw the dog running toward the stone stairway leading to the parapet. The nearest guards paced several yards away and clearly had not noticed the dog.

Collins struggled to his feet, every injury reawakened by the fall. Despite the pain, he managed a frantic sprint. The dog scrambled up the stairway. Collins reached the bottom as the animal gained the platform, then turned sharply toward the canopy. The dog's plan became clear. The canopy lay almost flush with the wall, and the dog could easily leap from the parapets to the entangled cat. Gravity would pull both struggling animals to the center where they might tear and bite each other to serious injury or death. Or the cloth could tear, spilling both animals to the hard ground. Collins quickened his pace, thundering up the stone stairs as fast as his screaming muscles would carry him.

"Hey!" someone shouted from the ground. A horse whinnied wildly. "Hey, you can't—"

Collins was not listening. He reached the parapets and turned sharply left, toward the garden and the dog, who had slowed to a lope.

"Stop," Collins yelled, trying not to look down. "No! Bad dog!"

To his relief, the dog whirled toward him.

"Bad dog!" Collins shouted again. "Leave that cat alone. Come here."

The dog obeyed, soaring toward Collins at a perilous gallop. Collins tensed to brace himself; but, at that moment, something sharp smacked into his left cheek. Thrown off-balance, he took a step to regain it. His foot came down on a soft object that screeched, then disappeared from beneath his boot. Collins staggered backward, the world spinning dizzily beneath him. The dog hurled itself into his arms, throwing him and itself out over the parapets.

Air slammed Collins, slinging his scream back into his face. He flailed wildly, panic overwhelming thought. He saw the moat rushing up to meet him, the dog twisting in midair. Then, he slammed into something much harder than water, incapacitating pain arching through his gut, agony spiking through him and overwhelming logical thought. He felt the world moving beneath him and grabbed on to keep from falling into black oblivion. His fingers winched around rope, holding him in place, and water splashed his face. A high-pitched voice sounded in one ear, over a disharmonious chorus of ringing, "Hold on, and you'll be all right. I promise."

Dazed and disoriented, Collins did as the voice told him. It reminded him of his tonsillectomy, awakening from anesthesia memoryless and suffering inexplicable pain. Then he had yelled for his mother, worsening the anguish in his throat, and he had cried for a long time afterward. "The cat," he croaked out.

"She's fine." The voice stayed with Collins, vaguely familiar, soothing, and the only thing he had on which to ground his reason. "You're fine. Lie still, and don't try to talk."

Collins closed his eyes, still clinging to the rope, and let his body go limp. He concentrated on tactile sensations, the steady movement and velvety surface beneath him. He tried to put the whole thing together. *I was in an accident. A fall. They're taking me to surgery.* Memory trickled back into his mind, and it did not fit the scenario at all. *Anesthesia dreams,* he reassured himself, but it did not ring true. He opened his eyes. The ground scrolled out beneath him: sticks, stones, grass, and dirt. He lay slumped across something hard, his legs dangling and his hands wound beneath smoothly braided ropes. *This is no hospital; I'm outside.* That discovery led to more. He smelled damp air and the distinct odor of horse. Shouts massed behind him, and birdsong wafted from in front. Finally, it all came properly into sync. *I'm lying across Falima, and she's carrying me away from the castle.*

Once Collins found the truth, it all seemed ridiculously obvious. Dyed as black as the horse, Korfius ran alongside them, and the voice in his ear could only belong to Zylas. Ialin had deliberately flown into his face, he had stepped on Zylas, and Korfius had completed the task by knocking them both from the parapets. The audacity of the plan floored him back to speechlessness. *We could have been killed.* He dared not move for fear of rolling beneath Falima's flying hooves. He knew they could crack open his head like a melon, and he could not take any chances. If he attempted escape, he might be worth more to them dead than alive.

The trailing shouts grew distant, then disappeared. Unable to fight for the moment, pain shocking through his body with every stride, he surrendered to the unconsciousness he had fought moments earlier. Blessed darkness gradually overtook him.

Benton Collins awakened with clear thoughts and a near-total lack of pain. Both of these realizations surprised him. Moving only his eyes, he glanced around an irregular, dimly lit cavern that smelled densely of musk. It reminded him of driving down a highway after a previous motorist had run over a skunk. Though a bit unpleasant, it compared favorably with the time he and some friends went hiking and one of the black-and-white striped animals ambled from the foliage. Before anyone could stop him, Collins' dog had leaped for the creature. So close, the resulting odor had burned Collins' eyes and throat. One of his companions had vomited, and the dog ran yelping to the car, tail wedged between its hind legs.

Zylas the man appeared from one of Collins' blind spots, circling to his head. The albino crouched, pale eyes studying Collins, hair falling in a milky curtain across his left cheek, features tensely sober. "Feel better?"

Much, Collins admitted grudgingly, but only to himself. "What did you do to me?"

Zylas blinked, but otherwise remained still. "Rescued you?" Clearly, the rat/man did not know whether or not he answered the correct question.

Collins had meant what had Zylas done to take away his pain, but he saw no reason not to continue the conversation from Zylas' response. "Rescued me?" He pushed up on one elbow. "Rescued me from going home? Or from a life of castle luxury?"

Zylas attempted humor. "Both?"

It was exactly the sort of thing Collins would have tried, but this time he saw nothing funny about it. "You tricked me to Barakhai. You lied to me. You put me in dangerous situations, then pretended to rescue me." He glared. "Why am I even talking to you?"

Zylas swallowed, still answering Collins' rhetorical questions. "To find out why I did those things to you?"

Though somewhat flippant, the response satisfied Collins. "All right, I'll bite. Why did you do those things to me?"

"Do you really want to know?"

Rage warmed Collins' blood. He wanted to tell Zylas to go to hell, to leave him alone and get out of his life; but curiosity would not allow it. He did have to know. "I deserve an explanation." He added bitterly, "But why should I believe anything you say?"

Zylas' shoulders slumped, and his head fell. "I'm sorry."

Collins gave no quarter. "Sorry I caught you? Or sorry you did it?"

"Sorry . . . I involved you in this." Zylas carried the expression Collins' mother wore when he disappointed her with his behavior. It never failed to make him feel guilty.

Now, Collins shook off the snap reaction. He had every right to wallow in spite and anger. "So you admit you lied to me."

Zylas sighed. "Let's say misled. I don't think I ever actually lied." Wrinkles creased his forehead. "So you're saying the king wasn't going to execute you?"

"Would I have been strolling freely around in the outer courtyard if he was?"

"That did seem odd," Zylas conceded. "Made things a lot easier for us to . . . to . . . "

"Kidnap me?" Collins suggested.

"But I thought—"

Collins did not wait for the rest. "You thought wrong."

"The others—"

This time, Collins let Zylas finish, but he did not. Instead, he went off on a different tack.

"Ben, the king wanted you to think you had some freedom. Had you tried to escape—"

"—the guards would have stopped me," Collins finished. "I know. He told me that."

"Once the king got the information he wanted from you, he would have executed you."

"I don't believe that."

"It's true."

Collins had proof. "He didn't execute Carrie Quinton."

Zylas went utterly still.

Collins sat, raising his brows in expectation.

A genuine grin broke out on Zylas' face. "Carriequinton is alive?" He did not wait for confirmation, but leaped to his feet and ran from the cave shouting, "Carriequinton is alive! Carriequinton! She's alive!"

Collins shifted to a cross-legged position, uncertain what to make of the whole situation. Out of his company, it had seemed so easy to surrender Zylas and his friends to the king. Now that they had come together again, the idea seemed heinous. Traitor or not, Zylas was still a human being. He did not deserve to die.

Zylas returned shortly with a slight woman in tow. Beyond her, Collins saw movement. Several others hovered in the tunnel behind them. Curious, he looked the other way. Another exit across from the first stretched into a blackness that contained several shifting shadows.

"Is Carriequinton . . . all right?" Zylas asked carefully.

"She's an adviser to the king. And she seems happy."

The woman spoke next. Small and mousy, she sported black hair and fair skin. Dark eyes looked out from small sockets. "Are you certain it was Carriequinton?"

"Trust me," Collins said, reveling in the irony.

The woman nodded.

Zylas resumed his crouched position in front of Collins, while the woman sat down beside him. "You requested explanation. I will give it to you."

Collins refused to let Zylas off the hook. "How do I know you're not just telling more lies?"

Zylas pursed his lips in consideration, then brightened. "I swear to God, with sugar on top, that I will tell you only the truth from this moment forth." He spat on his right palm and offered it to Collins.

The absurdity of the moment melted away most of Collins' malice. *Caught by my* own *lie.* Rolling his eyes, he spat on his hand and exchanged a shake before wiping it on his britches. *In my effort to pacify Vernon, I invented a new way to spread diseases in this godforsaken, Lysol-lacking world.* "Talk."

Zylas cleared his throat and sank to his behind. He studied the rocky ceiling, as if deciding where to start. The onlookers shifted, their whispers barely reaching him, uninterpretable. "Over the years, the royals have taken a stronger and stronger hand in the coming-of-age of *Randoms*."

Collins nodded to indicate that he knew. "King Terrin said he had to in order to separate out those creatures likely to murder others."

"That was, ostensibly, the original reason for doing so."

"Ostensibly?" Collins remembered having trouble with the idea of executing people who mutated to carnivores simply because they might harm someone. He recalled something more personal. "He said he had to execute your daughter."

Zylas' eyes watered, but he managed to suppress actual tears. "Trinya." His voice cracked, betraying the withheld weeping.

Collins continued, speech slowing as he watched the effect of his words on Zylas. "He said that's why . . . you . . . cause him . . . so much trouble." From the corner of his eye, he could see the woman cringing. She placed a hand on Zylas' shoulder.

Zylas could not hold back the tears any longer; they glided down his cheeks, pale dewdrops on a background of snow. "I was trouble long before . . . that."

Collins said nothing more, allowing Zylas to regain his composure.

The mousy woman stroked the fine, white hair and looked anxiously at Collins through beadlike eyes.

Zylas swallowed hard, wiping his eyes with the back of one white, long-fingered hand. " . . . before . . . he murdered Trinya and Erinal."

Collins shook his head. "Erinal?"

"His wife," the woman explained before Zylas could. "They were—"

"Seera . . ." Zylas warned.

She talked over him, "—childhood friends—"

"Seera," Zylas repeated, apparently her name.

"—and obviously deeply in love. I never saw two—"

Zylas' verbal prompting did not stop her, but his dark glare did. "Ben has more important matters to worry about than my relationship with my dead wife."

At the moment, Collins did not agree. The dead wife might have much to do with a situation he was continuing to sort through, hoping to fully understand. "What happened to her?"

Seera's face went as chalky as Zylas', and she placed a hand over her mouth. She left the explanation to Zylas, who rose and paced, clearly distressed. "She wouldn't let go." He dropped his head, hair flopping into ivory disarray. "She wouldn't . . . let . . . go."

"Of Trinya," Seera explained softly.

"The king's guards couldn't . . . couldn't . . ." Zylas remained in place, clearly waiting for Seera to finish his sentence this time.

Seera complied. "They couldn't pry the two apart."

Zylas finished in a rush of hissing breath. "So they tried to cut off Erinal's . . . her hands. But they couldn't get all the way in one—" He dropped to his knees, sobbing, and Seera rubbed his upper back. "Screaming. There was blood and—"

Collins grimaced, trying not to picture the scene. But he could not banish the image of a young woman pleading desperately, grasping for her terrified child with hands dangling from half-severed wrists. "Oh, my God."

"If only I was—"

Now it was Seera's turn to caution, "Don't. You couldn't be any closer than you were. You were a hunted outlaw. They would have executed you on the spot."

"But maybe Erinal and Trinya—"

"They would still be dead. And you, too. Then where would the rest of us be?"

"They wouldn't let me staunch the bleeding." Zylas was weeping uncontrollably now. "Why wouldn't they let me staunch the bleeding?"

Even Collins could answer that. "Because they wanted you dead more than they cared whether or not she lived." Zylas' grief ached through Collins. He felt helpless as a statue while his usually unflappable friend dissolved in front of him. The anger and bitterness vanished, replaced by a pure rush of sympathy so intense it left him speechless.

For several moments, they all remained quiet, drenched in a grief too intense to bear. Even the onlookers grew respectfully hushed and still.

Finally, Zylas spoke. "We should have known not to make a child, both of us distant descendants of Prinivere."

"Prinivere?" Collins blinked making a connection that seemed obvious but might prove absurd in this otherworld, where even the basic principles of science did not always apply. "Are you saying Trinya's switch-form was . . ."

"A dragon," Seera said, barely above a whisper.

A chill spiraled through Collins. "A dragon? Is that . . . common?"

Zylas looked up. "As far as any of us know, she was the only *Random* ever to become one."

"If Carrie told the truth," Collins pondered aloud, "then there are at least two." He met Zylas' bleary gaze. "Zylas, your daughter might still be alive."

Chapter 18

The conversation that followed left both men with unexpected hope. Collins came to understand that his companions had brought him from the castle to an area where dogs could not track him. Like the flowering tree where the group had hidden just before Korfius found them, the skunk odor that pervaded the quarters of Barakhai's *downcaste* garbage workers should hide their scent from second tier guardsmen.

After a meal and a bath, Collins felt more open to explanations. Alone in a straw-cushioned cavern with Zylas, he listened to the rat/man with an open mind. "You see, the less you knew, the safer you, we, and a pack of innocents remained."

"Maybe." It was a point Collins did not know if he could ever accept. "It might be the scientist in me, but I like to work with as much information as possible. The less my ignorance, the more I can figure out what to do to keep myself, you, and these innocents safe."

Zylas laced his fingers, dodging Collins' gaze. "I understand that now." He finally met the probing dark eyes. "But, at first, you didn't want to know that much."

"You mean when I thought I was going right home?"

"I guess so."

"But you knew I wasn't going right home. You should have told me that, too."

"I didn't know what the best thing was." Zylas threw up his hands. "It was supposed to be simple. Bring you here. Have you get the stone. Get you home."

Collins sat up straight, holding Zylas' attention now that he had finally seized it. "But you knew it wasn't that easy from the start. You brought others before me. Others who went mad. Others who *died.*"

Zylas closed his eyes and nodded sadly. "But you were different. I chose you much more carefully."

The words startled Collins. "You did?"

Zylas' lids parted to reveal the familiar, pallid eyes. "I watched you for a long time. Made a well-researched, long-studied decision. Surprised?"

"Very," Collins admitted. "Why me?"

"None of us wanted more deaths, and you are our last hope."

"I was your last hope?" Collins forced himself to blink, still stunned. "How so? My world has about five billion people at last count. You could always grab another."

"No. You *are* our last hope." Zylas thrust his hand into a pocket, emerging with the translation stone. "Our last of these, my very own, this one a unique treasure because it allows communication even in animal form. I was supposed to give it to you, but I just couldn't let it go. I won't put Prinivere through that spell she cast on you again for any reason. She nearly died, and she's not getting any younger. She's still weakened from it."

The details did not fit. Collins tried to clear his head, to force order to the last vestiges of chaos. "Why didn't the people of Falima's town guess what I was, given that I wasn't the first?"

"To them you were."

"Oh?"

"You were the first to leave the ruins before I could switch to man form and explain."

"Why didn't you just talk to me as a rat? You had the stone."

"What do you think drove our first visitor mad?" Zylas blinked with slow deliberateness. "And what was your hurry to go tearing off into the unknown, anyway?"

Collins felt foolish. "I was hungry. Very very hungry."

"I left you food."

Collins ran a hand through dark brown hair that seemed to have grown an inch since his arrival, and it felt wonderfully clean. "I–I didn't see any food."

"You didn't look."

Collins felt a warm flush of defensiveness. "You should have put it in plain sight."

"If I made it too obvious, you would have worried you had stolen it from someone else. Or that someone had laid it out for you, poisoned."

Collins doubted either of those possibilities. "I was too hungry to worry about things like that." He thought it far more likely he would have passed up the stems, roots, and insects as some science experiment rather than food. *Given how well-read I am, it took me stunningly long to realize I had entered another world.* "And how do you know what I would have worried about anyway?"

Zylas shrugged. "As you pointed out, I made mistakes in the past. But I want you to know this. You were the first one to leave the ruins prematurely and the only one who killed. The others kept searching for the way back home." The corners of his lips twitched, but he did not smile. "And I thought your need to find these might keep you there long enough.'' He drew Collins' glasses from another pocket.

Collins gasped, snatching the offering from Zylas' hand and planting them on his face. Instantly, the cavern leaped to bold relief. He had forgotten how sharp every crag could look. Each blade of straw became singular and distinct, its colors a gradual blend of yellow, white, and gold. He saw lines in Zylas' face he had never noticed before. ''Thank you, you horrid little thief.''

Zylas grinned to show he took no offense. ''You're welcome, you big ugly murderer.''

Though faced with a harsh joke, Collins forced a chuckle. He resisted the urge for a crueler one, though Zylas had given him the ammunition by opening his life's story. He did not want to discourage the albino rat/man from sticking with even the most difficult truths.

''You weren't supposed to kill anyone, and you weren't supposed to get arrested.''

Collins nodded, realizing a grimmer truth. At that point, Zylas could have abandoned him for another champion as they had not yet met or spoken. Collins could not have given away any information anyway, since he would have been executed before he found a way to communicate. ''How did you ever manage to get Falima in position?''

Zylas waved a dismissive hand, as if to proclaim the whole thing no bother. ''We'd been working on her for years, carefully trying to sway her to our side. You can see the advantage to having a horse-guard as a spy.''

''Yes.'' Collins wondered how much convincing it had taken to push her that final step knowing that it would involve turning herself into a wanted fugitive to help a man she considered a murderer and a cannibal. *No wonder she acted so hostile toward me.* He could understand why they had chosen Falima, a *Random* considered a lesser being than the other guards, at least according to her. He had to know, ''You took a huge and *unnecessary* risk saving me.''

"Unnecessary?" Zylas' brows rose with incredulity. "I had led you here. I couldn't just let you die."

It was not literal truth. Zylas could have let him die simply by doing nothing, though Collins knew he meant his morality would not have allowed it. "Ialin would disagree."

Zylas did not deny it. "As did Falima at one time. She came around. He will, too." From a pocket, he pulled out the folded, broad-brimmed hat he usually wore to shield his easily burned face and eyes from the sun. "Though I would spend my life for my cause, I don't expect others to do so." Anticipating some comment about those who came before Collins, he added swiftly, "usually. Besides, I had chosen you too carefully. We needed you." All humor left his features. "We still do."

Zylas looked so earnest, so pleading, Collins found it impossible to meet his gaze. He might have to refuse him. "What's so special about me?"

"You're smart and resourceful. You're willing to sacrifice for others, and you really do understand how they feel."

"Well." Collins felt his face grow hot, embarrassed by the praise he had elicited. "I try to be a good person."

"You are," Zylas said. "I knew it from watching you. Dogs obey all horse-guards and superiors, but they like people of good character."

Collins wondered if Korfius' loyalty sprang more from believing him royal, but he had to admit the boy seemed to have a deep affinity for him.

"And Prinivere supports you. That's the highest praise I know."

"Thank you," Collins said, though the previous lies left him wondering whether Zylas' tribute stemmed more from desire and need than truth. "So tell me. What, exactly, does the stone do?"

"What did the king tell you?"

Collins blinked. "Will that change what *you* tell me?"

"No," Zylas said firmly. "I just wonder . . ."

"He doesn't know."

Zylas grinned broadly. "Good."

"Nor do I," Collins reminded.

"Yes, you do." Zylas dipped his head with clear sincerity, wadding the hat in his hands. "It enhances magic, pure and simple. It would, hopefully, give our Prinivere enough power to help us. Maybe even enough to reverse this curse."

"Curse?"

Zylas stared, as if he found Collins' question the most absurd one ever uttered. "This whole spending half our lives as animals thing. You know."

Collins physically jerked backward. "You can . . . fix that?"

"Don't know yet. Prinivere needs to have the stone in hand—or should I say in claw—to analyze it."

"Wow."

"Yeah," Zylas agreed. "Now do you understand why we want it?"

"Yes," Collins said, though he shook his head. "But why don't you want the king to know? Stopping the switching helps everyone. Doesn't it?"

Zylas threw the question back to Collins. "Does it?"

Collins folded his legs and leaned against the cavern wall, considering. He wondered if his bland perspective made him miss something obvious to those whose lives cycled from human to animal on a daily basis. He supposed someone with perfect overlap might find some advantages over those who fully lost half or more of their rational time to becoming some lumbering, half-witted creature. *People like Zylas.* Collins shook his head. The very one he thought might have the least reason to change was the same one who daily risked his life for it. "All right, I give. Who would want to keep the curse going?"

"Don't you think there might be substantial power to remaining human full-time while those around you mark time for half of their existence? Hard to contemplate insurrection when you're awake and thinking a third of the day or less."

Collins suspected many of his fellow students managed to function on less. "Unless you have near-perfect overlap."

Zylas' hands stilled on the hat. "Now you know why I'm a wanted outlaw."

Collins returned to the point. "So you think the royals wouldn't want the curse removed?"

Zylas heaved a deep sigh. "I think it's time you heard the whole story." He rose to his feet. "From one who was there."

There? Uncertain, Collins followed Zylas with his gaze. Before he could question further, Zylas disappeared through the entryway.

Collins rose also, though he did not attempt to follow. The musky odor had become familiar; it filled his nose and mouth like a persistent aftertaste. He took a few steps in the direction Zylas had gone, turned on his heel and started back the way he had come. The world seemed to have turned upside down, spun around three times, then whirled completely around again. He did not know for certain who to trust anymore. His sympathies intuitively went toward Zylas, though he could not guess whether this stemmed from truly believing the albino in the right or just because he had gotten to know the man first and better than the other side. It reminded him of the movie *Butch Cassidy and the Sundance Kid*, where he could not help rooting for the criminals mostly because the story got told from their point of view. Only one thing seemed absolutely certain. He needed to get home to a world where science made sense and the studies that had taken all of his adult life and money had purpose. At the moment, he would consider selling his soul for a Big Mac, large fries, and a cup of fountain root beer.

Zylas returned shortly with a familiar old woman in tow. Prinivere seemed dangerously frail in human form, her skin a mass of paper thin wrinkles, her eyes deeply recessed, her hair thick but nearly transparent in color. She wore a light, shapeless gown that hung to her knees. She looked older than the last time Collins had seen her, only days ago.

Collins nodded and smiled in greeting. ''Good afternoon, my lady.''

Prinivere returned a feeble smile. ''Forgive my appearance—'' she started.

''You look lovely,'' Collins found himself saying, the words seeming foolish and yet, to his surprise, oddly true. Survival and great age had an almost inexplicable beauty all its own.

''She wore herself down healing—''

Prinivere interrupted Zylas. ''No reason to talk about that, my dear.''

Collins did not need the last word to realize what had happened. She had tended his wounds, which explained why he no longer suffered the pain of his falls. ''Thank you, Lady Prinivere. I feel very well now, but you shouldn't exhaust yourself for my bumps and bruises.''

Prinivere smiled, the wrinkles piling up at the edges of her lips. ''Healing magic is not expensive.'' She did not give him the opportunity for a reply. They could argue the point all day and still remain at an impasse. ''But I've come to tell you a story.''

Collins lowered himself to the ground in front of Prinivere. He still had many questions and hoped the story would handle most of them. ''Please.''

With Zylas' hovering assistance, Prinivere also sank to the straw. The rat/man took a space beside her.

Without further preamble, Prinivere began. ''A long, *long* time ago, when I was young, our world was much different. Humans and dragons had waged a war since long before my birth. It was not the type of war with many battles. Simply, the dragons raided the flocks of men when food grew scarce or they became too old and slow to catch the wilder creatures. And the humans found slaying a dragon a means to prove their courage or rescue their animals. More often than not, however, those clashes resulted in the death of the man.''

Collins nodded, recalling how terrifying even a feeble, elderly female dragon had seemed, though he had known at the time she would not harm him.

"They had spears and swords to pit against our claws and teeth, armor to thwart our spikes and tails. But they had no way to counteract our magic."

Collins' mind conjured images of brave knights riding off to slay dragons, only to return as charred heaps of bone in the satchel of some bypasser. Feeling he should say something, Collins inserted, "You'd think the humans would sacrifice a few sheep and goats to keep the peace."

Zylas shivered, but Prinivere only bobbed her head knowingly. "Yes, you would think so. For you realize what our friend, here, could not. These animals were animals through and through. The humans themselves regularly ate their herds and flocks as well as harvested their eggs, milk, and wool."

"It sounds very much like the olden days of my own world," Collins said. "Except, of course, for the dragons." He savored a situation where, for the first time, he seemed more in tune than his companion. Suddenly, he had found an explanation for the antique hunt scene tapestry in the king's bedroom.

Prinivere continued, "There were fewer people then, and they all lived within and around a single city, ruled by a kind and intelligent king named Larashian Elrados. He made peace with the dragons. Men could no longer hunt us for sport, and the city would welcome our visits. In return, they donated a portion of their crops, hunts, and animals to the oldest and youngest of us. Favors became as common as conflicts once were. It was not unknown for a dragon to carry someone on his back or to heal an injured man. And the people would help us with thorns and burrs, with flotsam caught beneath our scales, and they educated us about the ways of their civilization. To seal the accord, the dragons presented the king with a powerful talisman, a stone that could amplify magic. Though the humans could not use its power, did not even understand it, the king recognized that it had momentous significance to the dragons and accepted it with great honor and ceremony.''

Prinivere fell silent, and her gaze rolled toward the ceiling. Zylas placed a comforting arm around the frail and sagging shoulders. Collins waited in patient silence for her to continue.

''The peace and friendship lasted throughout Larashian's long and just rule and into his grandson's. Telemar, too, seemed kind and competent. So, when he requested a closer bond between our families, it seemed reasonable to consider the request. Not all of our kind believed it wise, but our elders finally agreed to allow a dragon to take human form with magic for the purposes of breeding with the king's eldest daughter.'' Prinivere heaved a sigh filled with ancient pain.

''Why?'' Collins found himself saying without thinking. Prinivere had explained the reasons, but they did not seem substantial enough. Kingdoms in his world had sealed accords with royal marriages and even exchanges of children; but he could not see any good coming of sexually comingling intelligent species.

''Why indeed.'' Prinivere's voice emerged in a puff of hoarse breath. ''With centuries of hindsight, I believe the king wanted to implant magic into his own line. We had tried to teach them, but people lack something in their life substance that we naturally have.''

''Or the reverse.''

Wholly jarred from her story, Prinivere stared. ''What?''

Under the full and intense scrutiny of both of his companions, Collins suddenly wished he had kept his thoughts to himself. Now did not seem the time for an extensive discussion of inheritance. Few enough species could interbreed, and all of those had common ancestors. Chimps shared about ninety-nine percent of their genetics with humans, yet that last one percent created so many differences. It seemed impossible to imagine that dragons and humans could cross-fertilize. *Magic*, he reminded himself. *Magic*. Still feeling the stares, he explained as simply as possible. "Perhaps humans have something dragons don't, something nature uses to protect them from using magic." Worried his words might sound supremacist, he added, "Because we can't handle it or something." Uncertain whether he had dug himself out or deeper, Collins changed the subject. "Why did the dragons want to do it?"

Prinivere ran with the question, to Collins' relief. "The dragons argued several reasons: that an important ally wanted it, that it would bring our peoples closer, that it would force all humans to see us less as animals. And one must not discount simple curiosity. They made sure the king understood the risks to his daughter. She was more than willing, especially once she saw the handsome, charming, mannered man our Ardinithil became. He stayed that way only long enough to get the job done, however, though she made it clear she would have liked to marry him."

"Dragons don't marry?" Collins guessed.

"We don't call it marriage." Prinivere's green eyes swiveled downward to meet Collins' directly. "But we do pair for life." She closed her eyes in a long blink. "We did pair for life. When more than one of us lived."

Three. Collins opened his mouth but glanced at Zylas before speaking. The rat/man shook his head ever so slightly and mouthed something Collins could not comprehend. He guessed Zylas had not yet discussed the two young dragons in the king's care and had some reason to keep him from doing so as well. It seemed unfair to withhold such important information from Prinivere, but he also knew Zylas always had his ancient ancestor's best interests in mind. When the right time came, he would tell her.

Apparently oblivious, Prinivere returned to her story. "Anyway, Ardinithil could have married her—human lives span so short a time, he would have become free to pair again still in his youth. But he had no wish to return to human form, as she surely would have wanted, so he refused. The king accepted this without obvious malice, and life continued much as it had. Until . . ." Prinivere trailed off, clearly lost in bygone thought.

Collins looked at Zylas, who shrugged. They sat for several moments in silence. Then Collins ventured a guess, "Until the birth of the baby?"

As if awaiting this cue, Prinivere returned to life. "Yes. The babies."

"Twins?"

"Dragons nearly always have twins. Occasionally singles. Rarely triplets. I once heard of four babies together, but only once in several centuries."

Collins suddenly realized why this particular interbreeding bothered him so much. "Dragons have live-born young?"

Prinivere turned her head toward Zylas, as if to get more coherent explanation for Collins' strange questions. Clearly equally befuddled, Zylas raised one shoulder and tipped his head without speaking. Prinivere returned her attention to Collins. "Don't all animals have live-born young?"

"Birds lay eggs. Reptiles and amphibians, too." Collins did not know if Barakhains categorized the same way as scientists, so he elaborated, "Turtles, alligators, snakes, frogs." He carefully omitted fish, not wishing to compare her to a creature they did not consider animal. *Dinosaurs.*

Zylas cringed, but Prinivere did not seem offended. "Dragons do not lay eggs."

"Oh." That now being obvious, Collins found nothing more to say.

"We have live-born young." Prinivere used Collins' terminology. "Like humans." She rubbed her hands together, looking uncomfortable. "Usually." She folded her fingers in an interlocking pattern, biting her lower lip. "We monitored the pregnancy with magic, and it soon became clear that the babies, both boys, were unhealthy. Usually, we magically ended such pregnancies for the good of our society, the well-being of the parents; but the king refused to give up on them. His attachment to the hybrids became an obsession that changed him, and he would allow nothing and no one to harm them.

"To our leaders' surprise, the unborn gradually regained their health; but they did so at the expense of their mother. Dragons don't sicken as humans do, which is why our healing magic works only on injuries, not diseases. It took our monitors many months to realize what was actually happening. Months passed, during which they sensed the babies growing stronger and the mother weaker before they realized the inherent and unconscious evil of the process. The babies were drawing their strength, the very essence of their survival, by draining the life of their mother."

Unlike most Barakhain science, this made sense to Collins. Undernourished women often became ill during pregnancy while the fetus, essentially a parasite, sucked whatever nutrients it could from her blood. No one he knew would consider that process evil, however.

"Once the dragons realized what was happening, they begged the king to allow them to destroy the unborn babies. He refused. For the last few months of the pregnancy, our requests went from wishful to desperate to angry. The king would hear none of it. Even risking the life of his daughter did not seem too high a price for the twins whose very existence he had facilitated for reasons that had once seemed pure and noble. We explained, we pleaded, we ranted, all to no avail. The twins whom nature intended to be stillborn thrived while the mother meant to lose them lost her own life instead."

Prinivere clambered to her feet, and Zylas scrambled to remain at her side. Her eyes seemed to blaze through their ever-present glaze of water. "The boys looked odd for humans, their eyes too long with oval-shaped pupils, their noses like . . ." She placed a hand over her own slitty nostrils. ". . . well, rather like mine in human form. They had points to their ears, and their skin looked more like dry scales. The humans feared them, and the dragons hated them. But their grandfather adored them. He smothered them with finery and servants, bad-mouthed those who shunned the boys, doted on them to the point of fulfilling their every whim. He demanded that the dragons train the boys in the ways of magic. The dragons, who could sense darkness in their hearts, still felt the boys should die. We refused, re-creating a rift between our societies. The boys grew up deeply spoiled and also deeply embittered."

Prinivere shook herself from head to toe, the movement strangely animal. "The firstborn, Shalas, wanted only to forget what he was, to live his life as a normal human. The second, Shamayas, resented what he should have become. He would watch us flying effortlessly overhead and desperately wished he could spend half his life in dragon form, as he felt he deserved. These desires became as focused and determined as the king's love for his hybrid grandsons, so much so that each developed a single magical ability even without our training. The boys' innate evil, the strong and covetous nature of their wishes, warped them to self-defeating talents. Shalas gained the ability to make others forget, but never himself. Shamayas could turn other's lives half-animal but not his own."

Collins grimaced at the horrible irony and wished his companions would sit. The story shivered through him like a horror movie, and having the two towering over him only intensified the discomfort. "So that's how the half-animal transformations came about?"

Prinivere held up a hand, curled like a claw. "Thinking they might find the significance of the dragon's stone, the king gave it to his grandsons. Their terrible powers mightily enhanced, the boys used them in a grander fashion. The first caused the populace to forget. The second inflicted hybrid lives on them, excepting only the king, his queen, and a few others of the royal line who struck their fancy. And, inadvertently, themselves, for they still could not affect what they truly wanted. Greatly desired magics fail on those with evil hearts. In this way, the king of humans achieved ultimate power. Inflicted with the curse, his enemies and subjects could not likely mass in rebellion. He and his direct descendants would rule forever.''

The ability to do such a thing went so far beyond his experience, Collins found it as difficult to accept as he once had his entrance into a world of fantasy. ''What exactly did the people forget.''

''What came before.'' Prinivere sank back into her sitting position. Though Zylas remained standing, Collins found himself far more comfortable. ''That they had prior lives, ones without the transformation curse. So stories of that time do not trickle down to those alive today. It takes someone like me, someone who was there, to tell it.''

Collins realized what had to come next. ''What happened to the dragons?''

''Our magic saved us from the effects of the first spell, but we could only temper the second. Suddenly, we found ourselves involuntarily human for part of every day, and that made us furious. A horde of dragons descended upon the castle. We killed the king and the half-breeds who should never have existed, but we could not reverse the evil they had inflicted without the magnifying crystal. We never found it. The crowned prince declared war against us, and the slaughter began.''

Prinivere's eyes grew even more watery, and a tear dragged down her wrinkled cheek. ''Armies and bounties—a man could become rich in a day simply by proving he had killed one of us. Our magic helped, but it has its limits. They wore us down and, one by one, they killed us.'' As she spoke, she sank lower and lower so that she had to glance up to meet Collins' eyes. Clearly, she believed herself finished, but he had to know one more thing.

''Some of you survived.''

''One,'' Zylas said, his voice seeming out of place after his long silence. ''Only one.''

''They knew our exact number.'' Prinivere now sounded as feeble as she looked. ''We had given them that, the means of our own extermination.''

"How?" Collins asked hesitantly. He wanted to know, though it would surely force Prinivere to relive the worst of her memories. "How did you survive?"

"I—" She choked, and Collins closed his eyes, suffering stabbing pangs of guilt for even having asked. He would never have dared press Joel Goldbaum's grandfather for details of the concentration camp he had narrowly escaped.

Collins said hastily, "Never mind," but Prinivere seemed not to hear him.

"One day, my mate staggered to our cave, mortally wounded." The tears flowed freely now, thickening her voice. "All my magic couldn't save him; we both knew it. And they had trailed him to the cave. We said our good-byes. Quickly, I cleaned up those wounds that the people could see, gave him as much strength as I could, and he charged from the cave with all the vengeful agony of an aggrieved cave-mate. They killed him—twice. By the time they managed to climb to the cave, I had made myself appear dead as well. They mistook me for their first kill, crawled off to die, and him for the second. They claimed our tail tips, as the bounty required, and left us both for dead."

A heavy silence followed Prinivere's story. Collins could think of nothing better to say. "I'm sorry. Very very sorry."

Zylas crouched, forestalling the obvious question. "She dared not leave the cave often, barely kept herself alive. She waited until long after the old-age death of the crowned prince and his successor before showing even her human self. She found a good man who claimed he would love her no matter what her switch-form, but she never let him see it. She did bear him twins, then left him to raise them, checking in when she could in human form. Once they had safely grown, becoming acceptable animals at coming-of-age, she mostly disappeared from their lives, watching only from a distance."

Though it sounded harsh, Collins believed he understood the reason. "She aged much more slowly than they did, and she would soon look younger than her own children."

Zylas nodded, "And they might figure out what she was, endangering all of them. But she oversaw their descendants, including, distantly, me. My wife, too, carried Prinivere's bloodline, which explains why our daughter . . ." His tone became as strained as Prinivere's.

Collins lowered a head that felt heavy with the mass of details laid upon him by people he had alternately considered friends and betrayers. He had so much to contemplate: to consider, internalize, or discard.

Zylas studied Collins. As if reading his mind, the albino said softly, "I'm going to lay one more thing on you before we leave you to your thoughts."

Collins met the pale gaze and nodded soberly.

"The king's newest law states that *Random* unions can no longer occur. Couple that with the previous edicts forbidding certain creatures from breeding as *Regulars*, and many lines will end. Where you come from, it may not seem like such a bad thing to eliminate rats and mice, snakes and opossums, and other animals you consider vermin. But to us, it's . . . it's . . ."

Collins filled in the word, "Genocide." He sat up straight and tall. "It's genocide, pure and simple. And it's very, *very* wrong." He could not come up with words strong enough to fit the outrage now rushing through him.

Zylas gave him a weak smile. "I'm glad you see it our way."

Chapter 19

THEY left Collins on his own for nearly an hour while the information they had given him swirled through his mind. Despite the quantity, it all came together with a strange and surprising ease. Zylas and the others had a desperate need and an honest battle that they could not fight without Prinivere's magic enhanced by the missing crystal, and the dragon's great age and frailness made time very short indeed. His education since elementary school had stressed the inherent fairness and validity of democracy. Kingdoms and dictatorships did not fit into his view of justice without the moderating influence of parliaments, congresses, and houses. America had been built by rebels; and though the system did not always work smoothly, as the most recent presidential election could attest, he still strongly believed in the underlying tenets of its governmental system.

Running footsteps seized Collins' attention. Worried about security, he lurched to his feet just as Korfius came skidding into the room. He charged Collins with the exuberance of a puppy, then stopped suddenly, as if uncertain what to do next. Wheaten hair fell across his forehead in an untended tousle, and his dark eyes glimmered with excitement.

Collins caught the boy into an embrace, struck by the thinness of his limbs. For an instant, Korfius stiffened. Then, his arms cinched around Collins' waist, and he buried his face in the royal tunic.

Falima came striding in after the boy. "Korfius, you were supposed to—" She broke off as her gaze fell on Collins, and she went utterly silent. She looked at the boy and man enwrapped together, and a smile softened her otherwise pinched features.

Korfius released Collins and took two steps backward. "You're back, Your Majesty."

Collins winced at the lie, finding it suddenly intolerable. "Look, Korfius. I'm not really—"

The boy did not let him finish. "I know. But I still think of you as my prince."

Now knowing what the king of Barakhai had decreed, what at least this portion of the populace thought of him, Collins did not take the words as a compliment.

Falima shifted nervously from foot to foot. Collins almost expected her to whicker before she finally spoke. "I'm sorry, Ben. I . . . should have trusted you sooner. Treated you better."

Collins was not sure he agreed. "I understand why you didn't."

"Still—"

"Still nothing." Collins felt embarrassed by Falima's apology. It would have taken him at least as long to force himself to associate with someone he considered a cannibal, let alone to treat him courteously. "I understand. You're a good woman in a bad situation. I know you've had to make a lot of hard choices. Giving up a life usually reserved for high-ranking *Regulars* to help a criminal stranger who seemed incompetent couldn't have been easy. I'm sorry I put you in that position." He extended his arms.

Falima moved around Korfius to take her place in Collins' embrace. He folded his grip around her, enjoying the warm softness of her. After the scrawny boy, she felt so substantial, so real. A rush of joy overpowered him momentarily, and the world narrowed to the two of them.

When Falima stepped back, Collins realized Zylas had also entered the cavern, quietly leaning against a craggy wall near the entrance. Dressed in his standard black, eyes eclipsed by his broad-brimmed hat, he wore a bold look of determination. A knife as long as a short sword hung at his waist. "May I assume from this you've forgiven one another?"

Collins' brow furrowed. "I wasn't aware we were fighting."

Zylas shrugged. "When he's out of switch-form, I'll send in Ialin, too."

Collins could not help picturing the glare of withering mistrust Ialin always wore in his presence. "I doubt you'll catch us hugging."

Zylas raised and lowered his brows, then nodded fatalistically. "Probably not." He flipped something into the air. Torchlight sheened from its surface as it spun toward Falima, and Collins recognized it as the translation stone. "I'm off."

Falima caught the stone in both hands, then gave Zylas a tortured look.

"Off where?" Collins turned toward Falima to confirm an answer he had not yet even gotten. He could hardly believe Zylas had so casually tossed over his most valued possession. The gesture carried an air of finality.

"To finish the job, of course. To get the crystal."

Collins blinked, confused. "Get the crystal? But it's—" Realization dawned. "You can't go to the castle. They'll kill you."

"Not if they don't catch me."

Collins' expression tightened into a frown. He hoped Falima would read the anxiety he felt. "You can't—"

"I can." Zylas adjusted his hat. "And I don't have a choice." His demeanor turned serious. "I'm sorry I brought you here;

and the others, too. It wasn't fair to expect outsiders to risk their lives for us.''

Collins started to protest, but Zylas silenced him with a gesture.

''With the first, I didn't realize the danger. Then, I convinced myself I could make changes that would keep them safe, that the significance of what I brought them to do outweighed any threat.'' Zylas repositioned his hat. ''You've convinced me otherwise. I've always been willing to die for the cause. Others already have. Now, it's just my turn.''

Collins did not agree. ''Your dying isn't going to accomplish anything.'' It was not completely true, assuming martyrs inflamed their followers as much in Barakhai as in the only world Collins had considered real until a few days ago.

''Who says I'm going to die?'' The question lacked the fortitude required to make the decision seem determined rather than insane. Zylas' earlier bold words contradicted the brave sentiment. They all knew that, alone, he would achieve little but his own demise. ''Have some faith in me.''

''I did, and I do,'' Collins insisted. ''Enough to expect you not to run off alone and half-cocked on a suicide mission.''

That brought a smile. ''You know, when I'm not holding the translation stone, you make a lot less sense.'' Almost immediately, the grin wilted and disappeared. ''There's something you need to know, Ben. Something I should have told you sooner.''

Now seemed as good a time as any for confessions. Collins braced himself for another horrible revelation.

''I told you Vernon and I have entered your world as a mouse and as a rat. You know that, once there, we don't switch forms.''

''The Law of Conservation of Mass and Energy.''

''Huh?''

Collins wished he had not interrupted. ''Never mind. Go on.''

Zylas dutifully continued. ''I've tried to go there in human form, but I can't get through.''

Collins narrowed his eyes in innocent perplexity. He studied his companion. "But you're not any bigger than I am, and I fit through all right. Easily, in fact."

"From there to here."

Collins considered Zylas' words, realization accompanied by a shiver of discomfort. "Are you telling me it's a one-way door?"

Zylas lowered his face fully into the shadows of his hat. "Only for humans."

"But I'm always . . ." The significance finally penetrated. "You mean . . ." Collins trailed off, then tried again. "No one can get from Barakhai to my world in human form." He looked at Zylas for confirmation; but, if the albino gave him any, he did not see it. "The people you brought here couldn't . . ." He remembered Zylas telling him that all of the others immediately looked for a way back to the lab rather than wandering off seeking food. No wonder Zylas had not had to worry about how long it took him to switch to human form in Barakhai. Those he lured to Barakhai became trapped. *Trapped. I'm trapped here. I can't ever go back.* The enormity of that realization froze his thoughts. He could not even contemplate the unlived future he no longer had in America.

Zylas waited long enough for the full force of understanding to seep in. "That's why the royals have not managed to find the portal."

Even when Carrie Quinton tried to lead them there. Of course, she thought she went to the wrong ruins when she couldn't go anywhere from there. Collins squeezed out the words. "I'm . . . trapped . . . here?" He turned a bug-eyed stare onto Falima. "I'm here forever." All at once, the details of that simple statement crashed down around him. A list of "no-mores" filled his mind: *friends, family, competent medical care, telephones, clean clothes, indoor plumbing, electric lights, heat, air-conditioning, Sony Play Station, pizza . . .*

"You're not trapped. Once I get the crystal . . ."

. . . email and instant messaging, real beds, blankets, James Bond movies, CDs . . .

". . . Prinivere can definitely get you home. In fact, she managed to get the first guy I brought here home without it, though she hasn't had the strength for it since."

Yeah, Collins remembered. *Home to the nut house.* "She can?" His monotone delivery revealed no hope; the claim sounded suspiciously familiar. *Wait a minute.* "You're playing me again, aren't you?"

Zylas jerked. "What?"

"Telling me the only way to get what I want is to do what you want first. That's how you got me to the castle in the first place."

"But this time I'm not asking you to do anything."

"You're trying to get me to go with you."

"Only if you want to. I'm perfectly willing to go alone."

Korfius and Falima remained tensely silent throughout an exchange that could only end in stalemate.

"I'll bet," Collins mumbled, a statement clearly well-understood by Zylas, who had picked up most of his English by listening to American conversations.

"Fine," Zylas huffed. "I wouldn't have you along with me if you begged."

Falima rolled a wild gaze to Collins, who had won the argument but surely lost the war. When neither of the men spoke again, she softly added, "Shouting at one another won't get at the truth."

Collins folded his arms across his chest.

"Ben, if you don't believe Zylas, why don't the two of you go back to the ruins and try? Either you'll get what you want or you'll find yourself trapped. Then, at least, you'll know."

Zylas' stiff posture eased. "I'm willing. You?"

Collins pictured them struggling through days of woodland travel, dodging hounds and horses, only to stand frustrating inches from the doorway that should take him home. Carrie

Quinton's inability to return should corroborate the claim well enough, and the details did finally seem to fit together. "Well . . ." He gave Falima a corner of the eye glance, certain a full look would make him agree to whatever she requested. ". . . you know you're still under oath. You swore to God with sugar on top. We shared spit and a handshake. If you break that promise, the powers-that-be here will strike you down." That hardly seemed a threat given Zylas' willing death mission, so he added, "And all those you care about, too."

Zylas' grin returned. "Can't have that happening. Want me to restate my vow?"

"Not necessary." Collins tried to sound matter-of-fact. "You promised not to lie to me, and you're still fully bound by that promise, you know."

"All right," Zylas agreed. His nostrils flared. "But only to you, right? I mean, I can still lie to the king's guards if I need to."

"Of course." It seemed ludicrous to talk about how Zylas could not lie to him while Collins maintained the illusionary significance of a nonsensical ritual he had only cobbled together to fool Vernon. "The first action Prinivere takes with that stone is to make me a portal?"

"First thing," Zylas agreed, holding out his hand to show he remembered he was still bound by his promise.

"And you know damned well I'm going with you." Collins tried to match Zylas' grin, though he felt anything but confident and strong. "Don't worry. I won't beg."

Falima loosed a relieved sigh. "Thank you," she whispered. "Thank you so much."

Zylas turned toward Falima, the smile that talk of the vow had raised turning cocksure and insolent. "I told you I chose well this time."

Falima did not argue. "And thank goodness you did."

Tattered and filthy, doing his best imitation of a hunted man, Benton Collins arrived at the outer gatehouse of the king's curtain wall. Guards peered at him over the ramparts, and the drawbridge ratcheted downward before he could utter a word. No sooner had the wood slapped the ground, then a contingent of six guards scurried to greet him, their expressions screwed up in concern and anxiety, their movements as jerky and skittish as a mother hen's. "Are you all right?" one asked.

Feigning a slight limp, Collins waved them off. "Fine. Escaped. Need to see . . . Carrie. And, if possible, the king."

The guards ushered Collins into the gatehouse more with their own forward movement than any particular words or guidance. Trying to look exhausted and pained, he tottered along with them, caught up in the motion. "His Majesty insisted we take you directly to the dining hall if we found you. We're glad you returned, Sire."

Sire? Collins wondered what the king had told them, then realized the obvious. The guards would all know by now that he had entered the upper quarters; which, to them, meant he had to be properly blooded, if distant, royalty.

Collins allowed them to fuss over him, through the second gatehouse, to the palace door, and up to the dining area. Someone must have rushed ahead for, when he arrived, the head table contained the king, Carrie Quinton, and a handful of other privileged guests. Her blonde hair hung in long ringlets, framing a face of beauty more exquisite than he had remembered. His escort joined the sparse array of servants at the common tables, surely more interested in observing his welcome than in eating. Maids still fussed over some of the furniture, suggesting that a meal had recently ended.

At the sight of him, Quinton rushed out from behind the table. "Ben, Ben!" She caught him into an embrace that thrilled through him, stirring an excitement he had not anticipated. He struggled to maintain his aura of fatigued relief as his body betrayed him. The hug became awkward as he found himself fixated on which parts of his body touched hers . . . and where. "You're all right. How did you . . . Did they make you . . . ?" She stopped speaking, withdrawing from his arms, ready to lead him to the head table. "Sit. Eat. Get your strength back, then talk." She ushered him toward the table.

Collins dragged after Quinton, surreptitiously adjusting his clothing, for once glad the linen hung loose on his narrow frame. He cursed the adolescent hormones that allowed a pretty girl to distract him from a life-or-death mission. On the other hand, he realized that, if he played this right, he could succeed at his task and win Carrie Quinton.

Quinton indicated the chair between her own and the king's. As surprised as unnerved by the honor, Collins glanced at King Terrin. The bearded face split in a welcoming grin, and he patted the indicated seat. "We're so glad you managed to get away. Did they hurt you?"

"Your Majesty," Quinton said as she sat, a hint of warning in her tone. "Please let the poor man catch his breath before you quiz him."

The smile remained in place, genuine, taking no offense at his young adviser's presumptuousness. "Of course, Carrie. You're quite right." He clapped his hands. Servants scurried to him, brandishing napkins, glasses, and bottles to fulfill the as yet unspoken command. "Bring a plate of food for our new arrival and anyone else who wishes it. Wine for me and the others."

A broad-faced redhead immediately distributed glasses, while a tall, thin man filled each one as quickly as she set them down. Others hurried toward the door.

Though Collins wanted to put off any questioning as long as possible, he thought it best to toss off a few crumbs. He addressed the king's question. "The fall off the wall hurt a lot, Sire. I was unconscious for the trip, so I'm not sure where they took me. Later, they gave me something that made me sleep and moved me again; but I woke up and managed to escape. They were chasing me." He plastered a stricken look on his face. "Did they . . . did they . . . did your guards manage . . . to catch them?''

King Terrin shook his head. ''We tried, but the rebels slunk away like the cowards they are.''

Thank God. Collins tried to display the exact opposite of the relief he felt.

The king patted Collins' hand with a palm the size of a bear paw. ''They won't bother you anymore; we'll see to that.''

''Thank you.'' Genuinely thirsty, Collins picked up his wineglass in a deliberately shaky hand and downed half of the contents in a swallow. Smooth and rich with the flavor of berries, it soothed his dry throat as well as serving as a vehicle for nervousness he no longer had to wholly fake. Necessarily vague, the plan did not anticipate an immediate meal with King Terrin. He had expected a chance to corner Quinton first, to spend some time convincing her to hand over the crystal she still wore around her neck. Zylas had assured him the rebels had a few spies placed within the curtain walls who might sacrifice their cover if the situation demanded it. At Collins' request, they would use the code word ''storm'' so he could identify or call for them, if necessary. The albino had also warned him to try not to let the royals lead him to the upper stories where none of the rebels could assist if something went awry.

''So,'' Terrin asked, not-quite-casually. ''Could you describe the rebels you saw?''

Collins nearly spat out his wine. He forced himself to hold it, though a trickle eased down his windpipe. He managed to swallow the rest before a racking spasm of coughs overtook him. He hacked for several moments, sucked in a long breath that sounded more like a wheeze, then lapsed into another fusillade.

Quinton sprang to her feet, patting Collins between the shoulder blades. ''Are you all right?''

Collins held up a hand to indicate he did not require her assistance. *That's all I need. A chestful of Heimlich-broken ribs to expel a molecule of liquid.* ''I'm fine,'' he rasped, wishing he sounded it. He cleared his throat, loosed a few more coughs, then regained control. "Sorry, Sire." He sounded as much hoarse as mortified. "Went down the wrong pipe."

King Terrin smiled, lightening the mood in much the same way Collins might have done in other circumstances. "I know I'm the king and people jump to my command, but you're permitted to swallow anything in your mouth before answering questions." The smile spread. "In fact, I encourage it."

Picturing people displaying their half-chewed food, Collins could not help smiling, too. "I'll keep that in mind, Sire." He found the title coming much easier than it had in the past. The king's easygoing manner comforted, and Collins wished he had a way to reason with him rather than lie. He shook off the temptation. The king had good reason to treat Collins well: not only to extract information about Zylas and the others but for scientific advice and, in the future, perhaps even trips to his own world to fetch items of use. Having little pieces of technology would make the king even more powerful than his half-animal subjects, and Terrin had reason to believe Collins might know how to get there and back. He knew the king had another side. He had suffered the royal anger and the results of a chase that had sent him tumbling down the steps, followed by a day and night in the dungeon. He believed and trusted Zylas. *God, I hope I'm not wrong.*

At that moment, a servant returned carrying a loaded plate, which he set in front of Collins along with utensils. It felt good to hold a fork again, even one as crudely made as the steel monstrosity he took into his hand. The plate contained a cooked fruit compote with sweet spices, roasted roots cut into cross sections, and a flaky fish chowder. Possibly hungry enough to even eat bugs, he devoured the food, unable to worry about manners. The king and Carrie Quinton exchanged glances that Collins believed were sympathetic. Likely, they believed the rebels had starved him. Though not true, the fare had been meager and coarse compared with what he had before him now. He could get used to food like this.

When Collins had devoured every bite, he finally turned over his attention to the king. "Please excuse me, Sire. I was . . . famished. And the food . . ." He could not think of a suitably complimentary word. "Wonderful. Better than wonderful. Delicious." *Oh, yeah. That made it clearer.* He continued babbling, "Just the best."

"Thank you," Terrin said simply.

Needing time to consider strategy, Collins took advantage of his deliberately ragged appearance. "Would you mind if I had some rest before we talk?"

The king stiffened for a moment, then regained his casual demeanor. Catching Collins' eye, he explained his discomfort, "The sooner we get after those rebels, the less time they have to hide."

"I won't take too long." Collins bluffed a yawn, stretching sleepily. "But I really need a bit of sleep to think clearly." The absurdity of his own statement struck him; he remembered cramming till morning on some of his most important tests.

The king gestured at Quinton. "Would you mind, Carrie?"

"Not at all." Quinton rose gracefully. "Come with me, Ben."

Collins' heart rate quickened, and he could scarcely believe his luck. The king had arranged the exact situation he needed, some time alone with Carrie Quinton. He rose, almost forgetting to appear tired in his excitement. The torchlight struck silver highlights through the thick, golden cascade of hair, and he could not help imagining the silky feel of it through his fingers. He followed her from the room to the spiral staircase, and she started up.

Eyes traveling to the muscular roundness of her butt, it took Collins a moment to recognize their destination. "Are we headed for . . . royal chambers."

Quinton glanced at him over her shoulder. "Of course."

Remembering Zylas' warning, Collins remained in place. "Won't we be intruding?"

Quinton laughed. "Intruding? Intruding on what? We've spoken up here before, remember?"

Collins remembered. He also recalled swords hacking at him as he tumbled down the stairs. "Of course," he said. "I just didn't want to be presumptuous." He covered with a smile. "Being rude to royalty can be fatal."

Quinton dismissed the comment with a wave. She descended a step and offered her hand. "Come on, you goof. *You're* royalty."

"I am?" Collins accepted Quinton's smooth, soft hand.

"For all intents and purposes." Quinton started back upward, Collins now walking at her side. He studied her in the light of the bracketed torches, scarcely daring to believe a woman so beautiful would allow him to keep her hand so long. Too much protestation would raise suspicions, and it did not seem so dangerous to enter the warded areas with only Carrie Quinton. "You've heard 'it's good to be the king?' Well, it's even better to be the king's adviser. Same good food, same comforts, same deferences—none of the responsibilities. They don't even expect you to be right all that often."

They reached the next landing and continued upward. Collins digested the explanation. "But don't you miss chocolate?" His own craving for something sweet tainted the question.

"They have chocolate."

"They do?"

"The royals do. I'll get you some."

Nearly distracted from his point, Collins continued as they walked. "What about fast food?"

Quinton turned him a searching look. "You mean lumps of grease doused in ketchup?"

Collins felt his cheeks grow warm. "Well, yeah. Stuff like that."

"No." Quinton winked. "But I can get the cook to fry you

up some salted lard and slap it between two hunks of white bread.'' She clapped her free hand down on their joined grip to simulate a sandwich. ''Primitive Whopper.''

''Gee, thanks.''

''Seriously, most of the fun of fast food is speed and not having to cook it yourself. Here, I don't ever have to cook again, or I can if I want to. I get what I want when I want it. And I still get things 'my way' if I request them.''

They paused on the next landing, and Collins noticed that the stairs continued upward for at least two more stories. Thinking back, the extension had been there the last time Quinton and King Terrin had brought him here, but he had not thought to question. He could not recall Zylas' explanation; their lessons on the layout of the castle seemed like a year ago, and he had taken more than one blow to the head since then.

Hand on the door latch, Quinton waited. ''You're not expecting to sleep on the roof, are you?''

Torn from his scrutiny, Collins glanced at Quinton. ''What?''

''Next stop's the roof ramparts, for the lookout guards. Then the top of the tower.''

Now, Collins remembered discussing the fact that some guards might climb the stairs past the royal areas to access their positions. Zylas had even mentioned the steps ending in a trapdoor that led to the top of one tower. ''Oh.'' *Duh.*

Quinton tripped the latch and pushed the door open to reveal a large bedroom. Tapestries hung from every wall. The first depicted a forest, with deer grazing placidly among a vast variety of trees, birds and squirrels cavorting in the branches, a rabbit peering timidly around a weathered oak. Another showed a pasture full of a mixed herd of animals. Horses raced regally through the background, a cow lumbering behind them. Sheep and goats filled most of the foreground. The third wall contained a picture of a young boy herding a flock of geese, ducks, and chickens. The last held a portrait of a ginger tabby cat stretched luxuriously on a canopied bed. A real bed, looking very much like the one in the picture, took up most of the middle of the room. Tied back with golden tassels, emerald-colored curtains surrounded a mattress clotted with woolen blankets. A blue ceiling harbored a realistic arrangement of painted stars. A beautifully carved wardrobe and a matching wooden chest completed the furnishings.

While Collins admired the bedroom, Quinton borrowed a torch from the stairwell to light the ones on either side of the room. She replaced the torch, closed the door, and sat on the bed. Shoving aside the bunched blankets, she patted a spot next to her. "Welcome to my room."

Collins approached. "It's wonderful." Wanting to remind her of their similar backgrounds, and his own sense of observation, he said, "I particularly like the night sky. I see Orion, so it must be fall."

"Yup."

Collins continued to stare. "You know, the pattern's a bit different here. How'd you get it so close to ours?"

"Kept making the artist do it till he got it right." Quinton pushed the covers to the floor and tapped the mattress again. "Went from memory, but I know it's not exactly right."

Only an amateur astronomer himself, Collins could not tell her how to fix it. He walked to the bed, not certain what Quinton wanted from him.

Quinton stood, gently straightened Collins' collar, then pressed her lips against his. Her large breasts conformed to his chest, and he thought he could feel the nipples against him. Instantly excited, he returned the kiss, thrusting his tongue between her lips. *She wants me. Oh, my God, this beautiful woman wants me.*

Quinton arched her body against Collins' and whispered in his ear. "I want you." Her warm breath stirred something so primal, he groaned. His legs felt rubbery, unable to hold his weight.

Together, they sank onto her bed.

Chapter 20

BENTON Collins lay flopped across Carrie Quinton's bed, basking in the afterglow and the wonder of the whole situation. *A smart, beautiful woman wanted me.* He stared around the canopy at the painted stars ignited by the faint light the torches provided. Hours ago, he would never have believed such a thing could happen. Now, the whole world seemed to have changed.

Quinton made a sound of contentment, which sent a wave of joy thrilling through Collins. He could count the number of times he had made love, now no longer on just one hand; but he still considered himself inexperienced. He had done his best with Quinton, holding out as long as he could, but the whole session had still lasted less than fifteen minutes. It delighted him to think he had satisfied her, too.

A trickle of guilt disrupted his joy, its source uncertain. Marlys remained far from his thoughts. He had assumed their relationship was over before he had even come to Barakhai. The fact that they had not officially broken up had to do only with his inability to contact her. The true wonder was that the relationship had lasted as long as it did. Once he realized that Marlys had nothing to do with the sensation pressing against his conscience, he puzzled over it. Some frail corner of his mind told him he had found his soul mate, and it was not Carrie Quinton.

The thought seemed madness. He and Quinton had everything in common: background, interests, sexual attraction. It seemed almost as if the world had conspired to bring them together.

Quinton sat up, reaching for her clothes. "Penny for your thoughts."

Collins studied her, the torchlight just right to capture proper details and hide the flaws. Her face held a natural radiance that required no cosmetics. The curls, disheveled from their lovemaking, looked even more attractive tousled. Pale as blue-tinted pearls, her eyes remained striking. Her large breasts, perky with youth, still excited him, even with his manhood freshly spent. Even the antiquated phrasing of her question did not seem strange or nerdish. "You're beautiful," he said.

Quinton pulled on her dresslike undergarments, then the actual dress, smoothing the skirting around her hips and thighs. "I'm intelligent, too."

Collins swallowed, afraid he had just made a fatal mistake. "Well, of course. But that goes without saying." Uncertain whether he had rescued himself yet, he added, "Ol' D-Mark insists on the brightest."

"Including you?"

Choosing humor over modesty, Collins simply said. "Well, of course." Then, finding a way to use both, he added, "Though he couldn't be quite as picky after you disappeared. Everyone thought he'd driven you to run."

"So that's what happened." Quinton laughed. "At least no one's worried about me." She pulled on the gold chain with the dragon stone.

Collins' gaze latched onto the crystal, and sudden shame

slapped him. He had allowed a tryst to distract him from his mission. "I'd venture to guess your mother's worried."

Quinton's lips pursed tightly. "I don't have a mother."

The words seemed nonsensical. "Everyone has a mother." Collins reached for his own clothing.

Quinton grunted. "Squeezing a child out the birth canal doesn't make a woman a mother."

Collins pulled on his loose-fitting trousers and tied them without bothering to look at his hands. "My biology training says you're wrong."

"Well my sixteen years in seven foster homes trumps your biology training."

All humor disappeared. "Oh."

"Oh."

"I didn't know." Properly chastised, Collins reached for his tunic. "I'm sorry."

"For the first two years of my life, the woman who claimed to be my mother left me crying in a crib for hours while she went out and partied." A shadow fell over Quinton's face. "They gave her four years to straighten out her life enough to get me back. Four *years.* An eternity for a kid. By the time they realized she wouldn't, I was too old for an adoptive family. In those days, they only wanted babies."

"I'm sorry," Collins repeated, wishing he had never raised the subject. It clearly hurt her. "You've done amazingly well on your own, given the circumstances you came from." Suddenly, his own problems did not seem significant at all.

"I realized she was rotten by the time I was three, but it took an army of social workers four years to figure out the same thing." Quinton finger-combed her tangled locks. "That convinced me I was smart. I always knew I'd make it through college, though without scholarships, jobs, loans, and lab assistanceships, I'd never have made it."

"You're incredible," Collins said as he put on his glasses,

meaning it. "Resourceful, determined, intelligent, *and* beautiful." He smiled. "And damned good in bed."

Quinton winced. "I don't know why I told you that. Since I got off on my own at eighteen, I've never told anyone."

Her confession made Collins feel even closer than their lovemaking had. "I have a confession to make, too."

Quinton turned him a look of innocent questioning. "What?"

"I can get us home."

"You can?" Quinton's tone sounded guarded, not the pure excitement Collins expected.

Nevertheless, he continued. "All I need is the crystal." He reached out a finger and stroked the smooth stone around her neck.

Quinton did not flinch. "I don't understand."

"What's to understand?" Collins' voice gained all the excitement Quinton's lacked. "With the crystal, I can get us back to our own world."

Quinton shook her head slightly. "Ben, this *is* my world."

"This . . . ?" Collins' grin vanished. "This—don't be ridiculous. I can get us home. To Earth." Doubting they had actually left the planet, he amended, "Back to civilization."

Quinton clenched her hands in her lap.

Collins studied her in silence for several moments.

Quinton stared at her intertwined hands. "I don't want to leave"

"But, Carrie—"

"I feel more at home here than I ever did there."

Collins wanted to say something, anything, to rouse Quinton. The idea that she would like Barakhai better than home had never occurred to him. "What if you got appendicitis?"

Carrie pointed to her right hip. "Appendectomy. Age nine."

"All right. Needed your tonsils out."

Quinton's hand went to her throat. "Tonsillectomy. Age six."

Frustrated, Collins tried something that could happen more than once. "What if you broke your leg?"

Finally, Quinton looked directly at Collins. "They do have healers here, you know. They handle broken bones all the time."

Collins huffed out a sigh. "Do they handle cancer?"

"No," Quinton admitted. "But I'd rather take my chances raising the dragons until they can heal me than getting poisoned with chemotherapy and radiation."

The dragons. Collins had almost forgotten them. Once the king's adviser/geneticist raised and trained them, King Terrin might as well be invincible.

"Carrie, please. I *do* want to go home. Can't you just let me have the stone for me?"

The pallid eyes narrowed to slits, then she dropped her head wearily. "Ben, I have another confession."

Collins fell silent, not certain he wanted to hear it.

Quinton's fingers twined like snakes in her lap. "When I first brought you up here, I just wanted to get some information out of you."

Collins closed his eyes, dreading the rest.

"But I found myself really attracted to you. Then, one thing led to another, and I never did ask any questions and . . ." She broke off suddenly. "Please look at me."

Liking the turn her admission seemed to be taking, Collins obeyed.

"I want you to stay," Quinton said with raw sincerity. "King Terrin wants you to stay and advise him. You'd have a life of luxury, the life of a prince."

Collins shook his head. "I—"

Quinton seized his hand. "I do want you to stay, too. I want to sleep with you every night. I want to bear your babies. I want to be . . . a *real* mother."

My babies. This was too much for twenty-three-year-old

Benton Collins. *From one session of sex to this?* Terror ground through him, and the urge to put some physical distance between them became nearly unbearable. He suspected her swift bond with him had something to do with those she'd lacked as a child, yet the understanding did him little good. He found himself hyperventilating. He needed air. *Too much too fast.* Worried about upsetting her, he reached for the crystal again. "Please, Carrie. Just let me have the stone. I'll only go to settle some things. To gather some comforts. Then I'll come back."

Water glazed Quinton's blue-white eyes.

"I will. I promise." The words came out without conscious thought. Collins could not even convince himself he would keep that vow. Spitting on his hand and sugar on top would not work for Carrie Quinton.

She spoke softly, her voice strained and hesitant. "Once we've established a life here. A baby. Things I know you won't abandon. Then, then, you can go back."

"Carrie." Collins cupped the crystal in one hand. "I can't wait that long."

Quinton jerked backward, then hissed in pain. Clearly the gold chain cut into the back of her neck.

Now that he had a hold on it, Collins closed his hand, unable to let go. "I don't want to hurt you. Just let me have it."

"No," Carrie said, then shouted. "No! Help! Help! I need help!"

Collins knew he had to escape and fast, but he would not leave without the crystal. He wrapped both hands around it and pulled.

Carrie screamed.

The door that led to the other chambers burst open. Three men with swords charged into the room, directly at Collins.

"Shit!" Collins gave one last desperate heave that snapped the links. Momentum hurled him to the floor, the stone clamped in his hands, the broken ends of the chain whipping his fingers.

His buttocks struck stone, and agony howled through his spine. Blood splashed his face, and Carrie shrieked again.

Two swords jabbed toward Collins. He recognized their wielders as men who'd been seated at the head table on his first visit to the dining hall. Now, he noticed only that they looked well-muscled and competent with their weapons.

Collins scuttled into retreat as the blades jabbed forward. His back jarred suddenly against cold stone, and he scrambled to a stand, smacking his head on something affixed to the wall. A wash of black-and-white spots swam down on him, stealing his vision. He bulled through it, only to find himself pinned to the wall by two swords at his chest.

"Be still," said a silk-clad blond who could have been, and probably was, the king's brother. "We don't want to kill you."

Menaced by swords, Collins was not sure he believed the man. The one beside him remained quiet. He stood half a head taller, skin and hair a shade darker than his companion's. He wore a beard while the other was clean-shaven, and his hairline was receding.

Collins tightened his hold on the crystal. He had come too far to give it up now, yet he saw no way out of this situation. His only advantage came if he believed Carrie Quinton's claim that the king wanted him alive. He glanced at the geneticist, who returned his look with hate-filled eyes. Her hands clutched at the back of her neck. It surprised Collins to find himself thinking clearly in a life-or-death situation after his utter panic at the gallows. If nothing else had come out of his trip to Barakhai, he had gained composure. *Fat lot of good that'll do me dead.*

Sweat dripped down Collins' forehead, out of proportion to the rest of his body. His scalp felt uncomfortably hot. "Carrie and I were just—" He flushed, finishing lamely. "—talking and . . . and . . . stuff." *Stuff. The new popular euphemism for sex.* Abruptly, Collins realized what he must have crashed against that now heated his head. *Torch bracket.* He needed a distraction. "Tell 'em, Carrie."

"He stole my necklace," Quinton hissed. "A traitor."

The men's heads swiveled toward her. Seizing the moment, Collins lunged for the torch with his free hand. The bracket tore a line of skin from his thumb, sending pain howling through his hand, but he managed to complete the movement. His fingers wrapped around the warmed wood, and he swung wildly for his captors.

The two men leaped backward, sparing themselves a burning but opening the way for Collins' escape. The fire flickered dangerously low, then steadied. Collins raced for the door to the stairwell.

"Guards! Guards!" the shorter man shouted.

Collins jerked the panel open, only to find the way down blocked by a seething mass of warriors. "Shit!" Clearly, the king had anticipated that Collins' allegiances might have shifted. Quinton had known from the start that she had formidable backup. "Shit!" he repeated, louder. He needed a distraction, anything to delay the mob below him. "Storm!" he shrieked the code word to any rebel in earshot. "Storm! Storm!"

When no one responded, Collins hurled his only weapon, the torch, at the horde, then thundered up the stairs. *Up is wrong. Up is wrong!* It made no sense to corner himself on a rooftop, yet he saw no other way. At least, it might delay the inevitable and place the choice of death or capture back into his own hands. The crystal bit into his palm, and another realization struck him. At least, he might get the object of contention into the right hands. Surely, he would find someone from the rebel forces in the courtyard. *At least, my death might not be completely in vain.* Though a scant comfort, it proved better than none at all.

Collins charged upward, pausing only to collect another torch from its bracket in the stairwell. A moment later, he reached the next landing, anticipating a flurry of guardsmen from the parapets. None came through the door, and Collins dimly realized that the rebels must have managed to handle those men for him. He continued to run, breaths coming in wild pants, legs pounding upward as if under their own control. Suddenly, he found a square ceiling over his head, and the steps ended at a trapdoor. Praying it would not prove too heavy, he bashed against it with his head and right shoulder.

The panel jolted upward, but the seconds of delay proved his undoing. A hand closed around his ankle, jerking him abruptly backward. Balance and momentum lost, he felt himself falling into someone's arms. Twisting, he thrust blindly with the torch. The taller royal retreated, beard aflame. He let go of Collins' leg. Collins threw the torch and launched himself through the trapdoor. He heard Quinton's scream, high-pitched and fiercely terrified, caught a momentary glimpse of her, flames leaping from her hair, before the trapdoor crashed shut behind him. Guiltily, he hoped her distress would keep the guards busy long enough for him to find a way down. He darted to a crenel and glanced into the courtyard below. Seven stories down, the goats, sheep, pigs, and chickens looked very small. "Shit!" he yelled. "Shit! Shit! SHIT!"

The expletive caught the attention of some of the animals, who looked up at him. Something buzzed in his ear, and he whirled to face a tiny bird, its wings fluttering so fast they seemed invisible. Collins could never have imagined himself so glad to see Ialin. "Here." He thrust out the crystal. "Take it."

Dutifully, the hummingbird zipped to Collins and seized the offering in a beak that seemed too small and slender to hold it. Ialin sank almost to the ground, then ponderously, inch by inch, managed to regain altitude. He sailed away.

The trapdoor thumped back open.

Collins dumped the bit of broken gold chain over the parapets, watching it twist through the air. It seemed to take forever to reach the ground. Below him, two goats struggled with a small hay cart. It was over. The rebels had won, but Benton Collins had lost. If he surrendered now, maybe they would not kill him. He thought of what he had done: double-crossed the king, burned royals, including Carrie Quinton, and delivered an artifact into the hands of a gang of thugs who planned to use it to destroy the king. *Oh, yeah. He'll let me live all right.*

The man who looked like the king's brother appeared first, guarding his head and throat as he charged through the opening. Then, Zylas' rat-head emerged over the battlements, panting around the translation stone. From the direction of his abrupt arrival, he had clearly waited on the roof ramparts, between the two towers, and had climbed the final floor of the tower from the outside. "Jump," he managed to gasp around the quartz.

Collins looked down. He could never survive a seven-story fall. The goats labored hurriedly beneath him.

"Jump," Zylas repeated, his voice a harsh wheeze. He clambered wearily onto Collins' hand, across his wrist, and into a tunic pocket. "It's our only chance."

A guard appeared beside the royal, and Collins could hear more clambering behind them. They approached him with slow caution, swords drawn. He had only two choices, and they knew it: leap to his death or surrender.

"Trust me," Zylas said.

Famous last words. Collins realized that, whatever his fate, at least Zylas was brave enough to share it. Closing his eyes, he jumped.

"Hey!" the guard yelled. "Hey!"

Air whooshed past Collins. His hair and clothing whipped around him in a savage tangle, and sheer terror scattered his wits. He screamed, utterly helpless, incapable of opening his eyes. Then, stems jabbed and shattered beneath him, slivering into his flesh like a thousand needles. *The hay wagon,* he realized before velocity carried him through the piled hay to the wooden slats of the wagon. Agony beyond thought thundered through him, and he knew no more.

Benton Collins awakened to a rush of pain that drove an involuntary groan through his lips. He opened his eyes to a whitewashed ceiling and a repetitive beeping sound that perfectly matched the rhythm of his heart. He tried to speak, but only a croak emerged from his parched lips.

A woman in a white dress with a pink stethoscope around her neck and scissors poking from her breast pocket peered at him. "Are you awake, Benton?"

Collins licked his lips and nodded weakly. "What happened?" He mouthed more than spoke the words, but apparently the nurse understood.

"You tell me."

Collins shook his head, wondering if his experiences in Barakhai were all some sort of hallucination induced by the pain drugs they had obviously given him. "Last thing I remember, I was taking care of rat experiments in Daubert Labs."

"That's where they found you this morning." The nurse turned, clattering some objects on a metal tray. "In an old storage room. Your mom's on her way. Couldn't locate your dad."

"He's in Europe with his girlfriend." Collins glanced around, still trying to sort real from imagined. "Am I going to be okay?"

The nurse returned to his bedside, smoothed his pillow, and rearranged the covers. "You broke your pelvis, your left leg, both arms, some ribs, and you've got a small skull fracture."

The list sounded terrible. "Gosh."

The nurse apparently was not finished. She picked up a spiral-bound chart from a bedside table. "Ruptured spleen, which seems to be healing on its own. Kidney contusion—you'll have some blood in the urine for a while, but that should heal. Pneumothorax."

The last word eluded Collins. Pneumo, he knew, meant air. "What?"

The nurse set the chart aside. "Lung deflated. They put a tube in your chest to reexpand it."

"Did someone beat me up?" Collins tried to smile.

The nurse shrugged. "Only logical explanation. Looks more like you took a bad fall, but that doesn't make any sense where they found you.'' She lowered her head, and strands of dark hair slipped from beneath her hairpinned hat. ''You're lucky that professor found you when he did. Said a very persistent dog led him to you.''

''A dog?'' Collins swallowed. *Is it possible?* ''Where is this dog?''

''In the pound,'' the nurse said.

''The pound?'' Collins tried to sit up, but pain and wires held him down. ''What if they—''

The nurse put out a hand to stay him. ''Don't worry. No one's going to hurt the hero of Daubert Labs. If you don't want him, there're about thirty others in line to adopt him. I think he's getting filet mignon for every meal.''

Collins had to know. ''Gangly hound with floppy ears. Brown and white.''

''That's the one.''

''I want him.''

''I'll let them know.''

''He's . . . my dog. Can you hand me the phone?''

The nurse gave Collins a stern look. ''I said I'd call. I'll call as soon as we're done here.''

''Thank you.'' Collins felt very sleepy, but curiosity won out over fatigue. ''His name is Korfius.''

''Korfius?''

Collins nodded.

''I'll tell them.'' She started out the door, then stopped and turned back. These are your things, if you want them. It's everything you had when they found you. I'm afraid they had to cut off your jeans.'' She smiled. ''I don't think you would have wanted them anyway. Dirty and bloody. You must have taken off your sweatshirt before . . . whatever happened. It needs washing, but it's salvageable.''

Jeans? Sweatshirt? ''Thank you,'' Collins said, accepting the plastic bag. As the nurse left, he poured out the contents: his cell phone, his watch, its face irreparably smashed, and a piece of paper torn from a scratch pad advertising a laboratory supply company. Scrawled across it in wobbly lettering were the words:

Ben—

Thanks from all. Me okay. Fall on you. You me pillow. Ha ha. You hurt too bad for Lady. Put old clothes and bring here. They fix, we hope. Korfius stay. Not send back. He want you.

It was signed only with a tiny paw print.

Collins lay back, imagining the effort it must have taken for the rebels to drag him, in animal form, even as far as they had. Korfius was *lesariat,* he remembered. He had gotten his wish to remain a dog forever, and now Collins had gained the smartest, longest-lived pet in the world. *My world.* He smiled through the pain.